# Jacob's Ladder

P.D.R. Lindsay

ISBN: 978-0-9876691-4-8

# DEDICATION

For John, a budding historian.

# CONTENTS

# ACKNOWLEDGMENTS

My thanks to Dawn Keur, zenato.com for her Cover design,
Grateful thanks also for assistance with research from the helpful
experts at the Victoria and Albert Museum, and the Royal Armouries.

# CHAPTER ONE

London, April 1642.

'It is nought good a sleeping hound to wake'

There was no need for secrecy, not now. The King had fled, his sycophantic Court and their hangers-on too. Parliament, John Pym and his fellow Members, had set a new guard at Westminster Hall.

Still, a man might be observed and noted there, and cautious men wished to go unseen. Who knew what would happen or might happen? A friend now might seize an advantage, turncoat, be an enemy later, best be careful.

The Thames though, was another story. Crowded with boats crisscrossing the water fast as shuttles through a loom, one boat and its passengers could hide amongst the many. A constant stream of these wherries ferried men to the Parliament stairs for Westminster Hall. All such boats were official. Parliament was busy. Clerks scurried behind their employers and were sent to hurry back and forth across the river, bringing and taking documents. All the same, these pale lank men, bent of back, scuttling like beetles, clutching their ink horn and quills, grasping their wallets of papers.

A mid-day boat load pulled up to the stairs and two clerks disembarked. At Westminster Hall they parted company, and by various back ways and stairs, the taller of the two took himself to the quieter small chambers behind the Great Hall. He found the door he wanted and slid unobserved into the room. Three men sat round a small ash table, one leaned against the mantlepiece, staring down into the empty fireplace. They all looked up when he coughed.

"Well?" The central man of the seated three spoke.

The 'clerk' bowed and straightened. He changed entirely as he reached his full height and let authority sit easy on his now squared shoulders. He looked quite different from that down trodden clerk. "Yes, I've let slip enough information."

"So," the man by the fireplace walked to the table, "the hare is off, the coursers follow. You are sure our quarry will go to Kent?"

"I've set a watcher. She talks to the chief household servant. Our quarry is off to Kent tomorrow."

"Good, so we have placed the two opposing families together. Now we must see how they perform. Can you be there to prevent any damage to our cause?"

The pallid man pushed a hank of limp hair off his forehead, his eyes lightened with amusement. "God willing, I believe so. I have organized a place for myself. We have friends there as you know." H e made a gawky bow. "I know I can prevent both families from doing us harm."

There was an approving murmur and some unkind laughter.

The standing man nodded. "So you go as a clerk again. Be wary, Master Clerk, do not overreach yourself this time." The authority in his voice bent the Clerk's head, but not his back. "Let us know what is needed. The good Puritan men of Kent would not be wanting to see supporters of the King in their county. We shall have aid from them there. I can control that, if you can manage the rest."

"I will, or rather our puppet will for me."

"Take heed, remember we need the good will of our quarry's family. Keep your methods civil, spill no blood. Never forget the King can offer much to the ambitious. See that nothing is offered to our quarry that they cannot refuse. And see that the two families do not compromise. Now London and the Thames are closed to him, His Majesty is seeking ships, sailors and soldiers elsewhere. He must have gold to pay for them. We can't afford to give the King chance to garner profits through either of these families. The more we can tie up any possible flow of gold the swifter he will be to concede."

"Amen," a heartfelt chorus.

A wave of dismissal, the 'clerk' bowed to the four, walked off, shrivelling into the character of downtrodden worker again. At the door he paused and looked back before he slipped out of the room. His companions ignored him. They left at irregular intervals, one by one, as silently and carefully. There was no need for secrecy, not now, but who knew what would happen or might happen? A friend today could seize an opportunity, turncoat, be an enemy tomorrow, best be cautious. If there were to be any tomorrows for a Protestant England they surely depended on secrecy today.

# CHAPTER TWO
## London, April 1642

Brothers! I knew it must be them I'd caught sight of, lurking in the shadows at the foot of the stairs. Who else would be sure I'd be coming from the Gamlen lawyer's offices at this time? Who else would lie in wait to escort me home and prevent me slipping away to find some amusement on the other side of the river? I paused on the half landing, debating whether to startle them with an apprentice boy's catcall. In the end I laughed, jeering down at them. "Do you think to spring out shouting 'boo' and set me all of a twitter, you great dunderheads?"

No response. That seemed strangely unlike my brothers.

The oncoming dusk made it hard to see, but peering down the stairs into the gloom it occurred to me that the dark shapes in the shadows held nothing like the bulk, breadth and height of Amos, Caleb and Samuel. Russet headed mountains they were. Like our father. My agile, light boned, fair haired looks were borne from our mother's side of the family. And that was where I'd have them, stone headed brothers or whoever, my quickness to their snail paced slowness. I placed my hands as far down each hand rail as I could stretch, thrust off the top step with a great push from my legs and swung myself down the flight of stairs, to arrow through the arched doorway and land in the street beyond. I bounced on both feet, with bent knees, and sprang round, hand going to sword hilt, to face whatever or whoever my nose for danger told me waited in that entrance way.

There were three men, but not my brothers. These had the look of a wealthy Lord's paid lifeguards, plain dark clothes, half cloaks, curled plumes on wide brimmed hats which hid their faces, and good workman-like swords. They stepped forward, swords hissing from scabbards, heedless of the busy street, or the people passing. I backed off on to the wider, firmer, paved part of the street, drawing my own sword. This was no jest, these men, whoever they were, advanced in life threatening earnest. I didn't like the odds and looked to better them. Idlers and passers by had melted away like frost in the morn. No help available in the street. I stared beyond the men, over their shoulders, and yelled. "Hurry up, you tardy idlers, there's one for each of you, I'll cheer you on."

They weren't fools, these three, to swing round and gawp whilst I ran off. They moved easily, forming a rough triangle, backs facing in, allowing one to see behind them. That one spoke. "Ah, a clever ruse, Master Jacob Emerick, but not clever enough." His voice mocked me. He touched his beard and looked down from his stiff-necked height at me. "I want..."

But I never heard what he wanted, for there indeed, in answer to my fervent prayer, were my brothers, unmistakable, coming out of a side lane, filling the width of the street with their bulk, striding rapidly, for all their rolling seaman's gait, in my direction. "Amos," I bawled, "Caleb, Samuel, give aid." I waved my sword above my head and danced backwards, away from the trio. My brothers' roars shook plaster off walls. The sound of their boots crashing towards me had my would-be assailants turn, stare, then run.

"Now," said Amos, regarding the vanishing trio with a grin, "what trouble have you been the causing of?"

I spluttered, sheathed my sword, and clouted him in his ribs.

"Tush, tush, you bothersome boy." Caleb caught my shoulders, spun me away from Amos. "Who were they? 'Tis a fine state when our little brother can't do the simplest task without upsetting folk." He was grinning too.

I shrugged him off impatiently. "I don't know. Nor do I know what they wanted, but the leader knew my name."

Samuel closed in so that the three of them made a wall around me. "It could be that Merchant we bested over the Dutch beer. He raged sorely at us, and you were the one who found us the trade and signed the contract." Amos and Caleb mumbled agreement. "I doubt they'll try again, but be thankful we came to walk you home, little brother and keep that document safe."

"In truth, my thanks, big brothers," I replaced my sword, "but..."

They halted abruptly, I cannoned into Samuel, bumping my nose on his bony elbow. Caleb hauled me upright. "Never say it's not there," he said, setting me straight on my
feet.

"I won't then."

They stared, three faces showing degrees of shock, fear and horror.

"In here," Amos said, veering sharp left and guiding us into the street's busy pie shop, "and give us your news."

Scant worry about finding a place to sit with those three giants to lift what they wanted out from under quieter customers. A table and benches appeared in moments, were set down in the corner over by the window where we settled. My concern fixed on who would pay for pies and beer. They'd left me holding the bill before now, and my purse was thin.

"Jacob, what's to do?" Caleb thrust a tankard into my left hand and a pie in my right. He always was cack-handed.

"We've the family meeting tonight, and I must tell all then." I bit into the pie. My brothers fumed, knowing I had the right of it. My information should go first to our father and our uncles, who were the senior Merchants Emerick.

I let them chomp their pies and swig beer before I spoke again, voice low, head bent towards them. "The kernel is this. Denzil Gamlen did change his will. He's left all to his other sister's child, a niece, one Mistress Loveday Maye." I saw their faces lighten. "Nay, it's worse than if it were left to Master Rolph Fawke as Gamlen originally planned. The Fowkes aren't going to lose that inheritance. This Mistress Loveday Maye is not of age and she lives with Lady Fowke." I took another bite and chewed thoughtfully.

"Well, little brother?" Samuel, pie devoured in three bites, leaned towards me and tried to snatch my pie.

I dodged his large hand, but he gained a chunk of crust. "Seems Mistress Maye's under the Lady's care and guardianship."

Three jaws ceased mastication, paused mid chew, and gave me the displeasing vista of partly opened mouths full of clumps of pie. Of a certainty my brothers did indeed bear a strong resemblance to oxen. They even swallowed together, then resumed their chomping, staring at me with three wide eyed stares. I sighed. Amos drew his face into a heavy frown, and his eyebrows crept up his forehead, but he drank a mouthful of beer and gazed at a point beyond my ear before speaking.

"Why is this worse than if Denzil Gamlen had left the estate to Rolph Fowke? We have our copies of the Emerick-Gamlen agreement. They are signed and sealed, fully lawful. Stop your guzzling, Jacob. You are our lawyer, explain. Tell us what we're missing."

I shook my head and raised my hands as if astounded.

Amos blinked, reached forward and knocked my hat askew. Samuel laughed. Caleb spluttered.

Brothers! It was their massively simple thinking which ruffled me so. There were so many threads to this Emerick-Gamlen problem, but you wouldn't think it to hear Amos, Caleb and Samuel trying to untangle the skein. I wanted to rap their skulls till their brains woke up.

"Reason it thus. Where is Rolph Fowke?"

"With the King."

"Aye, Caleb. And where's the King?"

"York, last we heard."

"Where are we and the lawyers and the documents?"

Samuel stretched across the table to clout me. "London, as we well know, you fool."

I dodged, hissing at them as at bad actors. They exchanged glances, and I knew there'd be trouble later. "Use what wits God gave you."

They couldn't.

"The Fowkes support the King. Pym, Parliament and the Puritans have driven the King and his Court out of London. Rolph Fawke would find it very difficult to come to London and make trouble for us." I gusted a sigh over them. "You great loobies. If Rolph Fowke had inherited, we would be saved from any attempts to call in the loan for at least a year."

Now they had a grasp of that one thread. Caleb grinned. "For if Rolph Fowke went to Kent to claim the Gamlen estate, the good Puritans of Kent might seize and restrain him."

"There you have it. Most of Kent supports Pym and Parliament with vigour. Rolph Fowke risks too much to go openly into Kent." Three nods, much thoughtful puckering of lips and brows. "But this Mistress Maye is going to Kent, and with Lady Fowke, to take charge of the Gamlen estate, and all its affairs. And you know what Lady Fowke will do?"

Once again my three brothers ceased chewing, then swallowed the remnants of their pies, nodding gloomily, three stalled oxen.

"She'll call in the loan," Amos said.

Samuel jibbed. "Our loan is protected. What of those clauses...?"

I interrupted. "Denzil Gamlen's lawyer believes she will try. With King and Parliament so at odds, the King needs money. Lady

Fowke could buy great favour and influence. And without that document, which Denzil Gamlen promised to write if he changed his will, we might well find the Merchants Emerick fighting in Law Court and King's Court."

"Why doesn't his lawyer have this document safely stowed?" Caleb waxed indignant.

"It never arrived. Denzil Gamlen died so suddenly, but it was written, for he wrote in the letter of instruction about changing his will, that he was sending it on to his lawyer with those deeds for the land he'd bought for us."

They gaped.

Ah, my brothers, good sailors who could read the weather, but didn't read the broadsheets, nor heard what I heard at the Inns of Court. They could smell a storm coming at sea and tell you how dangerous it would be, but not see the death traps hidden in this dreadful one brewing on the land between King and Parliament. Some of those same traps would be as deadly for the Merchants Emerick. That such practical men could be such dunderheads when it came to seeing the world as it really was, amazed me. But they'd paid for the beer and pies and came to escort me safely home, indeed they'd rescued me from three dangerous men. I looked at each in turn. "About our family meeting tonight. Is't possible that you three can claim ignorance of all I said?"

"What and lose a chance to mire you in Father's displeasure?" Amos nudged Samuel.

"I'll land you in Mother's if you try it. Stop your foolishness and promise to be mute."

They laughed, heaved themselves and me up, marched me to the door. "Never fret little brother, we'll be on your side. We need you to make safe for us and find that document. Without it we stand to lose all."

# CHAPTER THREE
The journey to Kent
April, 1642.

I departed for Kent and Gamlen Manor in the community of
Eikenthorpe, the following day. All were in agreement. If I could not
reach Gamlen Manor to hunt the document out before the Fowke
party arrived, and that seemed unlikely, I must go to Eikenthorpe and
negotiate with the heiress and Lady Fowke as though we had the
document. I had to prevent Lady Fowke taking legal action to force
the return of the Gamlen loan, and try to find the letter and deeds to
our land.

The whole family, uncles, aunts, cousins, my father and
mother walked me, under my brothers' escort, to our personal
Thames' dock. They were full of advice as they farewelled me.

"Remember what is at stake, Jacob. Take great pains." My
father spoke with anguish. "We must find out what has happened to
that document. I pray Denzil gave it to the parson's care. They knew
each other well." He embraced me in a rib crushing hold, again a
reflection of his disturbed thoughts. "Have a care, my son, for us and
yourself."

My uncles dwelt more on business. "God be with you,

nephew, watch out for the Merchants Emerick and the snares and traps set for you. Don't fall into them and fail us. The Fowkes won't be mindful of Denzil Gamlen's wishes and will destroy any papers they find."

My mother'd not been one for bussing and slopping. Kisses went with blessings and had to be earned, but now she gave me both. Her embrace firm, hazel eyes level with mine, she whispered in my ear. "I couldn't bear to lose another child. God keep you safe, Jacob, and beware." She twisted my long blonde lovelock between her fingers, her eyes filled, her face shadowed over. "I'll pray daily for your safe return." She stroked the lovelock gently as she released it.

Once there had been three broad, big boned, russet haired Emericks, my big brothers, and three light boned, fair haired Emericks, Kitty, Eva, and me. My sisters had been the family's poppets, as fair of face and manner as myself, though sweeter of temperament. Life had been easier when I had them as companions, but 'the Lord giveth and the Lord taketh away' and He took them last year. My mother lost her beloved daughters. I'd lost my right and left hands, my champions and fellow wits, my tricksters and supporters when our big brothers became too much to bear. Why the Lord needed my sisters more than we did, is one of God's mysteries, but sometimes it was too hard for my mother and me. I kissed her in return and the aunts, like a covey of sleek, neat partridge, bobbing heads, rustling, clucking and fussing, took their turns, bussed and blessed me as though I were off to far Virginia. "Go with God's goodness to protect and guide you," they cho) chorused.

I stepped into our wherry, and my brothers rowed me away. I took with me a full purse, full pack, and all the family's hopes. A heavy load indeed. It weighted my shoulders down all the first day of my journey. Oh, I held few doubts that I would be incompetent, unable to untangle any legal knots, but held many doubts about the honesty and honour of the Fowke family. All I could do was pray for the wisdom to find a way and thank the Lord my father had not insisted I complete the entire journey by one of our Emerick boats.

Down river to Brockleford in Essex, was enough for me.
***

I rode the final stretch into Eikenthorpe, five days later, in a fine April rain.

This part of my journey was much more to my taste than the river boat had been. The rain washed out the bilge stench, which still clung to my new gabardine, even above its own smell of felted wool. An insidious odour, it caught at the back of my throat yet.

Didn't matter that our river boats and coastal ships were scrubbed clean each day, below decks, especially on the older boats, those with sand and gravel ballast, it could be as noisome as the worst of the shambles before rain on a warm summer's day. Why wet gravel and sand should stink like a week of butchers' offal and discards I never understood, but it did. Amos swore he could tell which boat was which with his eyes shut, and I believed him, for each boat developed its own peculiar, pungent odour on a journey. I swear mine was the oldest and smelliest river boat, and that Samuel, may all pestiferous older brothers rot in hell, had arranged it so for me.

My horse snorted with gusto. I brought my mind back to the here of this straight road in Kent and the reality that the intermittent, thin drizzle had finally seeped through my gabardine, new though it was. I felt it cling damply upon my shoulders. "April, with his showers so sweet?" I said aloud, and brushed the brim of my hat free from the brilliant fuzz of tiny beads of rain. My mare flicked her ears back; I patted her neck. "Soon, Perry," I told the slanted ears. They pricked forward again.

I'd wasted three days searching for a good horse, an honest horse-coper was rarer than a hen's tooth. Every stable I visited, the men misjudged me. A rare green-one, a tomfool from town, they thought, come to provide them with amusement. I heard their sniggered comments made behind hands as these horsemen looked at my clothes and anticipated the pleasure of parting me from far more money than I should pay for some prinked up, over-preened old nag. I laughed out loud. Perry tossed her head again, as if in agreement.

I'd shown them, left them with empty purses, and a farmer happy with the fair price I'd paid for his home bred mare. I nudged her into a canter. Here I was, free of three overbearing older brothers, boats, ships and the sea, and with a task I'd relish if I were sure of success. To pit my wits against the cunning of Lady Fowke, to let her think she had the best of the bargain, whilst securing the Emerick/Gamlen loan, that was the challenge. God give me strength to face it and the wit to secure that which was rightfully ours.

The ground was still a mucky mess from the spring thaw, not good footing for a pleasant canter. I eased Perry back to an amble, seeking shelter for us both for our midday rest. The drizzle, which a rain-bleached sun turned to fractured rainbows, increased its intensity. Large drops splattered on my hat brim and Perry's mane. She shook her head and I watched the raindrops fly off in shining arcs, making flashy jewels of themselves. Pretty it might be but we were going to get much wetter. The stretch of open common land we rode through was without a leafy tree or bush to shield us from the rain. I guided her across the slippery  mud-churned road. She placed each foot with disdain, lifting her hooves free of the glutinous muck with comic squelching sounds. Once on the firmer ground I set her into a canter again, and we left the heath behind.

Two bushy may trees, growing on a little hillock, appeared on our horizon. I nudged Perry towards them. The trees, opening myriads of tiny buds, appeared leaf-thick enough to keep some rain off. Grass was scant on the hillock but growing thick and long between it and the road. I halted Perry below the may trees and looked up. Yes, they'd make a shelter. There should be dry earth beneath them, enough leaves for a cover, and the blossom not yet fully open. I gave thanks for that, having no wish to drown in the flowers' pungent musty smell. The mare turned her head to blow moistly over my rain darkened boot. She asked for rest too.

"And thou shalt take thy ease, my lady fair." I told her, ruffling up the crest of her mane with a gauntleted hand. One slow look round told me the landscape was open, the prospect clear, no hiding places for lurking ner'do-wells. No ruffian could creep up to take me unaware. I might be travelling in the well farmed, neatly villaged country of Kent, but rogues skulked everywhere. I had been careful, worn nothing ostentatious, travelled with or near other travellers, but anyone on horseback owned more than a vagabond or highwayman. The rain eased again back to that fretful drizzle. Lifting my right leg over the pommel I dropped to the ground. Perry nudged me hard in my ribs. "Patience, my lady, is a virtue." I eased her girths, covered the saddle, then removed my gauntlets to undo the bit buckles. Perry dropped the bit into my bare hand and slobbered messily over my fingers.

"You muck-worm." I shouldered her in the neck, shook my fingers in disgust and wiped them through the wet grass. Perry snorted, spattering more foamy slobber and stretched her neck to snatch at the thick grass on the slope. I pulled one ear, but gently, then took my packet of pastries from the saddlebag. It was three strides up the slope to the shelter of the trees, and Perry wouldn't wander with all this good grass to eat.

I wasn't the first person to stop here. Another man had taken shelter. He'd tucked himself back against the tree trunks, hunched in the shadow of the thorny branches, huddled in his cloak, his hat brim concealing his face. I hesitated. I hadn't made much noise, but surely I'd been heard? The question to ask myself was whether this man was a rogue waiting to surprise me, or a tired traveller sleeping too sound for his own well being. My pistol was out of reach on Perry's back, in the saddle holster. Should I fetch it or rely on the short travelling sword at my side? I fingered the hilt, easing it into my hand. Now to see if this man was traveller or rogue. "God give you good day, sir."

No reply.

Below me Perry tore at the grass noisily, spilling a spring scent of green sap. Still the man did not stir. I felt the bristle of hair at the nape of my neck, slid out my sword from its scabbard. This man sat concealed, wore a good black riding cloak, leather riding gauntlets and his boots were not muddy. Where was his horse?

With caution I extended my left foot to nudge the toe of the man's right boot.      Nothing happened.

Again I looked round, checking every side. No one lay hidden anywhere, there was nowhere to hide. No riderless horse grazed the tempting roadside grass. No one scurried off towards the horizon.

I crouched carefully, ready to jump away should the man startle awake. I reached out to shake him and felt the figure collapse beneath my fingers, falling forward. The feeling was unmistakable. I lurched back, my heart beating loud in my ears. It wasn't a rigid cold body, but I felt the absence of life, knew the feeling of death.

My brain stopped, my body stilled. I stared and stared as the man's hat slid slowly forwards, off his head, onto the ground. I took one step towards him and his head fell forwards onto his chest, startling me so violently that I found myself back down the slope clutching Perry's mane, my packet of pastries dropped at my feet. The mare snorted, upset by my rapid arrival. I leant against her warm friendly shoulder, breathing hard, fingers twisted through her mane for support. She nudged me then dropped her head, seeking more lush grass.

I smoothed my hands across her thick plush coat, more for my comfort than hers, then made myself walk back to the body. I had rather left it, for the consequences of being one who finds a body were grave, but graver still if the body was known. I thought I knew who this man had been, but I had to be sure. A pink balding pate and the fading brown hair were common to many men of middle age.

With reluctance I grasped the shoulders to turn the man over, out of the shade, and the body slid bonelessly towards me. I did know the man, or rather, had known the man. This spelt disaster for the Merchants Emerick and particularly for this Emerick. What to do? Dear God, what to do? No one else in view. I'd better make a rapid removal of myself and say nothing. It was not honourable but, for the protection of my neck, and the Merchant Emericks, it was sensible.

I drew in a deep breath to calm my heart and head, took another, steadied, then forced myself to examine the face again. It had a red tinge to the skin, puffed up especially about the mouth and eyes, but yes, this was Denzil Gamlin's lawyer with whom I had spent several days recently. What was his name? The horror of his death had driven my wits awry. Two disciples' names...er...Philip Jameson, that was it. There was something else I had to notice. His head was turned towards me, the cloak pulled away from the neck. Around the neck and tangled in the dark hood was a narrow pale cord, fine woven, possibly of plaited hemp. On the neck was the red weal showing where that cord had twisted the life out of the lawyer, in the Spanish fashion of the garrote.

This made havoc of my plans. I looked again to be sure, but the cord remained, a tangible visible object. Now my stomach decided to have a say in the matter and heaved. I backed off, taking the few paces down to Perry, my legs as unsteady as when I walked off our river boat five days ago. I gripped the saddle for support and swallowed my stomach contents back into place. What, in the Lord's name, should I do? I had to think clearly. Jameson had not died in a quick fight to protect himself and his purse. This was no clean kill with a blade. This was evil, a man's life sneaked out of him from behind, choked deliberately for...for what? His purse and horse perhaps, or those papers he carried? But here? How did he come to be here? How had I missed seeing his murderer? I needed to find out what had happened, to look carefully under the hawthorns and round the hillock, before I left.

Perry flung up her head, and I heard too what she had, hoof beats drumming on turf. The mare, ears pricked, gazed eagerly down the road. I hesitated, ran a hand over my forehead, then, remembering what it had last touched, wiped both hands clean in the grass. I dithered, rushed back to the body, hastily rolled it under the hawthorns, smoothed over the marks in the dry earth and slid down the slope to Perry. I wiped my hands again in the long wet grass near her and picked up my packet of pastries. Even if the rider stopped briefly he would see nothing, just me resting my horse and enjoying a bite in a sheltered spot. I placed the packet on my open saddle bag, held Perry's bridle with one hand and rested the other discreetly on the hilt of my sword.

The horse came on, cantering steadily towards me. I knew the rider had sighted me, his horse's flowing pace faltered, then recovered. When they were close, the rider eased his horse into a brisk trot. What a horse it was. I eyed it with regret. This was the horse I had meant to buy but could not find. A bay with a coat of rich lustrous brown, glossy like wet Thames mud at low tide, his luxurious mane and tail shone jet black. From the arch in the neck, through every smooth curved line of the body, this horse proclaimed himself a stallion fit for the King and he knew it, tossed his head for Perry to admire.

His rider was an unknown quantity. Nothing showed beneath the wide brimmed hat except a tightly wrapped cloak and boot soles. I prayed that he would trot past. I still needed to decide what I should do or say about the murdered man and wanted solitude and time to think seriously. The death of Jameson might be seen, to those who did not understand the complexities of Denzil Gamlen's new will, to be of advantage to myself and my family.

As the rider drew level the stallion nickered, side stepping, almost prancing on the spot. When his rider insisted that he move on, the horse jounced, then bucked. The rider was in no danger of being dislodged, but his hat was. It flipped off his head and skimmed like a gull across the grass. Perry snorted, amazed, and stretched her neck to gaze at it. I swallowed a curse and moved forward to pluck the hat from the clump of grass it rested on.

"I thank you, sir." The rider made his horse stand. Hatless, he was revealed as a young man around my age, or perhaps a couple of years older, in his early to middle twenties. He inclined his head in my direction and smiled. The smile improved his face considerably. "I can see I shall have to stop. I don't think Samson wants to miss your mare's company. We've had a long and lonely journey."

He had to be one of the homeliest young men I'd seen, his freckled face a commonplace bundle of jutting bones under flattened, dull brown hair. He was a startling contrast to his handsome mount. When he dismounted I had to look up. That wasn't a new experience. Accustomed to being the shortest in my family of giants, I looked up daily, but this stranger was nearly as big as my father or Amos. Leaner though, his body more bone than muscle, and with that crooked nose and lop sided mouth, only his wide smile stopped him being outright, frog-faced ugly.

I restrained all curses and managed a smile. It occurred to me that this young man was God sent, for it might be arranged, if I took care, that the two of us could find the body together. There was something about the man's whole being that exhaled a decent godly courtesy and propriety. I might be wrong, but I felt reasonably sure that he was not a thief or highway man, just an honest traveller. As such his first reaction to the body would be shock and horror, not accusations. I knew it wouldn't be difficult to counterfeit my own feelings when I saw the body again. My hands still shook from the first horror of finding it.

"Good day to you, sir. You were close behind me, I've just halted here myself. You're welcome to share the hawthorn shelter." I held onto Perry and watched the stallion. "That's a fine horse." It was easy to fill my voice with admiration.

"I thank you." The young man courteously bowed the slight bow of equals and accepted his hat. "He's of my own breeding. Master Nowell Merriot at your service." The care with which he dusted off the crown, and straightened the brim, before settling it back over his crushed and untidy hair, suggested a nicety about clothing that went oddly with that plain face.

I showed my packet of pastries. "I was about to settle under the shelter of those hawthorns. Master Jacob Emerick, at your service." We both bowed, then clasped hands briefly. His grip was firm, a courteous touch without any trial of strength. I leaned against Perry and watched the young man tend his horse in a swift and capable manner.

The wait felt an aeon. Forcing myself to stillness, easing my clenched fingers around the pastry, proved difficult. I made myself do it. When Samson settled next to Perry, eating as greedily as she, Master Merriot produced a packet from his belt pouch. .

"I've new bread and a good cheese here." He waved it at me, grinned and headed up the slope. I strode out behind him, close on his heels so that I might bump into him when he stopped, as stop he did with a startled exclamation. "What...?"

I echoed his 'What?', struggling to keep my balance and step around him.
The body was now obviously a dead body. It was lying face down under the hawthorns with its boots sticking out at one side and the hat at the other.

Master Merriot knelt down. "Some poor soul has met his end here, Master Emerick." He turned the body carefully by its cloaked shoulders, and I gasped as Master Merriot did. The lawyer's flushed face still shocked, and the cord and marks on the neck told their own story. I hoped my face looked as horrified as Master Merriot's, for he was staring at me. "This is no natural death." He stood up, looked around, then gazed at me.

I read suspicion in his eyes. Time to speak. "I don't understand. I saw no one riding in front of me, and you can see a good distance across this flat land. Did you see any traveller?" Master Merriot shook his head. "This man was a rider, look at his cloak, riding gloves and boots. Where is his horse?" I stooped and examined the ground around us and under the hawthorns. "I see no signs of a horse up here or other boot prints." I walked round the hawthorns, careful to step into any marks that might have been my previous footsteps. "How did the body get here? When did it get here? How long has this poor man been dead?"

Master Merriot still watched me, his blue eyes no longer showing friendship. "I don't know. I saw no other travellers." Did he hesitate? I wondered if he was not telling all he knew, and hadn't

Master Merriot touched the body in a way that showed lack of fear, or perhaps familiarity with the dead? No, it was all in my imagination. I was afraid of being accused. I stilled my panic and thought.

"I propose that we take him to Eikenthorpe, Master Merriot. Do you agree?"

He started to speak then checked, conning my words. "Sampson wouldn't carry a body. Would your mare?"

"I don't know. I'd rather not make assay. We must inform Eikenthorpe's authorities, the parish watch, or maybe the parson if there's not a Justice of the Peace there. Tell them what we found."

"We?" Master Merriot hesitated, glancing at me.

He wanted to ask more questions, questions I did not want to answer for I disliked lying outright. Time to intervene. "Look, Master Merriot, this poor soul came on a horse, where is it? And this cord, look at it." He did so, reluctantly. "This is the kind of cord you see tying reams of good linen paper, but is it specially marked in any way?" I knelt and examined the cord closely, touching the loose piece falling on the corpse's shoulder, turning it over, seeking marks.

Master Merriot stood off, shaking his head. "That looks like any piece of cord to me. You say you didn't see a horse. I haven't seen a stray horse. This is a puzzle...I don't see how...." He broke off and frowned. "I don't understand how the body came to be here." He wiped his gauntleted hands through the tussocks of wet grass, dried them on the inside of his cloak hem then removed them. "We'd better eat and ride on swiftly. Then someone can fetch this body before nightfall."

I nodded agreement. At least he had not accused me, and I'd done enough questioning and thinking out loud to make him think too. We returned to the grazing horses and stood beside them to open our lunch packets. I looked ruefully at the fragments of what had been tasty meat pastries and picked at the pieces. Had I convinced Master Merriot that the body was not of my making? I hoped so, but I must remain cautious. I had too much to lose. If some lazy or untutored officer of the watch counted my presence as finder the same as being the murderer, then God help me. And if those same officers knew of my family's involvement with poor Master Jameson then I would surely hang. Master Merriot was my witness that we found the body together and that he had me in his sight, riding towards me, before we found the body. Praise God, Master Merriot might be my salvation.

The pair of us began to eat, each with one hand kept in swift reach of our saddle holsters. Observing him cautiously as he was observing me from under lowered eyelids or with slight sideways glances, I did not know quite how to rank Master Merriot. I could see he wore boots of good leather, but they were not fashionably cut and shaped like mine, just plain well made riding boots. His brown cloak was thick, of oiled and felted wool, but it showed signs of wear, and had been re-collared. Master Merriott's family were comfortable rather than affluent then, or maybe he had a mother like mine, careful and prudent, who made the younger sons wear out the clothes. I wondered if Master Merriot had brothers. The only advantage of my having mountains for brothers was that I'd never shared their adult clothes.

Master Merriot's occupation puzzled me too. He did not appear to be a student, too old and worldly wise; nor an apprentice, his hair was too long, his clothes too fashionable. His hands had stubby fingers, but short clean nails. I met his gaze, seeing my doubt reflected in his eyes. He shrugged, looking uneasy, and when the flasks of light ale were empty, we remembered the reason for our haste and rode on together into another heavy shower.

A gust pelted cold rain into my face. I wrapped my cloak more closely and sighed. A sideways glance at Master Merriot caught him looking at me. I grinned in reassurance, but said an earnest prayer for a safe solution for us both. He hunched his shoulders against the rain and I echoed him, easing the damp cloth off mine. Together we rode at a brisk trot into a stretch of woodland. We kept to the centre of the road as the trees thickened into a well established stand. Master Jameson's death made us cautious. If truth be told, I felt fear. The murderer must lurk somewhere near and if he wanted to kill Lawyer Jameson, the Gamlen lawyer, he might also desire to kill the Merchants Emerick lawyer, me.

The trees were a bonnie sight, but I had no time to enjoy their beauty. I did think it remarkable that such good timber, of marketable girth, so near Eikenthorpe, had been spared the axe. Then the timber gave way to a well used coppice. Master Merriot's horse shied at the stacks of withies, posts and poles lying stacked and ready for use.

The road wound round like a drunken man staggering home. Eikenthorpe came into sight only in tantalizing pieces. Small views, framed by stands of trees or high hedges, showed well farmed land, cows or sheep on the lees and rough pasturage, a church spire, orchards beginning to bloom, roofs and chimneys of houses or cottages. Samson shied at two peddlers rounding a bend, on their way with full packs and plodding gait. A carrier's wagon creaked by and several foot travellers sloshed cautiously through the spring mud. A herd boy chasing three runaway pigs startled both horses as they rushed noisily past, making for the woods. Perry eyed them suspiciously, but Sampson shied again. I hid a grin, ruffling my reliable mare's mane.

"The orchards begin to blossom. We'll be here to see the cherries in bloom." My mother's small orchard would be nothing to the sight of these orchards.

Master Merriot broke his silence. "We may, that poor fellow won't."

As if I needed reminding. I opened my mouth to make a pointed response, changed it instead to, "God rest his soul." Then added, "Ah, here's the end of our journey." We had reached a ford and Eikenthorpe spread out before us. We waited as two empty farm carts, reeking of manure, trundled through the rocky shallows, and I noted that Eikenthorpe was more a large village than the market town I'd expected.

"It's a tidy settled place," said Master Merriot. He sounded surprised.

It was too, the buildings a pleasant mixture of old plaster and timber, or brick and timber. The whole place had a comfortable settled air, which we were about to disturb. "Aye and quiet too." The muffled village noises, compared to the friendly racket of London streets, sounded repressed, and no dogs came out to chase us. I smelt new turned earth, wood smoke and a light tang of well rotted manure, different from the tatterdemalion assortment of rich smells London produced.

Together we crossed the river in the wake of the wagons. Samson fussed about the water, Perry flicked her heels at him. A man, walking the river side path from the village, turned to watch us. His thin stooped figure straightened somewhat as he cast a sharp glance at our faces. "There's the first Eikenthorpe busybody," I told Merriot, "looking for something to gossip about."

Master Merriot hesitated as the road diverged. "We'd better seek the authorities."

"Settle into the inn first, show our money, and our worldly goods, then, when we have established ourselves as people to treat with respect, we can find whoever is in authority, perhaps a Justice, the Constable, or the Watch." Master Merriot gave me a quick glance. I halted Perry to explain. "Master Merriot, I do not want to find myself suspected of killing that man. We found the body, we might well be blamed. I am a lawyer, I know these things do happen."

Master Merriot's frown deepened. "I don't understand, surely...." He stopped and looked at me. "It makes no sense that we, honest travellers, should...." The comprehension grew in his eyes. "I see, because we are not known."

"Precisely, Master Merriot, we are strangers and we need to be seen as strangers with place and position. People with influence. To the inn, then?"

He nodded, looking thoughtful.

The only inn, The Moon and Stars, was an old stone building, blank walls to the outside. But the entrance, when we turned the corner and approached it, had been modernised, new, large windows set to each side of the archway gave the place a friendly lopsided appearance. The distinctive smell of singed hoof and the remote clang, bang of hammer on anvil told me that the forge was near. Good, Perry needed her shoes refitted. I rode her into the yard, dismounted thankfully, and watched as Master Merriot had to wait until the admiring stable boy summoned help to hold Samson before he safely dismounted. I risked a grin at him, and he returned it. We both stretched stiffly and watched the boys handle our horses.

Fashionable, well patronised by wealthy gentlemen, The Moon and Stars was not. However it did brisk business, judging by the filled stables. The stalls did not smell foisty, the water ran clear in a clean trough, and the boys worked under supervision of the head ostler. Living in London I knew that the showiest inns relied on reputation. I'd found that a quick inspection of stables and the kitchens of any inn soon told the true tale. And Master Merriot chose by the same principle, using his nose. I saw him check the water and sniff the hay. Clean straw and good fodder for the horse, the lack of bedbugs and untainted food for me summed up a good inn. The Moon and Stars passed that inspection. I'd expected to meet a few rogues and cheats on my journey, but not chinchs biting me every time I went to bed. There was no excuse in a decent inn for not turning and refilling the mattresses, nor scrubbing floors and strewing insect repelling herbs to keep bedbugs at bay.

I turned to Master Merriot. "Now we know our horses have good care perhaps we should make sure the beds are without unwelcomed visitors too."

Master Merriot snorted much like his horse did. "Aye, some inns are a disgrace, but this is Puritan Kent, where a clean house is expected." He winked.

I heaved Perry's saddle bags over the stable door and watched Samson fidget and fret. Master Merriot crossed the yard to help the ostler. The stableboys led Perry into large stall, giving her plenty of head rope. Like most females of my acquaintance, she enjoyed a little attention at frequent intervals, so I followed her in and leant on the manger. She arched her neck and blew softly at me. I ran a gauntleted hand roughly up her black shiny mane, to scratch as near her crest as I could reach. A good mare, my Perry, and affectionate. I wouldn't trade her, even for a Samson. She lowered her head and sighed at me through translucent, pink-rimmed nostrils, wanting more. I laughed, scratched her poll again, then stroked her neck softly. Time to hurry Master Merriot, secure a room, and report poor Jameson's ungodly end. I farewelled my mare and found Master Merriot. "Is Samson settled? We had best settle in ourselves and present our persons and our findings to the parson."

Master Merriot gave Samson's rump a farewell pat and turned to me. "Why the parson. Why not the Parish Watch?"

I laughed at the now docile horse with his muzzle deep in the manger. "Well, Praise the Lord, I know how to tame Samson if I have need. Give that stallion a manger of beans and chaff and suddenly he turns mild as milk," Master Merriot grinned and shouldered his saddle pack. "A wager? I'll bet you the parson is all powerful here." I held out my hand palm up, didn't tell him I'd ask my stable boy who was the law and authority in Eikenthorpe.

His eyebrows rose, he slapped my palm. "Agreed then. Shall we find the Landlord first and get a room, Master Emerick?"

"How are you placed for money, Master Merriot? Would you share a room with me and ease both our purses?" Ah, the sophistry of a lawyer; if we took a room together it strengthened my protection.

Master Merriot looked at me, and straight through my plan. "The better to give an impression of two honest young men travelling together?" He kept his voice low. "I am only here for one night, Master Emerick, but I will support you as you must support me. Let us be Nowell and Jacob then, and confound their suspicions. God knows, as we do, that neither of us harmed the man."

"Agreed." I grasped his arm and gently turned him round so that we headed across the paved stable yard to the inn door, strolling together.

# CHAPTER FOUR

As Nowell and I aimed for the inn door, a small boy, with a dirty face and bare legs, exploded into the yard, yelling with excitement. "Come see, Abe, come look, Simion, there's carriages. Warden Nicolls says it's the Fowkes come to take the Gamlen estate." The boys dropped their brushes and buckets and ran.

The groom whistled them back. "Nay, then." His tone was enough to make me start and feel guilty. "You put those tools away quiet and neat then walk. Don't be frightening the horses."

The boys sidled off, not quite running, to do as they were bid. I grasped Nowell's elbow and moved him forward. "Shall we observe this great arrival?"

He gave me a blank stare, then nodded. We strod e over the cobbles side by side and settled in the shadow of the arched entrance to watch. Even the groom came out to the gate, while the stable boys joined a trio of short haired apprentices amongst whom they wriggled and shoved. A goodly number of Eikenthorpe's population contrived to be in the street observing.

Only four outriders? Why such a quiet entry for Lady Fowke? The Fowkes were not known for their modest demeanour. I had seen the kind of display they had made in London. Puzzled, I watched and pondered.

The apprentice boys pointed and muttered, eyes darting towards any adult who might take offence with a hard hand.

"Hired horses, dull old plodders."

"Thought Fowkes were King's people. Don't want 'em in the manor here."

"Nay, Parson said 'tis Mistress Maye takes the Manor. She's named in t'will. Old dame Fowke'll be here taking her pick of her brother's best, then she'll be off."

"Where's the lord? Only two men at arms?"

Ah, the cleverness of Lady Fowke. I overheard the scraps of comments and conversation and realised what game she played. She knew how to think ahead and confuse her enemies. I would need all my wits about me if I were to deal successfully with her.

Nowell stood quietly at my shoulder. I watched as a slight smile curved the corners of his large mouth. We traded looks, sharing an understanding of the cunning of the lady. "She's not making much of a grand entry is she?" I murmured. "No sign of King's favours about her. Nothing to provoke the Puritans of Eikenthorpe."

He gave me a knowing grin. There was a lot more to Nowell Merriot than I'd ferreted out, but what I knew so far, I liked. I flicked another quick glance in his direction, but he'd shifted forward, looking into the coach and had moved slightly in front of me.

I leant near enough to speak in his ear. "She's too clever for Eikenthorpe folk."

Nowell glanced at me. "Aye," he said, then turned back to watch.

The blinds were raised in the first carriage and I saw Lady Fowke seated on the far side of the coach. A girl, no, a young maid, sat on my side of the coach. Lady Fowke's straight spine, stiff neck and trick of glancing over her nose put me in mind of a hawk about to bate. This young woman was all gentle curves to Lady Fowke's lines and angles. She glanced shyly at the crowd, smiling a quiet little smile. I admired her wide spaced eyes, the smooth white skin and high forehead. Soft curls touched her forehead under her coif and hat, curls of a tobacco brown colour, and she blushed, a pink cheeked tint, as she caught my eye. Not a traditional beauty, but those wide gentle eyes and slightly parted lips were alluring. Modest too. She did not tip her head or stretch her neck to attract admiring looks. Around me people muttered. "Mistress Maye" they said, with affection in their voices and smiled as they spoke. I took a long look at the Gamlen heiress, wondering how she might be of use to the Merchants Emerick.

As the coach passed she glanced back with a sudden stare. A warm smile quivered on her lips. For me? It was as though she recognized me. I smiled back, but now she crimsoned with confusion and would not look again. A mistake then. She'd believed me an old acquaintance, but I knew I'd never seen her. I'd surely have remembered her.

I tapped Nowell's shoulder. "I look forward to my visits to Lady Fowke, if that pretty maid is there."

Nowell snorted, it seemed his favourite method of expressing emotion, and frowned. "I'd say the lady will keep the maid out of your reach. She'll be promised, if not already betrothed. Use your noddle," he patted the crown of my hat, "the Fowkes marry for land, and position, you lawyers don't have enough of either for her likes."

Now there was an idea. Distract Lady Fowke with a proposal for a marriage agreement between Emericks and Fowkes whilst I found Gamlen's document. That might be a means to delay her. "I can but hope." I carefully readjusted my hat and flicked a finger under Nowell's nose. I knew that maid's arrival was preordained for me. I felt a grin as wide as Nowell's growing inside me and quashed it fiercely. Not yet. I had to present myself to the Eikenthorpe parson as suitably shocked. There were enough eyes watching here. To be seen grinning and clowning in the inn yard spelt disaster for us both until the cause of Jameson's death was sorted. "Keep a sober face," I warned. Nowell might not approve of me eyeing pretty maids, but he looked over his shoulder after the carriage before I swung him round into the inn yard again. "Oh ho! You're inspecting her too. Come, Nowell, let's secure our bags and find out from the landlord if I've won the wager."

Nowell shrugged himself free, then sighed. "That murdered man. Yes, we must arrange something, and swiftly, I can not stay above one night."
***

"Parson Paske's home," the innkeeper told us, "is next to the church. They're busy," he said. "They're doing some building."

The parson was indeed building, he was one of a party of men removing the outer cladding off the end wall of the house. He stepped forward through the swirl and pall of disintegrating plaster to meet us. The pale dust covered his hair and powdered his tunic so that he looked, not as a man of flesh, but rather one of stone. Statue of a saint? God forbid, I thought it, for he was all Puritan. I blinked and waved away the eddies of gritty dust that wafted forward in spirals of powdery mist and stuffed my nostrils full of a dry prickling. So this was Parson Richard Paske, this firm-lipped, upright man. Nearing forty, perhaps older, of middle height, obviously a sobersides Puritan from the cut of his hair to the cut of his coat, and very much a leader in his community. All the men turned to gaze after him as he stepped away from them. The boy'd spoken truly, Parson Richard Paske carried more influence than any constable and I'd won that wager.

"Parson Paske?" I let Nowell speak first and studied the house. The parson's home, originally an old fashioned oak framed house with wattle and daub in-fill and plain painted plaster, was being modernized and extended. Brickwork already replaced the plastered wattle in the main part of the building. The oak framing for a new wing stood in place. Stacks of bricks waited, squared up, ready for use.

I liked bricks like these, a warming ruddy pink colour, perfect for making pleasing patterns. I hoped to build my home in brick or even stone, one day...one God given day, when I had achieved that seat in Parliament, I would. I stopped wool gathering and turned to face the company who were now ranged about us.

"Master Nowell Merriot at your service. The innkeeper told us you are the person to speak to. We need your help and advice. Master Emerick and I stopped for a noonday break, not far from Eikenthorpe, by two hawthorns on a hillock." Parson Paske nodded. Nowell gathered breath, then spoke in a rush. "We found a man's body under the hawthorns."

Time for me to speak. First the polite bow and incline of my head then sober speech, that was the way to this man's reason. "Master Jacob Emerick at your service, Parson Paske. Is there a constable in Eikenthorpe? The man did not die naturally. He was killed."

The parson's gaze, from bright hazel eyes, rested on each of us in turn, making careful note of us. At least the man was thinking and wasn't shouting out 'murderers' and ordering us off into confinement. Still the risk was great. We must convince him of our honesty.

Parson Paske remained silent, his gaze steady upon us. It was a good trick if you thought the men in front of you carried some guilty secret or had a demon ruling their conscience. Nowell's fingers tapped on the hilt of his sword, but his face showed no guilt. I gazed directly back. I had done nothing. My conscience lay quiet.

The parson turned and addressed the group of workers. "Abdias, a constable's task for you. Take the cart out to those two hawthorns set on the little hill, just before the heath. These young men found a body there."

A babble of comments rose from the men.

"We will know more when the body is brought safely in to rest. Zachery, do you go with the constable and use those woodsman's eyes to see what you can see." The men moved off, half running.

I bowed and took Nowell's elbow. "We've done our duty, Parson Paske. Master Merriot, come, we can talk to the constable later, but now we must..."

Parson Paske interrupted. "I hope you will stay and explain how it came about that you discovered this body."

It wasn't a request, nor a demand, more an expectation that we would obey which I heard behind the polite words. I nodded, but Nowell protested. "I cannot stop in Eikenthorpe. I have business to conduct and time is pressing. It was an unfortunate chance that we found the body, and we can tell you little more than that."

"Yet you say no accident killed him. We must seek the truth of what happened and who this man is. Come and discuss your share in it with me. "

This time there was no doubt about what we had to do. It was useless to protest; we exchanged rueful looks, united in our reluctance to be examined by Parson Paske now, or at any time. The parson waited.

I stored away the fact of Nowell's reluctance and wondered what it was that Master Nowell Merriot wanted to hide. Did it concern that dead lawyer? I must find out, it might be important to know.

Parson Paske walked us round to the house door facing the green. Scattered under blossoming fruit trees in the enclosed front garden were yellow daffodils and white jonquils, and some tulips, like those expensive ones my mother cherished in her bulb pots, showed green leaf and bud. Parson Paske was visibly blessed by God's goodness.

Nowell nodded towards the small trees. "Are those cherry trees?" The wind sighed across the green and white petals floated past us, drifting down from the trees by the gate and spotting our hats and hair.

Parson Paske paused on the shallow step before the door. "These were of my father's growing, a dwarf tree that fruits later than any other cherry trees I know." He smiled. "My wife makes a much prized conserve from them, you shall taste it." A quick push and the door opened inwards. Parson Paske gestured, "Come through, we

32

can talk in my study, I act for the Justice of the King's Peace in Eikenthorpe, you must make your explanations to me." His boots tromped on the flagstone floor and he snecked the catch to open the first door on his left, ushering us through before him.

"Pray be seated. There, now explain to me what you are doing together here."

I walked to the window and stood with my back to it. Nowell settled on a broad stool. I knew I must speak first. I'd prepared what to say and how to say it on the ride into Eikenthorpe. I nodded at Nowell and began. "I am the youngest son of the Merchant family Emerick of London. I am the family lawyer." The words I made plain statements of fact. Anything of the braggart or hinting of self pride would damage my cause with this man. "I am here to discuss our business partnership with the new heir to Gamlen Manor. Denziel Gamlen was a business partner and his death has left unfinished business I am here to resolve." There, a simple statement that gave the bare bones while sounding frank and open. Should I add more? Perhaps to say how the family regretted Denzil Gamlen's death? It was true. His investments enabled the Merchant Emericks to expand, and I, personally, had been counting on the Gamlen connection and patronage in the future to sponsor me into Parliament. I doubted Lady Fowke or any of her family would be my patrons even had I secured a marriage agreement with them. No, safer not to speak words surplus to the bare facts. Parson Paske would only prate on about it being better to be away from earthly sorrows in God's heaven, and whilst true, I did not want to start the type of theological discussion this Puritan would relish. I would wager my new French flute the man enjoyed long theological arguments. I did not have time for that. I wanted Nowell Merriot to make his disclosures. When I knew what Master Merriot knew, then I might feel safe enough to say I recognized the dead man. The dangers of knowing and saying nothing were as great as admitting knowledge of Jameson. I held my tongue and let the silence and the parson's stare force Nowell into speech.

"I act in a matter of family business. We are Merriots of Brocklehurst, in Essex and breed fine horses. My stallion is to serve several mares in the area, and I am seeking good mares to purchase," Nowell said finally. "I shall not be in Kent above four days."

Nowell's words, picked out as they were spoken, I felt sure had been carved from a fatter source than he wanted to share with the parson. However I knew what I needed. Nowell did not know my world of Merchants and ships nor did he know London, nor was he a lawyer. I could safely suggest who the dead man was.

"We met by chance on this journey, Master Merriot and I. We both took shelter from a shower and so found the body. I think," I paused, altering my tone to sound hesitant, "I do not know, but I believe that the dead man was one of Denzil Gamlen's lawyers now attached to Lady Fowke. I met him recently, but this body..." I paused to allow an expression of distress to cross my face, "the face was altered somewhat."

Nowell's mouth turned down in distaste. "There was a cord round his neck," he explained, "he'd been throttled."

Garrotted, more likely, but I wasn't going to admit to any knowledge that might plunge me deeper into trouble. Some of my ventures in London led me to the South Bank and streets no respectable merchant man visited unless for the playhouses. What with those expeditions, and being around sailors on the dockside, I'd broadened my education rather more than I imagined Master Merriot or Parson Paske had. That included knowledge of things an old sobersides like this parson would regard as the Devil's doings. I wondered, with an inner grin, what he thought of playhouses.

Parson Paske pursed his lips, then nodded. "The parish and church wardens meet with me for supper tonight. By then we will have seen the body and will want to talk to you again. Now I must return to work. The removing of that plaster has been delayed too many times." He sounded resigned. "You may eat supper with us, until then..." he paused, reflected, then nodded. "Come with me."

God be praised, we weren't prisoners, although we were to be watched. I followed Parson Paske, waving Nowell through the door in front of me. The parson turned left, plodding down the hallway into the centre of the house. Nowell raised his eyebrows at me, but he followed, his boots making a noisy tympani in comparison with the parson's firm tread. Despite the appearance of the new, pale oak panelling and fresh laid flags in this passageway the house was much older. I could smell it, that scent of worn stone, aged timber, the must and dust of time.

From the passage we entered what once had been the Great Hall. Looking up I saw the rafters opened to the roof. The height and breadth of the place gave the impression still of the hall much as it had been two hundred years ago, a vast cavern. Parson Paske stopped and looked to his right. "Once the new wing is finished it will lead directly into this hall." He smiled "And if my wife and the servants can be persuaded to tolerate more noise and mess, then we shall also open the old wing into the hall, and Eikenthorpe will again have a place large enough for meetings and celebrations."

I guessed what sort of meetings Parson Paske meant. Travelling preachers, and Puritan fanatics, for if Parson Paske couldn't lawfully use the church for such meetings, because of those recent edicts from our King, then what better place than his hall? I felt my face shaping itself into a grimace and had to control my mouth, turning up the corners into a polite smile when I caught the parson glancing my way.

"I will send young Will to show you round Eikenthorpe and bring you safely back for supper." Parson Paske inclined his head politely, swung around on his heels and walked off to the breach in the wall where the new wing was growing. Faint swirls of plaster dust rose in the breeze of his passing and the raw moist smell of brick and new mortar tickled my nostrils until I sneezed.

Nowell fretted and tossed his head in frustration. "I have so short a piece of time to be in Kent." His voice rose in irritation. "I have many people to see and so much business to conduct." He wheeled about, would have walked away, but I caught his arm.

"It's best we wait and let this village accept us as finders not murderers. You and I know that the man was dead when we found him. We had nothing to do with his death. It was an unhappy accident that we found him, but these people must know this for themselves. Less haste, patience is all if you want to stay out of gaol."

Nowell jerked his head swiftly to the left. I turned. The young man coming up beside me was still a youth, soft edges, profile not yet firmed by a developed character. He could only be, at the most, seventeen or eighteen. His dark complexion was lightened by hot brown eyes. Obviously one of the builders, there was a shadowy pall of plaster dust following him. He had however ducked his head under the pump and his face, hands and hair were wet and clean. His doublet must have been hung up whilst he worked for it showed only the barest trace of powdery white though his shirt sleeves had grimy cuff edges. His feet and legs shone, fresh washed and bare. He carried his boots, splendid new bucket tops though modest in size, still reeking of fresh tanned leather.

"Let me put on my boots," he said, "for Parson Paske tells me I'm to walk you round." He squatted on a stool, rolled on his hose, tied them above the knee, pulled down the legs of his breeches and crammed his feet into his boots in a matter of moments. "There, Sirs, I am at your service. Will Verne is my name. My family farm at Little Yul. You are Masters Emerick and Merriot?" He bowed his head to us both.

Little Yul? That was part of our Emerick land which Denzil Gamlen had recently bought for us, but this lad would know naught of that. Stepping forward I offered him my hand. "I am Master Emerick, this is Master Merriot."

Will gripped my hand firmly, then shook Nowell's. "Well then, gentlemen, shall we walk round the important places of Eikenthorpe." He didn't smile so I kept my face still even though, behind him, Nowell's mouth and eyebrows quirked upwards in an expression of comic disbelief. "Follow me, please, gentlemen."

The sights of the centre of Eikenthorpe included the church, (overlarge for the present size of the community,) the forge, (a family affair and busy,) the Dame School (young children rhyming and spelling out their letters using Bible texts,) and the shops, (front rooms used as busy shops cum workshops whilst the family lived above and behind.) Nothing to touch London of course, but the cobbler was good and there was a glover who displayed plain but well made gauntlets and some women's pieced gloves such as my mother might like to wear.

"And what now, Master Will?" enquired Nowell. "My horse will need walking and another rub down if I am to continue on tomorrow. The stable boys can't manage him."

Will's brown eyes brightened. "You're staying at the inn? You own that stallion the stable boys talk of then?"

Nowell's eyes widened."Gossip already?" I wondered just how fast information and misinformation could travel in this village community. We both looked at each other and laughed.

Our contempt made too obvious, the lad scowled at us, and flushed, a dark glow beneath his olive skin. "This is a good place," he said.

"To be sure, no murder and malice abide." I meant it kindly, but didn't tune my voice kindly enough for Will. He glowered, the expression at odds with the almost girlish curls springing up around his face as his hair dried. I made certain Will saw me note the curls and the thick lashes fringing his pretty brown eyes. His fists clenched.

"My horse," Nowell said, stepping between the two of us and swinging us around by the elbow, "to the stables, good sirs."
***

Seen by candlelight, without the plaster dust covering, Parson Paske was a comely man. His skin remained pock free and few lines etched in his sorrows or joys. His brown hair was thick and springy, not yet thinning. Never a doubt or hesitation could I see written in his face; I felt sorry for any theologically troubled parishioners or those who could not see God his way.

His welcome was kind though, as if we were guests and not

compelled to attend because we were under suspicion of murder. "Thank you, both of you, for joining us."

I had regarded with approval Nowell's well made, unembellished clothes, fitting for the homely man he was. I hoped I'd never see Nowell in something like the slashed doublet and fine lace collar I myself wore. Parson Paske however cast a long glance at our clothes, though whether it was disapproval for the cut and cloth or just the colours he did not say. Nowell's light and dark greens and my claret and dark grey were hardly outlandish or garish. I met his gaze with a raised chin and I shrugged, making swift eye contact with Nowell. A bad Puritan may wear good plain clothes, as a good one might wear a well cut doublet, surely this parson understood that. We needed him to, for we needed a reasonable man right now, one who was not a Ranter. "Consider the man, not his garments," I told him and surprised him into raising his brows, a smile almost touching his mouth.

He welcomed us inside and closed the door behind us with a solid thump of sound. Nowell, following the parson, flipped my lace collar and pulled such a face of comic horror that I almost overset myself, had to catch my tongue between my teeth to prevent a burst of laughter. We must be careful to be sober during this meeting, but if Nowell twitched his froggy features into any more such expressions I would be hard pressed to maintain a seemly countenance.

The men in Parson Paske's study rose as he entered. I studied them all carefully, without staring. I looked each in the eyes and gave them an easy greeting. Six middle aged men, church wardens to boot, and the parson's choice I'd wager any odds. Perhaps they reflected the community, worthy and stolid, but how many were zealots or bigots, and how many were well meaning towards two strangers who had found a body? A murder in their parish must be dealt with, Nowell and I were easy suspects to choose. We sat where the parson indicated and faced the wall of stares, I thank the Lord that Nowell kept his face as peaceful as I made mine.

"We are satisfied that neither of you has done other than find a body." Six heads nodded in unison. Parson Paske continued. "The removal of all the man's property, his horse and bags, his purse and papers show we are possibly dealing with one or more thieves. We have seen your horses and looked over your baggage. You say you saw no one ahead of you, or passing you the other way? " He looked at me.

"I did not, sir, and I looked hard before stopping at the hawthorns."

"And you, Master Merriot?"

"I saw no one, gentlemen. No other rider passed. I think that a man on foot might have skulked away, but we saw no such man." Nowell shook his head as if bewildered.

I thanked God devoutly, if hastily, for Nowell's sharp wits. He could bear witness for me that I had nothing more than my mare and saddle bags, just as I could bear the same witness for him. So who had killed that scholarly and harmless lawyer, Philip Jameson, and why? His death seemed more than a casual thief's attack. Most thieves used a knife or cudgel, for to kill meant a hunt and the gallows. And the body had been hidden, arranged in such a way that a brief glance from passing travellers would let them assume the man was alive. Someone needed time to escape or establish himself elsewhere. It appeared obvious to me that his death might well have been because of his involvement with the Emerick/Gamlen loan. But now I could not say anything without revealing that I'd found him first, on my own, and then pretended to find him with Nowell. I could well hang for that, even though I had done nothing more. I schooled my face to calm stillness and sharpened my wits.

Nowell rose and inclined his head to the Wardens. "Indeed good sirs, we speak the truth, we only found a body and glad I am to have helped to have it brought to a Christian burial."

"So are we Master Merrick." An inclined head in his direction. "Your information, Master Emerick, will help us give some comfort to his family. We thank you for that."

I bowed my head. "His family will know where he

disappeared to, if not why he disappeared. I wish Master Merrick and I had been in time to help him live."

One of the six stirred. His companion laid a hand on his arm in a swift gesture. I eyed the line of faces. So not everyone was content with the parson's words. Or was it that they thought to lay a trap? I could smell more problems ahead for the Merchants Emerick and myself.

"Supper, gentlemen, and let us talk of other things."

Nowell and I rose. The wardens departed, and we made to follow Parson Paske, but my mind worried away at the murder like a dog at a bone. I could see how it might well be connected to my business and I wondered if these men had reckoned that too. I didn't like either idea at all.

Nowell went first, and Parson Paske stayed me with a hand on my arm. "Master Emerick, your business would have been with Lawyer Jameson?"

I nodded.

"Then you must remain here in Eikenthorpe until we have details of this business and know that Jameson's death is not to your advantage."

As I feared, but to protest or show any violent emotion would be useless right now. I attempted reason. "But even if his death were to my advantage, or the Merchant Emerick's advantage, that does not mean that I killed him. Nowell was with me when we found..."

"But Master Emerick, Master Merriot did not ride out with you from the inn you left this morning."

I stared at the parson. How had he discovered that?

"Consider yourself required as a witness and don't leave Eikenthorpe until we know what has happened. If you attempt to leave..." His look filled in the space left by the unsaid words, and it was not friendly.

# CHAPTER FIVE

Amos had guessed aright, although I would not tell him so. "Heart of Puritan country where you're going, little brother," he'd twitted me, "best leave your finery and wear decent black as long breeches and cassocks." Even my austere lawyer's garments, dark green doublet and breeches, plain collar, modest crowned black hat and simple leather gauntlets failed to gain the inn keeper's approval at breakfast. Strictly Puritan in dress and biblical in speech he viewed me and my clothes with disdain, looking down his empurpled nose and over his fat belly.

I smiled widely at him and enjoyed his disconcerted stare. Parson Paske I could understand, but this collection of villagers seemed more than like minded. They were of one mind. The innkeeper's black-brown tunic and breeches, of a serviceable woollen blend, and his clean pale linen collar, every man appeared to wear in Eikenthorpe. I thought about
young Will with his fashionable boots, and wondered what happened to those, like him, who took an interest in worldly things. Were they excused as being 'them', of the community, as I stood condemned because I was not? A sudden longing for the London multitudes, their rowdy disagreements and multiplicity of ideas, seized me.

41

London was a bigger pond to sail on and with more like-minded people to sail with. I had not thought how narrow a conformity village life must be.

"Can't fault the man's attention to cleanliness though," Nowell said from behind me, punching my shoulder to push me forward. He too suffered from the same disapproving gaze.

I looked at the soft white river sand strewn on the still wet, new washed floors and nodded. Some strict Puritans did hold that dirt and disorder were signs of the devil, their homes were clean, quiet and orderly. "The only pleasant thing about this inn, so far, Nowell," I murmured, careful to catch his ear and not the landlord's.

We followed him to our table by the window and settled down. "Clean, yes, congenial, no. His girth rivals his casks but his face tells me he's been sampling his verjuice instead of his ale, did you note that vinegary expression? No, the place is decent, but his humour..." I left unspoken the rest of my comment and tossed my gauntlets on to the table top. Nowell had swift enough brains to follow my idea.

"I wonder what would crack those features into a smile?" Nowell winked then started to cough, harsh choking barks. The innkeeper revolved sharply, pivoting on the balls of his feet. Nowell stopped mid-cough, his mouth split into a grin. The innkeeper glared. Nowell turned back to me, "Nothing."

A man of my heart, Nowell Merriot, a young man worth knowing and surely never a murderer. But then, who was? That thought stopped my grin.

The inn servant, a skinny woman in her middle-years, served breakfast ale, bannocks and a tiny portion of fresh butter to each of us. Of the motherly type, who liked young men, she smiled on us, told us it was too early in the year for much fresh butter or cheese, watched us eat and enjoyed our enjoyment. We settled down to oatmeal bannock, new soft skim cheese, some well smoked ham, and yesterday's bread crisped on the hearth and sweetened with a fruit conserve. When the landlord went upstairs she fetched us a cherry preserve so delicious it rivalled my mother's precious honeyed cherries.

A voice from the kitchens recalled the servant and I took the time, between mouthfuls, to comment softly to Nowell. "Someone welcomes us anyway. Will this double or treble our fee?" Nowell smothered his laugh as the innkeeper rolled past, scowling down at our table. "And you ride on, today?" I asked in normal tones.

He paused and gave me the kind of glance people give when they are angling for time as their brain sorts a reply. "I must remain for at least another day, Parson Paske's 'request'." His eyebrows quirked on the word, as his voice gave it a sardonic emphasis. "But I have letters for the Gamlen household. Are you riding there this morning? Shall we ride together?"

I felt my eyebrows rise and allowed my face to reflect my curiosity. Letters for Gamlen? What was Nowell doing? I waited, but Nowell stayed mum. "Yes, I'd welcome cheerful company." I shot another glance at the innkeeper and lowered my voice. "And shall we see the maid, I wonder?"

"I'll wager the lady keeps her close." Nowell frowned at me again.

"I'll believe that, but I'll wager the cost of a meal tonight I find a way to meet her." I knew. She was God's gift to me and the Emericks, a way to untangle the confusion of our business. I hoped to dangle a marriage contract as a means of delaying Lady Fowke or even persuading her into considering honouring Denzil Gamlen's agreement with us.

The arrival of the innkeeper's wife, clucking and fussing at the sight of the half eaten cherry preserve, put an end to our talk. It paid to mind one's tongue in front of strangers, especially when under suspicion. Gossip should not fly on the wind, especially in a Puritan community, but it always did, and well embroidered too. I finished my breakfast, eating the last of the preserve with gusto, ignoring the innkeeper's scowl.

There was nothing to complain of about the management of

the inn stables either. Perry's stall was cleaned already, she'd eaten, and fresh water filled her pail, the whole place was kept as clean as the inn and smelt so. Perry nickered her welcome when I spoke to her, stretching her neck to lip and huff in my face. She fidgeted so much under the dark haired boy's careful ministrations that I removed him to one side and took over, saddling her myself, but letting him do the bridle buckles.

The boy slid out after us as we clopped into the yard and joined his fellow stable boy to hold Samson's head so that Nowell could mount. I swallowed the temptation to tell him that the ladies' mounting block was handily placed. I let Perry play statue and watched as Nowell admonished Samson verbally before he managed to swing his leg over and settle into the saddle just as the fidgeting stallion tore his head from the boys' grasp.

Samson's squealing, skittish departure, accompanied by the noisy clattering of his hooves, brought heads to windows, bodies to doors, and a skein of children to follow after.

Nowell settled into the saddle and drove Samson forward. "Not a raggle taggle tail," he complained jerkily as Samson bucked and kicked his way across the green. The children ran behind, calling out at every start and plunge.

Perry tossed her head once, responded to my knees and walked smoothly away. "All wanting a sermon on Samson and your horsemanship, Master Nowell."

Nowell humphed, breathless from the effort of keeping his horse's head up and his heels down. He drove Samson forward. The horse seemed determined to unseat him.

I nudged Perry farther away from Samson's flailing hooves. "We're foreigners and strangers, new faces, different clothes. We are something to stare at." After Londoners' intense interest and nose-poking curiosity, I found the closed faces and slide-away, sideways glances of Eikenthorpe adults cold comfort. At least these children had a natural curiosity.

Nowell growled something and checked Samson's flying feet.

I pushed Perry into the lead. She ignored Samson and walked calmly through the ford. Samson stopped, dithered on tiptoe, then dashed after her, reaching the other bank in a more sober frame of mind. Nowell patted his neck, he arched it and settled down at last.

"Here's the other side to Eikenthorpe," Nowell said, pointing down the river bank to the right. "Home of the non-elect and non-chosen. Does that make them ungodly?"

The huddle of wattle and daub huts and patchwork of gardens hidden among the willows was unlovely, but then the people in them would be too. Drunkards, bone idle wastrels, sluts and whores, the ungrateful who took God's gifts and hid them under their bushels. I shrugged, thinking, with gratitude, of my more comfortable place in life. "God gave us our station in this world and we must make the best of it." Nowell wondered aloud about charity and what narrow minded Puritans would allow, a slip confirming for me what I guessed him to be. Then he caught himself, frowned, and said nothing more. Together we took the left hand path beside the river and Eikenthorpe fell behind us. April's weather was kinder this day and I looked forward to the ride, but it was short, for Gamlen Manor surprised us.

We came suddenly upon the house when the horses cantered round a long curve in the lazy river. The Manor had decorative paintwork between the oak timbers, garlands of stylized wild flowers in warm spring colours which cheered the heart. The orchard trees near the house unfurled a variety of green leaves and pink tipped buds. The gardens showed yellow narcissus, violets, primroses and fresh turned soil. The Manor looked a home, a solid contented estate, set snug between the river and soft round hills. I could see why the Gamlens had built and held there for so long. The contrast between Parson Paske's plain plaster walls and Denzil Gamlen's bright painted ones made me smile. "Now, there's a family home."

Nowell nodded. "Yes, solid and secure."

It was. The house grew like a tree from its tidy close and gardens. The first Gamlen had sited his home on the highest point of the land with the river well down hill for protection at the front and to one side. A dry moat only had been needed at the rear. Now it was kept a green sward for laundry. What looked like the entire household's linen sheets lay stretched across the steepest slope to catch the sun.

Nowell looked at me. "Lady Fowke setting the whole company about its ears already?"

I grinned. "Aye, one like her'll be insisting on a complete cleaning out and inventory of the estate. May heaven preserve the servants if they're found wanting."

Samson sidled as Nowell held him back. "I like good stone buildings." He waved his hand at the thick oak framing and decorated plaster in-fill between. "It amazes me that a house of timber and plaster can last so long. Do you think it will survive Lady Fowke?" We both laughed and he nudged Samson forward. The stallion plunged and leapt away, nearly oversetting Perry.

"We'll discover that soon enough, Perry." I slapped her neck and let her have her head.

\*\*\*

We were brought before the lady by her steward. Lady Fowke sat looking us over in a manner not at all civil. She was much smaller than she had seemed in the carriage. This impression of stature came from her character, not her height. She filled the long library with her presence. Our eyes turned to her as to a lodestone. I did not observe the amazing collection of books Denzil Gamlen owned for some moments. The steward waited until she had finished looking at us before announcing us again and then departing. I bowed, the correct courtly bow. Nowell did likewise. She sniffed audibly, took Nowell's letters, sifted through them quickly, tossed them on the desk, then dismissed him abruptly, almost angrily, sending him off after the steward. "Your reply will be ready by morning. The Steward will give you it."

Nowell managed a nod of farewell to me as he went. We'd meet back at the inn.

The crack of sealing wax recalled my attention. Lady Fowke had opened my letter of introduction and began to read it. I studied her as she read. I'd expected Lady Fowke to be slight and dainty, bird boned, but she was almost chuffy. Still hawk-fierce in her movements and words, her amber eyes, and that arrogant tilt to the head, set her off as one to respect. Her whole essence commanded my attention. When she looked at me down her nose, with her eyes focussed, directing her concentrated mind at me, I felt like some poor coney caught away from the burrow, waiting to be pounced upon. I tried a disarming smile, as though her eyes were not skewering me.

She froze me with a smile in return. It was a blast from the frigid north. "I am pleased to meet with the Merchants Emerick lawyer." Her look said I was exactly the sort of lowly creature she expected a merchant would send. "Do not think that I cannot understand legal arrangements. I know the law. We have much to discuss in these agreements my brother was foolish enough to make."

I bowed again. So, it was a fight, a straight thrust without even a 'Have at you, boy!' I withheld my thrust, drew in breath, kept my voice level and calm, and parried with polite diffidence. "I am here to discuss the Emerick-Gamlen contract. That is why I was sent, my lady, to make any accommodation with the heir that we can, within that agreement. There is space for some flexibility and we are prepared to be flexible."

She looked, and although she hooded her eyes swiftly I saw one glimpse of triumph. She believed she held the winning hand. Oh my poor family, my father's fears were realised. She had found the documents. "The contract finished when Denzil Gamlen died." She gave me the hawk stare. Then she pounced. "Well? You have brought what you owe me, in gold?"

I saw her register, with that raptor's eye, my brief moment of surprise and unease. Still I refused to be forced into unwise speech for I must appear the direct, honest man. "My lady, I would need a guard of six men to travel with such an amount. I am sent to go through the agreement with Denzil Gamlen's heir. His death is the time for any slight adjustment of the contract, and discussion about a possible rearrangement of the way the sharing of the profits from his investment in our ships is carried out. That was written in to our agreement."

"Indeed." Lady Fowke said. It was enough. It was a wall of a word and halted me. She stood in silence, looking at me, and I had to exercise great firmness to keep my feet from shuffling sideways across the mellow wooden floor. What a parcel of tricks she had for making a man uncomfortable and uneasy. I stood firm, raised my chin and returned the gaze.

"My brother is dead," she said, "and the Emerick-Gamlen loan is part of his estate. I am here to manage that estate on behalf of my niece, the heiress, who is not yet of legal age. My duty is to see that the inheritance is intact and complete. The agreement between the Emericks and Denzil Gamlen no longer exists." Her glance I expected to be triumphant. If she had found and destroyed Denzil Gamlen's document safeguarding our agreement surely it would have been, but the glance she gave me was watchful.

I inclined my head. It didn't hurt me to defer to her if it helped me slip under her guard. She was pushing hard, confident of the power of the Fowke name and of powerful help, even Kingly aid, more than we could call on. But the agreement expressly allowed for the same terms after Gamlen's death, and our copies of those papers lay safe in London. We could argue over that point for days, days which gave me an opportunity to mention marriage contracts as a delaying tactic, and even try to charm the heiress.

"From what I have seen," and here the lady pinched her nostrils together and sniffed, "we will need all the money to set this estate aright and provide a suitable dowry for my niece."

"Of course, my lady." I bowed my head again. Praise the Lord that the girl I'd seen appeared meek and biddable. Lady Fowke would be the kind of guardian who thought nothing of beatings, bread and water and imprisonment for children who did not comply with her wishes. I had my hopes, our Merchant Emerick hopes, set on trying to arrange a marriage settlement, and I wished the maid better than that kind of treatment from her aunt.

"Well? What do you have to say, lawyer-man?"

I thought of enlarging what I'd said with some fulsome compliments about her known skills as a guardian -- she had made the Fowkes wealthy through Star Chamber wards -- but decided against it as that beak of a nose jabbed in my direction. It was Lady Fowke I had to master, no matter who was the heir, and, judging by the look in her eyes, she had been expecting some words of that sort. With what contempt would she have returned them?

"My lady?"

"I want the loan repaid in full, Master Emerick."

To be sure she did. What kind of fool did she take me for? Did she really think we Emericks would give her gold to buy favours from the King? I composed myself to tread softly, began to explain about profit sharing, Gamlen's investments and the annual profit from this.

Lady Fowke pounced. "I understand the profit sharing clause."

She would, being Lady Fowke, understand that, but her words told me she'd read the original documents. Had she destroyed them? I watched as she waited for an answer, giving only a courteously inclined head in reply.

She glared and continued. "We have many expenses here and I need money, now."

She was blunt, overbearing. I opened my mouth again, but she gave me no chance to speak. "I can seize your ships." Direct to the point, even the kill. Perchance silence was my safest refuge. She stabbed me again with her fierce hawk stare, and I wondered if she modelled herself on England's greatest queen. That regal turn of the head, her tricks to unsettle you. She was old enough to have seen Queen Elizabeth, or to have known those who had. It was a shrewd presentation of herself. No one had ever taken our good Queen Bess lightly, and no one could ignore Lady Fowke.

"You will return tomorrow ready to sign papers and we will arrange where the gold shall be exchanged." Lady Fowke gave me a queenly dismissal. She believed she had won. I bowed yet again. "Now, you shall meet the heiress, my granddaughter, who will explain how the gold is to be spent."

"I would be honoured," I said, bowing myself out of the library. I smiled as I closed the door. One for me, Master Nowell Merriot. Now, how else, beyond a marriage settlement, could I delay signing Lady Fowke's documents without naysaying the lady too fiercely and provoking a show of Fowke power? She could organise a seizure of our ships. Her Fowke lawyers would find a way to do so. Perhaps I should begin the attack tomorrow with mention of the renegotiation clause?

A woman stood waiting in the hallway. She did not wear Gamlen livery like the grooms and stable boys wore, or a badge and ribbons in Gamlen colours as the house servants did. A Fowke personal servant then, one trusted, as far as the lady trusted anyone, like her steward. I wondered if Lady Fowke had removed Gamlen's main house servants herself, graciously granting a long leave, or even dismissing them, so that she was free to do and say what she liked without Eikenthorpe's long ears and trotting tongues catching her out. It would be like her to think of it.

"Come this way, Master Emerick, sir. Lady Fowke ordered that you are to take a little refreshment in the parlour."

I followed, treading carefully across the wide hall's wood floor, which was still a new pale hue, very conscious of my boots' clatter. Despite his sister's comments it seemed that Denzil Gamlen had been careful of his estate. This area of the house smelt of new timber and builders' glue, replaced floors and windows judging by what I could see in the rooms we walked by.

"The new mistress taking inventory?"

"No, sir, cleaning out the old to make all as my lady likes," the servant replied as we passed half open doors showing rooms full of bustle, furniture moved, chests opened, women with cloth bound heads chattering, enjoying a good clean out. "In here, please, sir."

She ushered me into a parlour where the thin April sunshine brightened the air and laid yellow squares on an oak table. Between the reflected patches of light a large platter of pastries, fancy breads and dainties, surrounded by small pottery bowls of soft cheeses, pickles and preserves, made a colourful show.

"Shall I pour you beer, sir?" The woman raised a jug and filled a large pewter tankard with sweet smelling tawny liquid before I even nodded. Denzil Gamlen always enjoyed my mother's best beer, and this smelt like a brew to equal hers.

"Mary, Mary?" It was a mild voice, low and light, a singer's voice. I turned and waited. I knew who was hurrying into the room.

"Mistress Maye, This is Master Jacob Emerick, to see about the Gamlen-Emerick business," Mary said. "Master Emerick this is the Gamlen heiress, Mistress Loveday Maye." I bowed and put all my pleasure into my smile, for my glimpse of her in the carriage had not deceived. Mistress Maye delighted the eye. She was as lovely as my sisters had been. Very like, with that same air of alert innocence that promised a quick wit, gem bright eyes, and silk soft cheeks. There was such a sisterly essence of gentleness and honesty about her that she made me want to take her hands and kiss her cheek as if she were my sister.

Mistress Maye curtseyed slightly, blushing to raise a bright pink tint high on her cheek bones and forehead. "My apologies, sir, for such an unmannerly late meeting."

I knew I'd stared longer than acceptable. Her wide apart eyes and her high forehead gave her face a come hither charm that some trollops I knew would make great play with, but Mistress Maye's dark ringed, smoky blue eyes held nothing more than a natural shyness at a first meeting. This was not a city maid to tease or flirt with those smooth London phrases I'd learned. Her hand, when I took it to lead her to the table, felt soft, smooth and warm, yet firm too. I did dislike limp damp hands that slithered in mine like a dead fish.

"Apologies are not necessary, I can see how busy you are." I accepted my beer from the servant, Mary, allowing her to seat me in the sun on the window seat. "My Lady Fowke makes an inventory?"

Mistress Maye laughed, a soft chuckle. She lived in no fear of Lady Fowke then. I felt pleasure that she was a petted niece, valued and perhaps loved for herself. "My aunt wishes to have this house cleaned and organized as all hers are. She finds her brother has been a little lax in these matters. Men are not good with housekeeping are they?" Her smile invited mine.

I obliged, after all she was the bonniest maid I'd met for some months. Why was it my mother never pushed such girls at me? Marriage didn't seem an onerous duty when this was the kind of maid available to wed.

"Have you tried the cherry tartlets?" Mistress Maye offered me a plate full of tiny pastries filled with preserved cherries, blood bright. Each was a scant scented mouthful, but I restrained myself, politely removing one.

"I don't know how Charity preserves the cherries so that each retains its shape. I must coax her to tell me."

Mary sniffed. "Aye, you do, Mistress, for she'll not tell me, but you can surely charm the receipt from her."

Mistress Maye blushed again. This time the pink warmed her neck and cheeks, also the little hollow in her throat, making visible a tiny beating pulse. "She'll be happy to let us know," she said as she seated herself at the far end of the window seat and placed the plate of little tarts beside me. "Do eat them up with me, Master Emerick, then I may tell both Charity and Grandam that you enjoyed them." She pressed another on me and took one herself.

I offered up a swift prayer of thanks and praise. Here was one like my sisters returned to me, a kindred soul with whom I could talk, share laughter and who listened with understanding. Mistress Loveday Maye was so like Kitty and Eva, it was a wonder. Even her laugh sounded the same, a light murmur of sound, pleasant to the ear. It would be a pleasure to hear her sing.

I applied myself to enjoying the crisp pastry and tangy

cherries, and let Mistress Maye tell me about her summers at the Manor. She'd been a visitor every summer since she was old enough to make the journey, and she loved the place. 'Twas Denzil Gamlen who introduced his sister, her mother, to Doctor Maye at Gamlen Manor. A fine love story Mistress Loveday made of it, for Lady Fowke planned a great match for her young sister. She had objected vigorously to such a disadvantageous marriage with a mere doctor. It was Denzil Gamlen who had helped the lovers and organised a private ceremony in the Manor's chapel. She told the story like a ballad and indeed it sounded like one, for Lady Fowke had been so angry she had never set eyes on her niece until this past Christmas, when she'd made her peace with Doctor Maye, and invited Mistress Loveday to the new built Fowke mansion in Hertfordshire.

"A romance worthy of a song, Mistress. Shall you set it to music?"

She smiled. "Not here near my aunt, nor whilst my father lives. My aunt won't bear reminding of my mother, not a word of sorrow sent to us when she died two years ago." Mistress Maye's face turned sad. "I miss her so."

It was a simple statement and touched my heart, for here we both were, bereft of loved ones and still in pain. I reached out and took her hand in mine. "I am sorry."

Mistress Maye, as perfect a companion as my sisters had been, shook off her melancholy, released her hand, and offered me more cherry tartlets. Mary tutted at us both. I used my special smile, a proven disarmer of middle aged women, the one I'd practised for years. Mary dimpled up and shook her head at me. It was a rare day when I couldn't wrap some goody round my finger and have her blush, smile and fetch me more of what I liked. She filled my tankard again.

Mistress Maye, in response to my questions, talked of her aunt's goodness, of presents, jewels and dresses, and life with the Fowkes. She was indeed a petted favourite, yet not much spoiled by it. I let my mind wander to reflect on the terms of a marriage contract that would tempt Lady Fowke, yet keep the Emerick fortunes afloat. Oh, Lady Fowke would be looking much higher for her niece, but if she believed that she could bargain with a marriage settlement for the return of some money, then she would be happy to negotiate, which granted me time to see what this honest young heiress knew of our Gamlen dealings. Denzil Gamlen had been a fond uncle, mayhap he'd told her something. And if a marriage settlement were agreed I would be only happy to comply. Mistress Maye was a maid a man would willing marry for her own sweet self as well as her fortune.

Mary coughed and inclined her head politely towards me. "My lady wants us to turn out the linen closet, Loveday."

"I have, Mary." Mistress Maye's eyes shone with laughter she did not voice, and she tucked herself further back on the window seat with a rustle of her sky blue skirts. Her pretty cutwork linen apron curved into her lap and her feet peeped out from under her hem. "Let us finish these cherry tartlets, Master Emerick, and there's a little cheese you might enjoy as you tell me about places you have seen. Did you really go to Spain?" I smiled at her, and proceeded to make inroad on the last tarts as I shaped a fine tale to tell of my rather dull trip round the Mediterranean learning the family business.

Mary beamed at us and poured more beer. Mistress Maye was a favourite with her too. I raised my tankard in a toast of appreciation to Mary and watched Mistress Maye eat the last cherry tartlet. Like my sisters, she smelt of ladies' soap, sweet and floral, with a pleasant earthy smell from her hair which escaped in glossy wisps from under the neat cap. I liked to be near a maid who was not shackled by a parent's presence into ramrod stiff, eyes down, mute obedience. My mother might not approve of the informality of our meeting, introduced only by a servant and not Lady Fowke, but even she would approve of the maid. As for my father and brothers, they would be smitten the first time Mistress Loveday Maye smiled on them.

There was another pressing aspect to bargaining with a marriage agreement. I could not foresee, no one could, what would happen between His Majesty, our King, and John Pym's Parliament. That we tottered on the brink of fighting I plainly saw. Who would win was not evident. The King had royal might, power and law on his side, if not the will and good wishes of his people. The mostly strict Puritan members of Parliament believed God gave them His blessing, and half England knew it to be true. Common logic decreed that the King should prevail, and my family might be persuaded that a link to the King through Fowke influence could preserve the Merchants Emerick if His Majesty prevailed over John Pym this year. That argument alone might convince my family to support a marriage contract. I must write today. Mistress Maye, not one to prattle or disturb a man's thoughts, drank her ale and let me muse.

"Would Lady Fowke permit you to show me through the house and gardens, Mistress?"

"Mary?"

"You need to speak about the garden to those boys and set them about their tasks. Now, you be firm with them, Loveday, or they'll be in the stable yard idling about. Steward Giff will walk with you and Master Emerick, and stand behind you when you speak to the boys. I'll send him round to you."

I gave Mary another of my smiles. This was heaven sent. A short space of time to whisper to the heiress and talk of Emerick and Gamlen matters.

Mary chortled. "Away with you two, I'll send Giff straight after." She turned herself around and headed for the door. "I'm to the kitchens, my lady has a special dinner in mind and the cook is awry."

Mistress Maye looked at me. Ah, those speaking eyes of hers. I looked too long and she, discomforted, gazed into her lap. I stood and bowed. "My apologies, Mistress, for staring. You have a little cherry juice on your right cheek." I directed my gaze to myself and carefully removed a crumb of pastry from my cuff lace. "Difficult things to eat tidily, pastry tarts." When I looked up Mistress Maye had a red patch on her cheek where she had scrubbed it, but her blush had faded. I offered a hand to assist her to her feet, but did not cling or clasp to hers.

Comfortable once more she swished her skirts straight. "Thank you, Master Emerick. Shall we walk through the hall to the ladies' door and the gardens? It's a pleasant way to the stables and I can show you Denzil Gamlen's collection of Italian paintings in the Italian room."

"I would be delighted to see them." I made another bow. "Did you know, Mistress, that my father and Denzil Gamlen went to Oxford together?" I opened the door with a flourish and gestured her through. "Perhaps we are kin enough that you may call me Jacob." Mistress Maye dipped a little curtsy, her eyes correctly downcast, shy again, but she agreed. Thank God indeed, here was the maid who might be honest enough to help me if she could. I offered her my arm and spoke cautiously of the long history of Emerick and Gamlen friendship, starting with my great-grandfather, who had grown up on a farm hereabouts, and ending with amusing tales about Denzil Gamlen and my father. Time tomorrow to see if she told her grandam any or all of my stories or held her tongue.

# CHAPTER SIX

The morrow brought an inquest, the coroner riding over from Wealdon, the nearest large town, at Parson Paske's request. Nowell and I, required as witnesses, had to show where we found the body. A party of stoutly Puritan jury men, the parson, the men who removed the body, and a doctor who came with the coroner, all walked to the hawthorn hillock, not an irksome task on a gentle April day. Nowell and I pointed out the place beneath the trees. Abdias and Zachary concurred, adding that they found no trace of Lawyer Jameson's horse or property, no sign that it had been hidden and removed, no sign of thieves lying in wait. Zachary, the woodsman, pointed out that the road, well used, had displayed only the usual forms of traffic, but that he'd swear an oath that four foot travellers, seven horsemen and three heavy carts had gone by that morning.

We tramped back in silence, through variable weather, drizzly showers, a shy peep of sun from behind the clouds, and more louring greyness; the sun appeared finally as we reached Parson Paske's home. There the inquest became formal. We trooped through the main door, marched down the hallway and stood in the large hall as the coroner instructed us all, at wearisome length, on our duties and rights. He told the jury three times what they might be asked to find. The coroner, Parson Paske and two of that panel of church wardens sat behind a long trestle table, stools and a bench were found for the jury, but Nowell and I had to stand through it all. We eased ourselves towards the nearest wall, close enough to lean the point of a shoulder against it for support, yet without the slovenly appearance of a slouch, as the coroner continued to instruct us all in his duties and rights. Doctor Matthews and his man waited before us. The doctor and I stood of a height, but his man came only to my shoulder, his heavy belly pouched over his belt, told of beer and overmuch food. He didn't look a suitable servant for the proper, neat and nice doctor. Still he had thick muscles and stout thews, more square and solid than round and fat, perhaps a useful guard to protect the doctor on his many journeys. He fidgeted from foot to foot until his master was called, then stilled, head on one side, listening. I straightened up, wanting to con any detail which might help me clear my name. Nowell did likewise. "Let us hope," he whispered on a thread of breath, "this doctor knows how to read death and has good news for us."

His man turned his head towards us sharply. "My master has much experience with unnatural deaths. If you did it he'll find out, and show how."

Nowell scoffed. "Better he show how we are innocent."

"Silence," the coroner ordered, his voice breaking as he raised it too fast. "Your turn to speak will come when I say so."

Nowell and I inclined our heads and stilled our tongues. The servant smirked.

"Doctor Matthews, explain to the jury how Lawyer Jameson was killed."

The doctor twitched his shoulders, tugged at his neck band and coughed. He gave a long lecture on the marks round Jameson's throat, and the cord found round his neck, concluding that Philip Jameson had been strangled with the cord.

"We knew that," I muttered to Nowell, as one juryman coughed noisily. Parson Paske sent a swift questing look at us.

"I know, Doctor Matthews," said the coroner, "that you have

studied in London, where you have many more bodies to examine." He sounded as if hundreds of corpses lay in the streets of the city daily. "Is there any way you can tell the Court when Master Jameson died. Had he been lying under the hawthorn for a day or less?"

"The body had lost rigour when I first saw it. That is," he explained to our puzzled faces, "a new killed body is limp, begins to stiffen after a few hours, becomes rigid and then slowly softens." The coroner looked up to speak, the doctor anticipated him. "It can take a long time for a body to lose rigour, or a few hours." He tugged at each side of his broad collar as he thought, cleared his throat and spoke again. "I believe that Lawyer Jameson had been dead for over half a day when the body was found."

Nowell touched my arm. I raised my brows in return. Now that was news we wanted to hear. Parson Paske bent his head towards the coroner and they talked. The coroner turned his head in our direction and beckoned.

"Master Merriot, come and give witness. Stand before us. When did you find the body of Master Philip Jameson?"

Nowell strode forward to face those at the table. "Master Emerick and I found the body around noon."

"Did you know Master Jameson? Had you seen him on the road or at an inn?"

Nowell shook his head. "No, I did not travel the main highway. I came from Leape where I had taken two horses to Joliffe's Manor there. I spent an extra two nights with the Joliffes for a mare they wished to breed had ripened and my stallion served her and then rested a day. I left them the morning Master Emerick and I found the body. I joined the main highway just before the stretch of open heath land."

Now that did lower jaws and focus eyes on me. The hunt was off and I was the quarry. Nowell spoke the truth as he must, but I feared the ensuing chase, both the wardens and some of the jurymen concentrated their gaze upon me. I forced myself to shape my body to an easy stance and keep a pleasant face.

The coroner leant across the table. "You travelled alone."

"From the Joliffes, yes."

Parson Paske murmured in the coroner's ear.

"You saw no other person, traveller, pedlar, labourer, no one, until you met Master Emerick?"

Nowell shook his head. Voices began to make themselves heard, but above the growing murmur, Nowell spoke, pitching his voice to be heard by all. "The only traveller I saw was Master Emerick riding before me. That stretch of common heath land is very flat and bare of trees. The road runs straight, and I saw Master Emerick riding ahead of me all the way to the hawthorn hillock, where he stopped and I joined him."

Praise the Lord, and God bless Nowell for that.

Parson Paske spoke for them all, even ahead of the coroner. "How can you be sure? The road after the heath is narrow and winds. How can you be sure that it was not another rider you saw on the heath?"

Nowell laughed. "Masters, have you seen Master Emerick's horse? My family breed fine horses, and I notice them. His mare is striking, angular, sharp rumped, her colour most unusual. She has black legs, mane and tail, and a light blue-grey body, deepening into a dark blue-grey on her rump which is scattered over with pear shaped white spangles. Her blue colour is rare, and I pushed my horse to catch up, intending to look the animal over carefully, perhaps make an offer. Only we found the body."

The coroner frowned, discussed Nowell's words with Parson Paske and the wardens, then dismissed him. "Master Emerick, stand forth."

I did, knowing that whilst Nowell had cleared me in his eyes, the coroner and parson would still see me as the most likely candidate for murderer. I schooled my wits to calm thought and my mouth to careful speech. I would not lie, but must not reveal that I found and moved the body before Nowell arrived.

"Master Emerick, how long were you at the hawthorn hillock

before Master Merriot joined you?"

"I had time to loosen the girth and cover the saddle, slip the bit and tie the reins. Then Master Merriot was upon me."

"You are certain you were alone, you saw no one?"

"No one, no rider, no cart, no walker."

The parson whispered to the coroner. The coroner turned to me. "Master Emerick, how well do you know the road?"

I allowed my face to show surprise, let my voice express it. "Not at all, good sirs, I have never been into Kent before. I travelled the main highway from inn to inn, following each landlord's directions."

The chief of the jurymen wished to ask a question. He and his fellows had been fidgeting ever since the coroner began questioning me. Finally the coroner turned his head. "What is it?" The juryman whispered. The coroner shook his head.

"Consider your answer to my next question with care, Master Emerick. Your family would have been advantaged by the death of this man, we know this..."

"Not so."

The coroner's face turned a rosy hue, his jaw trembled. Before he could speak again I began a speech I had carefully prepared. "I do not know how many of you, good sirs, had intimate acquaintance with Master Denzil Gamlen." I could see my polite addressing of them and my seeming change of subject puzzled the jury and wardens. The coroner and Parson Paske eyed me narrowly as though I were some blight on the cherries. I hid any sign of amusement. I might laugh later, but now I must convince these men that I had no reason to kill poor Master Jameson. "Parson Paske, could you tell me how many here would know of Denzil Gamlen's business affairs?"

"Few, if any, Master Emerick."

"I thank you. Then please, I beg of you, keep my confidences, Masters all. What I must explain to you is rightly only the business of the Merchants Emerick and the Gamlen heiress. I pray you keep silent on the matters I touch upon for I am here to negotiate for the Emericks, not with Denzil Gamlen, alas, but with Lady Fowke, who is managing all for the Gamlen heiress, Mistress Maye. I need every advantage I can hold."

There were hisses of indrawn breath and frowns on the faces of some jurymen. The parson pricked up his ears like a hound catching a note from a horn. The coroner continued to scowl at me.

"The Gamlens and Emericks have long been intimate. It's our family's fairy tale." I couldn't resist adopting a traditional story teller's stance and voice, just to vex the coroner and Parson Paske. "Long ago a beautiful Emerick maid captured the heart of a fair Gamlen youth. Their marriage began an abiding friendship between the families...." I broke off my performance before the coroner, whose face had mottled puce, took a fit. "When my grandfather began his merchant career he used Gamlen money. My father and Denzil Gamlen studied at university together, and Denzil Gamlen, eager to increase his investments, bought a share of our newest ships. His investments amount to a considerable sum." I paused to check for nodding heads and comprehending faces. "This past Christmastide Denzil Gamlen fell ill and changed his will. Because he had no wife or surviving children his estate he would leave to his nearest family. That is to his younger sister's child, Mistress Maye. To protect our mutual investments special agreements were to be drawn up." I looked at the coroner and Parson Paske to see if they followed where I led. "Legal agreements to be held by his lawyer and myself, giving the Merchants Emerick an extended period of time to repay, should the heirs wish for all in gold, and not yearly in profits from our ventures."

The jurymen appeared to be listening closely; I addressed them directly. "The Merchant Emericks do not have a copy of this document, Lawyer Jameson, following Denzil Gamlen's instructions, was to have a copy made for us. We never received it. Philip Jameson's death spells disaster to the Emericks, especially as any documents he had have disappeared."

So nearly there, now would they accept and believe? Some faces told me they might.

"Do you see, good sirs, how I could never have killed Lawyer Jameson? The Merchant Emericks needed him alive. He knew what the agreements were, he intended to find Denzil Gamlen's document and make a copy of that agreement for us. Lawyer Jameson worked for Denzil Gamlen with the Emericks, not against us. I had no reason to harm him and every reason to keep him from harm."

Tired by all the speechifying I exhaled and let my shoulders sag. I would have welcomed a seat, but Parson Paske and coroner wanted to ask more questions. I answered as politely as my mother taught me, although I longed to hurl the nearest stool at the parson, who insisted that there were ways I could have fooled Master Merriot, and enumerated some. I disliked his mention of the possibility of my turning back and waiting for another traveller to see me ride back to the hillock, it ran too near to what I did.

Finally the coroner stood and spoke to the jury. "We cannot accept Master Emerick's word without confirmation from Lawyer Jameson's office. We accept that he has only his own papers, and that Master Merriot believes he saw him before the body was found. Lawyer Jameson's papers are missing, as is his horse and baggage. Master Emerick has shown he has no reason to kill Lawyer Jameson, his reasoning is strong. Therefore I direct you to find the death as murder by person or person unknown. However," and here he turned back to me, "Master Emerick must not leave Eikenthorpe until we have received proof in the form of confirmation from Lawyer Jameson's office."

Nowell was free to leave and he did so, after giving details of where he travelled to the coroner, but I had to stay, only able to ride out to Gamlen Manor to attend to business with Lady Fowke.

# CHAPTER SEVEN

I saw Mistress Maye daily, Loveday, as I was now permitted to call her. It was she who gave me hope and kept me from despair. I felt as one tottering on the edge of a high place with jagged rocks to break me far below. The parson remained suspicious that I had knowledge of Lawyer Jameson's murder. We waited still for that confirmation from London. I found myself obliged to talk with him and the Wardens each morning, outside on the green, in front of the church, if you please, with any of the community who wanted to, looking on. The daily catechism followed the same pattern.

"Have you anything further to tell us, Master Jacob Emerick?"

I would shake my head at them all, looking each man in the eye, Parson Paske last of them. "I have told you all that I know, Parson Paske. There is no more to tell."

My family, all business-like as the Merchants Emerick, instructed their lawyer to stand firm, my father warning me to say nothing of the missing papers. Too late for that. He sent Parson Paske details of the Emerick dealings with Master Philip Jameson and of my actions on the three days before I left London. He even included my itinerary, and the names of the inns where I'd stayed, demanding that the parson send someone to confirm that I travelled alone and never met with poor Master Jameson, lending all the weight of what influence he had to clear me. I believe he added a discreet warning regarding my safety and what might happen in

Eikenthorpe if anything happened to me, but the parson did not share that message.

Loveday, though, on our third meeting, had listened to my tale of the missing documents quietly, then explained that she needed to write to her father to ask his advice and permission to speak of her uncle's plans. She would send a note that night. She knew of a messenger returning to her village in Essex. And no, she had not found any such document, but nor had her aunt, that she could say as a surety. With that to comfort me I faced the task of attempting to reason with Lady Fowke with more equanimity.

True to her word Loveday sent and eventually received a private message from her father and took me off to walk in the garden. She gathered what spring herbs and flowers there were, me holding the basket and learning what I could. With garden boys and gardeners around us for propriety, Loveday told me what her uncle had done.

She spoke quietly, talking of the flowers and herbs as she gave me them to place in the basket, in between each garnering she would add, in the same quiet tone, a piece of information about Denzil Gamlen's wishes. I had not thought she'd have the sophistry to be such a conspirator, but then I remembered Kitty's and Eva's ways with a secret. 'Twas a feminine wile to know and to hide. I struggled to keep my face polite and still as I heard the information, but I had promised to be discreet as a good lawyer should and must.

"Uncle Denzil changed his will as a safeguard. He believed that the divide betwixt King and Parliament might be too wide to bridge." She bent, searching amongst the dried bracken protecting her herbs and plucked a few new leaves. I knew them by their pungent smell. "Here's the first mint showing through, Jacob." I took the few leaves carefully. "Enough for a tisane of mint leaves and honey for my aunt," she added.

I sighed, but merely as a gentle exhalation. If Loveday heard, she gave me no sign.

"My uncle feared that with Parliament's pressure and the

majority of the country supporting them, the King might be deposed, his son asked to rule. Yet he also foresaw a darker future." She frowned, then pointed out a bed of yellow flowers. "See, all the cowslips are open. Wine making time, we must pick them today. I'll take a last posy of them for the house."

"Loveday," I curbed my haste and calmed my voice. "What did your uncle foresee?"

"A King who is excessively stubborn, strict Puritan Members of Parliament the same. Perchance, at worst, two armies fighting, at best, great civil unrest." Her face echoed my feelings as we contemplated that terrible future. "He wanted to preserve his estates here in Puritan Kent from seizure. The Fowkes are not Puritan, the estate is valuable, seizure would be a certainty."

A wise man, Denzil Gamlen, but I wondered if his plan would work.

She gathered the last of the winter savoury, helping me place it in the basket. "There now, let me see how the pennyroyal and other mints have fared the winter." Her voice changed, softened with delight. "Oh, look at all the primroses, such a patch of yellow to lighten our day." Which comment was so exactly what Kitty and Eva would have said that I closed my mouth on a sharp rejoinder, and on my impatience, looked at the flowers instead.

She picked a large bunch and we drifted, like the April breeze, to the next bed of herbs. "So Denzil Gamlen made you his heiress, Loveday." A sudden notion occurred. I touched her arm. "Did he expect you to marry Rolph Fowke?"

Loveday's peal of laughter, hastily repressed, reassured me. "Ah no, Master Emerick, my aunt has made a great match for Cousin Rolph. She plans an alliance with a wealthy Earl's family. That's where she went today, away for two days, talking agreements."

That sounded like the lady. "And what marriage alliance has she arranged for you?" I wondered if she knew of Lady Fowke's dealing with the Merchants Emerick, her haggling with me over a marriage settlement.

Loveday bent to inspect a clump of spearmint, removing the protective covering of dry leaves and stalks to look for new growth. "My aunt is not my guardian. My father is." She replaced the dead matter over the new shoots and straightened up.

Her words hit hard. I kept my mouth closed by clenching my jaw, paused to breathe, and then spoke as quietly as I could. I didn't want to startle Loveday into a shriek. "I hesitate to speak of something as private as the matter of a marriage settlement, Loveday, but Lady Fowke is certain she is to arrange one for you."

Loveday shook her head. "My father is my parent and guardian. He will have the right to say who I marry," and she dimpled, face flushing, as she added, "as I will have a say in the matter of a husband too. Besides, my aunt doesn't wish me to marry for another year or more. She needs me here. I have to manage the estate until all is settled betwixt King and Parliament."

She took the basket from me and made me stand, holding twine and scissors, whilst she fashioned bunches of what we'd gathered. I pondered her words and Lady Fowke's duplicity. Her ladyship, no fool she, could see I found the prospect of marriage to Loveday appealing, and, perfidious woman, tried to beguile me into a settlement, knowing full well that Loveday's marriage was not hers to arrange. Or mayhap she chose to believe she could overrule Doctor Maye on the matter of guardianship, for making marriage arrangements with me for Loveday she busily was. What a duplicitous manipulating female, I could trust nothing she said or did.

"Jacob, stop cloud gazing, listen. There is more to Uncle Denzil's will than you know. There was a private arrangement made last summer. My father agreed to this for my sake and I promised my uncle for his. I am to manage and hold the Manor here, acting as heiress, until Rolph Fowke may safely claim it. My reward is my aunt's gratitude, no mean thing, Master Emerick, for all you pull a face, plus a yearly allowance."

"Is't legal, Loveday? Did your..."

"Both my father and I signed documents."

"Your uncle cared for his Manor to fit up such a set of secret agreements. But what of the Merchant Emericks, Loveday? Denzil Gamlen promised my father a safeguard to ensure that last year's loan for our ships would not be called in at once."

She put her hand under my elbow, leading me down the gravelled walkway to the kitchens. "I was coming to that. If my uncle promised, then I believe he did write such a document for you."

"Then where is it?"

"Hush, Jacob, lower your voice. I owe much to my aunt, but I owe more to my uncle. He promised your father a document, I gave him my word I'd see his wishes carried out. I must do this, and my father agrees." We had reached the kitchen door. "I will seek out the papers and keep them safe for you. I've all the rest of today and tomorrow to search. I know where to look. Come again the day my aunt returns, and I'll find a way to get them to you."

"Have a care, Loveday. The possession and destruction of these papers is what your aunt needs to force the Merchants Emerick into repaying the loan."

"No, Jacob," her voice saddened, "my aunt needs nothing, no letters or legal documents, she would always find a way to force you to repay the loan. Thank God hourly for this divide between King and Parliament, or you would now be facing the King's displeasure and forfeits as my aunt demands. She only waits, you understand, amusing herself by tormenting you, until she knows how King and Parliament will settle."

Quick witted Loveday had the rights of it. Ah me, what a tangle this all was.

And now, here I was making my way to Gamlen Manor, hoping the document was found, but fearing it had not been. I walked along the riverside path taking care for my boots. Whilst not ridiculously fashionable, they did have large turned-over tops. Rolled high up the thigh when riding they protected my inner leg and prevented me developing saddle sores. But for comfort when walking, they were best worn folded back to the top of the knee, where the excess leather formed a circle around the leg, a large bowl-shaped circle. The left could catch the right in an unpleasant tangle and in no wise was I going to let them catch and pitch me forward onto the path, some local would surely see me. Besides the leather was still un-scratched, no scars marred the rich ox blood colour and I wished them to remain so.

The river Yul was not a great river like the Thames, rather one of those small chattering rivers, one side deepish and steady flowing, the other, scattered shallows, a broad width with rocks, pebbles and little pools. The Yul smelt of moss, rotting leaves and wet stone, different from the thick stew of scents the Thames gave off. No tang of salt and tidal mud here, just of growing things, sappy and green in a rich soil. I stopped to watch two small brown birds bobbing among the rocks. Yesterday morning I'd seen a mist-grey and blue heron with stabbing bill, and I'd heard a cuckoo. Two days ago I saw a kingfisher. Now as I walked to the Manor, I set my mind to quietly examine the problems I faced and observed the world around me. Large lazy fish rings circled in the deepest pool, and I startled two moorhens into clumsy flight. Their dangling legs and gawky progress made me laugh and did much to lighten my spirit. Of course Lady Fowke remained obdurate. How long, oh Lord, did I have to play her as an angler plays a wily trout? I could answer that myself, until Loveday found Denzil Gamlen's papers and gave them to me. Then I could take our papers and go home. Thankfully and rejoicing.

I ambled on down the river path, ignoring the sideways glance of two farm workers heading off with their hoes on their shoulders. The weather held promise of a sunny day, although April had as many moods as a spoilt child, and it was just as likely to cloud over and rain, but fields always needed weeding.

My father commanded me to write daily. Oh, those letters, it had taken one afternoon and most of an evening to write about the proposed marriage as part of the settlement. My father understood that a link to the Fowkes might aid us should the King come to agreement with John Pym's party, but my mother tutted over a marriage made without her approving the maid first and asked many tedious questions. Knott, the lawyer's clerk -- now there was a useful man and a discreet courier -- had carried the letter back to London along with some of Lady Fowke's documents.

Ah, a plague on Lady Fowke and a curse on her cavilling ways. I prodded another pebble into the water, it pinged off a rock and hit the bank, and thought instead about Loveday. A very special maid was Loveday, even to her name, an old name not much used, yet so apt for her. She told me she was born on February the fourteenth, thus her mother had chosen that name as meet and fitting. She was one of God's blessed children, no one frowned on her, all smiled to see her. She listened, didn't gossip or tattle, yet could speak lucidly and to the point. Her mother had schooled her well, and her uncle's library had been hers every summer. Yet she loved her garden, her herbs and simples, keeping house. She had more than a one sided grasp on the problems facing the country, and though her loyal heart was with the King, because of our oaths of allegiance, she could understand my views, being Puritan inclined herself. The Lord taketh, but He'd surely given in return. More than once I'd caught myself about to call her Kitty or Eve. Loveday wouldn't have minded. She knew all about my much missed sisters, as I knew about her yearning for her mother.

I stopped to lean against the broad ribbed trunk of a solitary willow tree and stared across the river flats at the meadow land. Sighing, I removed my hat and rubbed the itchy mark on my forehead where the band had pressed into the skin, ruffled up my hair, then set the hat on my head again. I ran my fingers lightly over the ribs of the tree bark, pushed off from the tree trunk, straightened my spine, and walked on, determined to stop fretting and enjoy this pleasant day.

I could live in the country, providing it wasn't Eikenthorpe. I felt bitter disappointment that the worthy folk of Eikenthorpe continued to look at me with glances loaded with suspicion. The coroner kept his word, and Master Merriot had been free to ride on, but uncertain times made people suspicious, and I knew poor Master Jameson. What stuck in my craw was the fact that Eikenthorpe people were as much self-satisfied as suspicious. I was not one of them. I must be guilty, if only of that. They did not wish me to be one of them. I was to be pitied for living in London. I could never understand Eikenthorpe and its wondrous perfections. I was the outsider, and I was not to disturb their world. That, I was sure, was what they feared -- a disturbance.

Rumours about me changed each day. I'd even heard it said that I might be a spy for Archbishop Laud, looking to report the doings of the Eikenthorpe church and have Parson Paske dismissed. I'd laughed at that one. Yet I felt their fear. These people, they had never seen London, but they thought they knew all about it. They looked at me and decided they knew me too. There were walls inside their heads and blinkers covering their eyes. In truth they knew nothing, yet assumed much, and, dangerously, believed their assumptions were truth.

Surely, I had managed to charm a goody or two into a quick smile, but the rest of the community fell silent near me, glanced sideways and guarded their tongues. Not even my regular attendance at the church services improved my standing with mine host or the Eikenthorpe young men I attempted to talk to. Parson Paske told me the information had arrived from the lawyer's office, but that did not mean I might not know something. Philip Jameson had been buried quietly and respectfully, but I knew I stood alone in a community needing to find a villain, and wanting to condemn me, the outsider, and not one of their own.

Someone's fat pied duck dabbled and splashed, enjoying its escape from the pond on the green. It was quite tame and quacked hopefully, cocking its head and reaching up its beak for a tidbit. I laughed. She put me in mind of Perry. I hoped the mare behaved herself, for the smith was trimming her feet, with only the stable boys to manage her. I'd not miss my time with Loveday, even for Perry, and the Manor wasn't a distance to walk.

I stepped out over that last stretch, eager to reach the Manor, and in the slow water of a deep pool at the bend of the river, where the willows hid the first sight of Gamlen Manor, something drifted into view. I watched it with idle interest, then slitted my eyes to stare. No, not a tree trunk or...a slow spin in the lazy current and the darkish lump turned a pale oval towards me. Dear Lord God, no, not another body. I wasn't finding this one.

# CHAPTER EIGHT

I turned on my heel abruptly, walked back down the path three paces, then swung round. I'd been seen on the path. There had been problems enough over Jameson's body. What I should do was make certain that it was indeed a drowned person, then walk on to Gamlen Manor and have some of the servants retrieve the body.

I stood and looked carefully at the river. The lazy current caught the mass again, the oval rolled and something that, pray God, couldn't be a hand, surfaced, showing a limp lace cuff, and a distinctive pink silk wrist darkened by the water to a puce.

I heard a noise, I didn't know if I'd cried out, but I found myself running, falling down the bank, slipping and crashing over the small rocks and pebbles. In the thigh high water I floundered to grasp at the flaccid body. Oh, God above, how could it be, yet it was. I'd guessed right. I had recognized that sleeve.

"No, oh no, Lord no. Loveday, oh, Loveday." I caught her in my arms. Her sodden weight nearly pulled me under. I staggered, stood firm and let the water pour off her and over me. I cradled her against my chest, touched my cheek against hers, desperate for the warmth of life. An ice frosted cheek returned my touch. No, it could not be. She was only limp and chilled from the water. It made me shiver for it cut to my bones 'til they ached with its winter chill. Loveday, too, she was only stiff from the frigid water. I squelched my way out of the pool and through the shallows, tripping and stumbling on the rocks and weedy boulders. I knew, with a distant awareness, that now my boots were awash, the leather stained, my stockings falling in soggy wrinkles and my long legged breeches soaked to the flap. What did it matter? Loveday, oh, how had Loveday fallen in? Dear God, what had happened? I'd heard nothing, seen nothing. Surely I would have?

"Let me, Master Emerick, let me."

I pressed my eyelids together, blinking several times before I could focus on the man who was trying to take Loveday from me. There was a face with lumpy waxen skin, dank brown hair, and drooping eyelids partly hiding dark eyes. Who? Of course, Knott, it was Clerk Knot, stood before me.

"You must tip her head down, Master Emerick, pull her arms and let the water out. She might breathe again." He reached out. What was he saying? I clutched Loveday closer, finally understood the words. Abruptly I rolled her over and Knott grasped her arms, tugged, then pressed her back. He tried again and again. No water flowed from Loveday's mouth, although her clothes still trickled water in little streams and waterfalls.

Knott shook his head and turned the body face up in my arms. He did not try to wrest Loveday from me, but he manoeuvred me round until the sunlight shone on her pallid face. "Strange." His hand lifted wet hair and the bedraggled cap away from her forehead, clearing her face. There were a few white May blossoms caught in the strands. "There should be some water."

I didn't care, I only felt the dead weight of the body, so different from Loveday alive. I'd swung her up onto Perry's back more than once and knew the feeling of the life spirit in her. There was none now. Loveday's skin was fungus white, no faint pink under-blush or delicate glow left. Her eyes were half closed, their innocence concealed. I could not free a hand to close them. "In God's Name," I begged the clerk, "shut her eyes."

Knott reached up with a trembling hand, gently he closed them. "Did you see or hear her fall?" He sounded bewildered and regretful.

"No, I heard and saw nothing. I just came upon her floating...." I caught myself, my breath snarling on a sob deep in my chest.

Knott pulled at his lower lip and frowned. "She's not...." He stopped and flicked a glance at me. A quick, sharp, rat keen glance which made the skin on the nape of my neck crawl. "There are only two pools between here and the Manor, which are deep enough to drown in."

I said nothing, but hitched Loveday up against my chest and walked on down the riverside path towards the Manor.

At the bridge, out of the empty land, came shouts. People appeared on the Manor side of the river. Two men lumbered towards us.

"Has Lady Fowke returned?" I shouted. "Fetch the lady, or find Mary."

"Make haste," Knott yelled. The men turned and ran.

"Did she fall and hit her head," I said. I couldn't think clearly. The enormity of the death staggered me. Why, oh, why, this gentle maid?

Other people hastened upon us, pushing, scurrying, calling out.

Knott reached out and slid his hand from Loveday's crown to her shoulders then turned her head away from me, touching her skull with little prods of his fingers. "No bump or broken patches," he said, "no water in her mouth and none came out of her." It was as if he were reciting a lesson, but one I did not know. I felt the words like a blow to my gut. Was the man saying she did not fall and drown?

The group arrived, panting and full of distress. Their breathless queries of "Who?" and "What?" stilled as they saw Loveday in my arms.

Servant Mary, puffing up behind, groaned, then reached out one hand to Loveday's cheek. Her touch removed any hope. Only then did she wail. My flesh bristled with more than goose bumps. The other women and men moaned or cried out. Not one was unmoved by her death, their faces showed their pain and disbelief. They wanted to know why and turned a concentrated anger on me. Knott stepped away, disappearing behind the group.

"What happened?" Mary's voice was sharp, her tears slowly rolled down either side of her nose.

I struggled to speak. "I found her in the river." I shut my eyes and saw again the dark lumpish bundle. "I waded in to fetch her but she was...." I raised my arms slightly to show them the body.

One young girl, the Manor goose girl, bawled, her breath gasping noisily in and out between her words. "I seen him." She pointed a wobbling finger in my direction. "I seen him holding her in the water." She blubbered afresh.

The murmur rose in a wave of sound. Every person stared at me, and I felt the weight of their suspicion. "Of course you saw me," I said, putting legal and Emerick authority into my voice. "You saw me wading in to the river when I found the body and went to lift her out." My voice cracked and I looked down, near to tears. "Clerk Knott saw me find her. He will tell you."

But Clerk Knott had disappeared.

The goose girl said nothing, just wailed and pointed at me.

"Hush now, Mattie," Mary said, but she sobbed too. "Adam, go and fetch the long board from the cart. Get Betty to put a decent cloth on it. Hurry."

No one tried to take Loveday from me, we marched as a group to the Manor, without words, our silence punctuated by sobs and caught breaths. The world around us took no note of the tragedy. I heard the chaffinch chink, the blackbird startle and a lark rose into the sky with his magnificent song. Loveday's favourite bird and she not able to hear it any more.

Knott reappeared, padding along beside me and I expected

him to speak up. He came on me so quickly he must have seen me find her body, must have watched me dash into the water. For sure he'd walked the path behind me. I wanted a word with Clerk Knott, but there was no time for more thinking. Lady Fowke came.

She stepped across the tender green of the ornamental camomile path, still wearing her travelling clothes and hat, to wait beside the knot garden. The light scent of camomile drifted on the air, and I nearly cried out. Loveday combed her hair with camomile water.

Lady Fowke, upright and controlled, had no tears. She gestured me away when I placed the body on the cart plank bier. But her hands, touching Loveday's eyes and folding her arms upon her breast, did so with regret and sorrow.

"Take her to her room," she said. "Tonight we will take her to the church." The men moved off as ordered. Some of the group followed. Her Fowke eye fixed me with that fierce hawk stare. "How, i' God's Name, did this happen?"

I was bone cold and heart sore, but my wits began to work. There were hostile ears stretched to hear me, and I intended to make sure the truth was told. "I walked from Eikenthorpe, my Lady, to keep our appointment." I saw the raised eyebrow and answered the unspoken question. "The smith is trimming my mare's feet."

The tangible hostility, the disbelieving sounds around me, threatened again, but Lady Fowke glared. I drew in breath and continued, careful with my words. "At the bend in the river, the one before this Manor, where there's a deep pool of water, I saw something which I knew to be a body. I waded in, hoping to help, and found Love ...your niece." I failed to say Loveday's name and bowed my head to hide my tears.

Zach, the stable-foreman, spoke out. "Mattie saw him, my Lady." He made it an accusation. The group pressed hard, threatening, eager for someone to blame.

Lady Fowke stared at her servants. Zach thrust the goose girl forward and she stood, struck dumb. She wrung her hands in her russet apron and shifted from one bare foot to the other. Lady Fowke grew impatient. "Well? What did you see, girl?"

"I seen him, holding her in the water." She knuckled away tears.

"You mean you saw me lift her out," I said, keeping my teeth clenched to prevent my shivering spoiling the words. "I think, my lady, that you'll also find that the clerk, Knott, saw me find the body." I looked round for him. He had vanished again.

Mattie sniffed and hid herself behind Mary. Lady Fowke sighed. "I cannot understand..." she let her voice tail away. "Would you, Master Emerick, take these men and see if you can find where Loveday fell?" It was almost a polite command from the Lady.

Zach, Abel and Jed accompanied me back along the river path, walking this time on the Manor side. Knott was before us. We found him kneeling beside the path at that first pool. Each man walked carefully, looking for slips or slurs in the bare earth or new turned clods and a crumbled river edge. I stood, shivering and looked down into the river, letting my eyes follow the base of the bank where it met the river like a little cove. Nothing there, and the men found no signs of a fall, nor were there snags like hidden roots or rocks on the path to tumble over.

"Boot tracks, women's pattens, bare feet," said Knott. "this track is well used."

We walked on slowly, heads down. But we could not find anything to show where Loveday had fallen in. The return journey, made just as carefully, allowed us to examine the ground again with the light coming from behind us. Still there was no place or mark to show how Loveday entered the water. The Fowke men muttered to each other and cast sideways glances at me.

"I'll not take much more of this," I told Knott. "I found a body, no one should say otherwise. And you must have seen me."

Knott shook his head. "Indeed I saw nothing, just you carrying a body."

I restrained, with effort, a snarl. That wretched clerk had been near enough to see. "I know you saw, you crawling worm, for if you did not then it's because you put Mistress Loveday in the water and I'll say so." I could speak no more as my voice failed.

Lady Fowke waited for our return, still standing amongst the camomile. She dismissed the men, told Knott to take himself back to his papers, and took me off to her library.

Weary with disbelief, numb from the icy damp deep inside my bones, I answered her repetitious questions dully and longed for quiet. "No, I'd heard nothing, seen no one. We'd found nothing to show how Loveday came to be in the river." Finally: "My lady, I am chilled through and very wet, may I borrow a horse and return to the Moon and Stars?"

Lady Fowke blinked, drawing her thoughts back from some distant place. "Go, Master Emerick, we will talk again tomorrow."

I bowed and withdrew, coaxed a warm cloak from Mary, borrowed a quiet horse and rode briskly back to Eikenthorpe. The sun hid behind a ripple of grey clouds, a late April wind blew down the valley. My hands stiffened so I could barely hold the reins, my fingers looked blue-white, but I no longer trembled with cold, I was rigid. If the landlord could be persuaded, a fire would be welcome in my room. Oh, Lord God, why Loveday? How did it happen? How came you to drown, you poor maid? I wept for Loveday and her short life on the whole of that return journey.

Good news gallops, but bad news grows wings. News of the death had flown. Parson Paske and several of his wardens clustered beside the parsonage gate. They stared at me. The breeze scattered white petals like tears over their dark jerkins. It was some comfort to think that even trees might weep for her. More petals sighed down on the wind. Every head turned in my direction as I rode to the inn. I nodded and trotted on, right now I wanted warmth, dry clothes and a hot drink. I refused to supply gossip about Loveday to these carrion.

The stable boy took the Fowke horse away. Perry nickered and stomped her feet. I rubbed her cheek, welcoming her warmth and gave her re-shod hooves a speedy examination. Good, well finished, hooves properly trimmed and shoes neatly fitted. "I'll be back soon," I said, rubbing her forehead at its centre whorl with cold stiffened knuckles.

There were no greetings inside the inn. I scuffed damp feet over the new cleaned floor, and the landlord glowered. He came forward to meet me. "If you come into the kitchens, Master Emerick, we can dry your boots and give you a hot posset against a fever." He tried to move me along in front of him, trundling me away from the stairs and my room as if I were a barrel.

"No, I thank you, dry clothes first." I dodged the arm and staggered upstairs, shedding the cloak, fumbling at my shirt strings. My room door was wide open. Mine host's clucky hen of a wife was bundling the bed linen onto the floor, searching through it as she did. One maid rummaged through a saddle bag, and a man servant was wrenching at my saddle. He appeared to be trying to undo the stitching to poke between the lining and the tree.

I exploded. "How dare you touch my things?" I had my short sword ripped from scabbard to the man's throat in a blink. "You leave that saddle." He looked about to spring at me. I whipped the borrowed cloak over his head and yanked him sideways, as I wrenched the saddle from his grasp. "If there's any damage done...." I examined the stitching. I wasn't worried about my money and private letters. They were safe, if damp, carried in my leather purse hanging on its special hook and hidden under the tabs of my doublet. But my other documents lay scattered around the floor, and my stout box made for the safe keeping of my pistols had been forced open. The lid swung by one hinge and the pattern of three woods inlaid around the lock had been splintered into sharp white slivers. That box my sisters had given me. "I'll make you pay for this." I roared. All the anger and pain of the day went into it impressively. The women scuttled into a huddle by the window. They skirted my pistols scattered across the floor. The man servant backed off, guilt and terror writ in equal parts across his face.

"We wanted to be sure you hadn't shot Mistress Maye." The

landlord spoke from the doorway, his tone truculent, his expression half shame, half determination. He watched the wavering blade anxiously.

I drew in breath and bellowed some more. It felt good. "You addle-pated moonling. You saw me walk out this morning without any pistols. How could I use the pistols when they were both locked up in that box?"

The landlord retreated. Furious and wobbling on my feet, I followed. I might be a small man, but I knew I could deal with a tub of goose grease like mine host. I rounded on the others present. "Mistress Loveday Maye drowned. There were no bullet holes in her poor body." I whirled back to the landlord. "I'll have your licence for this."

Footsteps sounded on the stairs. I glanced towards the door and the man servant kicked out. My sword flew ceiling-wards. I latched onto his flying foot and jerked hard. The landlord yelped, the women squealed, but the man servant went down with a thump. I snatched up one pistol and twisted myself around so that I watched both the door and the interior

Uproar from the door. Voices protested and bodies jostled. "No more, please, Master Emerick, no more, my friends." I turned my head. Yes, that was Parson Paske's voice and his arm held back a group of local worthies, including his wardens. Well, I'd make them apologize.

"Look at this. Is this how respectable visitors are treated in Eikenthorpe? Is this your hospitality?" I encompassed my upset room with a wave of one arm. Then I thrust the pistol under the parson's nose. "The flint is chipped." I turned and shoved the pistol's damaged firing mechanism under the landlord's nose. "Of what use is that flint now, you fat fool? Look at my pistol box. You will pay for all of this."

"Come, Master Emerick, we will talk in my home." Parson Paske's voice, low pitched, soothed. His arm held back the other men.

I eyed the group. Something didn't sound in tune. I had no intention of talking to anyone. "This is my room, fully paid for. I don't remember inviting all you people to meet me here."

"We must talk about Mistress Maye, about Loveday, Master Emerick."

I considered, something bode ill. I regarded Parson Paske. "Are you arresting me?"

"King's spy," someone muttered.

I looked down my nose and sneered. "Spy? You ignorant fool."

"Spy," young Will Verne hissed, as he squeezed his way through the press at the door.

I snatched up my sword but, as swiftly, the parson intervened. "That's enough." He addressed the men with him. "Master Emerick will stay with me until I am satisfied about today's affairs." That was the voice of command, as forceful as Lady Fowke's and as effective. "All Master Emerick's property is to be brought over to my home. All damage is to be repaired." The landlord shuffled and his wife's cheeks coloured to a hue deeper than her scarlet flannel petticoat. "Make certain, Peter, that Master Emerick's pistols and box are put to rights." They murmured.

I stood firm. "I do not agree. I've paid for my room here. There is nothing to show that Mistress Loveday Maye's death," my voice wavered, "was not an accident. Lady Fowke herself agrees."

Several men spoke out, but Parson Paske's voice silenced them. "And nothing to say it was not. No one can see how she fell into the water." He smiled and extended his hand. It was a peculiarly charming smile, which lit his face with an inner warmth. "Come, we shall find the truth together."

I reviewed my choices. A speedy reckoning showed me that Parson Paske's home was preferable to the local gaol. That was probably someone's dark cellar, or an old bull box, half midden, and half pig's sty. The parson could only hold me until Clerk Knott cleared me of drowning Loveday. "You will have to make room for my mare, Parson Paske."

"Of a certainty."

"I'll bring her." I turned on the cowering landlord. "Send me my bags and boxes, all repaired and made good, landlord, by tomorrow." I elbowed through the group. "Stand off, you men."

"Show him the way, Will," The parson called. Footsteps thumped down the stairs behind me.

I smiled to myself, ducked round the corner and was out in the inn's stable yard long before Will. Perry, nosing hopefully in her manager, whickered affectionately, blowing into my face when I slipped in beside her. I cupped her chin and blew back. She lipped my cheek as I reached for her bridle, slipping it off the hook as Will arrived.

"Move, Master Spy." Will shook, anger and sorrow clear in his face and hot eyes. Loveday, I'd swear, had been his first, love-from-afar, and he was in a rage of pain and fury.

"Spy? Guard your tongue, boy." I turned my back, dropped the headstall and bridled the mare. She shoved herself between us and nudged me. I leant one arm over her withers, thankful for her body's warmth and support, and walked out of the stall with her. In the yard she swung her head round and nudged again, as though asking me why I wasn't riding her. I rubbed her forehead, slid my hand to her withers, grasped a tuft of mane and swung myself up.

Will ducked under Perry's neck and grabbed my leg. "Oh no, you don't."

"Leave off." I pulled my leg back, then kicked hard, shoving him into the stable wall.

Will bounced off the wall, picked up a nearby broom and swung wildly at me. I ducked forwards, but it caught me across the cheek with a resounding thwack that rattled my teeth. I slipped sideways, wresting the broom from Will, then flung my arms around Perry's neck to save myself from crashing onto the cobbles. Will leapt, grabbing the edge of my doublet to pull me down. I let my weight collapse my body onto his. As I fell on top of him, his boot kicked me sharply in my ribs. It made me angry. Master Will was going to suffer for that.

# CHAPTER NINE

Will managed one hit to my head, a wild glancing blow, but his intentions were vicious. I rolled over, up onto my feet, pulling him up with me. Snarling, I struck back, but at half strength. Young Will, a mere bantam cockylorum, had obviously not learned to fight in earnest. I ducked his next badly flung fist and jabbed him in the mouth, a swift neat blow. He staggered back, flailing his arms. I managed a grin. A pity indeed that my brothers weren't here to see that. I stopped Will's next swing and clouted him on the side of the head. It was a good blow and hurt the boy, but he came on again. I thrust my leg between his, tripped him, and down he went on the cobbles with a thunk. I dived to pin him there for an easy finish, but behind me came a clatter of shod feet, and the cursed-be church wardens and community were upon me. Typically partisan, they laid their ungentle hands on my doublet, grabbed, then sat upon me, an unequal and ignominiously rotten way to end the fight. Not content with parting me from their young man, these men banged my head against the yard cobbles a few times as they dragged me away from Will. I cursed, kicking out swiftly, giving myself the satisfaction of hacking several arms and shins in repayment. I found myself swung to my feet, forced upright with a jolt that jarred the bump to my head.

Parson Paske had Will by the scruff of his doublet and a fistful of curly hair. "Will, think, boy. Master Emerick has no notion of riding away and leaving all his worldly goods behind. Curb your temper and desist."

Will muttered under his breath and nodded his head carefully. His lower lip resembled a bruised plum. I swallowed a smile then winced myself. Pain fingered the left side of my face. Those blows on the cobble stones. My cheek felt as though it was puffing up to reach my ear. My teeth ached from the head bashing I'd been given. Still I'd reckon Will had a worse head, with sore ribs and a stiff back to boot. I hoped that his every breath would ache for the next couple of days. That would teach him to kick his elders and betters.

Will, released, glared, but did not move towards me. The parson patted his shoulder. "Be easy, Will, we all seek the truth about Mistress Loveday."

I, held by many hands which pushed, shoved and pummelled me, staggered, my head whirling.

"Enough." The parson's voice again. "Let him walk with me."

The men murmured, but set me on my way with a shove that speared a shaft of pain to the top of my skull. Perry, standing bewildered, stepped towards me, huffing through her nostrils. I leaned against her shoulder, catching my breath. That, I supposed was a sample of what I faced now, until Loveday's death was explained. I'd settle that clerk when I saw him again, slipping off without giving witness. A plague on Knott, a pox on him and these stupid oafs.

We crossed the green as a group, the wardens a watchful circle about me, one supporting Will. Parson Paske ignored their presence. He looked Perry over and told me what a striking mare she was. He could see why Master Merriot recognised her. After praising her he pointed out the notable houses, as though I were a traveller passing through. The parson's own home was, he said, a family house inherited from his father and long time the Paske family home. I managed to reply politely, mentioning that the renovations seemed a good idea, brick being easier to maintain and sure to last longer than plaster. I didn't tell him I preferred the Gamlen Manor House's decorated plaster, all those garlands of flowers painted in bright colours. The parson's home stood stark, undecorated, exactly Puritan. A modest man, Parson Paske, correct to his glove tips and not one to make an ungodly ostentatious display of his wealth and well doing.

Ah, someone had warned the parsonage, or they'd heard the noise and come to see. The parson's wife stood at the door waiting for us. From the distance I thought she looked all Paske's wife should be, neat cap, tidy and soberly dressed, though not in grey or black, rather a muted blue. Close to her, I noticed her eyes, a clear blue. She offered her hand, begging me enter, her face warming with her smile. She looked directly into my eyes and apologized for the dust and noise, "Welcome, Master Emerick, to our home. I am sorry I didn't meet you on your last visit. May your stay with us be a comfort to us all." She then sighed, her smile now rueful. "And forgive the builders' disturbance. They will be finished within a few weeks." Her tone sounded more hopeful than believing, as she glanced at her husband.

She dispatched the wardens with a quick tongue and apt biblical quotations. I tried to smile, my best charm-the-ladies one, but my mouth failed, my cheek too bruised to move. At least she did not quote at me. I'd never beaten my mother at that game and I guessed that Mistress Paske could out-quote me too. "He has no need of your heavy hands, his word is enough," she scolded. "'He who smiteth first sinneth against the Lord,' you should remember that." My guards shifted uneasily. I stood, waiting for them to go. The parson nodded at them and they left, with obvious reluctance.

"Faith, Master Emerick will be staying with us until certain matters are examined and settled. Jacob, Mistress Paske will tend your injuries and make you welcome."

The parson's wife reached but did not touch my throbbing

cheek. "That's a bad bruise, come along in and we'll treat it." She took my arm to lead me. "Bring Will, please, Richard," she said over her shoulder. "He needs patching too." She tutted at him. "Ah, Will, I know you, acting in haste again. This time you've suffered. Perhaps now you'll think first before swinging your fist? Come and sit with Master Emerick and make your peace. Happenchance he'll teach you how to block wild blows from firebrand youths."

Will's face glowed a dusky red and he mumbled, but inaudibly. I almost pitied him. The parson took his upper arm in a friendly grip and propelled him down the hallway. Mistress Paske followed with me, taking me through the long hall, turning right, the way I had not walked before. I exhaled quietly, grateful to be gently steered. Mistress Faith Paske had a careful hand, she didn't jolt or jar me. Now the immediate danger had passed, the day's happenings weighted me down, a load so physical that every bone ached and my back bent.

"Here we are, Master Emerick." Mistress Paske Paske put a hand on my shoulder blades, guiding me to a seat by the fire. She exclaimed, and two lines formed a vee between her eyebrows as she scanned my face. "You are soaked to the skin." She gently pushed me to sit down. "Here, sit close to the flames and warm up."

"I thank you, Mistress Paske." I allowed myself to sink onto the fireside bench. My bruises throbbed and nagged. A smith started work in my head. I didn't feel like moving again.

Mistress Paske touched my cheek carefully. "That will be sore unless we treat it swiftly." She turned to Will. "Sit over here, Will, and mend thy manners." She spoke as an elder sister would, thrusting Will down on the opposite bench where he could see me and I could watch him. Then she smiled up at her husband. "Richard, there is a message come for you from Lady Fowke."

The parson's eyebrows rose. "Indeed? I thank you, is the messenger waiting?"

She nodded. "I've left him beside your study door." Her anxious eyes, scanning his face, told me much about their marriage, for her face didn't relax into a smile until he inclined his head in approval. Here was the kind of marriage my mother approved of. Three brothers married, a quiver of grandchildren, yet she urged me frequently to make a marriage of respect and understanding with a good, God fearing woman. Alas, all my mother's chosen godly young women were whey-faced, mealy mouthed and dull. Only Loveday.... Oh God in heaven, why did you take her? I groaned and held my head.

The parson dropped a heavy woollen blanket over my shoulders. "Faith will care for you. I have your word that you will remain here until we have examined Mistress Loveday Maye's death?"

I raised my head a little. "My word is given. I care about Mistress Loveday Maye."

"Then I will speak with you later." As he turned away Parson Paske smiled at Will. "And Will shall keep you company, until he takes your hand and promises good behaviour." Will scowled. The parson shook his head at him and departed.

Mistress Paske laughed and caught Will's chin. "Hold still and I'll have thy bruises salved." She reached for a small lidded basket sitting on the hearthstone. It was like Loveday's basket of simples and remedies. I wrenched my thoughts away. I refused to think on her turned to sodden cloth and cold clay. I watched Will squirming under Mistress Paske's hand.

Will's frown deepened.

"Hold still, Will," Mistress Paske's voice carried more command than I thought her capable of delivering. Certainly her meek countenance belied it. "Stop pulling faces and be easy."

I rested and let my eyes glance around to avoid Will's glower. I didn't choose to provoke a fight now, but Will and I would settle accounts later. I'd make sure of that. Instead I welcomed the heat from a fire made to roar by Mistress Paske. I sat so close my boots steamed. The fireplace nearly filled one wall of the room, and I started to feel my extremities again. I noted wearily signs of women's work, before my eyes closed themselves. Spinning wheels, spindles, children's little rush seated stools and toys, baskets of combed wool and distaffs of dressed flax, all things to remind me of women and the loss of one beloved maid. The smells drifting my way from a doorway to the left prompted my stomach to grumble. The scent of baked bread, herbs and hops made me hungry, and I could still feel hunger, Loveday could not. In this room where women's tasks were done, I regretted that I had not been earlier on the river path with a chance to see and to save. I leaned against the settle's high back and tried to relax, hoping my head would quieten even as my heart grew heavier.

"Loveday," Will said, round the cloths being applied to his mouth and chin.

"Hush, Will."

"He knows. He found her." Will struggled to sit up.

Mistress Paske pushed him back firmly and applied more salve. "Will, no more. Keep your peace, and let me finish this."

Will groaned, a sound of such distress which made me wince in sympathy. "Loveday," Will said again.

I opened my mouth, then exhaled noisily. Whatever I said would upset the boy. I'd seen Will several times since that first meeting here in the parson's home, always from a distance, his big brown eyes fixed on Loveday and scowling at me. Loveday was not a knowing maid. I checked. Had not been, I should say. I swallowed back the hard lump threatening to choke me. She had not toyed with Will. Her smile for him was the same for all young men. She never, had never, I corrected myself, favoured any man with more than sisterly affection, myself included. And indeed Will's worship had been from afar, he'd never importuned, merely gazed at Loveday from the back of the church or across the river, much to my amusement. But I'd tempered my laughter with recollections of my first love. At least Will's had been worthy, a true hearted, honest maid, who did not take advantage to demand gifts and favours from a besotted young man.

Oh, God, I prayed, let Loveday be safe among the chosen, one of the blessed as she blessed us. A kind of fierce anger rose up and gripped me, my heart constricted until my breathing faltered. I half rose, setting off protests from my bashed skull and bruised body. I leant upon the settle arm. "I cared for Mistress Loveday Maye, Will. How do you suppose I feel? Don't you think I would give my right hand to have been walking down that path in time to save her?" A sharp pain blinded me. I sank back feeling the silence my outburst had created. When I could open my eyes I found Mistress Paske and Will staring at me. Will's mouth gaped, but Mistress Paske's face glowed with sympathy. I'd swear she had tears in her eyes, their blue lightened with a sudden sheen. A kind woman, Mistress Faith Paske, who hid a soft heart and knew truth when she heard it.

"Say again, what've you said." Will found his voice.

"Before God, Will, believe me. I would give my right hand to have been on that path earlier. I would offer any prayers, promise anything, so that I could have pulled her safe from the water and not be the one to find her drowned in that pool." I closed my eyes to hide the picture of Loveday as I'd last seen her. Her flaccid white face swam into view behind my eyelids. I blinked them opened. Will still stared at me.

"Make me believe that you never saw her fall in. Give me your word that you did not do more than find her." Will's voice cracked. Mistress Paske kept a hand on his shoulder, but the boy showed no sign of rising to attack me.

I was too heart-sick to object to his insistence that I repeat myself. "You have my word that I found her dead in that pool. I know no more than you as to how she fell in or as to why. Here's my hand on it." I reached across and Will slowly extended his hand to clasp it. "As God is my witness, I found Mistress Loveday Maye drowned in the river. I would never have harmed that maid."

Will nodded, then buried his head in his hands.

"Praise God," Mistress Paske said softly. "Thank you, Jacob, thank you, Will. A friend is better than a foe." She smoothed her hand across Will's dark curls. "Don't grieve for long, Will. You should rejoice for Loveday. She is safe away from the pain and suffering of this earthly life." Will raised his head as though to speak. Mistress Paske touched his lips with one finger, preventing any words from spilling over. "Go home, Will, and rest. I know your mother has a good rubbing oil. See you use it soon or you'll suffer." She helped him to his feet and took him off through the kitchen doorway.

I closed my eyes and rested my head carefully on the settle back. There was a border of flowers with raised centres carved just at head height. I'd already found them apt at catching a piece of hair or nobbling the base of my skull. Something nudged my left boot. I stretched out my legs then felt a tug at the same boot. I opened reluctant eyes to peer down and see. A silent child of maybe eight or nine, her cheeks turning pink with effort, knelt, trying to catch hold of my boot. Puzzled I asked, "Now, where did you come from, and what are you doing?"

The child sat back on her heels. "Mama sent me, she's stirring a brew for you and warming the towels."

There was a little scuttering sound of rushes stirred over the stone floor and two more little maids joined the first. Their mother dressed them alike in blackberry purple woollen dresses with large homespun linen aprons. Their fine baby-fair hair, captured in plain linen bonnets, escaped in wisps to frame baby-soft faces. They stood like three images of the same child. So the oldest must have looked when she was younger, and so they would look as they reach the elder's age. Silently they regarded me with their mother's blue eyes, peach-down cheeks flushing, lips pursing with puzzlement. I managed a smile for them.

"Mama said to help you out of your boots," the oldest said.

I wagged my foot, then lifted the leg high above their heads. Suddenly pulling off the boot became a game. The thick wet leather clung and all three children had to clutch the boot and each other. They tugged, grew pink cheeked and fell over. Finally the boot came off with a rush, which sent them tumbling again. Little chuckles became open laughter. They left the boot on the floor and looked up at me.

I quirked my eyebrows at them, then prevented them removing the right boot by planting my foot firmly on the ground. The girls, uncertain, gazed with anxious eyes. I shaped a painful grin and lifted my foot enough for them to rush and grasp the boot heel. Then I raised my leg slowly, lifting the little girls up, the elder onto her toes, the younger two into the air. Still they clung. They gasped, made soft squeaking sounds, but held on, grasping the boot with eager hands. I lowered my leg slowly until finally all three stood firm, with a secure clutch on my boot.

"Now," I told them, "once, twice and a thrice..." They strove mightily, then toppled over each other with the boot between them. Accompanied by a chorus of childish gurgles and little chortles, I helped them sort themselves out and set them on their feet. They dusted each other down. I tweaked caps and aprons straight, then they fell silent. I looked round to see what had subdued them and there Mistress Paske stood, in the doorway, watching us.

"That's my good girls, take the boots to Silas to grease and dry."

Three little bobs and the girls linked hands to manoeuver the long boots between them.

"And see Lizzie afterwards, the bread oven is lit, she's making pastry. You can bake tarts with her."

Their faces brightened. There came a chorus of "Thank you, Mama," as they struggled through the doorway. I smiled then winced.

"Now, Master Emerick, Tabitha and I must treat that cut and those bruises and get you warm." Tabitha appeared from the kitchen carrying steaming hot poultice cloths, rue and comfrey scented, pots of ointment and warmed linen towels. Between them the two women peeled me out of my doublet, removed my wet shirt and salved, rubbed and pummelled me until I smelt like an apothecary's dispensary and felt like bread dough. "So cold and wet," Mistress Paske sounded distressed. "You must be careful not to take a chill to the lungs. We need to dry you." She talked as though I were the bed linen. I sighed and asserted myself. If I did not, these women would try to strip me like a child. I stood, or rather attempted to. Mistress Paske grasped my arm, steadying me.

"I fear that I seem ungrateful." I tried a brief bow. "Please I beg you, no more. I thank you. I appreciate your ministrations, but I can fend for myself." I bowed again and forced that smile of mine, the one for charming married women. It worked. They both blushed.

Mistress Paske stopped her maid's ministrations with a light touch on her arm. "Master Emerick is not Will, Tabitha. We forget ourselves. Please call Silas." She offered me the warmed towels and applied ointment to my cheek.

It was Silas who took me to the guest room. Silas, a steady man of middle height, weight and age, seemed blessedly neutral in his manner to me. He helped me out of the rest of my wet clothes, rubbed me down as efficiently as if I were Perry and wrapped me in warmed blankets. I welcomed the woollen warmth., I hadn't comprehended how cold my body still was until my fingers failed to untie my garters. Once I looked seemly, Silas called Mistress Paske. She appeared with a hot medicinal drink of potent smell and savour. Tabitha followed carrying warmed bricks and a warming pan full of embers to heat the bed. Mistress Paske offered me one of her husband's flannel nightgowns, and both women withdrew. I unwrapped myself again. Silas towelled me fiercely with more warmed towels and finished by rubbing my aching shoulders, arms and back with a skin-burning, oily liniment. Clad in the warm nightgown and rolled into blankets again, I collapsed gratefully on to the best guest bed whose hot linen sheets smelt of scorched cloth and ladies' bedstraw. Silas assisted me to roll between them and I shuddered, absorbing the warmth and quiet. Sleep, I craved sleep. Silas trod across the room, closed the door behind him and left me to find it. I closed my eyes and waited for it.

It didn't come. My head throbbed, drumming a petty counterpoint rhythm with my heart, and no matter how I turned my head, my mind would not rest. Images flashed behind my eyelids, my mind's eyes seeing what my heart ached for. Loveday eating cherry tarts. Will's scarlet face in church when Loveday smiled on him. Loveday, reduced from vitality to a soggy bundle in the river. The hostile faces around me at the inn. The fight and all that meant. Loveday smiling her slow wide smile. I turned over with difficulty for the blankets held me tightly, swaddled round me like grave cloths. I squirmed until I felt comfortable and shut my eyes again. This time it was Lady Fowke I saw, her hand held out for gold, then Knott's face as he swore he'd not seen me. Loveday laughed down at me from Perry's back, me swinging her round as I lifted her down, holding her a moment longer than I ought. She turned in my arms into that white skinned, dripping bundle.

I rolled onto my back and gave up hunting sleep in exchange for hunting reasons why. What had God in mind that He could give the world a gift like my sisters or Loveday Maye and then snatch them away? It beggared my beliefs, turning certainty into doubt. I rubbed my pounding forehead. Loveday had been mine by predestination, so I'd thought. Now I was wondering. Soon I would find myself before Parson Paske and those wretched wardens, answering serious questions about, not only Loveday, but that inconveniently placed, dead lawyer. It had to be faced. The Gamlen lawyer murdered, then Loveday drowned. Was there a connection or was I so wit fuddled that I looked for what did not exist? Had some hand, the same hand that garroted Jameson, pushed Loveday Maye into the river? How many of these village fools would see the tenuous link, if link it was, in a chain tied to the Emericks and Gamlens. Two murders, perhaps, two links in a chain, mayhap, but how many would set the linking upon me? Parson Paske might well and lead the others to see it too. I touched my head cautiously, caught my bruised cheek, and the smith in my head redoubled the number of horse shoes he beat upon. I exhaled a quiet groan and shut my eyes. Sleep, please Lord let me sleep. He did.
***

Click went the latch. The door opening woke me, and I opened my eyes to dusk. Praise God the forge in my head had shut down, although my mouth tasted foul. That must be the result of the herbal brew the parson's wife gave me. I pulled a face, rolled over to see the door and felt a catch of pain in my ribs. Will's footprints no doubt. Oh, I owed Master Will for that. Now, who had entered?

I eyed the wavering candle flame. Its height told me that one of the little girls stood there. She raised the holder so that the yellow light would shine on my face, and through the golden haze I guessed it was the elder daughter's face.

"Papa wishes to know if you are awake." Her voice sounded as gentle as her mother's.

I shut my eyes, rolled back against the pillows, drew a heavy bubbling breath. "No, I'm bedfast and snoring."

The candle flame wavered as she giggled. I snored more loudly. Through my eyelashes I saw the candle's light grow larger as she tiptoed near. Not yet, one more step, two more, now. I huffed out a great breath, but she'd had her hand up by the flame and shielded it. She squeaked, snatched the candle away and backed off. "Master Emerick, you must come. Papa needs to speak with you."

I sat up slowly, mindful of my bruises. I felt warm, but sore, still, better than I might have done. I flexed and stretched arms and back, then put my feet on the floor. "And which little poppet are you?"

"I'm Grace, Master Emerick." Cautiously she took a step nearer. "I am to lead you to Papa."

"Hold the light closer, Grace, I need my shirt and hose, and I can't find my breeches or shoes."

"You'll dowse it, and it's dark in the passage."

So she was afraid of the dark, that was an easy enemy to defeat. Ah, dear Lord, that I had only that childish fear to cure. "No, I won't. I don't like the dark either. Light the bedroom candles, and I give you my word that I'll leave your candle alight."

She heard the truth in my voice and came nearer. "Are you

really afrit of darkness too? Or do you have a girl of your own, is she scared?"

I laughed. "No, Grace, no daughters, and I truly don't like the dark." I did not tell her I meant the dark of things unknown. "My brothers have daughters and some are afraid of the dark too. Now wait for me outside the door, and I'll dress."

She went slowly, looking over her shoulder at my three bright candles.

I searched my bags for something clean and sombre, and I wondered if Mistress Paske would have dried my other clothes by now. As I tugged on clean drawers, tied my stockings, pulled up my grey breeches, I thought I guessed what Parson Paske planned.

"Master Emerick," Grace called. Her voice quavered so my shirt and doublet went on faster than the nightshirt came off.

"Grace, I'm finishing myself now." She pushed the door open to peep as I spent a careful minute arranging shirt strings, lace cuffs and collar. I combed straight my hair, re-braided my lovelock with quick fingers, tucking it well under my side hair for discretion.

"There now, we'll find your papa." I saw my shoes down beside my saddle bags and stuffed my feet inside as Grace huffed out the three candles. "Shall we go?" She drew in a deep breath and led the way.

The candle threw strange shadows in the passage. Doors and doorways, a chest, a chair, they became dark angled shapes. As the candle flame wavered so the peculiar shadows moved like strange creatures, sinister and scary.

"Now who would think that a square chest could make such a crooked shadow," I told Grace, as the shadow loomed at us. "And what about the chair further down, guess what its shadow will do?"

Grace gave a small sigh, crept closer and touched my hand. I closed my own over hers, knowing that this, more than my words, eased her fear. Her other hand stopped shaking the candle quite as much. She didn't hesitate at the right hand turn and there were the stairs, lit from below by ruddy firelight in the hall fireplace and the stars of four fat candles in two large branched holders standing either side at the foot of the stairs. When we were half way down the stairs and the shadows turned pale and faint I reached round behind Grace to pinch out her candle. The smell of snuffed wick told her what I'd done. She turned amazed eyes in my direction, and I nipped my thumb and forefinger near her nose. She squeaked, but I grasped her round the waist and jumped her down the last step. Together we landed, and I whirled her around, setting her back on her feet with a little bounce. She staggered, and I caught both her hands to steady her. She grasped them and dropped me a deep curtsey, using my hands to haul herself upright. "Now there's an honour," I told her.

She laughed up in my face. "Stand still, Master Emerick." She crouched to untangled the fringe on the hem of my breeches then smoothed a stocking wrinkle to the back of my knees. In return I retied her apron strings, tucked away some wisps of hair and pushed her cap straight. After she set the candle holder on the small table beside the banister she took my hand again. "Come this way, please, Papa is waiting."

I allowed her to tow me forward, teasing her about not being able to keep candles alight. At the end of the hallway she left me standing in front of a door. "Papa would like you to knock first," she said, bobbed and slipped away.

Ah well, I'd reckoned the parson was the school master sort. I wondered how well I'd keep my temper when Parson Paske started his lecture. I rapped firmly on the door and opened it, but stopped half way through as faces, not one friendly, turned in my direction. All talking ceased.

"Come in, Master Emerick." Parson Paske emerged from a group beside the table. At least he gave a welcome. This was the another pleasant family room, quite large and set for dining, the table, placed by the far wall, covered with good white linen and a rare arrangement of food. The smell made my mouth moist. Mistress Paske and Tabitha, with Silas following, came in through the far door, carrying more dishes.

"Let us sing grace, and eat well. We can examine Master Emerick afterwards."

I might have known. Trick it out how they may, some form of an enquiry was what they intended and so soon. I'd give them something to think about if they determined to pin Loveday's drowning on me.

# CHAPTER TEN

London. April 1642

The boats to and from the Westminster stairs still disgorged many people even though night's dark had taken over from dusk's smoky dimness. Clerks, Pym's supporters, groups of men who might be anyone, although clothing and bearing spoke of Puritan leanings, all frequented the wherries. Torches made pools of flaring, orange tinged light between which a skilful man could drift unnoticed.

Clerk Knott moved with a group heading for the House. Once inside he slipped away and took various back ways and stairs to another of those quiet chambers so useful for private meetings. He waited, leaning against the mantelpiece, kicking his heel against the cold hearth slab. He would have liked a fire. The journey had been cold and the ship damp. He hadn't had a hot meal for a day and a half, and he needed to wash away the smell of fish.

The door opened. Two men strode in, talking earnestly. Neither spared Knott a glance. They seated themselves around the small table and kept talking.

Knott shifted his weight, switched feet and kicked his other boot heel. Finally the door swung open. In he came, their leader, the man they had all been waiting for.

"Faugh! What a stench of fishy bilge water. Came down on a fishing smack did you?" The man's plump face creased into a quiet smile. "I hope you bring more good news. We've been doing well this week at keeping the King's purse thin."

Lean smiles lifted tight mouths.

Knott stretched himself to his full height and walked forward. "Yes, to both questions," was all he said, as he joined the three at the table.

"Well, what developments? Your return is unexpected, you'd only just travelled back to Eikenthorpe. How did you check Lady Fowke, master lawyer's clerk Knott? I presume your return is due to that success?"

The men laughed heartily, and one slapped his back. "Knott, an apt name for you, old friend. Did you tie Master Emerick in knots?" They laughed again.

"I came because Mistress Maye is dead." The three stilled, sat back to look at each other. Their faces became carefully blank, but Knott knew there was rapid calculation occurring in every head. "Master Emerick fished her out of the river and now confronts a hostile community anxious to blame her death on him. She was a well loved maid."

"How now! The heiress dead? How dead? Drowned? And does this alter the disposition of the Gamlen estate?" The shorter, clean shaven man spoke.

"Drowned it is believed for the moment, but I have doubts."

The men exchanged looks.

"And what hand did you play, Master Knott?"

The moments ticked by in silence. Knott loomed over the table and, in turn, stared each man in the face. "I do God's will for the good of all. What I have to do I will do." He walked back to the empty hearth and kicked the grate. "Her death works to our favour, to delay the legal settlement of the estate. I have no doubt Lady Fowke will claim all as soon as she may. The demand for the money remains."

"So, how can we prolong the delay until the King declares himself?" The third man extended his legs, crossing them at the ankles as he spoke.

"Leave young Emerick in trouble." Knott turned and walked back to the table, bent over them, rested his hands on two chair backs and smiled at the raised eyebrows. "Oh, I shan't let him hang, unless that is the only way to keep the gold out of Fowke's hands and the King's pocket." Not one man flinched. "I won't speak up for him just yet. I'd been out walking on the other side of the river and plainly saw him find the body and fetch it out. He had no hand in the death." He paused, scowling. "He's an arrogant young pup, cocky, well set up in his own regard."

"You don't like him? Doesn't he treat clerks well?" There was muted laughter before their leader spoke again.

"Careful, dear brother, Clerk Knott should remember we want the Emericks to support Pym and Parliament."

The clerk stirred. "Knott remembers. It's a dull slow game I'm playing, and the Emericks will never know of our involvement unless I deem it necessary." He straightened again to stretch his spine. "He's such a pretty fellow, Master Jacob, a fright won't hurt him." He drew in a long breath. "Parson Paske is no fool. He smelt something wrong about this death. He sent the chief church warden to get the London trained doctor from the next town. The doctor declared she was dead before she went into the water, not enough water in her, no froth in her mouth, and a mark on her throat."

The men exchanged startled looks. Their leader spoke. "So, you reckon this is a deliberate death, a murder?"

"It may well be. 'Tis a pity it were so, but if 'tis murder proved then we can prevent an Emerick-Gamlen settlement for many more weeks."

"Could it be said that Emerick killed her before you found him?"

"It is said and it would be a fine tether to hold the Emericks with if we could pin Jacob Emerick to it, but I doubt it. He'd been seen in the village walking out to the river path, was noted on the path walking towards Gamlen Manor before he found her. I can't do much against that, not as yet." He smiled, a thin toothy grimace.

The large plump-faced man sighed and dismissed them. "Just keep the money out of the King's hands, whatever way you can. I'm sure the Lord will take care of Master Emerick. But we send you to be sure of that." Another round of muted laughter followed Knott out of the room, as the men rose and went their separate ways.

# CHAPTER ELEVEN
## Eikenthorpe, April, 1642

I didn't stand long in the parson's doorway. I stepped forward, all brisk confidence, head high, shoulders squared, aiming like an arrow for the food. Parson Paske caught my arm and introduced me to a buxom goodwife. She didn't smile, but she didn't turn a shoulder either. He left us together and went to stand by the hearth. He simply looked round the room, and the chatterers and whisperers hushed.

"Let us give thanks for this food." I bowed my head to pray and tried to control my hunger. Parson Paske proved apt, shaping thanks within a short space of time and without letting a hot meal spoil.

"...and finally let the truth about Loveday, safe now with you away from earthly sins and strife, be told tonight. Forgive our grief because she no longer brightens our lives. Teach us to rejoice for her, safe with you in paradise. Loosen tongues to speak the truth and bind the liar with it. Mark him with your brand. Let him shake with fear before the wroth of your discovery. God bless us and keep us. Amen."

Loud "Amens" filled the room. My stomach gurgled. I straightened up, and Silas came to show me a place at the long table next to Parson Paske. Mistress Paske presented her husband with a pewter plate laden with a choice selection from the dishes. She wore, to my amazement, a coloured gown of moss green, and chestnut glints showed in the brown hair peeping under her neat cap. A Puritan community yet the women of Eikenthorpe didn't all wear sombre black or grey. There were several in the company wearing colours. I noticed gowns of russet brown, dark blue, and deep green but no lace. They all wore plain linen collars, caps and cuffs. I felt astonished and turned my eyes from the women to glance at the parson, all Puritan black and wondered that he allowed his wife a green gown.

Mistress Paske arrived at my side. "For our guest," she said, placing the laden plate in front of me. I appreciated the partisan treatment. A declaration of Faith, I thought with a wry inward smile for the pun. A good woman, this parson's wife. Tabitha presented a more modest selection to the woman beside me, and we all ate with enjoyment. The food tasted even better than it smelt and the fire, kept well fed by Will, sporting a vivid bruise across his mouth and chin, burnt cheerfully through the logs, hissing and crackling, flames brightly leaping.

Streams of conversation eddied about me. I kept my face still, my eyes intent on the food, eating hungrily, but listening carefully, caution being my watchword.

The men talked of planting and sowing, of sharing labour. They ate hugely, with a noisy enjoyment that spoke of hearty appetites from outdoor work. The women fed their men and themselves. No children were present. An important meeting this, with only the church and village notables here tonight, but they weren't baying for my blood yet. Each woman had brought her best cooking for the meal, and I listened to hints passed and the receipt for a fish pie shared. The women commented on household needs, reminding their men that more flax had to be planted this month, and better, finer wool was needed for their households. The sheep were kept communally, so why couldn't the ram with finest wool cover more ewes? Where was the new ram promised last year? The men listened, retorted with their own comments.

I ate steadily and continued listening. This was a community where everyone provided for themselves. All men called themselves farmers, even Parson Paske laboured on his large farm himself and shared the others' concerns. It was a bonding, like their religion, and a powerful one. Perhaps what I witnessed was proof of what I'd always thought, a common goal which benefited all was the strongest bond. Give people a purpose that they could see gave them all advantages, and they would work like a yoke of oxen with a good ploughman. The King didn't understand this. Good merchants and ship captains did. John Pym and the Puritans did.

The raised pie tasted good, excellent pastry with a savoury filling. I looked round for more. Will had the dish, disposing of the last piece in large mouthfuls. At his elbow sat a platter of those tiny blood-red cherry tarts. My own mouthful of pie clogged, lost its savour. Loveday. Loveday eating cherry tarts with me, or sneaking new bread for us, spreading it with blackberry preserves and eating it in the Manor bake house. Loveday laughing under the cherry trees, a scatter of blossoms decorating her cap and hair, Loveday so glowing with vitality, so unlike the lifeless bundle I last held. I closed my eyes against the sight, and pushed away my plate.

Mistress Paske appeared. She had a smile for me and addressed both her husband and myself. "Another helping of the trout, Richard? Perhaps a little more pie, Master Emerick? Ah no, I see Will has claimed that."

"Nothing, I thank you, my dear, except some more ale."

I shook my head, but Mistress Paske pressed me into also accepting a refill of ale. I liked this malt-sweet home brewed ale. My favourite brew was March beer, bitter with hops, but well made ale like this quenched the thirst easily, and a drink or two didn't loosen the tongue as quickly as March beer. Time to raise my head and look out for who might be difficult. I watched faces as the jugs circulated. All of them looked capable of raising problems.

When everyone had a full mug and an empty platter Parson Paske stood. "We are here tonight to examine Master Jacob Emerick."

I raised my brows politely. Inside my head an apprentice boy's voice cat-called. Let them try. I'd be all logic and sweet reason yet tie them in knots. I had not harmed Jameson and as for Loveday...I lifted my chin and regarded the company.

A square set man of mid-height, but dapper not stolid, and bright-white in his clean linen, stepped forward. He looked at me steadily. "Come, Master Emerick, give us God's truth. We know. Tell us why you drowned Mistress Loveday."

I knocked the bench over as I shot to my feet. "I? I drowned Loveday? How dare you speak such vile slander. How dare you besmirch my name and the honourable name of the Merchants Emerick. "

The man nearly stepped back. I knew I spoke through gritted teeth. The whole room felt my anger, saw my raised fist. I watched the faces changing, regarding me as a strong menacing presence. My head cleared. Be calm, you fool, I told myself. This was not the propitious start I had wanted. Fighting my rage, I picked up the bench, set it straight, then spoke slowly and clearly, pronouncing each word as though speaking to a simpleton. "I walked to Gamlen Manor to keep my appointment with Lady Fowke. At the bend of the river nearest the Manor I saw the body."

"And how did you know it was a body?" the buxom goodwife asked.

"I've seen enough living on the Thames." I smiled stiffly. "The Emerick home is built beside the river and we travel it often enough." I didn't tell her that the first body I'd ever seen was a disintegrating, soused mass with a livid bloated moon for a face, which I still saw when the night mare rode and terror struck my dreams.

The dapper man began again. "You must have heard a cry, a splash. How could you ignore it?"

"Do you dare accuse me of the dishonourable, the despicable act of standing by and watching Mistress Maye drown?" I eyed him. This time he did retreat one step. "There was no sound, no outcry, nothing."

"So you say."

I could have throttled the man. I reined in my anger, looked to reason, and began to speak. "There is nothing to show that Mistress Loveday Maye did not slip or trip into the water on her own."

The company murmured, inaudible comments from round the room.

I raised my voice. "Perhaps she had dropped a trinket or key into the deep water, and she fell as she leaned forward to fish it out. Or she could have waded into the shallows to rescue something and slid under that way." I stopped. Faces watched me, thoughtfully. I turned slowly, looking at every face in the room. "By what right do you accuse me of anything. No one can say that Mistress Maye's death is anything more than a dreadful accident."

"I am afraid we can, Master Emerick," Parson Paske's voice carried above the others. It silenced them all.

Some heads turned, people exclaimed. Silence fell as the parson rose and stood in the centre of the room. Every person turned to face him, questions written on their countenances though their voices stilled. I fought the impulse to sit. "I sent for Doctor Matthews from town. I was puzzled by certain aspects of Loveday's death and needed an experienced doctor's advice. The doctor feels sure that Loveday was throttled"

My legs gave out under me. I sat down in a heap. "Strangled?" My wits unravelled, and my mouth fell open. I couldn't find another word to say.

"The bones in her throat are broken, signs of strangulation. The doctor is quite sure."

"No. I can't believe it, who would..." disbelief and anger choked my voice.

"Dr. Mathews is certain," Parson Paske shook his head, "I want the truth about her death. This was an evil act, closely following another as evil, and I want no more Devil's work in this community."

I recovered my wits, closed my mouth and thought swiftly. I stood up, stepped around the bench and wended my way between the people. "Parson Paske, you have the information from Lawyer Jameson's office, you know how important he was to my family. You know that. I will swear now on the Holy Bible that I found the maid in the river and have no knowledge of how she got there."

The parson's eyes gazed steadily into mine. I didn't flinch. It was a kind of fencing, a duel, not to wound, but to see through the eyes into a man's soul.

"I believe him," Will said.

The dapper man jumped up. "No. Someone killed Mistress Maye, and it couldn't have been one of us." I glared at him. "This stranger had business at the Manor, he knew the family, he must have done it."

"Oh, such sound sense and cool logic. Any grammar school boy could reason better than that. Use your intellect and think like a man," I said, with a snort of contempt. "What is my reason for killing the Gamlen heir? The Emerick family needed her alive."

One of the church wardens popped up. "But we hear Lady Fowke demanded full re-payment." This was news to some of those present.

"More reason to harm the lady than the maid," Will muttered from his corner by the fire. Any smiles were hidden behind hands, any laughter turned to coughs before it became unseemly.

"I had every reason to wish the maid alive." I raised my voice. "What we need to know is who would wish her dead?"

Will sprang up. "No one could," he cried. Other voices called out, agreeing.

"Someone did. She's dead, not drowned by accident for Parson Paske says she was strangled, killed deliberately. Murdered. Who would want her dead?"

"You," called out the dapper man. Other voices clamoured in agreement.

"No," I shook my head. "Think. Lady Fowke and I were arranging a marriage settlement. I doubt very much whether any man with the prospect of Mistress Maye as his bride would have wanted to harm her. I certainly did not."

Will looked at me, startled, as did some of the other men, but not Parson Paske. It was clear he had learned of this already. No secrets in Eikenthorpe, even if there should have been.

The general talk rose from whisper to agitated hum.

The dapper man shouted, "Liar!"

"Listen," Will yelled, "let Master Emerick speak."

The parson raised his hand again.

In the sullen silence I spread my seeds of doubt. "I had the prospect of Mistress Loveday as my bride, a good marriage settlement for my family, and a satisfactory arrangement for settling our business agreements. I had no reason to want that precious maid dead." I looked at each man present and smiled my tight, polite lawyer's smile. "How many young men here thought to court her? How many fathers looked to improving the family fortunes with an alliance with the Gamlen heir? Even knowing what the stiff necked, overweening Lady Fowke would say?"

Several men, young and old, shifted uncomfortably.

"Who is a zealot, angered that powerful supporters of the King's one church inherited the wealthy Gamlen estate? Who was angry because the Fowkes would come, bringing their tainted religious ideas to disturb the harmony of your Puritan community? There are many reasons why any one of you would resent the new heir."

The room buzzed like a hive of disturbed bees. Expressions changed. Faces turned to Parson Paske. He watched me.

"Who did Loveday catch out in wrong doing? Who did she see...?" A great babbling filled the room. Parson Paske had to stand and shout for silence. I stood watching them all. Let me see but one sign of guilt and I would have him.

The chief of the church wardens spoke for everyone. "Don't you try your clever tricks here, you young whelp. We don't need you to stir us into turmoil. We're godly people, we don't break God's laws. " He removed his modest sugar loaf hat to wipe his forehead and other people chimed in, supporting him. He rammed the hat back on his head and braced his shoulders. "Let us see how godly you are. He turned to the others. "We'll put him to test shall we?"

One mighty assenting 'yes' came from all present. Implacable intractability. I saw no reason or logic that could move their prejudice. I knew three brothers with the same ox like immovability. Ruefully I accepted the fact that I'd have to face some ludicrous test and the thought was a bitter thing. I was a gentleman, my word was true, they dishonoured me. I turned my head to look at Parson Paske. I'd hoped for some justice from him. Parson Paske returned the look, but remained silent, as the church wardens settled what to do.

The chief warden poked a stubby finger at me. "If you had nothing to do with the maid's death then you won't fear to sit with her body tonight in the church."

I blinked. "What?" What kind of test did they have in mind? Not the old superstition about passing my hand over the corpse to see if blood would flow. Surely Puritans didn't believe in that kind of papist magic.

"And we'll watch you." The dapper man was bouncing on the balls of his feet. "If you're the murderer, if you harmed her, her spirit will come to accuse you and we shall see it. Then we'll know the truth."

No one dissented.

I sighed inwardly. That the spirit of a murdered person, on the night they were killed, would seek out the murderer before they went to heaven or hell, was an old belief, a religious superstition harking back to the days of Roman popery, for those without much learning. I'd have wagered a good hat that Parson Paske quashed such notions. That he did not boded ill. I bowed politely. "If that is the wish of the community then I agree." I looked round at them all. "I have nothing to fear."

Parson Paske looked at each person. No one said 'Nay', or shook their head. "Then I will organize a watch to be set over Master Emerick in the church."

I inclined my head. I had not harmed Loveday, and by no means would I admit to any fear, though I'd never sat through the night watches with a murdered corpse and didn't like the idea.

Will pushed carelessly through those present, drawing several sharp looks and one trenchant rebuke. He shrugged them all off. "I'll watch with you," he said, grasping my arm tightly. "We'll find Loveday's murderer."

Indeed, a fine gesture from the lad. I eased his grip, but with a friendly grin, that was an expensive sleeve he was crushing. I draped his arm over my shoulders and put mine round him to pat his back. "I'd like that." He thumped me cheerfully and grinned.

# CHAPTER TWELVE

The church smelt old and cold, not ancient though, no sense of centuries of fervour. It hadn't been part of an abbey, I could see that clearly. No, this was a newer church built at a time when churches were flung skyward as part of an optimistic rush by communities praising God and their prosperity. But the wool fortunes all those years ago didn't last long enough for Eikenthorpe, although a few worthies managed to build themselves elaborate tombs. The church, the over-large inn, the wide cobbled street at the centre of the village, all remained as signs of the hopes of growth to a charter and town rights. High hopes often went awry, as I was finding out.

Will clattered in after me, glanced across at me, then dumped his armload of cloaks and blankets beside the pillar nearest the knave table. The lantern, hooked over his left wrist, rocked from right to left and the yellow beams zigzagged up and around the stone curves of the pillar. He looked wan-faced in the light, his eyelids twitching, blinking often. I reached over and relieved him of the lantern. When I had steadied it, I avoided directing the beams into the transept where Loveday lay on her bier. All that could be seen of her from where we stood were the four star points of light, one flickering at each coffin corner. The tall fat beeswax candles, new-lit by the parson, burnt sweetly, giving clean scented, white light. The rest of the church lay hidden in deep, light-absorbing black. The community had picked a suitable night for ghost watching, cloudy, only half a moon, rain threatening, typical of late April, not even the stars brightened the gloom. The stained glass windows were invisible. The lozenge shaped spaces, shuttered on the inside, gave no variant to the dark, no paler pools of coloured dusk to relieve the inner gloom. I shrugged. A church should feel peaceful, reverent, almost comforting. This one watched and waited, not a pleasant atmosphere to be alone in with a corpse.

I moved nearer to Will. "We'll be thanking the parson's wife for those." I nudged the cloaks with my shoe toe. Mistress Paske had pressed the heavy bundle into a protesting Will's arms as I was marched off to the church, the church wardens four square round us like a guard. One now sat in each of the two porches, the others hovered somewhere near. "At least we're inside out of the wind. We'll be more comfortable than our guards."

Will managed a grin. "I want you to know..." he began, but Parson Paske called us to the bier.

Even the chill old-stone smell didn't mask the sweetly rotten scent of death. From the half sad, half shocked expression on Will's face he too had hoped that there was a miracle to come, an angel, perhaps some secret potion which would wake Loveday like Juliet. But the smell told us the true story. She was dead.

The parson watched as I stretched out to touch Loveday's death-cold hands laid one over the other on her breast. I wasn't shamed by the tears in my eyes either. I tucked a sprig of rosemary, taken from the Paske kitchen herb plot, between the stiff resisting fingers.

"Here's rosemary for remembrance," I quoted. Despite my mother's outward disapproval, all the family enjoyed plays, especially Will Shakespeare's. I could quote many lines. I'd found them useful to impress pretty maids. This was the first time I'd used that line in its true sense, and silently I promised Loveday that I would remember.

Will stepped up beside me. He could only stare, choke and turn away. Poor love-lorn Will.

I saw nothing in Loveday's face which told of murder. "Are you certain it was murder, Parson Paske? She looks like a drowned person to me."

"There are signs if you know how to look. And neither you, or the Gamlen Manor men, found anything to show how she fell into the river. The doctor learnt his skills in a London hospital, and, sadly, he has seen this type of strangulation before. The body always give signs." His voice changed, challenged. "You can't hope to avoid God's justice, Jacob Emerick, if you had any part in Master Jameson's or Mistress Loveday's deaths. There will be evidence to trap you."

I didn't drop my eyes in face of the accusing stare. Nor did I bother to hide the flare of anger he'd see in them. I'd not harmed Jameson, would never have hurt Loveday, and I was tired of saying so, tired of being asked to prove it.

The parson continued to regard me.

I regarded him in return. "Parson Paske, enough. You know I did not kill Jameson. Nowell Merriot and I found him dead. I hoped to marry Loveday Maye, would never have harmed her. I want an end to accusations, which you cannot prove. I am innocent."

The parson's dark eyes watched me steadily, but he gave me no reply.

I sighed. "Please believe me. I want to find out what happened as much, and surely more, than you do."

Still no words in response, but Parson Paske's jaw muscles tightened.

I clamped my teeth on my tongue to hold back angry words. How dare this man refuse to take my word, such an insult to a gentleman and to the Emericks. He'd accepted my word when I promised to stay at his home. I kept my face and my voice quiet. "Where do you want us to watch?"

"Settle yourself on the bench." The parson indicated a short backless bench against the side wall. "Will, I would prefer Master Emerick to be alone."

Will hunched a shoulder and muttered.

"Will?"

"I want to be here. I could be a witness for you as well as for Jacob too, if anything happens." Will did not sound as though he thought anything might happen. I swallowed down the anger and almost grinned. Good for Will.

Parson Paske stepped into our lantern light, gave Will his small lantern without a smile. "You will leave the church, young Will. You, Master Emerick, won't. And remember that you are watched." I nodded again. Will grunted something. "A peaceful night to you, Master Emerick. Come, Will." He gave each of us a steady look, then walked into the dark, his steps never hesitating until the door ring was turned, a draught disturbed the air, and he'd gone.

Will, following reluctantly, looked over his shoulder, held up his lantern to shine on his face, winked and departed.

I sat on the side bench, sprawled my legs in front of me and thought how best to arrange myself comfortably. Will sneaked back before I had time to shift the blankets or myself. "You'll catch it from Parson Paske."

"You need a witness," was all Will would say.

"I do so. I'm right glad to have you as witness. Let us contrive to keep warm," I pointed at the cloaks. "Who knows, we might even sleep. After all my conscience is clear."

Will laughed, an explosion of sound, took himself and the lantern back for the cloaks I'd dropped by the pillar, then toed the bundle forward. I stooped, swept up the lot, and tossed everything on the bench. "Cloaks, blankets, enough for two. Kind woman."

Will set the lantern safely to one end and grabbed a cloak. "You didn't kill Loveday. We won't see anything."

I cocked my head. This time Will sounded like someone in need of reassurance. He'd spoken brave words for the parson, now he needed me to tell him they were true. "No, you can be sure our night will be peaceful. I did nothing to hurt her, everything to help her, and she won't come to reproach me."

Will exhaled noisily, folded himself into the cloak, settled down on one end of the bench and wrapped a second cloak around his legs and feet. I, wishing my boots had dried, kicked off my thin leather shoes, tucked my feet up onto the bench and wrapped a blanket under them and around my legs. I pulled another blanket over myself, tucking the ends firmly under me. Finally I draped two cloaks over my entire body. I'd better stay warm or Parson Paske would hear about it. "Lantern left alight or dowsed?" I asked.

Will looked around the gloom, began to open his mouth, then said nothing.

"Shall we just let it burn out?"

Will shrugged. "If you prefer."

"You know if we sat back to back and leaned on each other we wouldn't have to prop ourselves against this clammy wall."

Will promptly turned himself about and I felt the warmth of his back pushed against my own. I leaned until we found our counterbalance. "That's better, you're more yielding than the parson or that wall." Will's back muscles jiggled as he laughed.

I shut my eyes and tried to breath slowly and steadily. I wanted to sleep through the night and be found in peaceful slumber, vexing the tired wardens.

"What could have happened to Loveday?"

Caught in mid-breath, I exhaled and started my steady breathing again. I spoke between slow breaths. "I don't know. If she were murdered who wanted to kill her?"

Will squirmed. "I can only think of what you said. That people here had reasons...I don't want to think that, but what..."

The northern porch door creaked open. A warden stepped stiffly inside, walked forward, held up his lantern, regarded us, said something inaudible, but pitched in grumbling tones, and went out again.

Will chuckled. "That's Luke Cooper. He'll be aching by

morning, more fool he." His voice changed tone. "You know Loveday came each summer to stay at the Manor?" I murmured an affirmative. "She's done...did so since I was nine. We all remember her, knew her, liked her. You only met her some few days ago. Sixteen days if I count aright."

I nodded, then realized that Will might not feel the movement, but he did, for he continued.

"Why would you kill her then? If Lady Fowke agreed to discuss a marriage
settlement you had no reason to harm Loveday and every reason to keep her well. Why would you kill her?" He fidgeted, obviously upset. "Why would anyone hurt her? For what reason was she hurt? There's a great secret hidden here."

"Can we find it out?"

Will pounced on the suggestion. "We could try."

"I still have business with Lady Fowke, I can speak with Mary and the other servants. Can you ask people in the village?"

Will's shoulders moved, another shrug. "I don't know. Does this business of yours, this money, does it alter now Loveday is dead?" I thought I heard a hint of suspicion.

"Loveday's death probably makes Lady Fowke even more determined to end the loan. My family need to extend it."

I felt Will relax. "I can help you," he said. "I know everyone in this community."

"Your aid is gratefully accepted, Will. Now in God's good name sleep, I'm weary. Reflect on the church wardens' fury when they find us peacefully slumbering with innocent faces."

Will laughed and wriggled down into the warmth of his wrappings. "I am not sorry I hit you, and I'll pay you out for that punch, but I'm glad you came."

I grinned to myself. So I'd found a friend, had I? Well, Will stood up for me, and one friendly supporter in Eikenthorpe was better than none. He wasn't so bad for a country boy, his wits worked. I yawned and settled my chin on my chest. It wouldn't be a comfortable night, but Will's friendship, as well as his back, warmed me. I resumed my slower deeper breathing and eventually slid into sleep.

The wardens interrupted us with regular inspections. My sailor's sharpened senses told my ears this as I dozed. The sea never gave second chances. My brothers and father clouted that into me by the time I was twelve, and I'd learnt swiftly to notice slight differences. The doors opening brought new scents on a waft of chill air, and the wardens didn't trouble themselves about silence. I'd register them in a conscious alert then sink back into sleep again. The same thing happened when the lantern used up its oil, and the darkness became complete. What brought me fully awake was that the pattern of the sounds had altered. The door handle turned with its familiar creak, then nothing. My ears waited for the door, the one on our side, to swish open with a draft of cold air. It didn't, so my ears told my wits and that made me open my eyes, wondering what had disturbed me. This time the door remained no more than a hand's breadth open, faint lantern light shaped its outline. I listened, ears straining. I felt the hair on the nape of my neck bristle for someone was looking cautiously round the door, checking the interior. Then the door opened slowly, only wide enough for a skinny figure to slip through. I kept my head lolling against Will's, hat brim against hat brim, and peered into the gloom. It was easier for me, used to the dark interior, to see the intruder, than for the intruder, within his lantern's circle of light, to see me.

Whoever it was had covered the lantern so that no beam of light could escape beyond the length of a short step. Will twitched, then a betraying jerk told me that he'd woken up. Secure in the knowledge that both of us were hidden in dense shadow, I nudged him and stretched slowly and smoothly, cautiously easing my stiff body. The shielded lantern, lifted only high enough to reveal the way, was directed towards the candle-lit bier. This late night visitor had come to see Loveday.

Will tensed and started to move. I leant hard against him,

nudging my shoulder into his. I grasped his wrist, squeezing it in warning. Then I spun round, the blankets under me slipping smoothly on the polished wood, and I took Will with me so that we both sat, backs to the wall, knees to chests, able to see what was happening.

The shrouded lantern gave us no hint as to who was abroad in the coldest hours of the early morning. A dark shrouded shape, with brimmed hat and heavy cloak, as most men wore, he advanced to the bier. I nudged Will, set a stocking foot down on the biting cold floor, and indicated with my hand, touching Will's, that Will was to circle round to the left. Before he could clatter his booted feet down onto the stone flags, I gripped them. Then I tapped my stocking clad foot against the nearest boot and moved his hand to feel my foot. Will touched my stocking and understood. He nudged me, then began to ease off his own boots. I clasped his shoulder in acknowledgment, rose and began a stealthy stalk from pillar to pillar. I was almost certain that the aisle was clear of obstacles, but I felt forward with each foot before putting my weight down on it. I wanted this man. Here was someone who did not know of the community decision, who thought the church empty of the living. Cautiously, without haste, I crept forward using a hunter's stealth. If only I had my pistols to hand. I didn't even have my sword. Surprise must be my weapon.

The intruder had reached the bier and stood looking down for the length of time it took me to slide behind the last pillar. I hesitated, I could not see where Will was, but I did want to watch what this intruder was doing. Heaven give the boy enough nous to wait.

The stranger rested the lantern on the bier, peeled off his gauntlets and bent over the body, touching the face, the hair. Hands fumbled at Loveday's neck. My feet moved without conscious direction. I raced forward. Will leapt out from the dark on the other side, his shadow arriving first, startling the stranger. His weight brought the intruder down in a heap beyond the lantern light. I slid onto the dark tangle of bodies to add my strength to Will's. I could not see who was who clearly until Will's now bare head, curls very evident, appeared in shadow form. An elbow crashed into his neck and the cloak snapped across his face.

This man could fight, and he wore a sword. He fumbled for the hilt as Will hissed out a warning. I rolled over and let my body block the intruder's movement. The man's hat fell off and we all three tumbled back into the little pool of light. The yellow glow revealed the stranger's face, stark white, set, with a crooked nose, freckles and a wide frog mouth.

"Nowell Merriot!" I sat back on my heels, astonished.

Will grasped Nowell's arm fiercely. "What were you doing to Loveday, you...."

Nowell flung him off much as a horse twitches away a fly. Will landed on his arse with a bump. "Jacob Emerick. In God's Name tell me what happened to Loveday." His voice broke and his face crumpled.

Will looked at us, eyes going from face to face, his bewilderment writ plain on his own. "He knows Loveday?"

"I'm not sure." I took Nowell's arm and heaved myself up, bringing Nowell with me. "What are you doing here?" I forced the suspicion out of my voice, keeping it curious but friendly.

Nowell ignored us both, turned back to the coffin, stared down at Loveday's body, and wept.

I remembered Nowell carrying letters for the Gamlens, his comments in the inn yard, and that smile of recognition on Loveday's face. Understanding dawned. I bent to grasp Will's arm, caught his elbow and hauled him to his feet. "I think Nowell did indeed know Loveday." Will gaped. I sighed and reached out to grip Nowell's shoulder. "Master Merriot, Nowell, hush man, you'll have the watch on us." I tugged his shoulder. "Come over to this bench and explain."

Nowell stood firm. "I have a keepsake to give Loveday." His voice was thick with tears. "I knocked both watchers under the chin with my sword hilt, they'll sleep awhile longer."

I tried not to laugh. Will exclaimed.

"Let me tie this round her neck," Nowell broke down again as he showed us a silver heart threaded on a silk ribbon.

I jerked my head to the left, indicating to Will that he should take himself around the other side of the bier, ready to cut off any dash for escape on that side. Will stared, nodded, then moved, picking up the lantern on the way. He removed the shields and held it up for Nowell to see what he was doing. I relaxed. Good, Will was thinking. Now, what to do about Nowell.

I watched him fumble pitifully trying to tie the slippery pink ribbon. His grief and shock hurt to see. I 'saw', with my mind's eye, Nowell hearing the news, wondering if it were gossip or God's truth. I knew how to begin.

"You know Mistress Maye well then? And you rode all this way hoping that what you'd heard was tittle-tattle." Genuine sympathy filled my voice.

Nowell finally fastened the ribbon, curved his palm around Loveday's cheek with a tender caress and looked up. The flesh on his face had melted, leaving skull-like bones prominent. His eyes looked tired, bleary with grief. "God knows how I prayed riding here. I could not, would not, believe that Loveday had died. I saw her only yesterday, knew her to be well. We arranged to meet when I passed through again in two days' time. She had something for me to take to her father."

Will interrupted, his voice rising. "You saw her?"

"We are...." His voice trailed away and he swallowed a sob, then started again. "We were to be betrothed this spring and married this summer's end, but Denzil Gamlen's sudden death and his new will delayed matters." Will's eyes grew round. Nowell groaned and leant over the bier. "Lord God, how could you let this happen?"

Will began to speak. I cast a warning look at him. "I found her floating in the river."

Nowell straightened. "You?" His voice cut the darkness. He

advanced, hands raised. "Couldn't you have saved her? Didn't you see?"

Will dodged the bier and gave Nowell a shove in the back. "Over to the bench and leave Jacob alone. He tried to save her, no one's thanking him, and half the village is hounding him."

Nowell staggered away, still too shaken for immediate physical retaliation. He gaped at me, then Will, pinching his nose to clear it.

I took his arm, guiding him towards the bench. "I found her in the river, Nowell. I thought she'd drowned. The parson says she was strangled." The lantern swung wildly as Will put out a hand to steady Nowell.

"What? Who would hurt Loveday?" Nowell collapsed onto the bench, amazed.

I eyed him. Certainly no one could make a pretence to that depth of emotion. His voice, his whole body expressed shocked surprise. Once the amazement wore off he'd be quivering with rage, not this shock. The problem was how to get him somewhere safe, yet keep an eye on him. He needed Will's help, but Will didn't trust him. I wasn't entirely sure myself, but several things stood in Nowell's favour. "Nowell, how did you hear the news?"

"The doctor rode into Undene and stopped at the inn. He was looking for a man, a church warden, I think, to carry a message to Parson Paske. I heard them screech and make an outcry. There can't be other maids named Loveday in Eikenthorpe."

Will's mouth opened and closed like a landed fish. Finally he managed to say, "Didn't you ask if it was truly Mistress Maye before you rode here?"

Nowell shook his head then buried it in his hands.

"Where's Samson?" I tapped Nowell's shoulder. "Is he tied up in the porch or loose in the church yard?"

Nowell raised his head. "Neither. He's tethered under the wall's shadow in the far corner. It's quiet and sheltered, safe from any thief or bothersome cur."

"Will, could you hide Nowell and Sampson for a while?"

Will paused to think, then nodded. "I'll take them home..." he hesitated..."the old shepherd's hut or the far meadow hay barn are empty..." he nodded again. "They should be undisturbed in either of those."

I took Nowell by the shoulders. "Listen, Nowell." He raised his head, brushing the tears away. "You can go home with Will. He'll hide you, then you can pretend to ride in to Eikenthorpe later today. That'll keep you out of the clutch of the wardens. Why did you have to knock them out?"

Nowell knuckled his temples. "I couldn't get in any other way." He shook his head. "No, I mustn't stay. I have to go back to Undene. I have work to finish. And I have good reasons for not wanting to be found here. There's some Puritan man seeking me. I need to...." His voice tailed away as he turned his back on us and returned to the bier. "I'll return for her burial, with her father." His voice cracked, and he sobbed again.

"Will, find him somewhere quiet until he's slept and recovered somewhat."

Will looked at the bowed head and watched Nowell pray fervently, his lips moving, his hands crushed together. "Our far meadow barn is not used now, it'd be quietest. That'll be best. I'll take him up there." He paused. "I'm not sure how I'll get back in here."

I pursed my lips, thinking. "Don't. Say we were woken by some noise. We investigated, found an intruder near Loveday, chased him out and discovered that someone had attacked the wardens." I smiled at him. "You're heading for Parson Paske to bring back some help. I'm virtuous. I promised to stay in the church so I do."

Will grinned then looked sober-faced as Nowell finished his prayers, farewelling Loveday with a gentle kiss upon her forehead. "Come, Master Merriot, let's take your lantern and flee." He grabbed a cloak, swung Nowell about, pushed him ahead. "Better fuss over the wardens when we've gone," he said. The door latch clicked behind them.

I sat for a moment thinking about Loveday, then I smothered myself up in a cloak, ambled across the church, waited by the door for a count of twenty, and hurried out into the far porch. The warden there slumped on the bench, moving his head in a muzzy, half dazed state. "What's happened?

"We disturbed an intruder and found Warden Cooper sprawled on the porch floor. Will's gone to find aid."

"Who came?" The warden touched his chin tenderly and groaned.

"Can I help?" The man accepted an arm up and leaned heavily on me as we shuffled into the church. Warden Cooper burst through the other door, angry words on his lips.

I forestalled him. "What happened? We chased out an intruder, then found you both knocked out. Will's gone for help."

Warden Cooper hovered between disbelieving me and accepting what he saw. He chose to believe his eyes. "I'll fetch Parson Paske."

He returned in such a short time that I assumed the parson had been one of those on watch around the church. Nowell Merriot knew something about evasion then and so, I hoped, did Will.

"I saw no-one myself," the parson said, "but if Will has gone for aid then I'll believe that someone else came."

It was not the time to challenge him for that slur on my honesty. I swallowed my choler and watched him organize new watchmen for each porch.

"There are still five hours to daybreak, Jacob, you must spend the full night here, or we cannot be sure of what you say."

Shut firmly inside again, I returned to my bench, rubbed my feet warm, wrapped them in two blankets, covered myself with more blankets and the cloaks then tried to curl up. The bench was too narrow. I padded my back with a doubled up cloak and leant against the cold wall. I envied Nowell his hay barn bed.

# CHAPTER THIRTEEN

I dozed, missing Will's warm back. The porch door's faint creak, that breath of cold air, and a flowery scent, disturbed me. I mumbled and stirred, but refused to open my eyes. I wanted sleep. No more disturbances, no more intruders, just sleep and a pox on the wardens, on the whole community. The scent faded. The Lord be praised. I was not shifting.

Some unknown time later I roused again. That plaguey draught brought more scents, chiefly lavender, floating my way. A deep rumbling made me twitch an ear. I mentally listed the possibilities: thunder in the distance? Will returning? I didn't care. I intended to sleep. I slumped further down, buried my head under the pile of cloaks and blankets, slowed my breathing. The rumbling increased, erupted as an ear shattering crash, followed by a flash of queer yellow light which penetrated my closed eyelids. This was a strange storm. Still, I wasn't troubled, if a storm wanted to rage, I simply wished it would do it elsewhere. The crash was repeated. I worked my head free of the coverings so that I could raised it sufficiently to see without moving the rest of myself. The small door, used by Parson Paske during services, stood ajar. Thick swirling smoke streamed inside, following the draught. It hung in spiralling coils round the candle flames at each corner of Loveday's bier. Someone had replaced the candles, for they were not the dumpy, flame spluttering stubs they ought to be, but tall yellow columns smelling sweetly of beeswax and honey. Between the far candle flames, beyond the bier, a figure stood.

I shot upright, my feet hitting cold stone before I knew I'd moved. "Loveday? Mistress Maye?" For one brief moment it was as though yesterday had never been. She was safe. I stepped forward gladly, then stopped. Comprehension nudged my wits. I had smelt death, held her body. So what was this? A trick. I snorted. A very stagy trick, such a cruel stupid thing to do, and what I should have expected from the nodcock worthies of Eikenthorpe. That tinny rattle of thunder, a shaken sheet of metal, and the wrongly coloured lightning, a special lantern with some apothecary's mixture. I laughed, a short jeering sound. "Is this the best you people can do? She isn't even like Loveday. Shame on you for making sport of the maid's death. What an ungodly disgrace! Call yourself decent, God fearing Christians?"

The church porch door on my side opened wide. Three church wardens and the parson appeared. I glared at them in disgust. I couldn't find the words to tell them what a cruel and wicked thing they'd just done.

"You gave yourself away." The dapper warden, not so trim now, smirked. "You started up, guilt on your face. We saw you."

I scowled. "Then I suggest you speak the truth. Daybreak may be coming, but there's insufficient light in this church for you to see my face from where you were hiding behind that porch door. Where you skulked not one of you could see my face." I walked right up to the coffin and stared across it into Mistress Paske's eyes. I sniffed so savagely in disgust that my nostrils pinched together. In the ensuing quiet I heard only Mistress Paske's breath whistling in and out. She began to reach out towards me. I stared her down. Her hand dropped. Turning my back on her I addressed the wardens. "You could have seen me if I'd stood here, by the bier, Loveday's bier, she who is dead, who, you say was evilly murdered and you play this...this schoolboy prank." I hoped my face showed the revulsion I felt as I looked down my nose at them. Parson Paske's face flushed, the wardens scowled. "Shame on you all, 'tis an ungodly disgrace."

The parson turned on his heel, walked to the bench, shook out a cloak from my pile, and returned to swaddle his wife in it. He ignored me. "Thank you, my dear. This will warm you, don't let the night air give you a chill."

Mistress Paske, bareheaded, her hair flowing down her back, tucked the mass of it into the cloak's capacious hood, and snuggled it over her head. As Loveday's spirit she wore a long sleeved, pleated white night gown under a white mantle and looked grateful for the warmth of the woollen cloak.

"You'd make a fine player on the stage, Mistress Paske, if they'd let women play-act." My inflexions were not complimentary. Even in the low dawn light, I could see her blush from throat to forehead. Her husband pressed his lips together, his eyes warning me. He put a hand on her shoulder, guiding her away. I squared my shoulders, gave the wardens a scornful look, "What was this fool trick to prove? Anyone with half an eye could see through it. I don't fear Mistress Loveday Maye's spirit because I never harmed her, and you have no proof that I did. I have been tolerant of your bucolic ignorance, but now we need to make things clear. Are you going to attempt to accuse me of murder in court? You'll need better proof than this. Indeed a mention of this trick in court will make you all a laughing stock."

"We'll hold you until we're satisfied. You're not cleared yet, boy." The men glared, turned and stomped out.

Parson Paske shook his head at me. "You will remain in Eikenthorpe until we are satisfied you did not have a hand in either of the two deaths." He turned away, supporting his wife, together they walked across to the opposite porch door.

Heads like iron, stubborn, irrational...stupid oafs! I stamped back to the bench to wrap myself up for the third time. No matter how firmly I closed my eyes, my anger forced them open. I enjoyed tricks and jests, who didn't? But what they'd done was a mockery of Loveday's life. I wondered how the parson's wife could have taken part. I'd thought better of her. But, oh, if only it had been Loveday's spirit, I could have found out who had harmed her. My hopes lay now with Nowell, who might know something, and young Will, who might help me hunt the murderer down. I must catch them both before Nowell departed, if I survived the remains of the night.

My eyes finally began to close of their own volition when the porch door creaked opened again, allowing lantern light to flood in. I swallowed curses. Who now disturbed the dawn? It was like trying to sleep in a market square inn the night before the annual fair.

The lantern and its bearer advanced. I smelt its hot metal and oil, then food, something sweet with honey. My stomach rumbled suggestively.

"You'll sleep better for having something warm inside you." It was Mistress Paske. Her basket clinked and clunked as she set it on the bench. Her lantern she hooked onto the wall bracket above the bench. The yellow light made a fuzzy circle about us both.

"I'd sleep better in a bed and without you playing pranks."

"Master Jacob Emerick, someone killed an innocent person. Loveday was beloved of all here. We want to know the truth." Mistress Paske began to remove the fleece wads, which protected the pots in the basket. "Then there is that poor London lawyer. When Denzil Gamlen's sudden death brought us all much sorrow we did not think that there might be more deaths. But you appear and we have two more, one which touches us dearly. We have to find and punish the evil doer."

"Your husband believes me to be that evil doer. You told me, Mistress Paske, that you believed me. I say again: I did not harm Mistress Loveday. I did not kill the lawyer. How many times do I have to swear this?"

"Don't raise your voice, I hear you and I believe you." She began to unwind the cloths wrapped around the pots in her basket.

"But that is not enough. We need to know who did. Here." She thrust a deep bowl into my hands.

I grasped it. My hands curved gratefully round the smooth warm surface. The scent from honey sweetened fingers of bread soaking in hot spiced milk distracted me. I gazed at the soft lumpy mess. "Mistress Paske, is this your children's breakfast? I haven't eaten brewis since childhood." I didn't know whether to be charmed or insulted.

Mistress Paske smiled. "It's warm and nourishing, enjoy it. Here's your spoon." She handed me a horn spoon, then removed two tall beakers from their protective wrappings. "You must seek out those who killed Loveday." She worried out one stopper then the other and the heavy scent of blackcurrant syrup rose with the wisps of steam.

I paused, spoon half way to my mouth. I raised my eyebrows. Thoughtfully, I swallowed the mouthful. "Indeed?"

"Indeed, Master Emerick."

I eyed the parson's wife. She sat on the bench, her basket between us, her own cloak now around her shoulders. She'd re-braided her hair, it hung tidily in one fat plait, and neatened her head with a plain linen cap. She'd also dressed herself in a woollen gown, a golden brown dress worn over her high necked chemise, the bodice mis-buttoned in her haste so that it sat uneven at the waist. Her full short sleeves ended above the elbow and her long, tucked shift sleeves fitted snugly to the wrist, the strings gathered and tied there neatly, very practical.

Mistress Faith Paske wasn't a fashionable beauty, she was rather like Loveday in some ways, another face with a high brow and innocent eyes, but she had a way of moving gently, slowly, like mist across a calm sea, soft and fluid. It was that grace which gave Mistress Paske such charm. That and her frank blue eyes, which she turned away from my scrutiny. I continued watching her as I spooned down the sops of bread and milk. She bustled over the basket, fussing, folding the cloths and patting the fleece down, hands busy, thoughts elsewhere. I finished, clattered my spoon into the pot, and observed her little start.

She drew herself up, lifted her head and met my eyes straightly. "Master Emerick, you must see that no one here wants an inconvenient truth. If you didn't kill Loveday, who did? You are a much better choice as murderer than an Eikenthorpe man." She pressed a split bap, spread with soft new cheese, into my hand. "I did what I did tonight because I hoped you had the wit to ask 'Loveday's spirit' to help you clear your name, or tell you who harmed her." She looked at me over the rim of her beaker. "In truth your wits deserted you. Couldn't you have made a pretense?"

I choked on a mouthful of cheese and blackcurrant, coughed, splutter out some words. "I'faith, Mistress Paske, and you speak of truth?" I spluttered again.

"Jacob Emerick," Mistress Paske's tone expressed, like a school master, her annoyance at my obtuseness, "my husband is a good man who believes that you are the sort of hasty, act-before-you-consider youth who might well have become involved in a murderous plot."

"Does he indeed." I gritted my teeth on several unseemly curses. "He goes beyond the bounds of reason. And as for youth? I've lived three and twenty years. Not much younger than you, I'd reckon." Mistress Paske dimpled. "Smile you may, but consider, I'm held here, treated as guilty of two murders, yet there is no proof against me. Parson Paske's wits wander. How would harming Loveday help the Emericks?" Exasperation raised my voice. "Does he take no account of the marriage settlement? It's Lady Fowke who demands the loan and will continue to do so until it's paid. Loveday alive helped the Emericks, Loveday dead..." I faltered over the word, "is of no help to my family or me."

Mistress Paske leaned towards me. "Master Emerick, Jacob," she patted my arm, "think." She spooned a generous dollop of fruit conserve onto both halves of another split bap, absently licking the spoon with a cat's neat lick, then she nibbled one half herself.

I stole the other half out of her hand, for the conserves smelt of peaches, and took another swig of syrup. "I do."

Mistress Paske cocked her head like a little Jenny wren and looked thoughtfully at me. "Share your thoughts. Why do you suppose these murders happen?"

I ruffled my hair with a weary gesture and yawned. "Your pardon, Mistress, but I am tired, I need sleep to think well." I finished chewing the crusty piece of bap, swallowed, took another bite, and considered what was least harmful to say. "I do not know, I cannot say." Would not say, as yet, but I wondered.

Mistress Paske snuggled herself deeper into her cloak, took a sip of her drink and attacked again. "The Gamlen lawyer and the Gamlen heir both murdered? That is outsider doings. You are the outsider, linked to both of them."

Shrewd, Mistress Paske, but wrong. I sighed. "That is spite, Mistress, the cursed ignorant spite of untutored rustics against the outsider." I rubbed my aching forehead, palmed my dry itching eyes. I wanted to sleep, my whole body yearned for deep untroubled sleep. If my mind were rested I could think, follow all the winding trails clearly and connect them. I felt I had missed some small but important thing. I had an answer locked away and a choice of keys, but was too stupid from want of sleep to fit the right key to the lock. What was it which needed finding? I knuckled my temples then rubbed my forehead vigorously.

"Have you a headache? See, knead your temples just here, scribing circles down behind your ears to your neck." Mistress Paske leant towards me and began to demonstrate with a light soothing touch. Then she jerked her hand away, pulled back from me, and stammered an apology.

I continued her actions and pretended not to notice the darker colour flooding her face. "I thank you, Mistress Paske, for the food, the lantern and those warning words. I will heed them, but now I must sleep." I slid sideways, tucked my feet up, pulling the cloaks over me. Mistress Paske dropped the blankets on top of me. I heard the basket lifted as I stuffed a lump of cloak under my head.

"Sleep, Master Emerick. The good Lord will make thing clearer in the morning. God give you peace. Rest well, Master Emerick."

My eyes grew heavy. My head nodded. It was as I slid down into darkness that I found a key to a lock I wanted opened. "Mistress Paske." Satan's imps! Had she gone? I floundered off the bench and out of the wraps. No, I could see her lantern. She had only reached the porch door. "Lawyer Jameson, Denzil Gamlen's man, did anyone find his letters and papers?"

"No, Master Emerick, I don't believe they have been found."

"Then how does Knott work, and how does Lady Fowke attend the business for the Gamlen estate?"

"Ah." She hesitated then bethought herself of what I should have. "But there will have been copies, surely, Master Emerick."

"But not the time to fetch them. Clerk Knott was here when I arrived. How did he have any papers when Jameson would be travelling with them all? What do you know of this Clerk Knott?"

Mistress Paske tutted, turned, walked back to me, and hooked her lantern on the bracket on the wall above my bench. She reached out and caught my shoulder, giving it a little shake as she would to her daughters or Will. "Master Emerick, Clerk Knott is a strict Puritan. He would not...."

I jeered. "And a Puritan cannot kill?" Treat me as a child would she? I'd show her. I caught her hand between both mine, tugging her closer. "What do you know of this clerk? I never saw him with Jameson before in their offices."

"Master Emerick...Jacob Emerick, let me go." Mistress Paske half laughed, half pleaded, her cheek colour darkening, the pulse in her wrists fluttering like a caught moth. She tried to ease her hand from between mine.

"Ah no, Mistress, not until I know what you know. Trying to treat me as though I were Grace? No, Mistress." I pulled her towards me until we were face to face and nearly touching. For one silent moment even our breathing stopped as I scrutinized her face and she, eyes downcast, refused to look into mine.

She twisted her hand, trying again to disengage. "Master Jacob Emerick, you let me go." Her voice, stern as she could be, egged me on.

My left arm moved around her waist to snug her closer. She had such soft tempting lips, it would be a delight to kiss her, also a just punishment for that play-acting she had done earlier. "Mistress Paske, you owe me a kiss to make up for this night." I tipped up her chin and found that her lips were warm and quivered under mine. She tasted honey sweet and I was loath to release her, but she pushed away even as I let her go. "How you dare to...if my husband knew you'd...." She stuttered to a stop.

"Mistress Paske, that was fair punishment."

She blushed again even more, her eyes wouldn't meet mine. She collected the basket and swished away on hasty feet, her head bowed.

I propped my chin in my hand and sighed gustily. Absently I smoothed my palm across the seat where Mistress Paske had been. I'd never had trouble attracting maids. Bold ones looked at me from under their eyelashes during church, sending messages which would scandalise their mothers. I ignored them, and the saucy forward ones who caught and squeezed hands surreptitiously. Kisses I stole from those who weren't maids, nor married ladies. Bussing the barmaid was a game, but kissing Mistress Paske Paske was foolish, lethally so, and the harm would go both ways. Good wives like Mistress Faith Paske did not make a game of kissing. I curled up under my covers, cursing the fact that I allowed myself that indulgence. Seeking the truth was my task, not extracting petty revenges. With my conscience chiding me I expected to remain awake, but to my surprise I slid into sleep.

\*\*\*

It was full light when Will shook me. "Jacob, oh, do wake up, Jacob," Will's impatience suggested that he'd been calling for some time. My head ached, muzzy, as though thick with too much rough cider. I raised dry eyelids, rubbed scalded eyes, and grunted.

"Jacob, Nowell's gone. I rode with him part way. He's work to do and some letters to collect, but he's returning for the funeral."

I groaned and stretched. "He had better do so for I need information. Are we supposed to have all problems solved and Loveday's killer found by then?" I wanted a pump to splash cold water over my head and shoulders and rose water to rinse round my mouth.

"Come on, Jacob." Will tugged my arm. "You and I are going to find out what happened at Gamlen Manor the morning Loveday died."

I groaned. "Let me wash and wake up first," I protested, as Will pulled me upright and pushed me towards the church doors.

"All fine and well, but hurry."

I hurried.

# CHAPTER FOURTEEN

Clerk Knott, newly returned from Lady Fowke's errands in London and a meeting with his colleagues at Westminster, meekly bowed his head and kept his face servile before Lady Fowke's onslaught. With his mind full of fresh knowledge about the King's doings, he barely felt the sting of her rage. He'd sent enough hares coursing through Eikenthorpe to keep young Emerick hounded for a goodly while yet and keep Parson Paske from the full truth. If his colleagues in London had not blessed his ideas with full support, they had not forbidden his ideas outright. He would serve his masters better left to his own devices.

He bore his vilification patiently, secure in his private knowledge about the future for the likes of her breed. But his determination to prevent any sizable sums of money reaching the King through the old hag or her kin polished itself harder than steel. He'd run that young Emerick through himself if that were the only way to stop the King gaining Emerick money. No matter what others thought, or said, John Pym believed that having the support of the navy and the ports would be the salvation of the country. As it was, the King, left ship-less, would have to gamble all on his army in a countryside full of resentment against him. Knott shuffled from foot to foot and murmured, "Yes, my lady," again, certain in his very soul that if Pym and his party had to defend themselves, they could succeed. The men who were the army were not the King's courtiers and companions. No, the bulk of an army was decent men, men forced from their home and families to fight, men for whom this King had little regard. But Pym's men, with good leaders, and God on their side, must, through the Lord's might, prevail, but only if he prevented that weakling Emerick giving way.

"Yes, Lady Fowke," he quavered into a silence as she swept to a halt.

The lady eyed him fiercely, then inclined her head, assuming a gracious dignity. "You will never again fail to return directly to me. You will never again stay to gossip in the village. You had no right or reason to speak to the parson, and you will suffer if this happens again." She looked down her nose at him and waved him away as though he were the rankest smell from an overfull privy.

Knott bowed himself out backwards and slunk off to find the other servants. He had set more snares for Emerick, trapped the parson with a half told tale, all of which now left him free to examine the other young stranger, Nowell Merriot. What information he'd gleaned in London made him want more. Merriot was not four square, of that Knott was certain. He smoothed his hose and tugged his doublet down. There was much to do. He must discover who had murdered Mistress Maye and why. He had his suspicions, but no proof and no reason why. He could not tie it with Lawyer Jameson's death. He knew how the Emerick-Gamlen legal affairs were to be settled. The maid's death must be different. Perhaps some of these servants would know about lovelorn youths or strangers visiting. A little gossip and he might find why the maid was dead. He'd spice their gossip with tales of that young cockerel, Emerick, and how he could have harmed Mistress Maye. Knott shuffled off down the hallway. He would like a word with tomfool Emerick right now, a word and a threat, something powerful to make sure that the Emerick gold stayed in the Emerick purse. He turned towards the kitchen. A flattering interest in food unlocked most cooks' lips. He would try what he could do with this cook. The reason for the maid's murder was in this house, the parson was sure of it and so was he.

# CHAPTER FIFTEEN

I wanted to wash away the tiredness and find a clean shirt before facing the household at Gamlen Manor. Will was only too happy to swing the pump handle. The parson's house boasted two pumps, one by the stone wall in the back yard, set over the livestock trough, yet handy for the gardens. The second, part of the renovations, stood new-housed in a lean-to scullery. The scullery floor had been paved, the pump surrounded by new brick steps wide enough to set down buckets, pails and the washed dairy bowls on. A neat and tidy arrangement, one, if she could see it, to tempt my mother into the sin of covetousness. I smiled as I pressed my aching eyes.

My mother had worked hard to persuade my father to have a new pump close to the kitchen door. She now had one, but was still trying to prevent mud being walked through the kitchens. My father never could see why the ground round a pump needed paving with slabs of stone or blocks of brick.

"Fetching the water was women's work and they had pattens to wear didn't they? If they slipped their shoes into pattens when they went outside then the mud would be left at the door wouldn't it?"

The discussion became most insistent during wet weather. The pump had been installed for just over half a year and I'd wagered a new embroidered shirt with my brother, Caleb, that my mother would have her paved yard before the year was out. I must remember to mention Mistress Paske's pump and yard in my next letter home. Meanwhile I wanted to clear the frowstiness from my head and gather up my wandering wits. I stripped to the waist, hung my clothes on the handily placed wall pegs, ducked my head under the spout, and splashed and spluttered.

"Here." Will shoved a round ball of pinkish soap into my hands.

My wet fingers released a gentle scent of roses. Startled I straightened, shook my head and blinked my eyes. My vision, blurred by dripping water, distinguished only misty shapes. I tossed my wet hair back, squeezed my eye lids together tightly, looked again. There stood the three little Graces, well wrapped in homespun knitted shawls, eyes staring, fuzzy fine hair loose about their heads, mouths rounded.

Grace spoke first. "That's our May Day soap."

"Oh," I looked again at the gritty soap, "thank you. Have you collected dew to wash in?"

"With Tabitha and Mama."

Still they stared. I smiled, then flicked a hand's scoop of water at them. The drops flew from my fingers, silvered by the slice of morning light from the outer doorway. The little girls watched them arch towards them, squealed, and ran away through the kitchen door.

"Hurry up." Will leaned on the pump handle and another gout of water sploshed from the pipe.

I soaped myself. "Sweet," I remarked. The grit was a little sugar mixed in with the rose oil. It smelt good, expensive ladies' soap, produced, I was sure, specially for May Day. I wondered if that was how Mistress Paske taught her daughters to make soap. It seemed like her to sweeten their lessons with a May Day promise, roses and sugar.

Another vigorously pumped spurt of water soaked me. "Enough, Will." I twisted my hair, wringing it out so firmly that the water landed on the stones with a splat.

The handle creaked to rest. Will cleared his throat loudly. I looked up and there stood Mistress Paske, clutching a bunch of dew wet herbs, with a little crock of dew water tucked under her elbow. Behind her skirts her daughters pushed and peeped. Mistress Paske blushed and turned her head away. Tabitha, in the rear, arms full of nubbly linen towels, tisked and elbowed forward.

"You should give us good warning you're bathing at the pump," she said. "'Tis not proper for little maids nor Mistress neither."

I refused to feel embarrassed. "I'd forgotten today you'd be about so early. A merry May Day to you all." I rapidly re-braided my lovelock and finger combed my hair behind my ears. Mistress Paske, a faint flush to her throat and cheeks, gave me a towel from Tabitha's pile. I accepted it with a bow of my head and draped it over my shoulders. "My thanks, Mistress."

Will reached down my doublet from the peg, to give me, but my shirt, Tabitha snatched from Will's hands, saying it needed washing carefully. Well, she couldn't do worse with the fine lawn than the inn.

"We've gathered May Day dew," the middle daughter, Ruth - or was she Hope? - piped up. "We're going to wash our faces and hair too. Then we'll be beautiful."

Will coughed his laugh away. I managed to hold my face steady. I put on a courtly smile. "Ah, but you little maids are like your mother, fair enough without the aid of May Day dew." I bowed extravagantly to them all, returned the soap to Grace, and departed through the scullery door.

Will hurried close behind. "All we needed was the parson to arrive in his breeks."

"Never you mind Parson Paske's rough tongue, Will. Wait 'til you hear Lady Fowke." I kept my voice light, rode my thoughts firmly. They'd strayed to last night's stolen kiss, and I rued the impulse which made me do it. Mistress Paske's blushing throat, so like Loveday's, forced a sigh, for Loveday was no more, and thinking on her wouldn't bring her back. "Breakfast before I ride out to face Lady Fowke, Will. But first Perry, finally breakfast."

Will muttered and humphed, but accepted my list. Probably he wanted another breakfast, for through the outer kitchen door drifted the sizzle of honey cured bacon frying. Parson Paske farmed as well as he preached. I had seen excellent hams hanging in the pantry and smelt the flitches of bacon smoking in the wide kitchen chimney. Besides which I needed time to clear my head and think out another approach to Lady Fowke. Will knew many of the servants, but he'd never manage the lady herself. If I could distract her, then Will could roam freely amongst the household, questioning all.

Perry expressed her pleasure at seeing me by nudging me roughly. She was anxious to be out. Will and I took a side each and brushed the spangled coat shiny. Will filled the manger with crushed beans and chaff while I walked Perry to the trough and let her slobber and huff as I pumped up fresh water. She slaked her thirst in slurping gulps then wiped her wet muzzle across my shoulder. I pushed her away and looked ruefully at my messy sleeve. Will appeared at the stable door to laughed as Perry snorted playfully and blew water all over me.

I reproached her in apprentice boy terms, and Parson Paske, walking into the yard, heard me. He frowned, but forbore to upbraid me. He wore stout muddy boots, old mended breeches and a patched cassock. Clearly he'd been inspecting his crops or beasts, but he lost not one whit of his dignity, although his old clothes looked more fit for the scarecrow than a parson. I received his permission to turn Perry into the old orchard and kept a civil face and tongue in the face of his distrust. Confound the man, I hoped he was as troubled by lack of sleep as I was.

"You are still under suspicion, Master Emerick, no travelling for you." Washed and shaved, the parson had only the blue shadows across his jaw bones and round his eyes to show fatigue. "Last night was not conclusive, Master Emerick, you will not attempt to ride from here without a guard."

Will emerged from the stable. "I'm riding with him, and we're only heading to Gamlen Manor, Parson Paske. We're seeking the truth about Loveday."

"Return by mid-afternoon. Master Emerick must face our charges tonight, Will. Clerk Knott is returned from London, and I shall hear his statement then."

"It'll clear Jacob."

"Fine words, Will, come and share breakfast with us, and give me proof of what you say." He walked on to the kitchens.

Will spluttered indignation and looked at me. I shrugged, led Perry through the gate and released her. She tickled my face with her whiskers as she blew warm moist breath in my ear, shoved me aside with a gentle nudge, and trotted away. I could not help but laugh at the foolish fond animal. Will slapped me on the back, urging me in to breakfast. I followed him, reflecting that my letter home, that painfully written explanation of the further problems I faced, would be safely on its way. I hadn't given it to Clerk Knott this time, but sent the letter through the government mail service. I no longer trusted Clerk Knott, and looked forward to catching him on his own. I had a clout or two for that mischief making man and some very sharp words. If he lied tonight...Will called for me to come and I walked through the kitchen, vowing to find Clerk Knott at Gamlen Manor and make him eat his words.

***

In the Manor stable yard I handed Perry's reins to a scowling Zach. Will grinned, winked at me and led his pony after the groom. Praise be for Will, he'd soon find out from the servants what had been going on the day Loveday was killed. Now, I had to find Lady Fowke. I breathed in deeply and squared my shoulders, patting my plain belt pouch. I'd decided last night that I would bring Lady Fowke, a month early, something I'd call the Gamlen dues from the investment. I hoped to quiet her demands with this ruse, but in such a fashion that she would have the name of the gold, yet not the substance. My boots crunched on the gravel of the stable yard, and I anticipated the approaching verbal duel with something akin to my previous confidence. The lady had been a trial, and I wished to be done with her.

Rather than walk round to the main entrance, I slipped through the laundry yard door, taking the path across the grass to the door into the ladies' walk. Loveday had always taken me this way, her private way to the ladies' garden and its door into the house. I felt her here, very close, so near indeed that as I opened the door, I paused, grasping the large ornamental ring handle in my hand, vowing to her that her murderer would not escape. The twisted metal left grooves in my palm and I examined them, marks of my pledge, as I ducked into the side passage which led to the main hall.

Nothing warned me, no strange scent, disturbance of air, prickling nape of neck or feeling of being watched. As I paused inside the door to allow my eyes to adjust from the brighter outside light, my hat was knocked off, my hair was seized, my head yanked back, and before I could react with an elbow slammed backwards, a thin blade pressed across my throat.

"Be still, little popinjay or your fine clothes will be stained with blood...your blood." The voice was low, pitched not to carry, but I recognized it.

"Knott." I could barely speak.

The knife pressed closer, the voice continued in that low pitch. "The same. Now listen closely, and do as I say."

I stilled, easing back slightly, leaning into Knott. A bare blade to the throat had to be dealt with carefully. Stillness first, action afterwards, if possible. Knott couldn't kill me here, not by slitting my throat. He'd have to make the death look accidental or as the result of a fight -- a cut throat was too obvious, too deliberate.

"What is it you want?" Every movement of my vocal chords grazed my skin against the blade, kept my voice a whisper.

"Ah now, that's sense." The grip on my hair and head tightened to an excruciating, scalp-lifting tear. The pain made my eyes water. I couldn't move. Knott moved. He forced my head down, twisted me about, then pushed me away as he released my hair. I yelped, straightening up, ready to pounce on him. He stood out of reach, but held the poniard blade steady, level with my guts. "Don't make me use it, Master Emerick."

It was a well kept knife, but it didn't shine like new steel. The blade sheen was dulled. Human blood dulled steel, over several stabbings of course, but a blade never regained that glittering shine, polish it though you might. I felt a spine chilling despair. This knife had been well used, and Clerk Knott clearly knew how to use it. He did not brandish his knife in a hand stretched at an arm's length from his body, with the blade pressed against my stomach. I would have had a good chance of disarming him then. No, this was the stance of a man who had fought with a knife before. Was Knott a hired killer then? But for whom and why? Was he responsible for Loveday's death? Oh, I surely believed him when he said he would harm me. I moved carefully.

"So now you know."

I raised my eyes from the wicked blade, so still and ready to strike, and gave Knott a furious glare. "Who are you?"

"What's in your pouch?

I closed my mouth and set my lips.

Knott's eyes narrowed, he scowled, but his hand remained steady. "Very well, young Emerick." There was a pause, long enough for me to feel sweat trickle down the back of my neck and break out across my forehead. Knott watched and grinned knowingly. "There's nothing you can do to harm me. Quite the reverse, in fact." The knife remained steady. "I'm here to see that Lady Fowke does not receive any or all of that Gamlen-Emerick loan."

A wave of dizzying weakness hit my knees. My mouth slackened, the words, "What? Why?" fell out.

Knott made a coughing sound. It might have been a laugh, his shoulders shook slightly, but the knife in his hand looked steady. "I will kill you rather than let any money reach the Fowkes. I will see your family destroyed rather than let any Emerick money reach King Charles."

I believed him. Knott's eyes shone with a fervour that menaced. What I couldn't understand was why Knott felt the need for threats. "We have no intention of repaying any money to the Fowkes."

"Keep it that way."

"Why, what is Emerick-Gamlen business to you?"

"Where do you stand, Jacob Emerick, in this quarrel between King and Parliament? Your family are good merchants, but only fair Puritans. What are you?"

I refused to answer.

The knife blade menaced me. "What are you?"

I bounded forward, swinging my leg up in a strong controlled kick, aimed at his knife hand. I missed, but hit his arm hard, knocking it, with the knife, well away from me. I let my fear turn to anger and slammed him into the wall, pushing his arm until he dropped the knife. "And what are you, Knott? Does Lady Fowke know what her clerk does? How will she feel when she hears what you've said about the Gamlen money?" I kept my voice low to match Knott, wondering, fleetingly, why I cared to do so.

"That woman has no hold over me. I work for the glory of God, through John Pym and Parliament."

So that was it, well, a part of it. Parliament's man, a spy. "And when will you declare war on the King?" My voice rose slightly, filled with contempt.

Knott's face lightened. "The King will raise his standard shortly. His will be the ungodly crime of declaring war against his own people. He will be the murderer. For the Lord God has prepared us, we are watching, and we will overcome the ungodly Queen and her papists who threaten our country, and the King's Archbishop, that papist pawn, Laud, who foists his one false religion upon us all."

A bigot, I had a ranting Puritan bigot on my back. Clerk

Knott, Pym and Parliament's man, was one of these fanatics. I hated fanatics, people who would do anything in the belief that they had the right of it, and God's blessing to boot. Knott might well kill me, if he thought it was God's choice. Under our 'good' King Charles we'd become a country of fanatics, each ranting about his version of paradise, each convinced of his righteousness. Archbishop Laud was as big a bigot as Puritan Pym and look where it was leading us. "I pray God it never comes to that."

Knott shook his head. "God's word is that it will." He stepped back and returned his poniard to its sheath hidden snug beneath his doublet. "I will be leaving here tomorrow morning, after this evening's meeting with Parson Paske. Nothing you say or do can harm me, for who will believe you? Make sure of withholding the money by signing no agreements, nor giving your word, and tonight I will say what you need to clear you of all suspicion of killing Mistress Maye. To be sure you don't provide Lady Fowke with what she wants I'll walk behind you and attend my lady with you." His smile was not pleasant. "You give her any money or use of your ships for her to give to the King and I'll give you into the hands of the Eikenthorpe worthies. To hang for two deaths."

It was a blow I felt almost physically, but Knott must not know. I acted the bravado and sneered. "Thou shalt not bear false witness, Clerk Knott. Doesn't our Lord hold that the truth is all that matters?" I glared at the clerk. "You know I was never anywhere near Mistress Maye or Lawyer Jameson."

Knott curled his lips in an evil leer. "Aye, but will I say that? Do as I ask, Master Emerick. Deny Lady Fowke." He moved to grasp my shoulder and turned me about.

I slapped his hand away. "Don't you raise a hand to me again." I dusted off my doublet and tugged my sleeves straight. "If you'd had the sense to enlist my support at the beginning we could have devised a goodly legal method of thwarting Lady Fowke and preventing her appealing to the King." I smoothed down my hair and winced when I touched my torn scalp. As it is..." I let my voice tail away, and I looked my disgust. "You have made an enemy of the Merchants Emerick, Knott. Unwise don't you think?"

Knott laughed. "But I know your ships have sailed, your coasters ply the London waters, there is little you can do now to hurt our cause. But when those ships return? I know you merchants. You'd be prepared to support anyone who would save your ships and your trade. Not one of your golden coins is to go into the lady's purse. When Mistress Maye stood as a bargaining point, you would hold back. Now she is dead you are not to be trusted. Here, God works through me alone. It is God's way to choose the best tools to hand, not use the ungodly or contrive ungodly lies."

I almost choked."And what, pray, is it when you lie to Parson Paske or spin lying tales of me in this community?"

Knott merely shook his head, his attitude one of absolute certainty in his righteousness. "I removed myself so that I could not say anything. But if I," and he leaned towards me and hissed into my face, "if I have to lie for God's cause it will be by God's design."

I drew away from him, restrained myself from spitting in his face, and strode towards Lady Fowke's library. Anger rose, fuelled by his insensate talk of Loveday's death. Let that lanky, pallid stick of a man try anything and I'd.... Well, I'd find some way of repaying the bigot with interest. I'd be wise to wear a poniard as well as my sword and keep my pistols loaded from now on. My spine still prickled, the anger I allowed, but fear lurked under my anger. Knott meant what he said.

"Allow me, Master Emerick." The clerk, all obsequious attention, opened the door. "Don't forget," he hissed, as I brushed past. I scowled at him.

Lady Fowke waved Knott away impatiently. "Well, Master Emerick? I see no gold. I warned you, I have powerful friends. I shall seize your ships."

I bowed politely again. I was aware of Knott's ear to the crack of the door. "Perhaps this will be of use?" I handed the letter of credit to her, then watched her pale ringed fingers crisply unfold the paper. There was a moment of stillness. I risked a quick glance up at her face.

Lady Fowke's eyes were firmly fixed on the seals at the bottom of the letter. Then they met mine, hot angry hunter's eyes, looking for prey. I kept my face still, my eyes patient.

"What is this?"

"A letter of credit. Present that in London, in person, to the people named and you will have the sum of money written there."

Lady Fowke struck with the speed of a falcon, wrung the letter of credit between her fingers, and tossed it to the floor. "I will have all monies and in gold." She was as certain and self-righteous as Knott.

I bowed and picked up the letter, handing it back to her. "I will see you in London, my lady, when you come to exchange your letter of credit."

She hurled it at my head. I caught it deftly by the seal tapes and stowed it again in my belt pouch. "As you wish, my lady. Please consider it. I will return tomorrow."

"I see what you are about, Merchant." She rose and her voice continued upwards. "It is beyond anything I have heard. I will have that gold, and I will seize your ships."

"Until tomorrow, my lady." I turned and left her. At the door I looked back. Lady Fowke was rigid, but her stillness was not that of inaction. She held herself back, her hands gripping each other, but her eyes said everything. I reckoned she was as dangerous as Knott and quelled a desire to run from them both. They deserved each other. Bigots, the pair of them, happy to ruin a good many people if it gained them what they believed in. Like to ruin we Emericks with their squabbles. A plague on both their houses. I shut the door sharply behind me and looked for Knott. Had he the wit to know that neither a Fowke or a Fowke agent could set foot in London now? At least he did not hide by the door. I looked up and down the passage way. Praise the Lord, he had disappeared. I had kept to his bargain and not given anything to the Fowkes, he had better stick to his this evening. I stalked off in search of Will.

Will held forth in the kitchens. Eating again, he waved his arms about, declaiming amidst a shower of crumbs. The round eyes and opened mouths of everyone around told of a powerful story. I listened and gathered he was telling them our amended version of what happened in the church, with Nowell turned into an intruder of evil intent.

"So mayhap it was the murderer come back. But we didn't catch him." Will waved a slice of pie at me. "Savoury pork pie, Jacob, it's good." I took a slice but winced at its reddish interior. It reminded me of Loveday and cherry tarts, cherries red as blood and Loveday deathly white in my arms. "I couldn't," I said, "it puts me in mind of Loveday." I spoke without design, but Mary sniffled, and some goodies tutted sympathetically.

"We've been through the household. There isn't anything missing we can see, nothing to explain why someone would hurt her." Mary shook her head. "She helped make the herbal concoctions, any medicines we used, the dyes and flavourings, perfumes and oils, but she wasn't killed for that." The goodies sniffed, and Mary wiped her eyes. "Who could a-done it?" Her voice rose in a wail and she wept again, burying her face in the cloths she held.

I could give a reason for the Fowkes wanting to harm her if they'd discovered she had those documents we Emericks needed, but Lady Fowke had been away courting the Earl and her only retainers at Gamlen Manor were Gif and Mary, neither likely to harm the maid. I patted her shoulder. "Where did Mistress Maye spend most of her time? Could she have seen something from a window? Did she catch someone at her herbs and simples taking what they might harm someone with? Would you please take me to see, Mistress Mary"

Mary sobbed again, sniffed and wiped her face. "Follow me, Master Emerick."

I left Will eating and speculating wildly with the servants as to who had disturbed us in the church. He winked at me as I left.

The still room faced south, was a charming little chamber and apparently Denzil Gamlen had used it to make perfumes. His flasks and bottles, starters and oils stood arrayed on shelves behind the door. The room still smelt faintly of various pleasant concoctions. All the rest of the room, neatly shelved, showed Loveday's tidy habits, herbs arranged by type, beakers, bottles and boxes labelled and stoppered.

I wandered from shelf to shelf, reading labels. This was women's work, unless you were a cook, or an apothecary of course, and Loveday, like my mother, had been a good herbalist. I knew so little about it. A check of the window showed it looked onto the ladies' walk, enclosed by high walls. She could have seen naught there.

"Nothing poisonous openly here, Master Emerick. 'Tis all locked away in the lady's store cupboard."

I poked a cautious finger among the packets on Gamlen's shelves, mostly they were half used, open packets but a neatly wrapped, sealed one caught my eye. I picked it out. "What's this?"

Mary held out her hand. "Let me see, Master Emerick." She took it from me and squinted at the tiny writing. "Oh, it's one of my lady's. She often made powders for her brother this past year. He turned sick at the Harvest Home, never regained his strength. Came to us for Twelfth Night, and my lady made him special potions, she thought he'd eaten too much of her rich food." She smiled with a servant's pride. "My lady's table is of the best at Christmastide, but he was ailing badly when he left London and they say here he just faded out of life." She gave me a doleful look and replaced the packet.

"Did Master Gamlen always join his sister for Christmastide?"

"Aye, since his wife died ten years past, for she'd not leave family out and he, her brother, all alone down here. He would make his yearly London purchases at tailor and bookman and go home after the Twelfth Night celebrations ended."

I walked slowly round the room again. "I can see nothing

amiss, Mary, you've the right of it, nothing happened here."

Back in the kitchens Will snatched up two pasties. "Venison," he said and shouldered me towards the door. "We'll find the villain who did it," he told the group at large and manoeuvred me outside.

"There's nothing odd happened the day she died." Will sighed. "They all want to help and all say the same things. Nowell told me...."

I held up my hand to stop him talking where others might hear. "So you did have time to question him." I walked him to the middle of the yard, out of earshot.

"I couldn't stop him talking, words ran out of him like new cider fizzing over the bung." Will kept his voice low, facing me. "He didn't stop until I sent him on his way to the inn." Will urged me forwards. "If I'm to take you back to Parson Paske in good time, we should talk on the way."

We reached the village before we had barely covered what Will had learned from each servant. Loveday had spent her day exactly as she had spent the others. No strangers had been seen, nothing marked the day out as unusual or different. We were heading across the green for the parsonage, allowing our horses to amble side by side, trying to conjecture possibilities, when Parson Paske's voice hailed us. Will muttered, but we turned aside. Walking towards us, sober black flanking rich claret, came the parson, Nowell and that officious Deacon.

"Come, Will, where are your manners?" I clapped Will's back and dismounted. "Well, gentlemen?"

The Deacon looked smug. "We have news, you won't like, Master Emerick,"

I shrugged, but noted that Nowell wouldn't look in my direction. I hoped he'd been wary, for if my suspicions were right he'd be branded another evil doer in the community's mind, and that put him in near as much danger as I was.

"Yes, you had every reason to kill Mistress Loveday, she was already promised to this man." The Deacon beamed with a most unchristian pleasure.

Mistress Paske's warning had made sense, and I'd since cursed my stubborn head for not pretending in church. This time I wasn't going to hide anything. If I'd never heard this news I would be astonished, so I didn't prevent my 'astonishment' from catching me mid-step with my eyebrows soaring into my hairline. "What did you say? Nowell, is this true?"

"In God's name it's true."

"Then why did Lady Fowke...? She was quite plain that the maid's marriage was hers to arrange. I was not the most favoured suitor, but the prospect of ships at her disposal allowed her to consider an Emerick-Fowke agreement. I sincerely believed that political considerations would have made her favour a marriage settlement with me." I gave a puzzled headshake, kept a mazy look on my face.

The Deacon did not understand, but Parson Paske had caught the political allusion, he frowned.

Nowell's lips twitched slightly, yet his voice was steady when he replied. "Lady Fowke did know." Here his voice faded as he struggled to hold back his grief.

"Perhaps Lady Fowke believed she could force Doctor Maye to agree to another, better marriage for Loveday?" I suggested. "That would be very like the lady."

Will had been following along, his head tilted, turning from speaker to speaker like a cock robin. "Then, as Master Emerick believed that a marriage settlement was likely, why would he harm Mistress Loveday? And beside even if he couldn't marry her what reason had he to hurt her?" Will shook his head until his hat slid sideways. "No sense in any of this. No reason to blame Jacob except he is the outsider. As well blame Master Merriot for harming the maid or that lawyer man. They are outsiders."

The Deacon puffed up his chest like a bantam cock. "Evil has been brought to our village and by whom? Not by the honest Puritans who live here." He glared at me and then Nowell. "Master

Gamlen kept his religious ideas in his own chapel and left us to worship rightly. You," he pointed at me, "have been in our church. You show the outward forms of pure religion, but the Lord sees your soul."

Parson Paske reached out and shook his arm. "Enough, Deacon. There's no need to warn me. I know, as God knows. We'll wait for the clerk's witness this evening."

I looked at Nowell, who gave me a faint grin. Will thumped my back and the three of us headed towards the parson's stable yard. We'd talk later.

# CHAPTER SIXTEEN

Clerk Knott arrived in time for the evening meal, escorted into the long dining room by Parson Paske, deacons and wardens tailing after. It was another family meal, I had guessed rightly, with all the church 'family' attending. Mistress Paske and Tabitha, with a dozen other wives fed us well. Wanting Will for the village gossip, and Nowell for information, I cornered them the room's length away from Knott.

"Pass that dish of pickled pork and tell us what you've heard, Will. You're our ears around the community. Keep your voice down and look like you're only interested in the food. Pour us some of that sweet ale, Nowell and believe me when I tell you I need to find out what happened as much as you do."

Nowell complied with a grimace, pouring the ale with a careful hand.

Will took his tankard and grinned. "But I am concentrating on the food, you should try this bread and cheese plait." He passed us both a chunk, but he lowered his voice and Nowell did likewise. I noted Parson Paske and Clerk Knott eyed us occasionally but made no move in our direction. I would have liked to overhear their conversation. Did the parson know who and what Knott was? Or was it theology they expounded to each other?

I let Nowell sigh over Loveday. "Why wasn't I here to help her?" Nowell's oft expressed regret, repeated after our every question to him, punctuated the conversation as a sad refrain. That and why the Almighty had not prevented such evil. Nowell took her murder as work of the Devil, and he scanned the faces around us as if he believed he'd see the Devil's mark on one of them. His knowledge of Loveday's family and life with Lady Fowke revealed nothing new. He had only come to Eikenthorpe to bring Loveday a packet from her father and letters to Lady Fowke. He understood well the lady's ambitions for the Fowkes. He'd feared she would wish to arrange a fine marriage for Loveday, but the maid and her father promised to stand firm. "What did you tempt the lady with?" he asked.

I shook my head. "Nay, not I." Honesty compelled me to add more. "I intended to ask about a marriage agreement as part of the Emerick-Gamlen settlement. The lady suggested it first."

Nowell sighed. His bleary eyes, the deep lines on his face aged him ten years, spoke of his devotion.

What gave me pause for thought was the reflection that Loveday was never mine to have, yet I'd been sure she was the Lord's gift to me. I'd assumed. I had to rethink several of my assumptions and quickly if I was to leave Eikenthorpe with my neck unstretched. Still between eating, drinking, and with questions and prompts, Will and Nowell managed to say a deal that I found of value. I chewed on their information as well as the meat and saw only more problems. "We don't have enough to set me free. They'll still find me the easy villain to chose. That clerk better speak the plain truth. He saw me walking on the path first and then go into the river...." I left the rest of the words hanging in the air to spare Nowell more wincing tears, and, if I were truthful, to save Will and myself the same pain. I couldn't understand how my plans fell out so badly, or why my carefully planned future should suddenly turn topsy-turvy. I felt as shaken as Nowell looked.

"Would it alter matters much if Knott lied?" Will's eyebrows lost themselves in his curly fringe. "We know him for a liar. We can say so, and he threatened you this morning, we can tell them that." He looked at the two men conferring. "Parson Paske knows something about that man, for he gives him more credit than he would a mere clerk."

"Well, he's not Gamlen's clerk, his clerk was a very different man. I know because I've worked with both Jameson and his clerk."

Will's eyes narrowed, but before he could speak Nowell patted his back in an older brother's condescending way. "Jacob found the body. He's not one of you, and unless he can point a finger and make good counter claims for a villain, who here, but us, will raise a finger to help him?"

Will choked. "But to blame a man for finding a body?" His voice rose.

I hushed him down with one hand, touched Nowell's shoulder with the other, reminding them both to stay quiet. I mistrusted Will's tongue with secrets. Nowell's I knew to be discreet. I'd warned them of Knott's actions and words, but to speak of them to Parson Paske was another matter. Would he believe me? I fingered the graze at my throat and heard again the threats. Knott had not hesitated. He would kill, he had killed before. But who else would want to remove the Gamlen lawyer and take his place? I needed some form of evidence, for Parson Paske would not believe me if I told him that Jameson had been killed by Clerk Knott. He trusted the man, knew of him.

My bite of oat cake clogged up my tongue. If I stood now and denounced Knott it was my word against his. Even the graze on my throat might have other explanations. Nowell had already chaffed me about careless shaving. Confound this whole Emerick-Gamlen tangle. I couldn't decide what to do or say, and indecision was a stranger to me. I, Jacob Emerick, who had always known what I wanted and how to get it, sat in this place, puzzled and confused, afraid of a miserable Puritan bigot. Perhaps it was because I sensed more. I could comfort myself with that, for this time I was out of my depth, sailing on dark water through a storm I could smell, but not see or understand. There had to be a way out, but I couldn't find it. All I conned was that Clerk Knott, who was no clerk, sailed on a ship loaded with trouble, probably powerfully gunned and manned, certainly commanded by a powerful captain. The Emericks might not be able to sail out of this storm if I jumped up now and steered them into it. There was no proof, just my reasoning, to mark Knott as Jameson's murderer, even though he had the Emerick-Gamlen papers which Jameson must have been carrying. I believed he had killed, but had nothing to accuse him with that would set me free. Loveday Maye's murder I could not understand, unless Knott had caught her with those missing documents.

Will ate heartily. Nowell pecked at little more than I could. If Knott lied, refused to clear me, or temporised, what could I do? Oh, of a surety, asking Knott a few awkward questions should plant seeds of doubt in Parson Paske's mind, even if I dare not denounce him yet. Calling Knott a Puritan spy, working for Pym's party, might only work in his favour in this community. This part of Kent was firmly Puritan, and, this it was that stuck in my craw, perhaps the Puritans of Eikenthorpe would welcome Knott and what he did for the good of their true religion?

Mistress Paske appeared at my elbow with large slices of spiced apple pie for the three of us. "The last of the stored apples baked just for you, Master Emerick. I hope you have thought what you will say, to convince these good men."

I kept my mouth still, but gave her a look in my best imitation of Lady Fowke. Her lips quirked upwards, she turned her face away. "Clerk Knott can clear my name. Whether he will is a different matter. I pray God he remembers the Commandments and speaks the truth."

Mistress Paske gave me a look.

Will muttered.

"I don't know why I am here, I can't clear you, Jacob, but I do believe you." Nowell's bewildered eyes, turned from my face to Mistress Paske's. All I could do was squeeze his shoulder and give him a shake in rough sailor fashion, hoping that he would keep his mouth sealed tonight, in case his grief lowered his guard. His secret, 'twas a surety, gave him as much to fear from Clerk Knott as I had.

Parson Paske called the room to order with a prayer for divine justice and truth. After which came the chorus of coughs, shuffling and settling down that always followed such lengthy prayers. The parson waited patiently, finally speaking when all were looking at him. "Clerk Knott, report what you saw on the day of Mistress Loveday Maye's death."

Knott rose, all servile clerk with awkward joints and humbly bent back. He bowed. I watched and appreciated the performance. He looked like some lank feeble insect, not a raving bigot. I knew that, without evidence, I could never convince any of those present that this humble Clerk Knott had threatened me or killed Jameson.

"Did you see Master Emerick on the river path?"

The silence that settled on the community settled like the absoluteness of death.

"Yes."

A universal in-drawing of breath.

"Did you see which direction he came from?"

"Yes, he walked from Eikenthorpe, on that side of the river."

A soft exhalation, in unison.

"Was he alone?"

"Yes."

A waiting hush, people leaned forwards in their seats.

"Did you see him enter the river and find Mistress Loveday."

"Yes."

A collective sigh rustled gently through the room. I watched the faces, some puzzled, some irritated, many disappointed. Into that silence bobbed the dapper Church Warden, thwarted but not relenting. "But," he interrupted, "that does not excuse him of strangling her."

"I think," Parson Paske said slowly and thoughtfully, "that we must accept that it does."

All began to discuss the problem, voices rose. Will slapped my back and even Nowell roused enough to pat my shoulder. Parson Paske kept his eyes on me, and I, remembering Mistress Paske's good advice, thoughtfully closed my own, muttering a thanksgiving. God alone knew how heartfelt it rose from my lips.

Oh, prejudiced Eikenthorpe would like to hang me for Loveday's death even though she did not drown and I had not touched her. Now was the time for action, whilst everyone waited and wondered who to blame.

"Master Emerick, there are some here who need to hear your oath." The parson advanced with a Bible in his hands. "Swear by Almighty God that you did not strangle Mistress Loveday Maye."

I took the book and holding my right hand on top of the Bible, my left supporting underneath, I swore truly.

"That was an oath, not something counterfeit or daubed with deceit." Mistress Paske spoke to her husband, but her voice travelled through the room. I heard no murmurs of agreement, but I felt the weight of worry and uncertainty float from me. The threat of hanging had rested invisible, but heavy, and it was a relief to feel it released. All I needed now was to be a genius of diplomacy and win over Lady Fowke. Oh, I knew I wasn't free of all suspicion, but no one would now try to hang me for the murder of Loveday.

"Master Emerick will remain our guest, until he finishes his business in Eikenthorpe. Then we can see him safely on his homeward journey." Parson Paske's voice insisted.

What I most wanted was private space to think and write down what had happened. That way I could, perhaps, perceive a pattern. Could I link Loveday's death with Jameson's? Until tonight Knott's silence had stirred up a puddle of misinformation which prevented others from seeing clearly. If he'd muddied the water, so that I could not find evidence of his acts, then who could? The whole mess needed great skill to unravel. I had God's gift of an intellect above the norm, yet I was sitting here, puzzled, lacking any understanding of which thread made a warp and which a weft.

When the talk eased and the singing began, Parson Paske took me by the elbow and walked me to his quiet study, informing me, as he did so, that he was a deputy lieutenant appointed to raise trained bands of men for Parliament. "More of that later. You have work to do to prove your innocence."

My mouth opened of its own accord as angry words fought to leap forth in a resounding yell of anger. I closed it hastily to think of better words. "I have just sworn an oath," I said, staring at the parson, "and told you the truth."

Parson Paske gave me the long level stare of one seeking to know if there was another truth. It was a stare to rival Lady Fowke's. Again my feet nearly shuffled guiltily under me, but I restrained them. "Sit down, please, Jacob, there is much to say." He seated himself behind his desk, the schoolmaster again.

My fingers curled into fists. If Parson Paske began to prate about the realities of truth, i' faith, I'd hit him.

"Two ungodly deaths in my community. Someone has unleashed a great evil and let the Devil do his work. I need to find out who, in this community, became his instrument in murder."

"And what if they are working for the Glory of God and the betterment of our country? What do you think of bigots murdering in God's name?"

Parson Paske paused, blinking twice as if my words had made him recollect something. "What do you say, Jacob? We are not Papists with an Inquisition to torture those who do not believe as we do." He closed his eyes and pinched the bridge of his nose. "You could help me."

I sighed. "My business lies in London. The only reason I came to Eikenthorpe was to make an agreement with Gamlen's heirs. When I complete that, I must return to London."

"You could find who killed Mistress Loveday. With my authority you may go anywhere, talk to anyone. Take some of the men, follow where she went on her last day. Search out and talk to all those who were at the Manor with her in her last days. Write down what each person knows, and by thinking, adding the little parts of knowledge together, you could arrive at the truth. The Lord gave you keen wits. Use them to find who has released evil in my community."

He stretched one hand across his desk in an appeal to me.

My suppressed indignation burst carbuncle-like, lanced by the parson's righteous words. "Pray tell me why I should, Parson Paske? Why should I be involved in putting this community's affairs to rights after what has happened to me? Who here is interested in putting my slandered name and honour to rights? Which of you will give me back what you have taken from me by suspecting me of two murders?"

The parson pinched the bridge of his nose again. He appeared weary and out of patience. "Your honour and good name matter not at all when it comes to the matter of seeking out this evil."

I growled, incensed. My family's honour, our good name, gave us standing as Merchants. Lose that and we lost trade. My voice soared to the ceiling beams. "You have sullied my name, the name of the Merchants Emerick, and left me open to calumny and dishonest treatment. Even that barrel of ale who calls himself a landlord hasn't paid me what he owes, nor has he repaired my goods. As you commanded him to. As you command me to help this community." I slapped both hands, palm down, flat on his desk, and leaned into his face. "Make good my pistol and that box. My sisters gave me that box. Treat me with the respect due to the Merchants Emerick and tell the community to do the same." I ran out of breath and words, could only glare.

The parson looked, not at me, but my hands, his mouth curved at the corners.

I pushed my face forward as close to his as I could. "If you dare to lecture me again, when you have not accepted my word, or proclaimed my innocence to all in this village, I swear I will knock you out of that chair and shake an apology out of you."

He leant back and smiled. That wretched man smiled at me, moving his chair and body beyond my reach. "Jacob Emerick." He stood up suddenly, tall and square, and I jerked upright, hands flying to make two fists. "Be calm." He walked round his desk and grasped my shoulders. "Jacob, hear me, please listen." He gave me a gentle shake. "Your arrival brought one death, now there are two. Such evil and for what reason? My people here are afraid, they look at each other. There is an evil loose, tainting the air, where there was kindness now there is fear. I will thank you if you can find our murderer, we need God's goodness back in our community."

We looked at each other.

"Jacob, if you do not seek the murderer I cannot. There are things happening beyond our community, great things which will have great effects, and I am a part of them because I am the deputy lieutenant appointed to raise trained bands. My first task now is to raise an army, and the money for a war I do not want. Justice for Loveday and the lawyer comes after." He released me and turned away.

Mistress Paske tapped on the door and entered, eagerly glancing from her husband to me. "Has Master Emerick agreed?"

The parson and I exchanged a look. He inclined his head to me, leaving me to speak.

The good Lord gave us wit and sense, logic and reason, but I felt more moved to turn stubborn, though, I knew better than to be the prideful boy. "I do not know if I can find the murderer, nor...."

Mistress Paske interrupted, pattering over to me, her skirts and petticoats swishing, her hand held out. "Tomorrow someone comes who can work with you." She caught herself, hand flying to mouth, looked anxiously at her husband.

Parson Paske did not frown, nor shake his head. He spoke to me. "This man could be of great help to you, Jacob Emerick. He has agreed to work with you."

Mistress Paske touched my arm lightly. "Please consider, Master Emerick." She stood beside her husband, and they waited for my answer.

"I have Merchant Emerick business to complete, as well you

know, that is my work." I could not harden my heart against Faith Paske's pleading eyes. "Give me a night's sleep to think on it."

Mistress Paske sought her husband's approval with a glance before she spoke. "Willingly." She smiled at us both. "Now come play the flute for us and stop your brangling. Your yelling scared my daughters."

"My apologies, Mistress."

She laughed and bustled us both out of the study, slipping her arm through our arms and so bringing us back to the company, all smiles, and all together.

# CHAPTER SEVENTEEN

The three men I met in the parson's hall in the morning came from the other side of the Thames, from Essex. Two were to help Parson Paske set up a trained band of men for Parliament's aid.

"Essex," they said, "was ready and able. As firm for Parliament and true religion as anywhere in Kent," they added, inclining their heads to me. Essex had been better informed, and more closely linked to Parliament than most other places. No wonder they had men standing ready and men training in preparation for the King's next move. Parliament had only approved the Militia Ordinance in March.

Mark and Benjamin Nesmith, the more military looking two, for their cropped hair, the buff jerkins, long riding boots, plain gloves and hats cried 'soldier', had fought in the Spanish Netherlands. Workman-like in appearance and attitude, they looked decent practical men who would teach serious soldiering, not fancy sword play. Will, taken away, protesting, to show them their training ground, and learn some sword skills, was in good hands. It was the quiet unsoldierly one Parson Paske meant to work with me, but he left introductions unsaid when first he spoke.

"Doctor Maye, God willing, should arrive tomorrow, for the

funeral. I would like you to speak with him, tell him what you know. It would be a great comfort if you had an answer to his daughter's death."

I refrained from speech, looked instead. The parson had a look for me, and the looks we exchanged collided. Had Mistress Paske been there she would have begged her husband's pardon for laughing, called me to order, told me I looked like a dog hackling up for a fight. The man between us served a similar purpose. He came to the parson's elbow, coughed and waited. Parson Paske recollected himself.

"Meanwhile, Jacob Emerick, let me introduce you to Master John Thurloe, a cousin and scholar who has a mind to help you unravel our puzzle."

If Nowell was a plain, even an uncomely man, Master Thurloe was a plain, ordinary man, nothing noticeable about him, except his hair, which ran smooth to his ears then broke out in a wavy bush to touch his shoulders. He was quite unremarkable and, when he looked me over for one instance, his eyes let me know that he knew I thought it, but cared not. Here stood another man at ease with his body, his mind and soul.

He was, she told me later, Mistress Paske's cousin, from Abbot's Roding where his father had been the rector. He dressed simply, but not in the Puritan costume of cassock and breeks. He could have been any age between five and twenty or five and thirty. His face, smooth over the cheek bones and brow, did not show lines. It was a face without much expression, reflecting naught of his thoughts and feelings unless he chose to do so, a good lawyer's face I would have liked myself. Mine gave my thoughts away too often, like Will's tempestuous face, which made a welcome contrast with Master Thurloe's as he clomped back into the hall.

"Will?" The parson's eyebrows rose.

"I'm sent to fetch the wooden foils we need for practise." He spoke with an ill grace, and his eyes flashed bolts of anger, his whole complexion dark with unsuppressed emotions. "I'm not to aid Jacob?

I want to know who murdered Mistress Loveday." Will was as readable as a child's horn-book. Parson Paske took him to one side, speaking firmly. Nowell would have quirked one eyebrow and split his mouth into that frog-faced smile. Master Thurloe merely stood beside me and waited.

I thought to provoke some reaction. "Do you have ideas about this matter, Master Thurloe, this matter of investigating Mistress Maye's death? How do you propose we set to it?"

Before he could speak, if he was going to speak, Will shouldered between us. Even his dark hair registered indignation, springing fiercely upwards above his frowning face. "My father and Parson Paske tell me I'm to train with the band. I'm to learn from these Essex men to be a soldier."

"Ah, Will, 'twould be useful to use a sword well. You could even earn Coat and Conduct money if Parliament pay men as they do in the King's bands."

He curled his lip at me, showing his canine tooth like a grumbling dog. "I want to help you find out who killed Mistress Loveday. I can learn fancy sword play another day."

"You will need to use a sword soon enough." Master Thurloe's voice surprised me. It sounded out from his chest, deep and tuneful. "How else will you defend your family, your faith?"

Will stared at Master Thurloe. "I don't know." He shrugged, turned his back and spoke to me. "You'll tell me what you find?"

"I will, and you take heed, have a care for yourself, remember what I said about asking questions for me."

He nodded, scowled again and stamped off to follow the parson's directions and find the practice swords. He knew who I spoke of, for I'd bethought myself of his and Nowell's safety and spoken quiet words in their ears about guarding themselves against Clerk Knott.

"You have concerns about your safety, Master Emerick?"

"Oh yes, Master Thurloe." Behind me I could scent the warm iron and starch on Parson Paske's wide white collar before I felt his hand on my shoulder. "Oh, yes, indeed, I have concerns, and neither of you," I swung round to include the parson, "neither of you, I can trust, to save me. Are you giving me whole cloth? Are you pinching at the truth? Do you want the truth, the small truth of who killed Mistress Loveday? Or are you so ensnared in the Puritan battle that small truths are lost, hidden by the larger affair looming over us all?"

"Harsh words." Master Thurloe glanced at the parson then back to me. "Do you have good reason for them."

"Aye, truly I have. You do not know." I turned to address Parson Paske. "How safe am I here in your home? The doors are open, people visit, come to speak to you, or to bring things for the kitchens, and my bedchamber is easily found. My clothes and goods have been turned over twice."

Parson Paske shook his head. "Believe me, Jacob Emerick, no one would dare. My wife or Tabitha have merely been caring for your clothes. You can trust me not to allow naught further. We searched your packs and clothes at the inn."

I shook my head. "No, I can trust your good wife. No one else. She and Tabitha know what was in my saddle bags to the last stitch and thread when I arrived. They know I did not have one of these." I took from my inner pocket an apothecary's vial, small enough to secrete in the palm of a hand. "I can trust Mistress Paske, for she knows that this has been placed there by hands other than mine. But you, parson? After what you've said and done these past days? Would you believe that something had been placed in my room or that I had brought it?"

His face told me his answer.

"I begged Mistress Paske not to tell you about this until I had spoken first." Again I showed them the tiny glass bottle. "Look at this vial. Poison of some sort? I have not opened it to find out. Who put it amongst my things? To make me seem a murderer? I believe so. I presume that it is to suggest that Mistress Maye was poisoned before she was strangled. Who will you believe, Parson? The one who points a finger and cries 'Search his packs again, look more carefully. I know we will find signs of a murderer there.' Or will you believe me, your wife and Tabitha, who can swear an oath that this was not in my pack or with any of my things when I first came here?"

The parson took the vial, held it to the light and noted it was only half full.

"Cunning you see, Parson Paske. It looks half used. Therefore I must have used the poison before. On Lawyer Jameson? On Mistress Maye of course, to quiet her before I killed her."

The parson and Master Thurloe exchanged looks. Master Thurloe took the vial and began to ease out the stopper. The parson checked him.

"Be cautious," he warned. "It may be a poison that kills if it touches you."

I looked from one to the other. "Can you see where this leads? First someone will come forward and say they are sure I have some poison, that someone at the inn noticed a little bottle in my bags. They will demand a search be made."

The parson took both our elbows and walked us before him to his study. Master Thurloe opened the door. We entered, and I was guided to a chair. "Sit, sit, Jacob. You surmise correctly. I have been asked to make a search of your things...." I began to ask who, but Parson Paske held up a hand and continued. "I refused because we had already searched, but as several people became insistent there was proof of your guilt, I promised a search would be made today. I understand their insistence now, and I am shamed, saddened and shamed for them." He took the vial from Master Thurloe. "To use this to prove your guilt is...."

I jumped up and strode to the window. "My guilt? I have done nothing bar find a dead man and maid." Through the window I could see the soft green of newly emerging leaves on the cherry trees and the daffodils fading and brown. I swung round sharply, about to speak, when there came an uproar, high voices and footsteps above, then thumping down the stairs. The three of us ran into the passage, jostling and sliding to the foot of the stairs. At the top Tabitha clutched one little maid, Mistress Paske had her arms full of the other two. Someone slid through the kitchen doorway, disappearing before any of us could see more than a man's dark clothed body. Master Thurloe and the parson gave chase. I ran upstairs to the women.

"What's to do? Who was here?"

The little maids broke free, chattering, pointing and pulling. Mistress Paske stood dumb, white with shock, and Tabitha wrung her hands. Grace reached out and tugged me towards her. "It was that man," she whispered, "that man here again."

Ruth chimed in. "He tried to put this in your shoe." She offered a folded slip of paper. I opened it. It was an apothecary's note for belladonna.

I remembered the vial. "Did he give you a little bottle to hide?" Ruth shook her head, so did Grace, but then she looked at her youngest sister and it was Hope who smiled and piped up, "I did."

Tabitha clucked and tutted, as well she might, and Mistress Paske shuddered, knelt, pulling her daughters into the circle of her arms to speak softly to them. "Never...always ask me, tell me, when there's a stranger come in the house. To hide something in our home, especially Master Emerick's room, is wrong."

"But," responded the littlest, "it was the Warden's man."

Parson Paske and Master Thurloe, hurrying up the stairs, heard this. "Who, poppet?" the parson requested. "The Warden's man. Which Warden?"

But Hope did not know, and the fact that she had been wrong stopped her mouth and opened her eyes wide in dismay.

"Nay, then, my little chick." I scooped her up. "You thought to help and you have." I turned to her father. "Look at this, Parson Paske." I thrust the note into his hand as I swung the littlest maid around to face my room door. "Come, show me what the man did." I took her into my room, the rest following closely, watching so carefully that Hope made shy, hiding her face in my shoulder. I held her close, rested my whiskery chin on the top of her neat capped head and gently wobbled it, tickling her. She giggled, nestling closer so that I could slid a finger under her chin and chuck it. She was as warm as new bread and as soft and sweet smelling.

"Now, my chick, Grace will be the Warden's man. You show her what to do." I set Hope down and Grace held out her hand. Hope towed her to the chest and patted it. On it sat my box of pistols, newly returned, splintered wood restored. "That's a good poppet." But Hope only had eyes for her father and mother, to measure her act in their eyes. When they nodded she scampered happily over to the bed, tugging Grace with her. At the bed she squirmed her little hands a short distance between the top and second mattress. "He did this." Then she took Grace to my shoes. "He gave me the paper to put here, but Tabitha called."

Mistress Paske, still pale and quiet, took her daughters away, exchanging a long glance with her husband as she did. She said, without words, how near she felt harm had come to them. Tabitha's sniff and look as she followed after said the same, only more sharply.

The parson agreed. He turned to me and Master Thurloe. "What worries me is..." his face turned to the bed.

Master Thurloe nodded. "Aye, cousin, what he might have placed there, more poison?"

Before I could speak Parson Paske did. "I will go and ask Tabitha if she knew the man, try to find which Warden is involved."

I recollected one scowling face. "Your dapper Warden Henty shows dislike of me beyond reason. Mayhap it's him, Parson Paske." He humped and trod off down the stairs. I turned to Master Thurloe. "And you did not see who the man was?"

"No, he had gone, and Cousin Richard was anxious for his family." He walked round to the far side of the bed. "Shall we turn these mattresses and see what we find?"

I made a bundle of the bed linen, placed it on the chest, and took my side of the top mattress. Thurloe lifted up his side of the mattress with ease, mine seemed to stick in one place. We exchanged a look and I stopped tugging. "Master Thurloe, can you roll your side of the mattress towards me?" He did so as I considered what harmful thing might be under it. He saw it first and called out. Together we manoeuvred the mattress until we could just see a dark something, a rounded lump of leather?

"A shoe?"

I shook my head. "No." I carefully poked at the mass with my dagger's point. "More like gloves or a gauntlet." Master Thurloe thrust a hand towards it, but I warned him off. We looked at it, and each other, then flipped the mattress over.

"It seems to me, " I said, coaxing the thing out and letting it flop onto the floor with a plop, "that this might be something of Mistress Loveday's set here to prove I was the murderer."

"Likely," Master Thurloe came round to my side of the bed and stared down at the lump on the floor. "Am I correct in thinking that I smell..." he broke off and examined the mattress. "My house-proud cousin," he said dryly, "will not be happy at this nastiness staining her good feather mattress."

We looked together at the sticky brownish red stains. I grimaced at Thurloe. "Indeed she will not." We left the mattress displayed so that Mistress Paske and her servants could find and make good the damage, and I, using boot toe and dagger's point prised open the sticky clump. "That," I said "was one of my riding gauntlets. The dark stains and brownish liquid would be," I bent and sniffed, "ox blood?"

Thurloe inclined his head. "Mayhap, or pig's."

I kicked the offending gauntlet across the floor. It hit the wooden door frame with a moist thud. "Why would they do it? The blood is still sticky, could not be from either of those poor dead bodies." I followed Thurloe down the stairs. "They are not protecting the guilty, for I dare swear that no one from the Eikenthorpe community laid hands on either lawyer or maid."

Thurloe paused at the foot of the stairs. "You think not? What is it you believe...no, we'll talk in the study. I am going to report our sad news about the mattress to my cousin." He managed a smile. "I suppose she will forgive you more easily than the man who placed it there." He turned left toward the kitchens, and I turned right for the study.

The parson entered on my heels, almost fidgeting in his distress. "This is a sad affair, Jacob. Such mortification I feel, that my Warden could stoop to such folly."

"So, it was Warden Henty? Then he's brought trouble upon himself. He owes me a new pair of riding gauntlets."

"Indeed, indeed. As I see it, Jacob, it is more than he. The man here just now was the inn's servant, but my daughter is correct. Warden Henty brought him to this house some days ago. It seems several people have conspired." He grasped my shoulders in a forceful hold, turning me to face him so that our faces came near to touching. "Find me the murderer, Jacob Emerick. Suspicion hangs under every eave, working on my good men, their families. The women fear to chat, but gossip, wicked gossip, flies. People look askance at each other, fearing their neighbour might be the one who killed Mistress Maye."

Master Thurloe stood in the doorway, waiting for the end of Parson Paske's speech. "You and I, Master Emerick," he said, "could do this together."

Could I? I wanted to know who had killed poor Loveday. I had been afraid it was my involving her in the search for Denzil Gamlen's documents which had caused her death, but the lady had been away when Loveday died. I reckoned the paper I needed Loveday had found, and sent to her father. Lady Fowke would have crowed triumphantly over me if she had found those papers. I gathered my thoughts and found the parson gazing anxiously at me. I looked him in the eye and nodded. "Answer me this, Parson. Do you see two separate murderers?"

Master Thurloe moved to the window, watching us both. The parson exchanged an understanding glance with him. "Jacob, the two deaths are linked, we are sure of it, and you, because of your knowledge of the Gamlen affairs and Philip Jameson, can find the connection."

A knock interrupted us. Grace and Ruth arrived carrying a tray between them. "Mama said to bring you this," Grace said. They slid it onto their father's desk, bobbed to us and pattered away, leaving a rich spicy scent behind them. On the tray a plate of pies bubbled gravy at the seams, three mugs, and a pitcher of small beer, warm and piquant with apple and nutmeg, sent wisps of scented steam curling upwards. Master Thurloe poured the beer, and we waited impatiently for the pies to cool.

"I am of your minds, gentlemen. It would seem that I am, my family is, the link between the two murders. But I believe there are three strands woven here. Mistress Loveday, Master Jameson and the third, as you well know, is Clerk Knott." I watched for reactions, Master Thurloe gave none, his face and body expressionless, but Parson Paske's eyelids quivered and his nostrils flared on an exhaled breath. "I wonder why you are so certain I am the link only and leave Knott and his masters out of the reckoning?"

More silence, no attempts now to open their mouths and explain.

"The Merchants Emerick have a long connection with the Gamlen family. We have shared investment in our ships. When Denzil Gamlen died so suddenly he had just made a new will in favour, not of his nephew, Rolph Fowke, but of Mistress Loveday Maye, his niece."

Still only a polite listening attention from both men.

"This Loveday told me. Her uncle had a shrewd mind. He understood which way the political winds might blow. He intended to save his estate intact if the King and Parliament came to fighting." Master Thurloe stirred and glanced at the parson who parted his lips as if to speak. I held up a hand.

"Lady Fowke wants money. She is attempting to break the Emerick-Gamlen agreement and have the loan repaid. I dare say she expects kingly gifts if she gives money to the King. We have ships, and with London standing behind Parliament and John Pym, the King cannot seize what he wants. Lady Fowke is demanding all the

Gamlen money, and the use of the best of our ships, our fine new pinnaces."

Both men exchanged 'as we guessed' looks, and Parson Paske offered round the plate of pies. I reached for one, juggling it from hand to hand, trying to cool it. Master Thurloe broke his open, hissing when hot gravy spilled into his palm. He licked it away, muttering. The parson smiled, leaving his pie to cool a little longer. I cautiously pulled my pie apart and waved the halves through the air.

"Jacob, you have given us but part of your reasoning. Why do you involve Clerk Knott?" Parson Paske picked up his pie as he spoke.

Master Thurloe frowned. I looked twice to be sure his face made such a revealing expression. It had. I wafted my pie halves through the air again and began to explain.

"In London, I attended the Gamlen lawyer, Master Philip Jameson." I gave them both a steady look. "I knew his staff. The legal clerk presently with Lady Fowke and claiming to be Jameson's replacement is not one of them. I have never seen Clerk Knott in those chambers. Philip Jameson's man with the knowledge to assist Lady Fowke, who assisted me, was a clerk named Nathaniel Breane."

Still a listening silence, but it seemed I had given these men no new bones to gnaw on. They knew more than I had. They knew Clerk Knott was a Parliament man. That told me much about them and the measure of trust I could give them.

"Loveday's death is a nonsense until you weave the events together with my coming to Eikenthorpe." Here I paused as though to take a bite of pie, but it was guilt that gnawed at me. Was it my coming to Eikenthorpe which put that sweet maid in her grave when her life was scarce begun? I wanted to rage at someone, anyone, even the Lord, for such futile waste. "I hope and pray it was not only my coming which caused Mistress Loveday's death." No response. "The root to all the evil action lies in Gamlen's money and a certain group's efforts to keep it out of Lady Fowke's hand, and therefore the King's purse." I drew breath for a resounding finish. "Question Clerk Knott, find how he came to replace Nathaniel Breane. Ask who sent him here. Demand to know who, and I believe there we will find our plotters, and the murderer. Two lives have been spent to prevent the King having Emerick gold and Emerick ships, and neither death was necessary. If we Emericks had been openly consulted and a request had been made honestly and frankly I believe Mistress Loveday Maye would be alive." I glanced from one carefully blank face to the other. "But you both know this, do you not? You know who is responsible for her death." Another thought struck me. "Dear God in Heaven, is this why you are happy to see me fitted to the crime?" My voice rose and a blazing anger made me shake. "The waste of two lives because a group of bigots preferred to work by deceit, rather than through honest intercourse. Puritans, who kill, self righteously, in the name of their God."

The parson closed his eyes and bent his head, as in prayer. Master Thurloe, however, straightened his spine and raised his head, the lawyer asking questions. "Do you believe Clerk Knott capable of killing."

"He has threatened me." I touched the graze on my neck. "Held a knife to my throat and warned me not to let Lady Fowke have any Emerick money."

"Clerk Knott?"

"Yes, Parson Paske. Your Clerk Knott, or whatever his true name is, your Parliament man here to stop me at my work."

He rose and walked out of his study.

Master Thurloe smoothed down his doublet and set his sleeves straight. "I believe, Master Emerick, if Cousin Richard is about his business enquiring of Knott, that you and I had better be about something too."

I stared, my wits flopping around like a landed fish. "Is this all? After what I have told you, you say we should be about our business. The parson says naught, leaves, you say to find Knott. Does the parson take the Warden and threaten imprisonment? Or does he warn Knott to flee?"

"Have no fear, Master Emerick. Cousin Richard is seeking the truth, and the man, Knott, will not evade him." Master Thurloe walked over to me. "Master Emerick, I know Knott is not the murderer. He is under orders, yes, but killing has no part of those instructions. Come, man, swallow your pride and tell me what you suggest. Let us be John and Jacob, and work together."

To my shame I could not. I shook my head and his words died. There was no place for friendship here. In my mind he would always be that man Thurloe, meddler and informer, who might harm the Merchants Emerick. Howsoever, it was politic to use the polite form of address. "Master Thurloe, if we should be busy and doing, then shall we visit the hawthorn hillock where Master Merriot and I found the body of Lawyer Jameson? I have an idea that might explain how the body arrived there without either of us seeing another horse and rider. It's but a short ride if your horse hasn't rested fully."

Thuloe nodded. "Well then, Master Emerick, to the stables. I would like to see where you found poor Jameson."

We set out with Thurloe mounted on Parson Paske's horse. Perry refused to amble, but pranced and cantered, delighting in her exercise. She tossed her head most unmannerly and danced round Thurloe's plodding gelding. "Perry," I remonstrated.

"Perry?" Thurloe looked my mare over carefully. "Ah, an apt name. "

I managed a laugh. He was making an attempt to be civil and it behove me to make an effort too. "Aye, all those pear shaped spangles on her rump make it a certain name for her."

He nodded and checked his gelding to avoid another of Perry's starts, but by the time we reached the hawthorn hillock she had calmed herself and settled to a brisk walk. We halted and sat, looking up at the hawthorns, now in full bloom and drowning us with their sour musky scent.

"The body lay hidden under the trees, but neither Master Merriot or I had seen anyone on horse back or leading horses, nor was there anyone vanishing in the distance. Lawyer Jameson was dressed in well used riding boots, gloves, riding cloak and hat. His horse had disappeared. Young Will Verne claims he would hear about it if someone around Eikenthorpe had found a horse and quietly kept it. He did investigate, says there are no stray or strange horses in the area."

"Hmm, so did Cousin Richard, with the same result. You think, Jacob Emerick, that the body arrived as a body in, say a cart?"

He was quick. "How else? Will and I discovered that Lady Fowke had two cart loads of goods sent on before her and that Knott was with those carts on the last stretch of their journey. That would include this stretch." I pointed to the road ahead. "But those carts turned off this main road and made their way to Gamlen Manor on the old bridle-way past the Verne farm."

"Ah." A slight sound, but full of understanding. He tilted his head towards me in the fashion of a blackbird listening for a worm. "And?"

"And I believe that Knott and the Fowke servants met with Lawyer Jameson in London, killed him for his documents, let Knott take the body on in the cart whilst they took his horse away with them."

"No, believe me, Cousin Richard and I know about Clerk Knott."

"Shouldn't you rather say that you and Parson Paske know what Knott told you and no more?"

A slight approving nod of his head, then Thurloe dismounted. The gelding dropped his head to graze and Thurloe left the reins loose. Three strides up and he stood by the hawthorns. He looked round slowly, walked round the bushes, came back and scanned the area. "I see." But what he saw he didn't say. Down the slope, back to his horse he went, in silence.

"Do you ever share your thoughts, Master Thurloe?"

He mounted. "You were described to me as a little cockerel, puffed up in your family's pride, strutting in fine feathers with a small wit you thought greater."

"Hah! That would be friend Knott."

"No."

"I wonder at Parson Paske then, not a Christian judgement."

Thurloe tutted at me. "Cousin Richard? Not his. Not one you will know, Master Emerick. You must understand that the business of merchant families, like your own, is not just yours any more. Others are watching and needing. We hope to prevent a war."

I steadied Perry, who made to shove her way forward. "And you, are you a watcher?" I turned my head to observe Thurloe.

"No, Master Emerick, I have tasks to carry out." He spoke out frankly, open with me for the first time. It was like speaking to a different man. "I intended studying at the Inns of Court, but the King and Parliament make all things unsettled. My family affairs keep me occupied. Lord..." he paused, did not give the name, continued "my patron and his fellows in Parliament, have work enough for my skills. My family wish me safe from...." Again he did not finish his speech, instead he turned to me. "What will you do when the fighting begins?"

I shrugged. "My family have tasks enough for me. To procure trade agreements and keep our ships safe is no easy duty."

"Unsettled times are bad for all." Thurloe urged his gelding to trot on and we returned to the parsonage in a more companionable manner than we had set out. I had learned several things and found Master Thurloe easier to work with than I expected. I wondered what Parson Paske had accomplished with Knott, and if he would tell me, as well as Master Thurloe. The arrival of these men from Essex had been planned, each had a role to play. The Nesmiths were openly soldiers, but what more was Master John Thurloe than a cousin come to stay?

There was no time to ask, for when we crossed the ford I saw Nowell Merriot with a group of strangers in the church yard, and Parson Paske beckoned. Doctor Maye had arrived.

# CHAPTER EIGHTEEN

Nowell had me by the elbow and out of the stable so swiftly I had scant time to make Perry comfortable. "I have stayed overlong in Kent, Jacob. Will you give me your word that you'll write to Dr Maye and tell him what you discover concerning  Loveday's death? It is right that he should know all."

We were walking swiftly to the church. "I will, Nowell. Shall I not write to you too?"

"I will find out for myself," he said grimly.

"How will you do so, when you are travelling, looking for aid for the King?"

He startled so violently his elbow jabbed my side, then he stopped, staying me with his hand. "Do others know? Has Parson Paske found me out?"

I soothed him. "Be sure that you can trust me. No one has spoken out in my hearing or asked me questions. I have not seen Parson Paske glance your way. Remember that only Will and I saw you in the church with Mistress Maye's body. Your grief then made you speak over-free." I clapped his shoulder and flung back my head as if in good humoured outrage, for those watching to think we exchanged pleasantries. "I guessed what you would hide, a game that

Master Thurloe is playing here also, with that Devil's spawn, Knott. You are safe."

We strode on. Nowell managed a smile, a faint echo of his frog's gape. "In the course of things we would have been wed next year, my Loveday and I."

His arm went over my shoulders, mine round his, and we sighed in unison. The words did not exist with which to talk away the pain of Loveday's death, and it was futile to try. "It's the why of it all I cannot understand." Nowell smiled faintly again, admitting nothing, knowing I knew. As we came into earshot of the parson, half the village, and the strangers, talk ceased. The strangers, Mistress Maye's family no doubt, for their sad faces told me so, greeted Nowell. Nowell bowed, introduced me.

"Doctor Maye, this is Master Jacob Emerick." The doctor bowed. I bowed in
return.

Straightening up, I found myself looking into Loveday's eyes again, those dark ringed, smoke-blue eyes, and started. Her father, as short as I was, thickset and with thinning grey hair and skin, bore no other resemblance to his daughter, but those eyes proved difficult to meet as an honest man should. Tears threatened.

"If my daughter had drowned it would be hard to forgive you, Master Emerick, for not being on the river path in time."

"I found it hard to forgive myself, Doctor Maye, when I discovered her."

He looked me over, then nodded. "Why any person would wish to...." His eyes flooded, he pressed his lips over words he couldn't speak. Parson Paske took him by the arm and led him into the church. Nowell pulled me amongst the remaining four people, introducing me to them as we slowly followed.

"Master Emerick, this is Mistress Susannah Tunnace, Loveday's aunt, Doctor Paul Tunnace, her husband, is a doctor in Ramsdene, the next town to our own."

We bowed and murmured greetings.

"These are the brothers of Mistress Susannah's husband, Master Noah Tunnace and Master Abel Tunnace." Nowell's fingers resting on my forearm, nipped me in warning as he spoke their names. I exchanged slight bows with Masters Noah and Abel Tunnace, who had the look of the Nesmiths, soldier-short hair to fit under a helmet, plain hats and gloves, buff jerkins and serviceable short swords. More military men back from fighting Spain. For some, like these two, the spoils of war, if you had good comrades and were cautious, need not be death. The Tunnace brothers looked canny enough to have loot stored away to turn into a small business or farm. I could guess why they had come to Kent.

The servants from Gamlen Manor, Lady Fowke and her people, the entire village, over-filled the church and spilled out into the church yard. I walked in with the family and saw Loveday's coffin set in the church where she had been placed on the bier that night Will and I watched. Primroses, cowslips, white wood anemones and green leaves covered the plain wood.

Parson Paske made the sad service memorable. Of a certainty he was not grieving. He rejoiced that Loveday had attained salvation. He spoke a farewell for her, his belief that she was safe in Heaven, a comfort. Such a goodly and pure a maid was chosen, predestined for her heavenly reward, we all should know and rejoice. Maybe so, Parson Paske, but she'd left friends behind whose hearts ached. Mine included.

The coffin was carried by Will, Nowell and the Gamlen Manor steward plus three men from the village. Parson Paske warned me to stay back and let those who had known her longest have the honour. If people thought this a punishment they were mistaken. I'd recent memories of carrying two other young women, as bonnie as Loveday, to their graves, and wanted to carry no more. I watched another ending, another life cut short, buried away in the dank graveyard ground. The damp heavy smell of graveyard earth, redolent of old bone and decay, filled my nostrils yet again. I'd learned to hate it. Useless to rail against our Maker, but to lose my sisters and

Loveday Maye, three maids I cared for, for reasons I knew God could have prevented, shook my innermost beliefs.

Mistress Paske guided the family, and chosen few, into her home like a clever goose girl, never rushing, but getting the people there as she wanted, Nowell and myself amongst them. She spoke to each of us as she moved us along. "Shake off those morbid thoughts, Master Emerick. Find the murderer for Doctor Maye and send him, comforted, on his way tomorrow." She tapped my arm as she walked past, all brisk and busy, the good huswife, meeting my eyes only once, with a warning. In the great hall the three Graces, appointed helpers today, carefully fetched and delivered to her instructions, with a shy smile for me when they passed nearby.

Glancing round the throng, I saw Master Thurloe made one of a knot of men with the Tunnace and Nesmith brothers. Far enough to be out of earshot if I spoke to Nowell or he to me.

"Let me know how you go on, Jacob, and find the murdering demon. I'm with you. There's only one mind and hand in the two deaths." Nowell gripped my hand. "God keep you, Jacob and keep you safe. May we meet again in better times." I gripped his hand in return and wished him God speed. He made his other farewells. Doctor Maye clasped him like a son, and Doctor Tunnace and his wife cried out against his leaving, but he touched their hands, turned sharply and left.

"We haven't seen his horse," Grace and her sisters whispered behind me, plaintive, but not expectant. If they had whined I'd have turned away, but it was hard to ignore the plaintive voices and the hopeful eyes of those little maids.

"Come, we'll slip out quickly and watch him ride away. Be wary, Samson is a stallion and not to pet or approach."

Three grave nods, they joined hands and Grace tucked hers into mine. We edged away, down the passage, through the kitchen and out into the stable yard

Samson had been briefly installed in Perry's box whilst she kicked up her heels in the orchard paddock. The doors stood open,

Samson stamped snorting. I swung the three Graces up on the flat topped of the low wall behind the water trough.

"Mind now, stay safely up here, poppets."

Three grave looks and nods.

It sounded as though Nowell needed a hand with Samson, and I knew Parson Paske's men were busy. I went to help. Inside the box Nowell stood backed into a corner. Samson, stamping and fretting, snorting noisily, restrained only by Nowell's hand on his bridle, formed an angry, shifting wall between Nowell and that wretch, Knott.

"I'll have all those messages you carry, Master Merriot." Knott swayed, trying to dodge round Samson and transferring his dagger from hand to hand, ready to strike.

Nowell faced me, saw me, but craftily he didn't jerk or move his eyes. He eased his bridle hand on the right, letting Samson swing his hind quarters to the left, Knott's way. Knott stepped back a pace and I smashed my fist onto his wrist so that his hand opened and the dagger dropped into the bedding. Then I had Knott by the scruff of his neck and seat of his baggy breeks. I ran him into the wall, letting Samson's quarters catch him on the rebound, allowing me to barge him into the doorframe. We spilled out into the yard, Knott going down under me.

Nowell needed no words from me. He had Samson out and himself in the saddle whilst I thumped Knott into stillness. Samson plunged and half reared, hooves pounded over the cobbles, and, amidst little squeaks and oohs from the three Graces, Nowell departed.

I left Knott prone and wheezing to rescue Grace, Ruth and Hope. Their round eyes, open mouths and tightly held hands showed their fear. I smiled as I lifted them down. "Did you see Samson. Isn't he handsome, a mighty terror? Do you remember your Bible? From the Book of Job? 'Hast thou given the horse strength? Hast thou clothed his neck with thunder?...The glory of his nostrils is terrible.' That's why we must be cautious with a stallion."

They didn't cry, but three lips wobbled as they looked at Knott raising himself to hands and knees.

"Stallions are dangerous and strong. Samson is. They can hurt people who don't know what they are doing." I jerked my head in Knott's direction and the girls nodded, departing, I hoped, with less fear.

I went to Knott, dragged him to his feet, shook him. "Why bother Master Merriot? What did you want of him?" But Knott staggered off without even a curse, dazed stupid.

The three Graces reached the house, as I went to shut the stable doors. The bottom half door dragged, catching on something. I shoved it back to see. A quick glance showed nothing, a careful prod with my foot dislodged a folded brown packet, no bigger than a scrap of paper, at the edge of the brown bracken bedding. Small enough to enclose in one palm, and thin as a folded sheet of fine paper, it cried out 'secret', but whose? Knott's or Nowell's? Hearing footsteps crunch on the gravel I had it tucked into my inner pocket before Master Thurloe reached me. He came without the parson, but with, to my surprise, raised eyebrows and anxious face. "My small cousins say there was trouble."

"Knott had his knife out threatening Master Merriot. I clouted him."

"Why?"

I dusted myself down, and straightened my cuffs. "Knott didn't say, and he can thank God that horse of Nowell's did not eat him. As it was, it stamped on him." I smiled at Thurloe, glad to have spoken the truth, but kept a friend safe.

A blank-faced stare, a faint smile and Thurloe took my arm, leading me inside. "I hear Lady Fowke is leaving tomorrow morning. We could visit Gamlen Manor and examine the servants and Mistress Loveday's things when there's only a housekeeper present."

"Lady Fowke leaving?" I stopped in the long hallway, my thoughts racing. "She said nothing about leaving at our last meeting."

Thurloe nudged me on towards the parson's study. "Gamlen

Manor, what's it like? It's an old Manor with a moat isn't it?"

Master Thurloe, the informer, well, he could find out for himself. I had had enough of this spying and taking sides. Nowell was a man whose company I enjoyed, what did it matter that he was for the King? Thurloe's company I could do without. I touched the little packet in my doublet pocket, pulled a long face over Thurloe's questions and went before him into the study. "You'll see tomorrow," I said over my shoulder.

Master Noah Tunnace had spread a large map on the desk, now cleared of Parson Paske's papers. There were coloured markers from the fox and geese board dotted about it, and Master Abel Tunnace wrote notes with a slow pencil into a book.

"Ah, Master Emerick, you have ridden round Eikenthorpe how many tracks and small roads lead to the main highway?"

"I didn't come here to count roads."

Noah Tunnace's look told me that was not the answer he wanted. Mine asked what more could he want from me.

"How many land owners here would...?" Master Thurloe behind me must have made a sign for Tunnace looked over my shoulder, then closed his mouth.

"I know nothing, Master Tunnace, except that the Merchant Emericks are negotiating with the Gamlen heirs." I turned to Thurloe behind me. "And how will I achieve agreement if Lady Fowke leaves?"

"Where will your ships be if you don't reach an agreement?"

There was no harm in telling all those listening ears, and hopefully the news carried by Thurloe to his masters would bode well for Emericks in the future. "The pinnaces would be safe out at sea on long trading voyages. Out of reach of any grasping hands." I did not tell them our pinnaces had already sailed, my brothers captaining them on their maiden voyages. "How far do you think Master Pym and Parliament can push the King to reach a settlement?" I looked at the faces.

"Who will break first, Master Emerick? The King or John

Pym?"

I heard again Knott's words, that the King would be first to openly declare war against the rebellious factions. I wondered what choices he had been left with and who pushed hardest, the papist Queen or Puritan Pym.

"What will you choose to do when the Royal Standard is raised?"

"Go to sea." I could, but I'd rather not, and I was not telling these men more of our business. I bowed politely. "Excuse me, gentlemen, but I have an agreement to settle before Lady Fowke departs." I left them and went to saddle Perry.

It wasn't until I was well down the river path when I remembered that slim packet. In the shelter of the willows I sat easy, loosened Perry's reins to allow her to snatch at the spring grass and slid the small square from out of my hidden pocket. It was done up in oiled and waxed cloth, finely stitched. Why did it need waterproofing? I remembered an old tale about messages hidden in wine barrels and wondered how this message must go and to where. I had no qualms about using my dagger to slit the skin open. The paper message inside, unfolded, barely covered my palm. The writing was minute, some sort of doggerel. If it were the results of Nowell's information gathering, I hoped it wasn't his only copy. Now how could I destroy it? I couldn't let Knott, Thurloe, the Tunnaces, indeed any of the Eikenthorpe community see it. If it were Nowell's, he had a quick mind, he'd surely remember the contents. I thought of the kitchen fires at the Manor. Easy to throw an armload of wood on as a favour for the kitchen maids and burn this and its wrappings. I put the paper back in my pocket and gathered up Perry's reins. Hoof beats pounded behind me. I wheeled Perry round, my hand on my sword hilt.

"Jacob, it's Nowell." Will's red face, hatless head and shirt sleeves spoke of disaster. "Knott's raised the Tunnaces and trainees to go hunting him."

"He'll be safely on his way."

"No, Jacob, listen. He went to Gamlen Manor. We saw him, and the Nesmiths sent Ben Foley to tell the Tunnaces. They say he's the King's spy."

"That was said of me. Who says such things?"

"That cursed clerk told them. He says Nowell has been visiting all the Manors and Estates gathering news for the King." Will's voice and face expressed shock. "What do we do?"

"And what are they doing pray, sending you out to train, making maps, asking the parson about the local gentlemen?"

Will's face made me laugh, first scowling as he thought, then guilty understanding dawned. "They are doing the same."

"Yes, two sides prepare," I sighed, "and not for peace. You know the country, Will, how can we warn Nowell?"

Will dithered. "But, Jacob, should we help...if he's one of the King's men?"

"Will, whatever he has been doing cannot have grave significance for you. He's been here a few days, probably trying to find out where the arsenal is and talking to known supporters of the King. What have Eikenthorpe people been doing but the same for Parliament?" I made Perry move closer to Will's pony so that I could grasp his arm and shake him. "Will, do you bear Master Merriot any malice?"

Will's frown turned to a grin. "Nay, he's a proper man. Aye, I'll do this for Loveday. The truth is as you say, he can't have been doing more than looking and talking. We're doing that too." He turned his shaggy gelding's head and applied his heels. "Follow me, there's a way across our farm that will take us out onto the road, ahead of the chasers and well beyond the wooded stretch they're searching now. We can catch Nowell before the hawthorn hillock."

A gentle nudge and Perry turned smoothly to follow Will. We trotted to where the path lowered itself to river level, and Will made his nag scramble down the bank and into the water. We forded the river cautiously, then heaved up the opposite bank. Will set off at a canter. I urged Perry after him. The track, as such, did not exist. We crossed pasture, followed a sheep trail, then down over arable land, always skirting buildings and people. We rode fast, hard work for the gelding who was puffing when we spied Nowell. Will had been correct. We had found him before the hillock. We reined in on the road and waited.

Nowell cantered up, steadied Samson to a stand, and looked at us. "Trouble?"

"Knott has the trainees out after you. Ride hard." I hesitated a moment, wondering about handing him the note, but I refrained. It might be Knott's and I feared Will's tongue. "Go safely, Nowell and...."

He cut my words off with a, "Will, is there another road?"

Will shook his head. "Just tracks. Get over the open heath quickly, after that look on your right for oaks being felled. Ride into them, but not on the logging path, keep that on your left hand. There's a ditch or two to jump and then you'll find the oaks taper into farm land. You'll see a cart track, follow it to a barn, look right and you will see an old bridle path going across pasture and lees beside a river. Take that and it will return you to your road and well out of their reach. Hurry."

"God's blessing on you both and my grateful thanks." Samson, urged forwards, plunged away, his hooves sending divots flying.

"Can your horse manage another race, Will, until we're clear of the hunters?"

"He'll have to."

For safety and his nag's breathing I left Will on his farm land to amble home and prepare excuses for his absence. I returned to the river track and Gamlen Manor much cheered to know we had kept Nowell Merriot safe from the likes of Knott. Would that I could do the same for the Emericks

# CHAPTER NINETEEN

Gamlen Manor would be left in the hands of Mary as steward-housekeeper, so the stable boy told me. All to go on as if the lady remained and cracked her whip.

"So, young Dickon, the household is secure, no one turned off, and you might yet make an ostler."

The boy, all thin leg and bony elbow, grinned, leading Perry away with a careful hand.

I walked the familiar way from stable yard to house, going this time to the Manor's main entrance, to make my way in like a gentleman.

Two armed, liveried servants, ones I did not remember seeing in the house, stood beside a locked and banded trunk in the open hall. Otherwise I would not have known Lady Fowke was leaving. I sensed no bustle or lady-inspired rush and Knott was nowhere about. It was Mary who took me to Lady Fowke, who made us wait as she carefully wrote and set her seal to a list of instructions for Mary

"This is what you have to do, con my instructions well, Mary, for I will not tolerate any deviation after I am gone."

Mary curtsied, head bowed. "Yes, m'lady."

Only the fine new lines at the corner of Lady Fowke's eyes

revealed the pain of Loveday's death. As predatory as ever, she swooped on me. "Well, Master Emerick?"

"God give you good day, Lady Fowke. I am informed you are leaving. Can the Merchants Emerick assume that the agreement I have been discussing on our behalf will be acceptable to you?"

She pounced. "No. I'm to the King, and you Emericks will lose your ships and cargoes. I will have an end to my brother's agreement, the return of the gold and the use of those ships." Thwarted she may have been, but, for her, it was temporary. She demanded and insisted as if she believed that all must, nay, all would, give way to her.

I bowed and bit hard on my tongue to hold back angry words. The Emerick-Gamlen agreement held, but any good arrangement we could have settled, beneficial to both Emericks and Fowkes was lost. She had refused to compromise, wanting all her own way, and in this fight she would lose all. Doctor Maye had information to use, and I would seek it once his first mourning period had passed. I managed a civil tone for a polite "I am sorry, my lady, for it was a profitable agreement." All in vain.

She looked down her nose at me, setting my person at naught. I was less than the oak planks beneath her feet. "For the Emericks, perhaps, but we Fowkes will have it overset," she flashed, her temper rising swift as a river in flood.

"Doubtless your lawyer and I will settle on some agreement, my lady." I bowed with a magnificent flourish. "God be with you on your journey, and keep you safe, my lady." It choked me to say it, but I remembered my family, and my manners.

She snorted and gave me the hawk's glare. "If," she said, "my granddaughter's death was in any way due to Emerick interference, I will see you all swing for it."

I found no words to nay-say the lady, shook my head. "We all suffer from Mistress Maye's death."

She turned away again, walked to the window, refusing to speak.

I wondered how she could leave without knowing who the murderer was. "Shall I give this copy of our proposed agreement to your clerk?"

"No. He is away to London following my instructions." The look she directed at me came straight from Hell, a hot blast of pain and anger. "That parson tells me you are seeking my niece's murderer. Do you think he is one and the same for the two murders?"

I bowed. "I do, my lady.

"Make the monster suffer for what he did." One tear escaped her, slid down her cheek. She turned sharply away that I should not see.

I bowed again. "My lady," I murmured, and left her with her misery.

In the kitchens I found Master Thurloe had arrived, and so had Will. How he had escaped his training and silenced Thurloe I did not know, but Will heeded no one, went his way, as determined as I to find the truth about his dear Loveday's murder. The kitchen staff, augmented by the gardeners, stable hands, and probably some farm hands too, stood round the hearth and tables. The very air quivered, disturbed.

"We can't know of every moment of her day," Mary said. "I was close to the maid, and I didn't know all she did."

Heads nodded, people murmured, one spoke for all. "We have our tasks and Lady Fowke watched over all, we needed to be dutiful to keep our places here."

More murmurs of agreement. I could see that they wouldn't have dared stray from their allotted tasks as they might have done with an easier master who trusted them.

"What of strangers?" This from Will.

Thurloe, with a placid face and calm reasonable air, spoke softly. "Perhaps there were visitors from Eikenthorpe, or villages beyond. Did anyone come to deliver or fetch and may have seen Mistress Loveday on the path or in the presence of another person?"

No one would say. They shook heads, refused to look at each other, and swore not.

"No one would say differently," Will whispered, as he slid into place beside me, "but they would know." We looked at each other. "Knott went where the house servants could not always go. As did Giff and Mary."

I considered. "They fear for their friends and neighbours."

"I doubt we'll ever know." Will sounded resigned.

"By listening and speaking quietly to each person alone we may find something. It's a lengthy task and one to be done without threats on our side."

Thurloe eeled his way towards us. I patted Will's arm as if in sympathy. "How is your soldier's training? Be hasty, Will, start talking, Thurloe's on his way."

"The Nesmiths are teaching us to be soldiers." Will's voice told the tale, as did that face of his.

I reined in my laugh. "Good training they'll give you, for they must have survived many battles."

Thurloe joined us, heard and added, "My Lord Wessex had the Nesmiths training the bands in Essex. They know their work, make good muster-masters."

Will shrugged off Thurloe's remark. "I'm more use working the farm. The March rain put us behind with the sowing. The King will keep, next winter's feed won't. His Majesty has to settle with Parliament. He surely knows that."

Thurloe turned to me. "And what is your opinion, Master Emerick?"

"Oh, I think we had rather hear yours, Master Thurloe. You speak with more knowledge than we have, being from Essex."

He caught my meaning before Will had only puzzled it through part way. "I am not the Earl's man," he said.

It might be true, but I did not believe so. Thurloe came from Essex, where Richard Rich, Earl of Wessex, had been preparing men for war. I believed Thurloe to be Wessex's man and probably

Wessex's agent. I looked him over again and he looked straight back, the corners of his mouth curving upwards. He would keep his counsel, and I had nothing to prise his oyster mind open and find his pearls of knowledge. I gave up.

Thurloe turned to Will. "You should leave the questioning to us, young Will, and return to your training."

Will sighed. "We were sent off to chase a supposed spy. I searched my allotted area, found no one, and now I have a field to sow." He gave me a wink, a friendly thump on the arm, and left us.

Thurloe humphed, muttering. I hid my grin and managed a sober comment. "I believe food will be as vital to an army as it is to his family."

Thurloe shrugged. "No doubt, but now we need men trained to fight." He sighed and indicated the crowd of people."Join with me, speak to each of these people about Mistress Maye."

I raised my eyebrows. "Will's talked to them all. They remember nothing."

I received a look equal in severity to Parson Paske's at his most school-masterly. "But we have not spoken to them, nor compared answers. That is important. When you need to find things out, Master Emerick, it is only by asking the same questions several times of several different people, then comparing those answers that a pattern might emerge, a fact be discovered."

So this was how Master Thurloe spied and pried, by repetition and comparison, by quiet questions and analysing answers. It made a sense of sorts. I nodded and we began.

I listened to Thurloe's quiet questions, dropped into general conversation with each individual of the staff. Thurloe spoke as though he were alone with one person, and his voice never rose to be audible to others beyond that person. It was as though the two of them were alone, yet those questioned felt safe amongst their fellows. I used that trick myself. It was successful. As I noted answers in my head, I compared them with what Will told me each person had said to him. Not much of matter when Will reported. Yet I elicited, not names, I knew enough of a close community not to ask outright for names, but descriptions of who had delivered or fetched that day, and where people moved about. He'd not mentioned the comings and goings of the men from other farms, his own visit, nor the journey to the mill, heedless, feckless, addlepated, young whelp. I'd broil him finely for missing those details when I saw him. Between us, Thurloe and myself coaxed the inside staff into remembering what they did the day I found Loveday in the river.

"Nothing to any real purpose now, but several people to find and question. We have a collection of mayhaps and might have beens, and perhaps some helpful negatives," I remarked to Thurloe, as we walked together to the stables. His reply was an abstracted grunt.

We questioned the outside staff, grooms and lads, the gardeners, in like fashion and received the same vague answers, lacking in precision. We thanked all for their help and promised to use what we'd learnt with discretion. Silence seemed prudent before the stable-boys, but after Thurloe mounted his gelding he kept silent all the way to the parsonage. I wished for Will's or Nowell's companionship more than once on the journey. I would have delighted in the chance to take the ideas floating around my head and, by wondering aloud, raft them together into something solid and sure. So much to think about, yet it was the why of Loveday's death that puzzled me.

Back in Parson Paske's study, the map still lay spread on the desk, but the Tunnaces had gone, out chasing Nowell. Master Thurloe and the parson discussed with me the answers we had gleaned. We sat around Parson Paske's desk and I memorised everything, writing cryptic notes on a sheet of the parson's paper. Thurloe had an astounding recall of each person and what they said.

Thurloe noted my scribing and tapped his head. "You should learn to remember by rote. Your head is safer than paper."

I shrugged. Perhaps, if I were a spy, but legal contracts were best written down. I turned to the parson. "The more we question and garner answers the more questions we find to ask."

Parson Paske did not smile. "Indeed, Jacob, that is how we will find the truth. It is only by asking all the questions that we can find the one answer we seek. You have your notes. It is for you to compare."

I foresaw a long and tedious time before me and checked the childish imp within which wished to ask Parson Paske to pray for a sign from God, preferably a thunderbolt to strike the murderer. I smiled to myself, picturing Parson Paske's face at such a demand.

"Write out the names of those who came to Gamlen Manor that day, Jacob, and list those who were seen on the river path or about there."

My well cut pen slid across the well prepared paper as I made the lists. The study book case held one shelf with a neat stack of paper. On the desk sat a pen holder full of fresh cut pens, a filled sand shaker and ink pots. Mistress Paske knew her duties, a huswife of excellence whose husband should surely prize her above rubies. A thought glimmered in my mind. Perhaps that explain his acquiescence over the green dress, a reward for her excellence. I must ask her, if only to see her blush in confusion. Teasing Mistress Paske or the three Graces gave me the only source of amusement I had in Eikenthorpe.

Thurloe broke the silence again. "We should question all those on both lists separately, Master Emerick. Then compare our impressions." I nodded.

A knock on the door heralded Tabitha with a tray of honeyed bread rolls and tankards. We helped ourselves and talked of other things.

"How important, Master Emerick, do you imagine the navy could be if the King declares all those who oppose him as traitors and raises his standard against them?"

I walked to the desk and looked down at the maps. There was the Thames, with Essex one side and Kent the other. London held the river, and the river flowed down to the sea. Whosoever held

London and the ships could block the river, hold back ships from the sea and blockade the ports. I tapped the map and looked at both men. "I believe the navy is the key which could prevent a war."

"But who will control the navy?" Thurloe looked at the parson, they both looked at me. Then Thurloe rose and walked to stand beside me. He pointed to the map. "London is for Puritans and Parliament. The people of London drove out the King. We hold the docks and waterside, we are able to control ships there. Now the navy is deciding. Not just the admirals, but officers, ship by ship and man by man. To stay with their liege lord, his Majesty, King Charles, as they swore an oath to do, or mutiny against their King and support Pym and Parliament. It will be a hard choice, but many sailors know the rough justice of the Papists in Catholic ports, they fear King Charles will bring in a Papist army. We can hope. If we have the navy we can prevent foreign mercenaries from arriving or foreign ships from landing arms and munitions. We can sail into our own ports and harbours to reclaim them from the King's men." A good plan and one well thought out. Thurloe must have discussed it thoroughly with his masters.

The door latch clicked. "May I enter?" And Mistress Paske came in, holding a taper and her candle-lamp. She proceeded to light candles. "If you need more light the rushlights are in the box on the mantle." Her glance took in the map. She sighed. "It surely won't come..." her voice trailed into silence.

"Thank you, Faith." Her husband, usually so stolid, showed he could also smile and he did. With approval.

Mistress Paske flushed, gave him one of her own, turned towards the door, hesitated, then returned to the three of us clustered round the desk. "Do you really believe that if we cannot find agreement with His Majesty, and it comes to blows between his men and ours, that we can possibly defeat the King?" Her look she directed to her husband, but her words were for Thurloe. "His men can pay to arm and train all those beholden to them, and all those they can force into their armies. They can buy fine horses for their cavalry." It pained her to speak the words. Her face said so clearly, yet she continued. "His will be an army led by men who have campaigned in Scotland and Ireland."

"Put your trust in the goodness and mercy of God. Where is your faith?" Parson Paske's rebuke made Mistress Paske flinch. She bowed her head. I didn't feel inclined to smile at the inadvertent pun, nor his words, for his wife spoke with good sense. Help and experience the King had in plenty.

"Forgive me, Parson Paske, but there are many merchants whose thoughts wander in the same direction." I felt more than saw Master Thurloe's attention, a fierce concentrated like a ray of sunlight.

"Oh, never look askance at the Emericks, Master Thurloe, we will hold for our beliefs if His Majesty, our Sovereign Lord, King Charles, refuses to give them freedom. If Parliament can hold London and the navy can hold the river and coastal waters then we Emericks are safe for a while. But will Pym have the power to persuade His Majesty? We would all like to know that."

The only answer was silence, the silence of caution, of furrowed brow, sideways glances. I returned the glances, bowed and withdrew, wanting to wash the dirt of the day from my hands and comb my hair before supper. Mistress Paske followed. She took a candle-holder from the hall table and lit the candle in it with hers. I had one foot on the bottom step when she laid a hand on my arm.

"What do you think, Jacob Emerick, can unskilled men defeat the King's trained army? I see no hope if we should fight."

I found myself patting her hand as I would her daughters'. Her hand twisted under mine and clutched it tightly. "What happens to our men? To young Will, my Richard? They are not warriors but farmers, parsons, shepherds, potters, weavers, brewers, not born to fight, nor kill."

I shook my head. "It cannot come to war, we cannot fight our neighbours. Your husband knows this commandment."

"And so does the King. Oh, why can he not give a little?"

I gave her hand a gentle squeeze and released it. Even in the dim light of our two candles I saw the confusion in her face, the pulse beating in her throat, as she realised she had taken my hand. "Ah, Mistress Paske, we can only pray for sense. If our King Charles cannot be seen to give way too much, we must help find ways to camouflage his bending."

"His Majesty is not the only person who cannot compromise." She gave me a sad half smile and bustled away to the kitchens, skirts swaying, soft slippered feet scuffing slightly on the rush matting. I shook my head to order my thoughts and climbed the stairs.

The opened window warned me this time. Just a scent of cold night air, through the gap between open door and frame, but enough to make me pause at the door. I knew the window had been closed. There were three possibilities, Nowell, Will, or Knott. After this afternoon's hunt I doubted Nowell was that foolhardy, and Will would have found us in the study. I put the candle-holder safely down beside the skirting board and watched eldritch shadows creep down the hallway.

"A secret visit, Master Knott?" I opened the door a bare hand's width, keeping it firmly between myself and where I guessed he stood. Knott was too handy with his knife, besides I had already pasted him once today, and he'd be wanting vengeance.

"You complained to the parson about me." Knott's voice came on a breath. "You spoke to that spy, young Merriot. Tell me what you know about him."

He was moving out from behind the door. I waited till I reckoned he was reaching out to yank it open and slammed it hard back towards the wall. It rammed into something solid. Success. I'd caught him. His knife jammed on the door edge then clattered onto the passage floor beyond my feet. I leaned hard into the door and crushed Knott to the wall.

Knott was strong, but I had my feet braced firmly against the door frame and continued pressing on the door. Knott objected. His words were indistinct, but his voice sounded in sharp protest.

"What trouble are you trying to make now, you miserable wretch?"

"Let me out to speak, and I will tell you."

"I don't trust you, ranter man. You and your knife, here in the parson's home."

His grunt was followed by a fierce thrust against the door.

"What are you doing, Master Emerick?" The soft little voice beside me nearly undid me, for I started. Only the bracing support of the door frame behind my feet stopped Knott's heave from freeing him.

I couldn't see which of the three Graces it was, but I knew their voices. "Fetch your father, little one, now. There's a bad man I've pinned behind this door."

A faint ooh, and a draft, I heard feet pattering downstairs.

"Parson Paske's fetched, say what you need to me now or before him."

The noise Knott made was more fitted to a mad dog than a good man.

Up the stairs clattered Parson Paske. "What's this?" More noisy feet and Master Thurloe and, ah, good, the Tunnaces had arrived to crowd behind the parson.

"Clerk Knott," I said and stepped away from the door. "With his knife," and I edged it over to the parson's feet with my boot toe. Knott shuffled round the door, both hands covering his nose. Thin trails of blood striped his fingers, a drip hung at his wrist, bulged, splattered on his breeks.

"What do you mean bringing violence into my home? Look at you, man! Best let my wife see to your nose whilst you remember what I told you."

Master Thurloe thrust a large handkerchief between Knotts' fingers. I heard Mistress Paske downstairs, soothing tones to calm her little girl's words, high pitched in distress.

"I will not have my family upset by your actions here. What

ails you, man, that you come by stealth into my home?"

"He let the spy go." Knott's voice was muffled, but the tilt of his head indicated me.

"You never told me Master Merriot was a spy. Of what and for whom?" I turned to the circle of men behind me. "All I saw was Master Merriot being threatened by Knott in the loose box. I knew nothing but that. Of course I disarmed Knott. Should I rather have let him stick Master Merriot in the gut before stopping to ask questions?"

No one replied.

"Now I find him hiding in this room, waiting for me, and he had his knife in his hand."

I drew my sword. "Shall we end it here Knott? Spill blood on the parson's clean polished floor?"

Breath hissed, but no one moved. I expected to be grabbed, restrained and abused, but no one did. I continued my actions and pricked the point of my sword into Knott's gut. "Tell me, what is it to be? An explanation or a stab or two where you'll feel it. In the loins perhaps?"

Knott shuffled back a little, no one moved though Thurloe's arm restrained Parson Paske. The Tunnaces stood by.

Knott lifted his bloodied face and spoke. "You couldn't do it. You've never killed a man, and you would never dare here and now."

Perhaps the others guessed the same, but Knott had rubbed my temper raw. Besides I'd thumped him the stable yard and enjoyed it. I whipped my blade up as if to prick his throat, but leaned in to kick him hard, right in the codpiece. As Knott bent over with a moan, I caught him on the point of his chin with the sword hilt. His knees folded, and he sprawled on the floor.

"Now you'll have to wait to find out why he was looking for you." Thurloe sounded amused. "Noah, could you and Abel remove friend Knott?" The Tunnace brothers hooked their arms under Knott's armpits, yanked him up and away down the stairs.

"To my study with him," Parson Paske called after them.

"Now, Master Emerick, have a care. Master Knott has powerful friends."

"And they need Merchant ships and Merchant families like Emericks, Parson Paske. Master Clerk Knott has taken a personal spite, has been placing my reputation and honour in doubt, trying to fit my neck in a noose."

I saw the parson's look, and gave him one of my own. "Let me question him, in your presence."

"Very well."

After Mistress Paske's ministrations in the study, Knott, reeking strongly of winter green, rue and comfrey, recovered enough to exchange quiet words with Master Thurloe, the Tunnace brothers standing guard over the two of them.

My sharp ears could not pick out any of Thurloe's conversation, prick them though I did. It carried some import, for each man held the other's gaze steadily. I feared that Master Thurloe spoiled my game. Time to interrupt.

"Lady Fowke sent you to London, Clerk Knott. Why did you remain here if you are her clerk? And what did you want, Master Knott, waiting with your knife in your hand, in my room?"

He sniffed, holding a wet cloth full of herbs to his nose. His hands, restored to their usual greyish-white, squeezed the cloth in rhythmic contractions. He appeared frail, even harmless.

"Seeking to take my life? One more to add to your tally of two?"

His hands stilled.

"Where did you kill Lawyer Jameson? You carried his body in Lady Fowke's carts, the ones bringing her goods and chattels from London to safety in Eikenthorpe. Did you walk as he rode, and when he dismounted to rest you garroted him and left him under the may bushes?"

Knott said nothing. Thurloe watched. Parson Paske cried, "Proof, Jacob, proof."

"The cord that garroted Jameson was fine legal cord, used to bind reams of legal paper. Some offices have their own paper specially made, it comes bound with a cord named for that office. Jameson's cord was just such a cord, cord from his own office. He was attacked by one with access to those papers and that cord. And who was there, supposedly working with him?"

Knott squirmed. Thurloe looked from him to me.

Parson Paske glared. "Is this true, man? Did you have a hand in his death? Only God has the right to give or take life. His, not ours, Master 'Knott'."

The way he said 'Knott', told me the parson did indeed know him by another name.

"If it is God's will...?"

"God's will to take a life? Never!" The words exploded from Parson Paske. "I shall not have in my house anyone who has broken God's commandment and claims that he did so because it was God's will."

Knott sighed and straightened his spine. He raised his head and looked the parson in the eye. "I did not kill Philip Jameson."

"No?" I let my disbelief show. "You brought his body here and were happy to let any other man take the blame and hang for his murder." I glared at him and thought of Jameson's wife and family, who might never have known what had happened to him or where he was. They had not been able to farewell him or see him buried. "You are a despicable worm, a ranter. You prate of godliness, and know nothing of true godly behaviour."

Knott's look, from dark eyes full of contempt, with his assured stance, his 'I am right and godly good' air gave answer enough for me. "Here's your precious zealous Puritan, Parson Paske, possible murderer of Jameson. Certainly breaker of the King's laws, to wit the removing and hiding of a body. Ask him what he knows of Mistress Maye's death."

Master Thurloe lifted his hand. "Enough."

"Oh no, it's far from enough. There is much that involves this man in the two deaths. I am seeking the murderer, as you requested. Yet you cry 'enough'. Why? Because he is one of Pym's men. Does that protect him from our law? And what about God's laws?" I paused to draw breath, damp down my temper. I advanced on Knott. "It's bigots and stubborn block heads like this driving us to war." I wheeled round to the parson. "Is this what Pym's party brings us to? Such bigotry, which allows murder if it aids the great ideal? Such ruthless determination to have our way that we cannot help the King bend a little or bend ourselves to achieve a peace?"

Both men sighed. I stared at them. "Do you want the murderer brought to justice? I begin to believe you do not." I glanced from Thurloe to the parson.

"Clerk Knott has an important task in hand." The parson spoke with reluctance.

"And what do you know of this?" I asked him.

The parson turned his head, looked at John Thurloe. Thurloe nodded.

"Jacob," the parson rose, walked towards me. "You know of the ascent of popish practices in our English church. You know what our King is doing. He will not bend. We cannot." Parson Paske's voice, though filled with regret, did not falter.

I looked at the parson in disbelief, but it was Thurloe who continued.

"In the past decade we've had Irish and Scottish wars, we have Papists openly working at Court, now we have Papists waiting to return to our country and burn us all. The king has asked them to aid him." Thurloe reached out and tapped my shoulder. "We know he has."

I shook my head. "You want a war?"

Both men gazed at me. Knott buried his face in his herbal concoction.

Now it was I who cried enough. I stood up again. "Parson Paske, you will tell the community I am cleared of any suspicion, that you know I found the body of Master Philip Jameson and had no hand in Mistress Maye's death." I stomped to the door and swung round to fix my eyes first on Parson Paske, then on Master Thurloe. "You should also tell them that you know who the murderer is, but won't arrest him as he is a 'good' man, a Puritan, one helping bring us to a civil war." I banged the door behind me and pounded my temper out on the stair treads. Home seemed a wonderful place right now and even my great ox-like brothers better company than any I'd found here.

# CHAPTER TWENTY

I expected Parson Paske to come and reason with me. I expected to begin another discussion about that demon's spawn, Knott, with John Thurloe. Instead there was silence. I fumed, I acted like a testy lad and kicked the wall. Finally I calmed and wrote in my journal, thought long, perched on a stool by the window, using as much of the twilight as I could gather to eke out my single candle. Little useful could I write, but I did scribble a line or two as a farewell for Loveday.

> 'Ah, cruel maid, to stray so far ahead,
> To leave behind the love we give,
> To accept that heavenly love instead.'
> Now I remain, alone to live
> In sorrow, left behind.'

Poor stuff I knew. I wasn't happy with it, but muttering a few more rhymes and wrapping my lovelock round my fingers didn't help either. Oh, I'd made a fine speech but I wondered if perhaps I'd made a fine fool of myself, storming out like Will might have done. I swore under my breath. Damn Thurloe, who drove me to behave like a callow youth and not the cautious thoughtful family lawyer I knew I could be.

Outside my door came a pit-patting, a child's chortle, then scuffling, to herald a knock. The three Graces entered at my call.

Papa talked men's talk and Mama readied supper in the kitchen. Would I hear their reading before they went to bed?

A quick temper doesn't help matters, but I had chewed more humble pie today than ever in my life, being asked to do this women's work was too much. Oh, I'd hear the little poppets, but in my way.

"In your Papa's study then."

They squeaked, shaking three bonneted heads, but I had them by the hand to make a chain, then a circle. I galloped us round and around, then out through the door and down the stairs, with much sliding, clattering and giggling. We rushed into the study with nary a knock.

"A bible, a bible, we need the big bible," I sang, swinging my tail of little girls into a circle again. The great brown leather-bound bible on the bookstand beside Parson Paske's desk was too fat to grasp in one hand, nor could I pick it up easily with two. I'd come to make a bother of myself and looked now to become a fool again. Thurloe, the Tunnace brothers and the parson watched, astounded. Knott, free from any restraints, and quite his own man, consulted their large map, ignoring us. If the little maids had not been there I would have knocked him down again.

"Use your mother's bible." Parson Paske addressed his daughters and frowned at me. This time it was the three Graces who led me round and out to that snug room beside the kitchen where I'd had my bruises dressed by Mistress Paske. A long time ago that had been.

Beside the fire was a chair with the three Graces' rush topped stools set about it. Where my mother might place a foot rest was a small willow hamper. Grace and Ruth lifted first the cushion then the lid. Hope bent into the hamper and brought up a bible, a handy chapman's copy, the blue of the thin board covers faded where it had been handled many times, the sprouting bookmarks telling their story of long use. I took it from her. I knew nothing of educating little children, but hearing them read? That should be simple.

Grace read her allotted passage from the Epistles. Dry stuff for a little girl. Ruth had the ten commandments to read and learn. Hope sought the alphabet letters in the story of Noah, making words where she could. I gave up on their tasks, settling instead on the Psalms. We could sing those and I needed music to soothe my temper. We started with Psalm 23 for them all. Grace and I read it together, then Grace managed alone. Ruth read it with me, then with Grace, finally managing most of it herself. I put Hope in the middle and stood behind the three of them to point out the letters as Ruth and Grace read it again. Then I borrowed one of their recorders and played a simple version for them. We sang it. Swift to catch the tune, the three Graces also knew the words, although Hope's words weren't always those written. Ruth and Grace chuckled, and told me they had never learned this tune, so we were very pleased with ourselves and the pleasant noises we made.

When their three voices could carry the tune every time, I gave them a simple harmony to memorise and practise without me for a brief space, whilst I visited the study door and leaned my ear against it.

It was a solid door. I heard only a murmur, until someone stood up to leave. Chairs scraping and feet moving sent me creeping back towards the girls who, good students that they were, still sang happily. I hid in our doorway as the Tunnace brothers paused in theirs, one in, one out, so that those inside raised their voices to be heard at the door. I also could hear, but only tantalising snatches.

"We can use..." Parson Paske said . Feet moved obscuring more words.

"That carries too great a risk, if he knows now..." Master Thurloe?

A jumble of mumbled words as two spoke together.

"You have endangered all with your tricks...will never trust us...could have been of use..." Parson Paske's voice again, falling off as if he turned from the door's direction.

"We'll cope. He's safely hid with us...Master Emerick's pride...he won't forget." Master Thurloe for sure.

Then clearly at the door. "Information as to what I have found must not be free to fly to those who can inform the King. He must not return to London with that information until I have prepared. I have more of the same work to do in Essex." Knott, that thin dry voice.

But none of it of any use, or making much sense to me. As the men left the room, I sped through our door. Moments later Parson Paske found me with the girls, conducting their singing. He arrived, the intention to complain of our behaviour writ clear upon his face. Fortunately our singing stopped him protesting overmuch, and he let his daughters teach him the tune, singing away heartily, a vibrating bass under their soprano sweetness. Mistress Paske came, her hands full of wet pudding cloth, with Tabitha and Lizzie, to see what was to do and sang with us. It was, for the Paske home, as near noisy as I'd ever be likely to hear.

Thurloe joined us bearing two flutes, he played one himself, gave the other to me. I played tenor to the main tune and we sang for our supper. I knew several different versions of Psalm music new to them, so we had a fine time learning those, and then Thurloe taught me two very old songs I'd never heard either.

Knott and the Tunnaces had gone when we finished. Lizzie returned to the kitchen, the three Graces said their prayers with their father and went up to bed, their mother and Tabitha gently chivvying them along like ducks moving their ducklings away from the pond. I watched them go, remembering my mother's like behaviour, then turned on the parson.

I gave the flute back to Master Thurloe and looked at them both. "Come now, gentlemen. What is it you want me to do? You asked me to search out a murderer, to work with you, Master Thurloe, to find out what happened to Mistress Loveday Maye. I find you a likely murderer, yet you protect him."

Silence, a thicket of it round them both. I tried again.

"If Master Jameson was killed to allow Knott to take his place, it is a surety that Mistress Maye was killed to delay settlement of the Gamlen estate, thus preventing Gamlen gold reaching the King. Both killings were done by the same hand, and that hand was Clerk Knott's. Why does he go free?" I kept my tone as civil as possible, but oh, I longed to rough up the parson's calm. As for Master Thurloe, I wanted to rattle his pate 'til his ears rang.

Parson Paske shook his head. "Jacob, Clerk Knott did not harm Loveday. He followed you along the river path, and he had been at the mill. I have spoken to the miller and his family. Knott was with them when Loveday came to harm."

I felt all my certainty vanish like breath expelled from the lungs with a body blow. "What of Jameson?" I stuttered.

"Where is your proof, Jacob Emerick?" the parson asked.

I had none. Mistress Paske's entrance stopped my mouth. I needed time to sit and reason again.

"Master Emerick, with my husband's permission I have a tale to tell about the last visit I had from Loveday." She seated herself in her chair, tucking her skirts neatly around her. She paused and looked at her husband as she settled her hands tidily one in the other, palms up.

"Yours is the story, Mistress. Tell it as you will."

"Then I will begin at the beginning. I came here, to my husband's home, in the spring, eleven years ago. My first visitor was Master Denzil Gamlen. A kind man, he made me welcome, and because Eikenthorpe has always been his family's home, where he led others followed." She checked, sent a quick glance at her husband, who nodded, shifting his weight to settle deeper in his chair. "To have a welcome from the leading land owners as well as my husband's parishioners made my life easier."

I wondered at that. Had Parson Paske been expected to find a different kind of wife, one nearer his age, from his own community, a women more sombre, less attractive, a Puritan bigot, clad in those dark blacks and greys? Mistress Paske might not have been the ideal for the Puritans of Eikenthorpe. I looked from wife to husband, speculating how unkind Eikenthorpe could have been without Denzil Gamlen's open approval.

"Denzil Gamlen took an active interest in our community, he enjoyed a friendly relationship with us, came to the Sunday evening service, often stayed for supper. Every summer Loveday came with her parents. Her father might only stay for a few days, but Loveday and her mother stayed all summer. After Loveday's mother died, Master Gamlen brought her often to visit me." Mistress Paske paused, reflecting. "I think he felt the need for a woman in Loveday's life, poor heart-sore maid, so troubled by her mother's painful death. And so we talked of women's things...." Mistress Paske blushed, a rosy flush spreading across her cheeks, let her gaze drop to her hands on her apron. "None was better than she for consolation and company when my last baby, our blessed boy...." Here she turned her hands over, gripped them together and looked towards her husband. He had tucked his chin, hiding his face, staring down into his lap. Mistress Paske deliberately released her hands, drew a breath, and continued, "departed this earth so early to go to his heavenly home." Her fingers curled and uncurled, the only sign of her pain and agitation. She observed them moving and quickly folded her hands together again in her lap.

"We shared a loss, you see, and thus we could share other things. She came to me...I know that she was troubled those last few days. The day before you found her, she came to tell me...some small thing it was, she said, just a small pother, a thing she couldn't understand. She would wait first to discuss it with those it concerned." Mistress Paske cleared her throat. "I fear those concerned did not stop at discussion. Loveday knew something, and they did not like her knowledge."

I stirred uneasily. "They? You think, then, Mistress Paske, that perhaps Loveday had found out the murderer and was killed for it?"

Mistress Paske looked at her husband, then at me. "I do not know, but there are so many questions. Why was she coming down the Manor side of the river, on the far path? She didn't go to meet you. You were on the village side of the river. She would know that. Who was she trying to reach?"

I sat still, thinking. "I assumed...."

"Assumptions are useless. Think, Master Emerick, think, based on what we know." Even the parson raised his head at her tone.

Wood ash fell as the logs burnt away, red sparks glowed, floated upwards, extinguished. I threw a log into the hot ash, then a handful of wood chips around it. Small flames crept up the log which began to hiss, singing in the rising heat. I let my frustration spiral away with the curls of smoke drifting up the chimney and drew in a breath redolent of pear wood and hot wood ash.

"If 'tis not Clerk Knott, then who? I am confused."

"Come now," Thurloe said, briskly, "surely you have enough snippets from everyone to put together? What is Master Knott really doing?"

"Murder."

The parson scowled, his wife flung up her hands, Thurloe muttered.

I continued, determined to make my point. "I am sure he knows what happened to Lawyer Jameson. Murder most foul."

Mistress Paske looked at her husband and Thurloe, her mouth opening to ask questions. The parson shook his head.

I held up my hand to stay the questions. "He has documents, which he must have taken from the body. I assume he works for the Puritan faction in Parliament. Collecting information for them, stopping the Fowkes gaining anything for the King, trying to hang me."

The parson bent towards me. "Come, Jacob Emerick, there's a tangled skein here, far more complex than that. Can't you unravel a thread or two?"

"How? And at what further cost to my honour and good name?"

"Oh dear Lord, make this boy's wits work." Two red patches flamed a warning high on Mistress Paske's cheek bones. "Make this fool see beyond Knott. Think, Jacob Emerick, think. Can there be two separate acts of murder, linked perhaps, but involving two murderers? "

I sat there with the little brown packet a lead weight in my inner pocket, surrounded by deceit and duplicity. Nowell and Knott, Thurloe and Pym. What to do? Who to trust? I watched the remains of the log smouldering in its ashes and thought hard. Finally I made my promise, gave my word. "I will try again."

Mistress Paske's eyes shone, her husband nodded, their faces reflecting satisfaction.

Thurloe expressed his appreciation by giving me information, not that I hadn't guessed, but he confirmed the truth of my guesses. "I gather special information for Pym's party. I was not sent here to watch you, that is Clerk Knott's task, but I could assist you."

I nodded. At last, an exchange of information that would help we Emericks. "There is a document, Denzil Gamlen promised to write. Did he leave it with you, Parson Paske?"

"I have no knowledge of any such paper."

Thurloe exhaled. "Knott told us that Mistress Maye searched the Gamlen account books and family records. Did she find any thing of note, something which led to her death?"     The     fire crackled as Parson Paske tossed on another log. Mistress Paske rose and put a taper to the rushlights so that a pale circle of light enclosed us. She settled down within the circle, only I, leaning against the fireplace surround, stood in the dark. The hidden packet scraped against my ribs. I kept my hands still, not reaching for it and answered Thurloe with a nay.

"What do we know about the two deaths?" Mistress Paske looked at me.

Thurloe raised his hands, palm outwards. "I would choose to

believe that both deaths are related. I do not think we could have two murders here."

Parson Paske bowed his head. "Amen to that."

"As I understand then..." I stopped to think and grasp the bits and ends, the scraps floating in my head, tying them together with my words. "We have Lawyer Jameson killed for one of several reasons: robbery, the murderer stole his horse and possessions, or for some legal dispute the murderer lost, or for a paper he did not have." I twisted my love lock tightly round one finger. "Yet for Mistress Loveday's death I can find no reason except the documents we Emericks needed. They would have given Lady Fowke reason." I tugged the lock over-fiercely and unwound it. "I cannot, in fairness, see the lady strangle her niece, nor was she at the Manor the day it happened." I exhaled noisily. "Only that cur Knott had a clear motive to kill both, and you quit him of both deeds."

"The deaths are not political deeds. I swear that." Thurloe sounded sincere.

"Yet you are here because you believe the King will raise his standard and declare War. You wish to make sure he never returns to London until a peaceful agreement has been made. Therefore you bring the Tunnaces and Nesmithes to prepare the men of Kent and Essex." I looked at Thurloe. "I know you are with the Earl of Wessex in thoughts. The Earl has raised bands of trained men and is going to prevent the King reaching London. You are here to see that this happens in Kent and prevent those in who might favour our King from giving him any form of aid or succour."

Thurloe nodded.

"How do you know the King will declare war? How can you be sure?"

Parson Paske steepled his fingers, looked at me over them, then replied. "We know. Cousin John brought us news, my family have links to many men around Pym."

"And perhaps," here I glanced at Thurloe, "in Essex, the Earl of Wessex, the Lord High Admiral, with his men in Parliament has knowledge too. Perhaps knowledge direct from the King's party? What is the Earl doing?"

Master Thurloe hesitated, decided and spoke. "He has persuaded the navy to stand with Parliament and is using ships to block supplies coming in for the King." He saw my face and nodded. "Yes, before the King has raised his standard. And my Lord Warwick has moved arms and ammunition to London from Hull."

"But that will only provoke His Majesty." Despair twisted my gut.

Parson Paske sighed, nodding to Thurloe, asking him to continue.

"You think our King has not been trying to buy arms and ammunition overseas? You think that he is not organising Catholic armies to come to his aid? How do you think he will pay for them? With money he does not have? Or with concessions to the Papists? Master Emerick, war with our King is inevitable. He is bringing the Papists back."

Mistress Paske cried out. Parson Paske frowned her down before he began to speak. "If merchant families like yours ally themselves with the Admiral and the Navy, we can stop the war within weeks and force our King to negotiate."

Thurloe nodded. "Hence Knott comes here to prevent Lady Fowke obtaining any part of your loan, ships or cargoes, or benefit from the Gamlen estates."

Exasperation made me terse. "Why did no one come and speak to us about this in London? If, instead of plotting and conniving, we Emericks had been asked, openly and honestly, to withhold our boats and ships, we would have been able to reassure you on that. And you would have spared me much pain and anguish, perhaps even saved two lives. Have you reflected on that, Parson Paske, Master Thurloe."

"Don't shout, Jacob, please," Mistress Faith begged. "My daughters have been upset enough this day."

I swallowed some of my rage. "The Emerick-Gamlen loan

agreement includes a clause allowing the Emericks to repay the loan over a period of time after Gamlen's death. Denzil Gamlen promised to make the period ten years and wrote a special document. We do not have to repay money or give a percentage of the cargoes. We do not have to allow the heir use of our ships."

Thurloe and Parson Paske exchanged pleased looks.

"However, to ensure this I had to return with one document, promised by Denzil Gamlen and which his lawyer, Philip Jameson, had instructions about in the form of a letter."

"Then soon, home you must go, Master Emerick."

I stared at Thurloe, then the parson, a sour taste in my mouth.

But Thurloe raised his hand. "Ah, one moment, Cousin Richard, I think...had, Master Emerick? You say had? You do not have this document?"

"No." I drew breath...what should I tell them? How safe was it to let John Thurloe and thus Clerk Knott know what might be in Jameson's papers? Should I tell them of the documents Loveday was sure she could find? No, to know all that gave them power. If they found the letter or documents they'd use them against my family. "Did you not know," I addressed Thurloe and the parson, "when that wretch, Knott, killed Jameson, he took his papers. Knott might well know where this Emerick-Gamlen document is."

"No." The parson shook his head in denial. He turned to his wife. "Please send Silas to me, and we should have supper."

Mistress Paske left us. Thurloe sat down, his forefinger smoothing across his lips in a thoughtful manner, thinking hard.

"Well? An answer please. What has your skulking and conniving gained? And what better result might an open and honest approach have gained?"

Parson Paske raised his hand for silence as Silas entered. "Silas, would you find Clerk Knott and tell him he is to come at once? You might find him in the inn."

Silas inclined his head and departed.

I raised my eyebrows. "Clerk Knott was supposed to carry Gamlen papers for Lady Fowke to London." Thurloe gave me a look I understood. "Ah, could his masters have him copying those papers? Though I doubt that the lady gave him ought of great value. She's too knowing to let important things out of her hands."

Thurloe murmured agreement, but Mistress Paske and Tabitha interrupted, bringing in supper and we stopped talking to eat eggs and ham, bread, fruit cheeses, and fresh syllabub.

Knott arrived as we finished. Silas stood behind him, urging him forward. Master Knott glowered at us equally.

Thurloe waited until the parson dismissed Silas. "Where are Philip Jameson's papers?"

Knott looked surprised. "I have them."

"All of them?" I asked. "Including the ones he carried when you killed him?"

Knott turned on me, snarling. "I did not kill him."

Thurloe spoke again. "Did you read all those papers. Did you con each carefully?"

"No, I handed them on to..." he paused, "to London," he finished.

I scoffed at him. "You didn't harm him, but saw what happened, and never raised a hand to help him except to take the papers?"

"That's not for you to know."

"No, but God knows...."

"You, you dare speak to me of God, you little jackanapes." Knott dived for me. Thurloe hung on to him. Parson Paske moved in front of me. Knott ranted and spluttered, struggling in Thurloe's arms.

"Be still, man." Thurloe shook him. "You return to London tomorrow, you must take Master Emerick with you. Together you can go through all the papers you took from Lawyer Jameson. There is one he needs, vital to the Merchants Emerick. Master Emerick will know which one." Knott yelled and struggled. "Oh, hold your noise, you fool. This document denies the Fowkes any part of the Emerick-Gamlen money."

Thurloe released Knott who glared at me. "What about..." he began, but the parson intervened.

"Think, Knott, think man. If Master Emerick journeys with you, then you can be sure that he will not pass information to Master Merriot as he journeys home."

I felt my eyebrows arch. I know my eyes boggled. "I pass information? More slurs and slights! And in truth, you think I will make a journey in the company of this devil's spawn? With his knife for company?"

"And myself." Thurloe was curt. "I wish to talk to some people..." here he paused... "in London," he amended.

I turned to Mistress Paske who had returned to see what the shouting was about.

"Well, Mistress Paske, I can see that you must be my witness, for if I fail to reach London safely I expect you to start a hue and cry for my body." I jested only in part.

Mistress Paske took my words seriously. "I give you my promise, Master Emerick, please send me word of your safe arrival."

The parson protested, Thurloe glared, but I bowed to her as to a queen and thanked her gravely. Her eyes flicked a swift glance towards her husband as she blushed.

"Well then, gentlemen, I ride tomorrow, but I will return to finish my other task. I will not let Loveday's murderer escape. God give you good night."

I took a candle from Mistress Paske and myself off to my room. Now that I could leave Eikenthorpe freely without further fear of trial for murder I felt strange, giddy, head detached, floating above my body. I knelt by the bed and thanked God from the bottom of my heart. It was only as I undressed that I thought again of that wretched packet of Nowell's and wondered when and how to destroy it.

# CHAPTER TWENTY- ONE
Brockleford, May 1642

The journey back to London differed greatly from my first journey to Eikenthorpe. This time there was no stopping at inns or travelling the main highway with others for company. A swift departure, on a fine May morning, one of those when the warmth comes early and the wind smells of summer. I had a sad farewell from the three little Graces and a dignified one from Mistress Paske, all Puritan and proper as Mistress Paske should, though her fingers may have lingered in mine as she spoke her regret that my stay had been enforced. A good woman, Mistress Faith Paske, and a right godly friend she had been to me.

We rode fast, our fit and fresh horses well able to keep the pace, but we took no liberties with them, although we hoped to travel thirty or forty miles a day, using the longer evenings and clear moonlight nights. We stayed with Puritan ministers or Pym and Parliament supporters known to Thurloe or Knott. We rode a mazy winding way, not the straightest way, but on local pathways and by roads. We often received accompanied guidance from the host or his men.

Master Thurloe took care to keep between Knott and myself

at all times. I doubt that the two of us exchanged more than a dozen civil words each day, Knott affecting not to notice my disdain. Thurloe, suave and correct, introduced me as the youngest son and legal advisor of the Merchants Emerick, giving me my rank amidst strangers, and therefore ensuring polite treatment. Knott kept his mouth shut and behaved, in public, like a lawyer's clerk should.

What they did or said after supper I never knew. If I wasn't tired and hadn't been encouraged straight to my bed, usually shared with the son of the family, I found myself seized by the ladies and younger members of the household and made to sing and play the flute. Neither Thurloe nor Knott attended our musical sessions, and the participants kept me close. It showed the measure of trust given, and allowed me to return the same, easing my conscience in bushel baskets about my many attempts to eavesdrop on the nightly meetings, and keeping my dagger under my pillow.

As for Nowell Merriot's note, listing I knew not what, in that doggerel, it never left my ribs, bandaged there firmly. I had determined to burn it, but could not find a private opportunity. Privacy was essential, but there was none. I took great care never to fidget at its hidden place, and I also made sure Knott and Thurloe had no chance to search my belongings, though the family papers of importance were kept safe at all times, carried in my hidden purse beneath my doublet.

Waiting to cross the Thames I railed against Thurloe's decision forbidding me to send messages ahead asking an Emerick boat to come and take us swiftly to London. Any of our boats would have taken us, horses and all, to the city, but we crossed by ford to the Essex side of the Thames and thence, not straight on to London, but to Brockleford. Now I understood why Thurloe disdained our Emerick boats and why Knott watched over me. Brockleford was Nowell Merriot's home place and Loveday's too. I feared Knott planned some mischief for Nowell, but we proceeded to the Tunnace house in the centre of the town to the north of the market square and we were expected. A group of plain clad and military clad men swept

Knott away. Master Thurloe followed, leaving me free. I watched the stable boy, and made much of Perry, then walked out through the stable yard gate to find Doctor Maye.

Everyone knew where the doctor lived, and I only had to walk down a side lane, through a cobbled alley to the bridge. The doctor's house stood back from the road, over on the right, on the other side of the bridge. I set off cheerfully and saw Thurloe coming across the market square. He caught me up on the bridge.

"Do you have urgent messages for the doctor, that you stalk off in haste?" He huffed and puffed.

I quirked one eyebrow and remained silent. Thurloe grasped my elbow, a bone pinching grip. I drove the elbow into his stomach with some force. "Leave be."

Thurloe doubled over and released me.

"I thought he might like to know that there is a strong possibility that 'Clerk' Knott knows who killed his daughter."

This time Thurloe grabbed me by the wrists and wheeled me around. "Whatever Knott's involvement with the lawyer, we told you there was none with Mistress Maye. You are not to stir up a broth of trouble for Knott, and give needless pain to Doctor Maye."

"He did for me. Clerk Knott deserves a mouthful of his own physic. Why should I be silent?" I pressed my hands together, pushed upwards, jerking my wrists free. Then I slammed the palms of my hands into Thurloe's ribs. The force of them made him cough air from his lungs. I snorted, making it sound a threat. "Keep your hands away from my person, Master Thurloe, and show a little respect."

"Ah, Master Emerick," he gasped, "you know what happens to the prideful."

I shrugged and scowled. "Why preach at me? If your friend Knott had had less pride, he and I could have worked together. He chose to work on his own, saying he was God's instrument. Is that not pride? He believed only he could prevent our money going to the Fowkes. Is that not pride? Your man Knott worked without consulting me, spoiling my efforts. Is that not a result of foolish pride?" My voice rose in anger. "Is it not, Master Thurloe?"

Locals were stopping to stare. Thurloe sighed, clapped my shoulder and forced a smile. "We have no need to act the part of players out here. Give me your word that you will not accuse Knott, or in any way suggest to Doctor Maye that we know who harmed his daughter, but are reluctant to act. Do not hurt the good doctor more."

I looked my amazement at him. "You can say this?" I had him.

His mouth twitched, he actually frowned. "Swear, Master Emerick, or I will come along to stop your mouth."

I scoffed. "You might try." I extended my hand. "You have my word. But I shall demand yours in not keeping silent when we have proof of what happened to his daughter."

He gripped my hand fiercely and gave his word, more willingly than I'd credited him.

I crossed the bridge and found the doctor's house. He had a good housekeeper and gardener, no signs of neglect outside or in. The garden, crowded with the green growth of spring, recalled Loveday sharply to my mind. I stopped at the gate, blinking my eyes until I could see again the spring flowers, and rows of herbs showing new leaves and neat wooden labels. The doctor himself stood visible in a bay window full of pots of seedlings and young plants. His housekeeper answered my knock, the doctor looked up, noticed, recollected my face and beckoned. Honest man that he was, Doctor Maye greeted me without joy, but as a good man would. I found myself looking into Loveday's eyes again and was not ashamed to be embraced and weep a little.

"I learned when I became a doctor," he told me, encompassing my shoulders with his plump warm arm, "that those the Lord taketh are often those who we need most. I struggle to comprehend still."

I returned the embrace and acknowledged his words with a

nod. Since my sisters' deaths I had foundered more than once in what I knew to be my understanding of God's goodness. Uncertainty disconcerted me. I had always known surety and preferred that state, but for now it was enough to share the pain with Doctor Maye and wonder at God's work together.

I delivered Mistress Paske's message, a proper one of love and concern for the doctor, and learned that Lady Fowke had not returned what had been requested of Loveday's to her father.

"Oh, her fine clothes and jewels I did not want," he explained, "they were bought with Fowke money. But the trinkets we gave her, and the woollen shawl made by her mother that Loveday cherished, I would like. Ah, and I do dearly want Loveday's writing box." The doctor managed a smile and a shrug at himself. "Twas only a simple wooden box, one Nowell Merriot made for her, when yet a school boy, but I would like to have it for both their sakes. Was nothing left with Mistress Paske? My lady promised to do so."

No, my lady had not, and Mistress Paske had given me nothing but words. I promised to seek the things on his behalf. I knew that Mary, at Gamlen Manor, would allow Mistress Paske to look them out. The doctor, pleased, called for refreshments.

"It's not a valuable box, but I remember how Loveday and Nowell would leave messages for each other in it. He'd made a double lid with a secret lock, a place for them to hide..." he paused, his voice catching and managed a faint smile at me..."safe so they thought, but I always did know it held their secrets. Nowadays Loveday keeps...kept her letters hidden in there." He turned from me, blinking tears away. "If she had been writing a letter to Nowell or myself she would put it there, away from Lady Fowkes' eyes, until she could send it privately by her little goose girl friend. I would like to have her last words to me."

There it was. The one piece of information I needed. I stood, holding my mug of mild beer, with Parson Paske's words about speaking to many, listening to all and asking questions, sounding again in my head. The doctor, in all innocence, had given me the link in a chain of knowledge which could bring me to Loveday's killer.

Again I heard certain comments repeating in my head. Nowell's voice, those words he'd spoken in the church: 'She had something for me to take to her father.' Mistress Paske wondering why Loveday was on the other side of the river.

I gathered all my scattered wits, comforting the doctor as best I could. "Mistress Paske will surely search for you."

He agreed.

How much dare I trust him? He gave Loveday permission to tell me family secrets. He was isolated from Knott and his ilk. Thurloe he did not know. "Would Loveday hide those documents Denzil Gamlen had written for my father there?"

"You do not have them?"

I stared. "Indeed not. Did Loveday write to say she'd found them?"

The doctor nodded. "We knew where Denzil Gamlen would have documents stored safely."

I stared. Was this why the murderer struck? We needed the box. I needed time to think clearly. "We must find it, Doctor, but where is it? I must find it. Mayhap Mistress Paske might guess."

The doctor agreed and farewelled me with kind words. I strolled pensively back to the stable yard.

Perry's stall, clean and quiet, seemed the best place for private thought. Perry agreed. She tugged hay from the rack and nudged me occasionally to remind me to rub her cheek bone or stroke her sensitive muzzle. I leant against the manger and petted her as I linked the separate fragments into one coherent idea.

Loveday had confided, not in Lady Fowke - indeed who would? - but in Mistress Paske. Worried, she said she had to speak to someone about a small thing troubling her. She'd arranged to meet Nowell the next day, not at the Manor, but in the village church. Again she wished to be away from the Manor. Doctor Maye told me Loveday had a writing box with a secret lid within a lid, in which she kept her secrets, private things like letters and notes. Was this what she wished to give to Nowell? Did it seem reasonable to assume the 'something' for Nowell was her writing box, and she wanted to give it, or its contents, to him privately, keeping it safe from someone at the Manor?

Loveday had nothing in her hands when I found her. We knew she had been in the water for a short time. Thurloe and I had discovered she'd left the Manor that morning, no more than twenty minutes before I found her. Her wooden box surely was able to float for longer than that, but I had not seen anything floating near her in the pool. I leaned my forehead against Perry's neck and shut my eyes the better to 'see' the pool and river bank. I was nearly sure there were willows and a hazel hedge on her side of the river and that at least two willows had great gnarled roots going down the bank to the water.

Not one of us had ever found out or reasoned why Loveday floated in that pool. We knew she had not fallen in from the bank, but could she have walked the path a short way farther down, where there were rocks large enough for stepping stones? Could she have stepped from the stones to the small stones and gravel of the inner shore by the bank to walk back to the willow roots? Indeed I couldn't remember if there was a broad enough inner shore for her to step on, but if...all these ifs...if there was and if she reached it, might she have hidden that box among the roots, before meeting the person who would only need to bend and seize her neck? What she did with the box and whether it contained the reason why she was killed I was in a fever to find out.

"That must be what happened," I said to Perry. "I need to talk to Will about hiding places. Surely it is what the maid would do."

"And what might that be?" Master Thurloe's head appeared over the wooden wall of Perry's stall, he rested his arms on the top, waiting.

"I have to return to Eikenthorpe. I think I know what happened to Mistress Maye and where she left her father and Master Merriot something which could explain everything."

Thurloe hauled me off to the Tunnace parlour and made me explain in front of Clerk Knott, himself and the Tunnaces. I did so reluctantly, anxious that Knott should not have a chance to send someone for the box before I saw what she might have hidden in it. There was no difference, as far as I could see, between the Fowkes and Knott's people, when it came to making damage for the Merchants Emerick.

Knott refused to be interested. "The matter of the maid's murderer can wait. We have to reach London with my information quickly. Lawyer Jameson's papers are there, and my masters need what I have for them."

"No matter? When someone else might reason as I have and look?" Indeed my fear was that they had looked and found the box.

Knott remained obdurate. "No, we must leave for London tomorrow."

I looked at Thurloe and swallowed my frustration. "I am not your prisoner."

"No, indeed not, Master Emerick, but we need you to find that document and intercede with your family. It is important your family understand and make the legal arrangements which my patrons approve..."

"Oh, as you will it then," I interrupted, shrugging and making myself sound tetchy and peeved, "but I will return to Eikenthorpe after three days. Do not delay me longer." Then I removed myself, as in a huff.

# CHAPTER TWENTY-TWO

I had little time. Thwart Knott and Thurloe I must and find that box. I was sure Loveday had attempted to reach someone, Nowell, by my reckoning, that morning, with those documents we Emericks needed. She had been sending them to her father for safety. I had to look. It wasn't only for the Emerick papers that I was in a fever to find the box. I would like to finish that final task she had set herself, deliver her messages, then run her murderer through with my sword.

To gain my freedom I took myself to the kitchens to entertain Mistress Tunnace and her cook. I charmed those goodies, one so thin and the other so short, 'til they cooed like contented turtle doves. I sampled their cooking and led the talk to medicinal herbs, my mother's, then Loveday's. It took a little coaxing to extract the details of the best local herbs, but soon Mistress Tunnace felt easy enough to treat me as family. It helped that I sat on a stool and used my small-boy's grin. It never worked on my mother, who boxed my ears if I tried it, but it was a sure success with unsuspicious and kind natured dames like these.

"We are that overstretched with all you visitors, Master Emerick."

"Jacob, to you, Mistress."

Both dames reddened and flustered. "Well, then, would you grant me time, Mast...Jacob," a little cough and a peep at me, "to run again to market and the bake house, by you taking my seeds to the doctor, poor man, with this, his favourite sweet bread? He should have some seedlings ready for me." Mistress Tunnace, smiling hopefully, offered me some of the same sweet bread, buttered with a generous hand.

"My pleasure, dame." I bowed graciously and waited, enjoying the bread, until all had been safely gathered into a basket. This was better than I hoped. I was being directed to the doctor's. I left openly through the front door with it and the plump and clucking Mistress Tunnace on my arm, she delighted to be shopping, I delighted to find a way to freedom. We parted company at the bridge and I strolled to the doctor's, a man with legitimate purpose.

Once through his door, I begged for his aid. "I must leave, now, secretly. Can you help me to a cloak, a horse and the way to Master Merriot's, I have need of Nowell."

"But why, Master Emerick, why?"

I told him my reasoning.

He listened, nodded, put me in his little cart, hidden under a horse blanket, and drove me out of town to Nowell's home. He chatted as he drove, whistling, a thin reedy sound, but tuneful, when people were near, to warn me to keep low and hidden. His voice barely reached me above the rumble of the wheels. I lost it entirely when the pony's shoes struck rocky footing. It was only when we turned on to something softer that I could hear clearly.

"Now, we've come to the farm lane. You know the Merriots breed horses? They'll have a swift one to loan you. I'll tell the Tunnaces I implored you to return and fetch Loveday's box for me when I bring your mare to my stable. I'll see her safe to the Merriots' for your return."

Perry had been my biggest concern. Thurloe and Knott could dance on Tyeburn's tree for ought I cared. I thanked him heartily.

"No, no, Master Emerick, 'twould be payment enough if you

could but bring me Loveday's last letter. Ah, I would sleep easier for having that." The poor doctor faltered, heaved a sad breath, and when he'd recovered himself, said, "You may emerge, Master Emerick. No one but the Merriots shall see you now."

The Merriot home, what I saw as I peered over the side of the cart, was a modern version of the fortified manor. Built as a hollow square, the low stone building, looked rather like the Eikenthorpe inn, walls outside without windows, a massive wooden gate, now open, to guard the entry way -- the whole a strong plain dwelling without embellishment or airs.

"Christopher Merriot," said the doctor, "bought, built and moved out to this bigger farm when he married a silk merchant's daughter." He guided the pony through the arched entry way and paused on the other side.

The interior area was not as I expected. It took the form of a square. But the square was divided into two neat halves, separating the farmyard side from the house, by a strong post and rail fence. The right half of the square was plainly farm yard, stables, lofts and barn, a neat lane led into it from where we waited. The fence, swathed in climbing plants and shielded from the house by shrubs and bushes, stood three rails tall, straight and strong enough to prevent even an oxen's incursion. The left side of the square, in front of the house, made a small but gracious garden, laid out with a gravel walk, edged with low box hedges, between which were four flower beds, stone seats and a sundial. Ornamental shrubs in great vases flanked an imposing carved doorway.

The doctor laughed at my face. "It always amazes," he said. "When you meet Mistress Merriot you will understand why Christopher Merriot did this for her."

"I've no time to be mannerly. I need to flee, Doctor Maye. That rogue, Knott, will surely give chase."

Before he could reply an ostler appeared. "I'll take him, doctor." He wore no livery or badges, merely plain, dark working clothes. Of the doctor's age, he also looked too thin for his height. It was his overlarge mouth told me who he was, it was very like Nowell's.

"My thanks and a good day to you, Master Merriot. This is Master Emerick, whom Nowell knows. We have come on urgent business. Is your son hereabouts?"

"To you he is. Welcome Master Emerick, we are in your debt." He bowed his head then turned to the barn, calling for one Micah, who came running. "Put the doctor's pony in the usual stall." The young lad led the pony away, and we followed Master Merriot round to the house entrance.

I fretted with impatience to be off, away before the hunt was up. I caught at the doctor's arm, but he patted my hand. "Wait," he murmured.

I restrained my feverish imaginings, in which a vengeful Knott chiefly figured, and followed Master Merriot along the hallway.

"Marianne," he called.

She came in a bustle along the passageway, slippered feet flying over a paved floor, petticoats swishing, skirts rustling. "My daughter, Master Emerick." We both dipped our heads politely.

Mistress Marianne Merriot, poor lass, was very like her father, with the same dull brown hair and sharp nose. A real Long Meg, as tall as Nowell, with the same plain features, but not, praise God, that mouth. She stood, wrapped in a large apron, with her hair scraped tightly off her forehead under a large linen cap, and brought with her the damp woollen smell of dyeing cloth.

Mistress Marianne offered her father a moist, rose scented towel. He wiped his face, then hands thoroughly. I took care not to stare; Master Merriot had not appear soiled of face and hands, nor were we offered towels. Perhaps it was his peculiar custom. An unusual household this.

"Marianne, find and conduct your brother to your lady mother's parlour." She whisked the towel from him, dropped a correct half bob, and returned, without a word or smile, from whence she'd come.

"Come, Master Emerick." The doctor touched my shoulder. I turned and followed.

The parlour, facing the garden, with four long windows giving clear views of it, made me wish for a rose water dampened towel to sweeten myself. It was not an English room. A dark green and pink floral silk gleamed on the walls, all the embroidery colours blended, soft and harmonious, entirely female, sumptuous, expensive and foreign, like the lady occupant. Little wonder that Master Christopher Merriot wanted a rose scented towel before he touched her. I kept myself from wiping my hands on my trousers with difficulty, feeling I would soil the very air about her. Mistress Merriot might be of an age with my mother, and have a quiver full of children, several of whom gathered round her, but I had never seen a more beautiful or exotic woman. Master Merriot took his wife's hand and bowed over it. My roaring impatience dimmed to smouldering embers as I made Nowell's mother (and he so frog faced ugly,) a court bow to honour her. Indeed the lady might step into her carriage and be off to the King's Court, for her clothes were all in the height of fashion, as the Queen would have worn. Her dress was lambent silk, dyed in costly pink shades, Brussels lace adorned her collar and cuffs, and pearls gleamed in her hair and ears. Mistress Merriot was surely not English, for she had true black hair, gleaming in the light with shiny blue overtones, akin to the Florentine merchants' ladies I occasionally saw in London. She wore it cap-less, tied up into a knot of dangling curls on the top of her head, the newest of London hairstyles. Her face and features were perfection, flawless, her skin gleamed, her eyes shone a blue-black as deep as midsummer's midnight. From head to foot she looked some great lord's wife.

"My lady, this is Master Emerick." Master Merriot's voice, his whole demeanor, were a wonder. Courtly, reverent, he plainly cherished his wife for the rare beauty she was. The children, two older girls, another girl and two little boys still in petticoats, stared at me.

"Right glad I am to meet one who helped my son." Mistress

Merriot's voice astonished, well tutored to musical cadences, but as English as her hair and face were not. Her voice had been trained to be a charming part of a beautiful whole. This was a woman raised to be married to gentry, for her family's betterment. I knew. My sisters had been raised as two such maids. I gave the lovely face all my admiration. "And right glad I am to have helped." I bowed again and wondered how this Merriot marriage had happened. Mistress Merriot's beauty gave her entrance into any of the great families and surely her family had riches enough to buy her a lordly gentleman. It was a puzzle, one to ask Nowell about some other, less urgent time.

The lady remained seated, beckoning me to her side. My boots tramped on the polished wood floor, then scuffed over the woven carpet, floral patterned, all a-tune with the wall coverings. For a fleeting moment I smiled at the thought of my mother tushing and tutting at the needless extravagance of that carpet, and of her gazing in amazement at the magnificent embroideries on cushions, screens and hangings. My mother's stitching was plain, her embroidery simple, nothing like the brilliance running riot across the linen stretched over the large embroidery frame Mistress Merriot and her daughters worked on.

The two older daughters, graced by their mother's hair and features, and promising to be as lovely, curtsied to their mother, to we visitors, took their little brothers and sister by the hand and led them to the window seat to read. I remembered the older girl, Marianne, and felt a twinge of pity for her plainness amongst her lovelier sisters.

"How may we help, you, Master Emerick?" Mistress Merriot made the polite query, but her husband did the calculating with a swift glance at the doctor and myself. He knew we wanted Nowell.

"Something about your daughter is it, doctor?"

"Indeed, Christopher, Master Emerick has discovered something."

"Then we had better discuss this quietly and discreetly . Excuse us please, Madam, and if Nowell...." But Nowell arrived with his sister.

"Master Emerick, Jacob, have you news?" He stepped eagerly towards me. His sister, much improved by a smile, and the absence of cap and apron, obeyed her mother's welcoming gesture and slipped across to join her.

"Forgive me, Maman." Nowell bowed to his mother.

"Go gentlemen, and God speed your errand."

We hurried after Master Merriot to the back of the house, to a small secure room, furnished with a work table and stools, a locked cupboard, and a desk. Nowell closed the door behind us.

"Well?"

"I need a horse, cloak and the means to return to Einkenhope. I think I know where Mistress Maye hid something of importance, something which might lead to the man who killed her."

"What is this? How do you know?"

"I don't know, Nowell, I've reasoned it out from what the doctor told me. I am certain she used her writing box to keep hidden something we need to discover, and that she hid her box before she fell into the pool. I'll swear Knott did not have the box or anything like it on him when we found her, and I believe I have a good chance of finding it."

Nowell's face showed a dozen expressions, finally settling into pained curiosity. "Why can't you ride there?"

"I'm brought here with Knott by the Tunnaces and John Thurloe. They want me in London to find a missing document and force an arrangement on my family with Knott's masters." Nowell's eyebrows rose. I smiled. "They refuse to let me go back to Eikenthorpe until that is accomplished. I must leave my mare and go now before the information I gave them can be used by them or by others." Master Christopher Merriot's face showed a dawning of comprehension, he nodded.

Nowell looked at his father. Master Merriot spoke. "Very well, you go too, Nowell. I'll come after with remounts for your return. Take the horses we were sending up to..." he collected himself, but it wasn't hard to guess where staunch Merriots would send their horses for sale, "and ride them each in turn." He took his son to the door and said something in a soft tone. "...the King's reward," he finished. My ears took note and I thought of the hidden packet.

The doctor, meanwhile, farewelled me with promises again about Perry and explanations to Thurloe. "I'll assure Master Thurloe of your quick return." He hesitated, then spoke again. "Be wary, Master Emerick, for, if what you think is true, then someone else may be watching for you, or spying on you now. Let caution be your guard. Look behind you as well as before you. And bring me a letter from my daughter."

He hastened me after the Merriots, leaving us in the front entrance. Nowell escorted him to the stables, and Master Merriot took me to the kitchens, calling for Marianne as he passed the parlour.

She came, with a sigh, to stand in the doorway, coloured silks in her hands. "I'm sorry, my dear," he called over his shoulder, "only you can do this privately. Pack enough for Nowell and Master Emerick to travel light and swift to Eikenthorpe and return here."

She caught her breath, but, "Yes," she said, turning to request her sisters to take the silks from her and beg her mother's pardon.

"Now, Master Emerick, you head to the kitchens. I will go and help Nowell. Marianne will find you and guide you to us."

I stood my ground. "Master Merriot, Nowell cannot return to Eikenthorpe. They know him. They've chased him out once, believing him the King's spy."

"You'll need him. He knows that box."

"He might be taken. Parson Paske might hold him."

"You'll have to watch for my son again, Master Emerick. Peise the situation, peise and judge it for him. Mayhap you'll keep him safe in the shepherd's barn on that young Will's farm." He laughed at my expression and slapped my back. "Follow your nose. The kitchen's along the passage. Ask for a traveller's packet."

In the kitchen the cook basted, the cook's assistant beat a mixture in a bowl, and young scullery boy tended the fire. They barely glanced at me until Mistress Marianne swept in behind me and headed into the pantry. She began to select cheese and oatcakes, wrapping the food in linen cloths and placing it in a small basket pannier. Cook bustled in to argue her choices, and I enjoyed a lonely slice of pie before they noticed. The cook frowned and grumbled herself off, but Marianne scolded and laughed together. It much improved her, the rapid changes of expression across her face gave it a pleasing liveliness.

"Master Emerick, and you a grown man and guest. You're as bad as Nowell or my father. How if that slice of pie had been put by for the children or Maman?" She took the food basket, gave me a linen wrapped packet and a worried look. "Have a care of my brother, please, Master Emerick." She touched my arm hesitantly. "He shouldn't go back to Eikenthorpe."

"I agree, but he has a need and feels honour bound to help. I will watch over him."

Mistress Marianne gave me a small smile, just enough warmth to turn up the corners of her mouth and make her eyes lighten. "Thank you, Master Emerick. If you would follow me."

We arrived at the stables by the back door. Nowell, enveloped in his thick brown cloak and dark hat, waited for me. The horses, all well bred greys or blacks, stood ready, two light greys saddled, two blacks and two dark greys carrying leather packs with leading reins linking them to the saddled horses.

I took the offered cloak and hat, watched Master Merriot fasten a pack to each black and listened.

"Ride through the night," he told Nowell, "change horses frequently and watch yourself."

Nowell swung onto his horse. I accepted Master Merrick's leg up and settled into the saddle. "Be mindful at all times, Master Emerick, and bring my son safely home." He stepped back. "God speed."

We departed through the farm gate, going across the Merriot fields at a steady pace, Nowell leading. "I know the way," he said. "Let me guide us, and you watch our rear."

# CHAPTER TWENTY-THREE
Journey to Eikenthorpe, May 1642

I thought our ride to London swift. Nowell's pace was swifter. The moon gave us good light, and at dawn we came to a farm where the Merriots had an arrangement to rest their horses. The watch dogs stirred but knew Nowell, and growls turned to grumbles not noisy barking. We slept in the hay 'til noon, the horses watered, fed and cosseted, rested too.

In the late afternoon we swung the pump handle for each other, and splashed away the dull heavy feeling in the chilly water. We ate in the kitchen with the family. It was a small farm. Only family lived there, although one worker came daily for field work. They'd just killed the spring calf, so we ate fresh veal. It tasted good, more so after a night snatching bites as we rode and a day with an empty belly.

We left as the moon rose. "I'll take the light greys on to my lord," our host said. "He wants all you have and soon. Ride safely in God's care."

We departed, again crossing the farm land. "Going to the local lord are they?" I gave Nowell a knowing grin. "And thence to the King?" Nowell gave vent to one of his distinctive snorts and increased the pace, taking us on to an old bridle way. I was glad of the moon and Nowell's knowledge of the country. Nowell also considered my riding skills. His was the skill that made managing horses look simple, without effort. I had problems leading one horse and riding another young horse. Oh, nothing to unseat me, for I had ridden regularly in London, but enough to yank my arms occasionally and make me grateful to Nowell for his patience.

We had come to the end of the meadows, a narrow spinney lay ahead. Nowell eased into a walk, and we paused in the darkest shadows by the trees. Nowell looked ahead, I watched behind. We both listened, checking the horses for any signs that they sensed a strange horse near. Nowell turned his face towards me. "Wessex and Pym are not the only men to see a dangerous future and peril for our King and country. The King's loyal subjects are readying bands and training men too."

I swore. Our horses fidgeted, clinking their bits. In the spinney a tawny owl hooted. "For pity's sake, Nowell, is there no way we can see another ending? Can nothing turn the King's mind from forcing us all to his way, without heed to what will happen? Can he not give at all?"

"Ah, Jacob, that chance has gone." Nowell sounded as disconsolate as I felt. "But our loyalty is and must be to the King."

"It's not as simple as that, as you well know." I took the little packet out of my hidden pocket. "You dropped this in the stable."

He couldn't see in the dark, but he knew what he had lost. "You'll give it to me?"

"Aye, I did try to read it but..." Nowell laughed softly at me. "I reckon I know what it is, a list of names, but I don't think it can hurt for the King to have, it's merely confirmation."

"I would be grateful to have it, Jacob. It is valuable to the Merriots. Yes, I gathered information for the King, but there is little support in Kent." He reached out and took the packet, grasped my hand gratefully, and took the lead again, making for the centre of the spinney.

I concentrated on ducking stray branches and thought how

simple it was for the Merriots. They were not Puritans, and though Mistress Merriot was a merchant's child, as a woman she would not appreciate the difficulties our King put in the path of merchants, even those like her father, who would do business with those of the Court and could curry favours there.

We paused again at the far side of the spinney, in a pool of moonlight, and I continued my thought, but out loud. "You are not a Puritan, my friend. Your worship is not affected by Laud and the King's edicts. Your breeding and selling horses is not affected by what the King does. People always need good horses."

Nowell stroked his horse's neck, his head tipped my way, listening.

"Nor, I dare guess, are you as feared of the Papists as we are."

A swift glance came my way.

"I've seen your mother. I suppose her mother, your Grandam, to have been from Milan and so reasoned you have a little sympathy for Papists."

"You're a good merchant to know where quality silk is found. Yes, my mother's family are Milanese. Many people have reasoned as you. We protect my mother from their malice, and she attends church service on Sundays."

He did not say Mistress Merriot was not a Catholic, but I let it rest. Something had startled a blackbird badly. It flew up in the dark, chink chinking an alarum.

We listen and waited. Then a vixen barked.

"Only a poacher going through. Come away, Jacob. Down here there's a track to the old ford. If we make good speed we can cross at low water."

We did. The ford, an ancient one with paved footing, was not wide, but straight. With Nowell managing all the led horses I suffered no upsets, even though my black halted mid-crossing, pawed at the water, and thought about rolling.

We stopped close to the Thames, still in the pitch dark of

night, only the scent of meadow sweet and honeysuckle telling me summer came, and this wild ride was not some fond imagining, but happening, in verity, in this year of 1642. Nowell brought us to another farm the Merriots used when moving their horses into the Kent. We stabled ourselves and them in the barn, waiting for daylight before disturbing the family.

Unsaddling a horse in the dark was a slow business, but soothing. The touch of the warm velvet-thick coat, the smell and sound of a horse settling himself in for rest, calmed. I was tired, hungry and weary of travelling. On a boat, I would have become tetchy. Here, the soft muzzle nudging, and the damp breath blown in my face, the slow breaths and steady chomping from the horses made gentling music. I leaned against the black's shoulder and rubbed his poll. How were we to ride into Eikenthorpe and find the box? Openly, or hide Nowell in Will's barn? I couldn't decide which was the surer method.

We ate what was left of Mistress Marianne's cheeses and some cold veal, washing it down with what was left of the much shaken home brew, sitting in the empty stall next to our nags. The smell of clean dry bedding and the horses' warmth made me sleepy, but tomorrow we would be in Eikenthorpe.

"I don't have a plan, Nowell. I thought we could use young Will's sheep paths to reach the river. You could wait with the horses in the sheep barn and Will and I would search."

Nowell stopped munching. I waited for an explosion and a demand that he should search too. None came.

"That's as good as any plan I can think of. What if you don't find it?"

"Then I have gone back on my word and a given promise, all for naught." There was a bad taste in my mouth, and it didn't come from the stale beer.

"And if you find the box and proof of a killer?"

"Ah, Nowell, these men are only concerned about Loveday's death as it affects their matters with the King. They have assured me it has naught to do with their immediate concerns, and those are to be their first consideration."

Nowell cursed them, a strange, irreligious and blasphemous collection of expressions, some foreign. One of the horses sneezed loudly.

"Well, expressed, oh, equine companion. You concur with my opinion of his mangling of the English tongue."

Nowell laughed and clouted my shoulder. I thumped him back ,and we forgot silence as we tussled. The noise we made disturbed the dogs and brought our unknowing host upon us in a panic.

\*\*\*

It rained for the final miles to Eikenthorpe, heavily as we passed the hawthorn hill and Jameson's last earthly abode. Hate it though I did, I accepted the rain as a gift, for, muffled from toe to head in our cloaks and hats, we might be anyone, thus we became invisible to the overly curious and watchful. Nor would anyone recognise the blacks as horseflesh of mine or Nowell's. "We could reach the river in this downpour, and no one would recognise us."

Nowell pondered for a pace or two. "Find the thing without Will's aid? And perchance we keep him safe from Parson Paske's homilies and Eikenthorpe's wrath? That's right and fair."

We followed the sheep trails and cattle tracks down to the bridlepath, and I permitted myself to think we had achieved secrecy and avoided Will. In the ways of perverse providence, the lad then appeared on the far side of the river, hatless and with only a short cloak, riding a neat bay horse. He saw us, drew his short sword and yelled. I looked at Nowell, holding back my laugh. His eyes stared, his mouth opened. "What," he managed to say, turning to me, "is the fool doing?"

Will now set his horse at the river and charged us. He crossed in an excess of spray and whoops. As he plunged up the bank at us, I collected my horse, ready to move right. "Veer left, Nowell" We parted, and Will's horse took him between us. We both swung round to face him. Will's horse, a hard mouthed nag, proved difficult to turn one handed, and Will struggled to manage it and the sword. I started laughing. "You'll get yourself killed doing that, you young fool."

He didn't hear, finally yanked his horse around and trotted up to us. "Declare yourselves," he demanded, waving his sword in a way more dangerous to his horse's neck than us.

"You'd be dead by now if we were villains. That's a poor method for one to tackle two. All we have to do is...." I drew my sword, Nowell drew his and we rode either side of him, points levelled and steady. "Either of us could have spitted you, Will Verne, like a lamb for roasting."

"What?" Will's sword wavered. He sheathed it and looked around. "What in God's name are you doing here? All of the band are out. We are to stop any strangers and ask them their business."

"Like you did? Is that how the Nesmiths taught you to approach two men on horseback?" Even through the rain I could see Will's face darken, his cheeks redden.

"I..." he cleared his throat, "I hoped to...." Then he laughed. "I thought to startle you."

I remembered the Will I knew, who had at me in the inn stable yard. "Hah! Think? You didn't think. You dashed at us all anyhow. Had we been an enemy, you'd be dead."

Will shook his head. "Not I." He looked at Nowell. "You will be if anyone finds you. What's to do?"

"Naught if you're to stay safe, Will. Jacob and I come to seek something Loveday put by for us."

Will opened his mouth. I flung up a hand, and his speech died aborning. "Will, use the mind God gave you. For once in your life reckon the consequences. You live here, you must be at ease here, must be comfortable with your neighbours. You can't be seen to associate with us."

"If you say so, gentlemen." He grinned and nudged his horse around us. "I'll follow to see what you villains do."

We exchange scowls, but Will, heedless, fell in behind.

The grey sky darkened, clouds loured, the rain pelted upon us. Nowell swore, in Italian, if I heard aright. I patted my poor wet horse, hunched my shoulders under the borrowed cloak and hoped for a swift end to everything.

We plodded along the riverside path, following the Yul's course, until we saw Gamlen Manor across the water meadows. Here our path divided into three, we rode down the narrowest, already muddy, but closest to the river. The horses squelched through the ooze, churning up the rich scent of river silt. We smelt dank, of wet felted wool, both reminded me of finding Loveday's body. I turned my mind to other thoughts, of Mistress Paske and what she might know about hiding places Loveday could have used.

We rode past the first bend and there we were, at the second curve, where the pool lay, its surface pinked into concentric circles by the rain. Yes, there were, even when the river ran fuller than before, enough pebbles and sand to make a shore in the bank's curve. Loveday could have stood there easily, reached the place by stepping on those rocks.

We halted under the willows, looking at the snarl of knotty roots along the bank beneath us. I dismounted and cocked my head at Will. "Here, boy, make yourself useful." In fine London style, I pushed my reins at him. Nowell did likewise.

Will told us how to use them.

"Tush, boy. Such language." I exchanged my shocked tone for a serious one. "You asked how to help us. Then hold the horses."

"What...Jacob, why have we halted here?" Will dismounted in haste and grabbed all our reins.

"Keep guard and watch for us, Will."

"Why, Nowell?"

"Best for you not to know."

He looked at us both, then said something extremely rude about our forefathers.

I shook my head at him. "Bringing shame on your family, young Will, to speak in such a manner." I pushed Nowell ahead of me.

Five paces took us to the lower part of the bank. A staggered line of broad rocks led like steps to the pebbly bay. I stepped on them with care, mindful of my boots, then stood, staring at the bank. Three main roots knotted themselves around each other twisting down to the water. Two larger roots curved over and under those three, twisting along the full length of the bank, to disappear into the soil again at the end of the bay. Numerous, finger thick roots interwove between them all. What might Loveday have done?

"She wanted to reach you, Nowell. She was followed perhaps or felt threatened. Where could one, in urgent haste, put a box that might stay safe and yet be found?" It was a puzzle.

Nowell removed his gauntlets, draping them over the edge of the bank. He began searching carefully and methodically from ground level to bank top. I started at the other end of the bay and poked and peered in every hole, niche or nook that looked possible. Just as we decided to give up the search, Nowell found, accidentally, leaning on the topmost horizontal root, a sizeable pocket opened behind it, a snug dry cavity.

"Did Loveday know of this?" His voice fell away. He stared into the space.

I thought he'd found the box, hurried to see, slipping over the pebbles and sliding into him. "Is it...?" It was empty.

Will's booted feet appeared in my line of vision. I looked up into his puzzled face. "It's empty," I repeated, unable to clear my head of any thought, but that. I had been so sure. I turned to Nowell. "It should be there. Knott couldn't have sent someone before us could he?"

"We were wrong."

"Then where is it? The doctor doesn't have it. Would Lady Fowke have been able to find it?"

"Where is what?" Will's foot swerved past my nose. I looked up, startled. "Explain yourself."

"Nowell made Loveday a wooden box, a writing box, but he

made it with a hollow lid for Loveday to keep private things."

"Why would she...?" Will's face lightened. "She knew."

"Hush, boy, let me think." He crouched down to hear better as I caught Nowell's shoulder. "Listen. It was not false reasoning. The box is here somewhere. Think. She has something she can't keep safe at Gamlen Manor. She tries to tell Mistress Paske, but stops. Why? Loyalty to her family, I believe. She knows you are meeting her in the church, so she speaks out at the Manor, asks one question she shouldn't have, and someone follows her. She realises she must hide what she carried." The ideas, strung together, still made sense.

They also made an image of poor Loveday, desperate to reach aid, hurrying as far as this river bank, knowing she was followed and hiding away her box. I wasn't the only one to feel anger. Nowell's face, full of wrath, looked at me.

"Who might find the box? Will, is this a well known hiding hole?" As I waited his reply, I began searching again. "Look once again, Nowell, we might find it yet."

We didn't, but Will found his tongue and made suggestions.

"Children. Down by the river, that's the place children dally." He grinned. "I remember, taking messages or fetching a pail of sand or grit, we could make time to play a bit. This pool is good for fish and frogs."

I agreed. "Yes, it would be a child who'd swing on tree roots down beside the water here. Who?"

"Who?" echoed Nowell. "Will, who is likely to pass here every day? Does any child work at the Manor daily?"

I remembered the doctor's words. "The goose girl."

"Mattie." Will supplied her name. He looked thunderstruck.

"What is it Will?"

He swore. "I should have thought of that. I knew Loveday was kind to Mattie. I could have had this box..." his voice ended in a sigh.

Nowell crossed the stepping stones before I'd turned round. "Let's find her," he said, climbing the bank and walking back to take his reins from Will.

I thrust my hands up towards them both. "Heave me up." They obliged, running me up the bank to the path, where we each collected our horse and mounted.

"Where do we go, Jacob?"

"Where we'll find Mattie, I think. The one safe place for you, Nowell. Gamlen Manor. Are the Fowke servants there, Will?"

Will tussled with his gelding, who didn't want to turn round."Yes, and..." Nowell nudged his black and the horse pressed against the bay gelding, shouldering him round, forcing him to move.

"And?"

"Mattie'll be there. The geese are nesting and she'll have them safe away beside the poultry yards. Those ganders are fierce and she has to keep them in."

"Then we must ride on to the Manor, and fetch that box."

# CHAPTER TWENTY-FOUR

The rain, turned to a steady downpour of fine drops, hid us well. Will's short cloak had a hood, he covered his head, and the three of us became any three travellers going about our business.

We reached the Manor in minutes. Will took us to an open barn behind the stables, and we rode inside. Will dismounted, shoved his horse in a stall, and headed for the stable yard.

"I'm to tell Housekeeper Mary that Master Emerick," here Will dug a knobbly elbow into my ribs, "and I are to collect what is remaining of Mistress Maye's to take to her father. She'll let us search over the house."

Nowell led his horse into a stall and nodded. "Where is the goose yard?"

"Go around the barn to the back, seek the walled enclosure 'twixt the dairy and the cow byre. Mind the dogs. The geese will be there, some sitting and some with young. Watch yourself, they're ill tempered until they can take the goslings to water." Will grinned again. "They'll have you running."

Nowell laughed, shaking his head.

I handed him my reins. "We will keep the household busy, Nowell, seeking that shawl, some receipts, mayhap a book and the box. Do you, softly now, coax Mattie to tell you where the box is. Tell her Loveday left it for you, and with things in it for her father."

"I've sisters of my own, Jacob, I can persuade young maids as well as you." But a swift smile flashed across his face.

Will and I left him and walked through the stable yard to the house. The maid servant who first attended us, whispered, in a most pert fashion, that Mistress Mary kept the Manor as Lady Fowke commanded, overruling all, menfolk as well, with a kind face and warm voice, if you did as asked. I frowned the maid down for her frowardness and revised what I would say to Mary.

"What may I do to help you, gentleman? I thought you'd be back in London, Master Emerick."

I explained that I had returned on Emerick business, but had undertaken an errand for Doctor Maye. "He wonders if his daughter's shawl, trinkets and her writing box were left behind here. Lady Fowke promised to send them to him and yet they are not with the things he received. He begs that you would give them to me that I may take them to him when I return to London today."

Mary flung up her hands and exclaimed in surprise, "Why, my Lady commanded me to look through and organise all, and I did not..." her voice dwindled away, she covered her mouth with her hand and thought hard. "Well, I don't know I'm sure. I can help but little for my Lady herself cleared Loveday's room. I'm certain she would have taken the trinkets and box for the doctor. She never asked me." With much sniffing and sighing Mary stumped ahead on her stout legs, leading us through the house into all the places where Loveday used to be. She looked thoroughly for us and we helpfully suggested places to search. The shawl she had tucked away for her own self. "M'lady oversaw all, and this," stroking the shawl, "and some old gowns and petticoats she intended the parson's wife to have for the poor. I kept it for remembrance of my dear maid." She swiped the corner of her large linen apron across her eyes.

Will muttered and patted Mary's shoulder. I rolled the shawl up into a neat bundle, sailor fashion, and thanked the housekeeper gratefully. She knew of nothing else. Lady Fowke had taken Loveday's books of herb lore and receipts, her fine clothes and any valuable bauble or jewel. She was sure Lady Fowke had returned Loveday's trinkets, those her father and mother had bestowed upon her, along with her Bible and prayer book, in the parcel sent to the doctor.

Finally we came to the small rooms near the kitchens. We stopped in Loveday's place of work next to the still room and drying room. Here she'd studied her herbals, concocted her remedies for the household and written down the receipts. I wanted to search the room carefully. I hinted, but Will was slow, only finally understanding my nods, winks and head jerks, when I moved behind Mary and gestured to her and then the door. He coaxed the housekeeper into taking him to the kitchen to talk to the other servants about Loveday's things, particularly the box, dwelling on Doctor Maye's need for it. I lifted down every book and flicked through the pages, searched behind them, down the back of the shelves and in any possible crack or corner. I intended to replace everything neatly, but time swept on apace and I'd be far away from Mary's wrath when she saw the disorder.

It was in the cupboard near the fireplace, a well aired and dry place where Loveday had stored the powdered herbs, that I found one small thing, a packet, with a few grains of powder hidden in one corner. It had slipped between the shelf and the back wall. I checked it against the other neatly filed packets, but couldn't find a match. There was no label or writing on the packet, but a faint smell might tell the knowledgeable what the contents had been. I hid the thing in my inner pocket, hoping that Doctor Maye would know.

I strolled into the kitchens, seeking Will, and found him eating. Nothing out of the ordinary there, but the circle of servants centred round one of the stable boys, a stocky lad with a cast in one eye.

"Listen to Luke, Jacob," Will said. "Go on, Luke, tell us again."

"That Mattie, she got a bead necklace from Mistress Loveday. Sez she give 'er it to take a packet to the parson's lady."

"Now tell Master Emerick when this was."

"Mattie said the day afore he," pointing at me with the crust of bread in his hand, "found 'er in river."

"This is news, Will. I think we need to see Mistress Paske, to ask her to speak to Mattie." I smiled at the company. "Doubtless, she'll have those letters that Doctor Maye wants so."

I swept a courteous bow, collared Will, and went out before anyone could ask questions. We made haste for the goose yard and Mattie.

The yard, small, grassy and with mounds of old straw for nests, was full of hissing geese and flapping cackling ganders. Mattie was not in sight, but Nowell was, balanced on a ledge half way up one side wall, with a phalanx of ganders beating their wings below him.

Will and I leaned on the gate and chuckled.

"That's an odd perch, Nowell." Will slapped my back, and his chuckles turned to loud laughter. "Couldn't you persuade Mattie to find you a better one? What did he say about coaxing young maids, Jacob?"

Nowell said nothing, but the look he gave Will spoke of debts to be paid.

"Where's Mattie, Nowell?" I had to shout, for the ganders had registered us in their territory, increased their racket, turned and ran at us. They thrust their long wicked necks through the gate bars, stabbing their beaks like knives. Will struck, grabbed two necks and held on to two ganders. I hesitated, missed the first time, finally grasped the other two ganders. Nowell dropped off the wall and ran at the remaining gander, who flapped, lost courage, squawked, and raced away to his wives. Nowell strolled to the gate, all unconcerned. Will let go first one, then the other gander's neck as Nowell started to climb. Nowell vaulted over in a flash, spurred on by the furious attempts to buffet him.

"You young whelp!" He cuffed Will who would have returned the blow with a like one.

I restrained him. "Leave be, Will, you asked for that. We have to find Mattie, Nowell. She's been telling people Loveday gave her a bead necklace as payment for taking a parcel to Mistress Paske." Nowell's mouth opened on a question, snapped shut as I answered before he asked. "She says Loveday gave her the parcel the day before she died."

Once mounted it was a quick, although nervous trip along the river path to Mattie's poor home. The rain, as we were in want of it, had ceased. The clouds lifted, people would be moving about again. Nevertheless we reached the huddle of hovels that were Mattie's little community without seeing anybody. There was no one there either.

A sad sight, those pauper's dwellings, ill repaired wattle and daub with holes for chimneys, brushwood bundled and stuffed together for roofs and mismatched driftwood or crooked thinnings as fences. One scraggy old nanny goat browsed the river bank, tethered round the willow tree trunk. She was the only sign of prosperity we saw, not even a lurcher to work the warrens. One roof hole dribbled a thread of smoke. Even the few vegetables and herbs in the gardens struggled to thrive. It was as if hopelessness seeded the very air, tainting all it touched.

Will, at home in his own community, and practical to boot, shook his head at the squalor and pointed to the left. "Mattie lives with her Grandam who owns that cot. Her mother's been dead a few years now. Her father was crushed by a great tun barrel at the brewery, before Mattie's young brother was born. Parson Paske, he sees they get a bit of reading and writing from the Bible, but the sins of the father rest heavy on the children and they're not of the elect are they?"

Nowell snorted.

"Careful, friend," I warned him, "this is Puritan country. You cannot doubt the rule of the elect. Will doesn't, so don't start him wondering. He has to live here." Will stared, Nowell shrugged.

"Now, one to the back, me, one stays here with the horses, you, Nowell, and Will, who is known, shall flush out young Mattie into the garden."

It was a good plan and should have worked. As I waited at the back of the cot, in case Mattie tried to slip away unseen, I heard Will knock, calling, "Grannie Tratt?" He entered, I heard the door dragging over the floor. I strained my ears, listening for conversation, but it was Will let out a bellow, in fright it sounded. Nowell called. I ran round and in through the door. There stood Will, looking down at a bundle by the fire, a stiff awkward bundle which had fallen from the seat wedged into the wall, a rude plank seat placed to gain the most heat for its occupant.

We had found another body.

"What...? Who...? Is this...?"

"It's the Grandam." Will looked at me. "She's cold dead."

Nowell demanded to know what was happening. I sent Will to him and crouched beside the crone. She was old, very old. Death could be a natural cessation in God's time, but after my earlier experiences in Eikenthorpe I wanted to be convinced this a natural death.

Nowell came to the door and started to speak. "Don't ask questions, man, make a light. We must know that this is not another murder." He found a bundle of kindling and thrust it into what was left of the fire, then brought the spluttering torch to me. Together we looked for blood or wounds on her head and hands, anything rather than open the ragged blankets wrapped round her which smelt strongly of piss and old woman.

"Closer to her face again, Nowell. Yes, ah, yes, I did see. Look at her eyes, Nowell, look carefully and tell me what you see."

The old woman's open eyes stared, eyes of blackest black, with only a thin band of colour around the blackness. We shuddered at the sight. Nowell brought the spluttering remnants of the torch even closer.

"Have a care."

He raised his arm, allowing the last of the kindling torch to give a flare of light, looked again, then walked outside, dousing the torch in the fire as he went. I followed. "Why are her eyes so black and big? 'Tis not natural."

"No, that it's not." I received a rapier look. Will called a warning, but Mistress Paske was upon us, dragging by the hand a pinch faced, trembling Mattie.

We all spoke together, the whats? whys? and wheres? colliding with each other and good sense. Manners won and we allowed Mistress Paske to speak. She noted Nowell, pursed her lips at him, and scolded us roundly, as though we were all little Matties.

"Inside all of you," she commanded, "stay out of sight and..." her voice ceased as she saw our faces. "No, ah no, I hoped..." she said softly.

"Yes, Mistress Paske, another death. Mattie must explain how it came about, for we know she has some things of Loveday, things Nowell needs to take to Doctor Maye. And I want the contents of the box she hid." Mattie squawked and cowered behind Mistress Paske's skirts.

We waited impatiently until Mistress Paske cleaned and laid the body out and sent Will to find the Warden and bring the pauper's corpse basket. Will argued all the way to his horse. "Tell my husband I will explain when I return, but that you know nothing. And you don't, do you, Will?"

Will spluttered.

"That's why you go."

"I'll remember every word for you," Nowell promised.

The look Will gave us would have soured milk, but he went.

Mattie remained sobbing by her Grandam.

Thanking God for my family's wealth, I crouched beside the girl and offered my bribe. "Would you like your Grandam to have a proper grave plot in the churchyard?

Mattie sobbed on. "You can have a good wooden coffin for her and a stone cross to mark her place."

Mattie raised her snotty wet face and tried to stop crying.

"Here." Mistress Paske brought a dipper of water, and with a clean cloth from the basket of things she'd brought, she wiped Mattie's face, and patted her soothingly. "I believe your Grandam would have liked a real burial and not the pauper's plot. Master Emerick has promised you. I know he keeps his word." Here she shot me a glance full of questions, obviously wondering what I was doing back in Eikenthorpe. She patted Mattie again. "Tell us how all this came about."

Mattie's eyes stayed fixed on her Grandam.

"Come, let's sit on the old willow out on the river bank, and you can tell us what happened." Mistress Paske took Mattie's hand, I followed behind. Outside Nowell had collected the horses and stood behind us, half hidden amongst them.

"Mattie, what did Mistress Maye give you to take to Mistress Paske the day before she died?"

My raised hand silenced Mistress Paske. Mattie's eyes darted a look left, then right. She squirmed and bent her head over her lap.

"It was only some receipts I'd asked for, wasn't it Mattie?" Mistress Paske's kind eyes glistened, "Loveday always remembered."

Mattie nodded, but wouldn't look at me directly. The telltale giving her away was that she didn't look into Mistress Paske's face either.

"Mattie, what else was there?" I kept my voice toned down to a soft coaxing.

Nowell leaned towards the girl. "Mattie, you do want that proper burial for your Grandam?"

Mattie nodded.

"Then speak truly so that her soul, hovering near us now as she waits God's call, will hear and be glad."

Mattie sobbed, one body shaking sob, snuffled, nodded again and began. It was a tale quickly told. There had been several packets of remedies for Mistress Paske to use with the receipts. Mattie couldn't read much, but she did recognise the one tied up by itself like the packet Loveday had given her once for her Grandam's aches and pains.

Mistress Paske sighed. "Ah, Mattie, if you had asked me, I would have given you it.
To take it is stealing and breaks the Seventh Commandment. Why didn't you ask?" Nowell hushed Mistress Paske, and I cheered Mattie by promising neither Nowell or I were going to complain to Parson Paske about the stealing. She swore that was all she'd had from Mistress Maye to give to Mistress Paske, and she'd only kept and used that one remedy for her Grandam's aches. "Then what about her bead necklace you have? That was in her box. When did you find Mistress Maye's box in the hidy hole behind the willow roots?"

Mattie stared, shocked that I knew so much. She cried out that Mistress Loveday wouldn't mind. She knew that Mistress Loveday meant it for her, but finally, after much yowling, she told us everything.

It seemed that Mattie showed Loveday the hidy hole, and sometimes Loveday left a letter which Mattie took to the inn for the postal service to collect. Loveday paid her with a basket of food for the family every week. It was when Mattie had looked in the hidy hole the day following Loveday's death that she had found the box.

Mistress Paske scolded. "Mattie, you knew that was too valuable for you." I touched her arm and she paused, pressed her lips together to stop further words.

"What did the note say? Mattie, there was a note." It was a good guess and impressed her.

"For my father." The words hurried out then, as she rushed to explain and wipe the frown from Mistress Paske's face. She was going to give it to the parson, to send to the doctor, only she opened it, just to look-see, and found two more packets of a remedy. She'd known what they were because they were very like Mistress Loveday's packet but written on. 'For Denzil Gamlen,' they said, 'for his pains.' She hadn't meant to touch them, and she hadn't touched the letters and papers, God's truth she hadn't, but with the rain coming her Grandam ached so that she had stirred one into some of the nanny's milk and given it to the old woman this morning.

I think all of us struggled to make sense of it. Nowell's eyebrows rose, Mistress Paske looked as if someone had hit her. I felt as if some one had wrapped a blanket round my wits.

"And where is the box and all its contents, Mattie?" I asked, eager to see those packets.

Mattie squirmed, would have run, but we had her hemmed in.

"Mattie, you stole, and your Grandam is dead. That should be punishment enough, God's punishment because you broke His commandment, but what do the Church wardens in Eikenthorpe do to thieves?" Mistress Paske drilled each word out crisply. Mattie looked up quickly. "What will they do to you, and what will happen to your brothers and sisters?"

Mattie threw herself down in the mud, wailing loudly.

"Get up, child and take me to the box." Mistress Paske extended her hand and tugged Mattie to her feet. "At once. Let us untangle this sad affair."

We went inside and, Mattie delved in the bedding where she and her sisters slept. A miserable pile it was with lumps of wood wrapped for pillows. Mattie's pillow was Loveday's box.

Nowell had more right to it, and I let him clasp it. Mistress Paske watched Mattie.

"Mattie, you know the Wardens will want to whip you for stealing. If you return all Loveday's things I will plead for you. Where are her trinkets?"

All hope gone, Mattie wept, tried to procrastinate, but finally showed us the pocket in the wall near her bed. She'd secreted them there.

Outside again, we heard Will call a warning. Nowell thrust the box at me, and fled to his horse. "Will's barn," he whispered, as he ran past. We all went out to stand on the path, making a great to do about Mattie having found Loveday's box and not delivering it to Mistress Paske. Mattie howled so I'm sure the parson, Wardens Hugh and Thomas never saw Nowell disappear, with us making such a plurality of noise and pother, and a mounted Will dragging at my horse, effectively blocking the river path.

After the Wardens departed with the body, Mattie walked with Mistress Paske, back to the parsonage where her brothers and sisters sheltered. Parson Paske and I exchanged guarded disclosures as we strolled behind. Will listened in so closely from his horse that his ears must have pricked nearly as sharply as the nag's.

"And you say Mattie told you the packet was for Master Gamlen, Denzil Gamlen?" Parson Paske's voice could rise no higher.

"When we examine the box I think we will understand. These are muddy waters, it's difficult to see beyond the knowledge that Mistress Loveday died because of something in that box."

I let Will speculate, peppering the parson with 'What if this...?' and 'Suppose that...?' And he asked a question I'd been waiting to ask privately. "You won't punish Mattie for killing her Grandam will you? She didn't know she was hurting her Grandam."

Parson Paske frowned him down, telling him it was matter needing much thought and prayer, not idle speculation, but he could not see how the child would have known.

At the parsonage the parson and the Wardens talked briefly in the library then went to deliver judgement upon Mattie and her brothers and sisters. Mistress Paske followed, leaving Will with me, both looking at the box.

"Mattie could not read well," said Will, running his thumb nail along the join between lid and base, "so I expect she made a mistake." He tapped the box. "We could open it and be sure."

"Not without witnesses. I want the parson and Mistress Paske to see. I'm sorry Nowell's not here. Bear witness for him."

Will scowled, opened his mouth to protest, then shrugged. "As you say. For Nowell and Loveday."

Parson Paske returned alone, and did his best to remove Will. Will and I outfaced his authority on behalf of Doctor Maye and Nowell.

"I shall ride with Jacob to Brockleford," Will announced grandly, "to tell Doctor Maye all that has happened. Nowell's family live nearby, I shall tell him what we have discovered. I am a witness to the truth."

I hid my laughter at the parson's expression, then challenged the parson's right to investigate the box and its contents. "Loveday hid this box, and what is in it, for Doctor Maye, for her father. 'Twas he gave me the task of finding it and returning it."

Parson Paske's arguments slowly dwindled. He inclined his head. "Very well, then, Master Jacob Emerick."

At last. I could open Loveday's box.

# CHAPTER TWENTY-FIVE

It was clear Mattie had jumbled the contents of the box. I slowly spread everything over the parson's desk. The lifting of the door latch made me pause, until Mistress Paske came in, cupping Loveday's trinkets in her hands. The parson frowned. I feared he might object to her presence, so I spoke first. "I would appreciate Mistress Paske's advice, Parson Paske, for she discovered Loveday's trinkets, and the truth about the box, which we might not have done."

Parson Paske gave me one of his looks, as he gestured his wife to him. "Sit here. You can make good Loveday's beads." She nodded, gave a hesitant smile and sat down, her hands already busy untwisting and separating the links and strands.

I turned back to the box and told out loud each item as I removed it. "This is a letter." I let my eye quickly skim the contents, refolded it. "A completed letter to her father, not for us." I picked out the note, it was the last note she had ever written. The words and appearance told me so. There were no proper greetings as in the letter to her father. The letters were ill formed, smudged, obviously penned in haste. I remembered Loveday's neat writing and sighed, paused to recollect myself, then read the brief message as steadily as I could.

*'Something is amiss, Father. I am afraid. I dare not write of what in case of prying eyes, but oh, if I am correct, then it is truly a great evil. Send these papers to the Merchants Emerick. Tell Master Jacob, he'll know what to do to set things aright. I've given this to Mattie. After this morning, I fear the worst. Pray for me.'*

There was no more to read. I cleared my throat and blinked my eyes. No one challenged my decision as I placed the note with the letter. It was for her father to have.

Next came the packets. Mattie had replaced the emptied one, and I picked it up along with the matching full one. I passed the emptied packet to Parson Paske. He leaned towards his wife, and she moved closer to see. They studied the inscription.

I showed Will the full packet. These packets had been carefully made from bands of coloured paper and sealed with wax in the form of several little flowers. All most prettily done, with an inscription written by Lady Fowke, to her brother. I recognised her strong hand. I showed the writing to them all. "This is from Lady Fowke to her brother. I know her writing well. Mattie gave her Grandam the contents, and her Grandam died." I looked across at the parson. "Did you note her eyes, Parson Paske, the Grandam's eyes?"

"Indeed, Jacob. I cannot understand it. I know, once having seen this before, may God forgive the evil sinner who killed his wife, that poison can do this."

"Did you observe Denzil Gamlen's eyes? Were you called to his death bed?"

Parson Paske shook his head. "He was prepared for his coffin when I saw him, eyes covered."

"This might have a bearing on the matter." I took, from my hidden pocket, the empty packet I'd found at the back of the cupboard at Gamlen Manor. "There's a fragment of powder in here. I discovered this little packet earlier today, hidden in the herbal cupboard at the Manor. I'm hoping that Doctor Maye can sniff out the poison, or test and discover it from the powders in either packet."

We bent over the two packets, as if our close scrutiny could make the powders speak. "I am no expert," Parson Paske said, "we will leave that to the doctor."

I agreed and found Will breathing down my neck as I examined the box's remaining contents. The Paskes watched in silence, but their eyes spoke of a dawning understanding. There was a letter from Nowell, which I put with Doctor Maye's, and two plain everyday packets of medicinal powder, marked again in Lady Fowke's hand. Then a list, or perhaps receipt, on a scrap of paper, in Loveday's hand. It simply read: *Plain: 3 parts, 3 parts, 2 parts, 1 part, 1 part. Gift: same parts plus 2 measures of nightshade, hemlock or yew? No taste or smell when mulled in wine.*

"Ah." Mistress Paske clapped her hands over her mouth, only her eyes remained visible, rounded with horrified understanding.

"What is it?" Will looked at each of us in turn. "Is it the receipt for what's in the packets?"

The parson nodded his head slowly, looking at me.

I tucked the scrap of paper back in the box. "I think so, Will, I think it may be. Let Doctor Maye experiment and then perhaps we'll learn the truth."

We passed around all the packets again with care. Mistress Paske opened one corner to look at the contents. "So much wickedness," she said, "I don't want to believe it." She carefully tucked in and folded down the corner, then handed the packet back to me.

The box was empty. I made to close it, as if finished, hoping differently, but sure Parson Paske would not forget Loveday's mentioning of the Emerick papers. He did not. He looked at me and then the box. "The Emerick papers?" he enquired.

I made a wry face. "Believe me, I do not know which papers she secured for us. Possibly the land titles Gamlen held for us." I would say no more for I would not trust the parson.

The parson flapped his jaw like a hooked fish. "Land titles?"

I gave him a wolf's smile. "We bought land in Eikenthorpe, parson. Denzil Gamlen had the use of it for us." I saw Will frowning and laughed. "No, Will, we won't claim your farm. It is an investment for us. The Merchants Emerick need land if we look to advancement through Parliament. My task, I pray." The parson's eyebrows rose. "But now, can you see a way to open the lid? There's a cavity in it."

Will pushed carefully up then tried pulling down and up. Nothing happened. I tried, then gave the box to Parson Paske. He twisted the lid. When that failed he turned it about. Mistress Paske, watching us, suggested sliding the domed lid. It eventually slid right, forward and to the left and, when a catch was released with a pin, the whole lid fell open most ingeniously. I grabbed the thin bundle of paper on top, tied with legal tape and neatly sealed. Loveday had included a note, slipped under the tape, addressed to me. All appeared neat and tidy, so I assumed Loveday had tucked these papers away some time before her death. I read the note to myself first then shared a little.

"These are for the Emerick family from Denzil Gamlen. They are the deeds to our land, and some letters. They are important to us and private. Now I have them I must return, first to Doctor Maye, to let him have what is rightfully his, and then to my family."

Will grumbled under his breath. Mistress Paske bent her head and sighed gently. The parson tried to speak, then threw up both hands in defeat.

"You will hear what you need to hear, Parson Paske, but my family's business is ours alone. It does not bear on these poisoning in Eikenthorpe. And yes, poor Jameson was killed in London for these documents, a cruel irony, for he never had them."

Parson Paske scowled, but kept his peace. I replaced what needed to go into the box, and we all gazed at the four packets lying on the desk. We sat in a state of confusion, stunned by what the presence of those packets of herbal remedies might mean, and trying to weigh the importance of Loveday's receipt. Two deaths and one planned so artfully and cruelly.

It went hard against the grain for me, a Merchant's son, who'd watched his sisters groomed to be wives of gentry, who had hoped to become a Member of Parliament and gentry himself, to believe that those whose company he sought, could stoop to such a murder. "It's Loveday's death I can't fit. Lady Fowke could have poisoned her easily. Why was she strangled?"

Parson Paske spoke finally. "We need a period of reflection and prayer to give us full understanding. You have found much and revealed more, Jacob. I thank you for that." Mistress Paske sent her husband a pleading look, he nodded. "Ah, yes, and perhaps you would spend the night with us? Delay your departure until tomorrow so that we can enjoy your company once more."

I nodded, but before I could speak, Will bounced up and announced that if he was to go to tell Master Merriot and the doctor all that had happened, then accompany me to London, he needed to seek his father's permission. "And Jacob had best come along to prove there was an invitation."

Oh, mightily done, Will, for he released us to secure Nowell and hide him away from prying eyes. But at my personal cost. The prospect of taking Will to London, I did not relish. A mental image of him loose in that great city made me quail. I'd have the tiresome task of watching over him and warding him from harm when I had a deal of legal work to catch up on and make right for my family. I winced inwardly and slapped the boy's shoulder.

Will rushed me back to the stables, leaving Mistress Paske to chastise Mattie for her lies and the parson to settle where she and her unfortunate sisters and brothers should now make their home. We disturbed our unwilling horses and made them carry us, at a gentle walk, along the river path and up the farm track, to Will's farm.

Nowell had his nag well settled in the sheep barn, resigning himself to another night in a stable and not a bed. He listened to all we said, but demanded food and drink before he could comprehend it all. "A meat pie, or two, bread, cheese and a tansy, might be a sufficiency. Come Will, what can you provide from a raid on your good mother's larder?"

Will paled. "She counts every morsel. There is nothing she has in there uncounted."

I laughed at his expression. "Think, lad. What might go unnoticed? Is there no hen strayed and laying out. Can you not take a dipper of cream and a squirt of fresh milk?"

Will looked at me, frowned then shrugged. "Aye, I can find a hen. I can take the last of the roots, turnips, carrots and parsnip. There's a pile of soft ones my mother sorted out that she'll not miss."

Nowell groaned. "Food, don't talk about it. Fetch it. How can I think about poisons when my belly's hollow as a drum?"

Will and I made a swift raid down to the farm house. Will entered the dairy, I waited by the rear window. We left the dairy light of a small pannikin of cream, one dripping bag of new cream cheese from the back of a row of many, and the cow byre lost a clucky hen and her eggs. Will hid the result of our scavenging in the centre of a pile of chop and hay which he pulled up to the barn in a hay sack. "I told them I have to feed the horse," he explained, winked and added, "but I didn't say which horse."

I grabbed a corner of the sack and we heaved together. "You'd best let me speak to your father soon and explain why we are here."

Will grinned. "In my own good time."

"Ah," Nowell exclaimed as we came through the door pulling the sack, "at last." He and Will used a base corner-stone, one of the flat ones which extended into the barn, like a hearth, and lit a very small fire. Soon eggs and cream coddled over the low flames. Nowell and Will, clearly practised at this poacher's style of outdoor cooking, had the hen reduced to pieces and spitted on sticks before I could offer an alternative suggestion. Instead I fed the horses whilst Will and Nowell argued over the best use of the still dripping cheese. Will snatched the cheese from Nowell and tipped a goodly half into the pannikin with the eggs when a voice broke in on their argument.

"What, in our Lord's name, do you think to do?"

We all startled like deer, and Nowell jumped sideways so that my body shielded his. Will glowered, his face darkened and he scowled ferociously. His attitude, and the intruder's young appearance, told me this was an interfering older brother. Will had my sympathy.

"A fire, Will, near fodder."

In truth the barn stood empty, apart from our horses' hay. I recognised the tone, this was the first born brother, and plastering on the elder part in that tiresome way older brothers had of loading on guilt. Sometimes it was more than a younger brother could bear. I'd never born it with patience from my three big brothers. Will looked to feel the same.

"At my request, Master...?" Whatever ill feeling went on between the two halted and the righteous young man introduced himself. He was broader and heavier than Will, of the same height, with those same velvet brown eyes, but with brown wavy hair.

"Hamnet Verne, and if you are a visitor then you should have been made known to my father, as Will well knows."

"Then perhaps you would do me that service, and let Will settle the horses." I had him by the elbow and turned away from Nowell. "I am Master Jacob Emerick, and I have a request to make of your father, if you would be good enough to take me to him." I flourished a half bow and Master Hamnet could not politely refuse.

"Will, you had best come and pack your things." I turned, spoke to Nowell as to a groom. "Eat, Noah, and make ready the horses for our journey. Ride on ahead to ready our change of nags."

"Pack? And where is Will..."

I moved Master Hamnet through the barn doorway. "I should speak to your father before you, Master Hamnet." I frowned and urged him on. "Will is needed to bear witness to Doctor Maye."

Hamnet's mouth opened and closed. I'd caught his attention now and he wouldn't have thought for the third man, except as a groom, until we'd gone. God Bless Nowell for his quick wits. He'd be away before anyone came to look.

Master Hamnet made haste and had me in the farmhouse and introduced to his mother and father in short time. This was a family farm, the house plain, grown from something much smaller over years, the timber frame and plaster in-fill age darkened at one end, the brick chimneys in odd places. I'd seen the farm outbuildings outside, snug to the house, standing in good trim. It was the same inside, clear that the Vernes held hard work as a godly attribute. Mistress Verne had many hands to help her, poor Will had a gaggle of sisters, four, two younger, two older than he, all with the family brown eyes and plenty of the family curls escaping their fetching little caps. They gazed at me and their battery of stares, along with their father's disapproving humph, made me try my charms first on Will's mother. She looked a brisk goody, with Will's brown eyes and dark hair, although hers was tamed under a well fitting coif.

"I need to ask a favour of you, Mistress Verne."

She recognised me from church meetings and smiled politely. "A favour, Master Emerick?"

"Will is needed to bear witness to things we discovered about Loveday's death. He should speak to Doctor Maye and to Master Merriot and to the Gamlen estate lawyers in London." I turned to Master Verne. "With your permission I would take him with me tomorrow to Doctor Maye in Brockleford and on to London."

There was a babble of words from them all.

"He will ride with me to Essex and then we will ride with Master Thurloe, Clerk Knott and the Tunnace brothers to London. He will return to you by Emerick boat, in the company of the Masters Tunnace, as far as Brockleford and ride his own horse home from there."

Master Verne quietened his family with a firm, "Be silent." He then faced me with a frown. "Does the parson know all this? Is this his idea and does he enforce the request?"

"He is aware of the need for Will to go with me. He will support it. It is my pleasure to ask you to give your son leave to come with me, Master Verne."

Will's father huffed and humphed. He had a thick collection of iron grey curls, which he scratched through as he thought. He stared into my eyes. In his eyes I could see distrust. My anger rose again.

"Don't doubt me. You forget yourself. You will have heard Parson Paske clear me of all charges. I am a decent godly man, and of the Merchant Emericks."

"Aye, that's what I fear."

"What? That the Emericks will remove you from this farm?"

He burst into loud speech, but his wife tush-tushed him hastily, bustling forward, her hands twisting her apron askew. Master Verne's words died. Sisters and brother watched, faces anxious or fretful, edged with worry.

In the long pause, a period of thick silence, the Vernes waited for an axe to fall. I reproached myself for my clumsy failure to appreciate their concern. Of course Denzil Gamlen would have told them who owned the land. His death must have brought them as many fears as we Emericks had.

"Why should the Emericks remove a good tenant? I'm not here to change that arrangement. Here, shake my hand as a sign of goodwill between us. The land is still yours to farm."

In the babble that followed I learned they had feared greatly. "We did not know if the Fowke family had any rights, or what you might do." Master Verne gripped my hand, wringing it painfully before I could remove it. His loquacity, for his relief loosened his tongue, led to me learning that Will had been set to watch me. I laughed. Master Verne laughed in turn and slapped my back.

Mistress Verne drew me to one side and spoke quietly. "Now, sir, we are plain people, not wealthy, this journey to London, well, we don't wish to see our boy getting notions above his station in his head. A farmer he is, and will be."

"If I can get a farm and there's little chance here." Will had arrived and stood in the doorway, bootless, hatless, hair springing up, face full of indignation. "I need my own land."

One of his sisters laughed. "You've to catch a girl with prospects or a widow with a farm," she teased. Will growled some comment, but the tension eased again.

"Am I to go then? It's not like I'll be pressed for an Emerick sailor, or turned over by highway men. Though I may stay and make myself a builder. Jacob tells me there's much building going on in London with skilled men wanted. With all this work I'm doing for the parson, I could soon be calling myself a builder's apprentice."

His father nay-sayed him, his sisters teased some more.

"You'll be speaking to Doctor Maye, Master Nowell Merriot, and possibly be witness at a meeting of the Emerick and Galmen lawyers. Then you'll return home down the Thames, on one of our Emerick trading boats, Will. That is all. And..." I addressed Master Verne, "that is all he will be doing." A glance at Will's disappointed face explained why Mistress Verne ducked her head to hide her smiles.

"Come, Will," she said, "let me find you something to wear in London." They left us.

Permission given, I eased set shoulders and began to charm the family as best I might. "Master Verne, the future is uncertain, but I'll send Will home with a legal paper giving you the right to farm here in our name. Whatever happens, whether Pym or King prevail, you will have the papers to make yourself safe here."

The sun came out in all their faces. Tenant farmers had much to fear from unknown landlords, Gamlen had been a good one, they'd not known what we would be. Will's sisters brought sweet ale and Master Verne offered a pipe. I thought of Nowell in the barn and hid a grin. It was good they did not know that the Royalist spy they had helped to drive out previously, sat eating their food in their sheep barn. Soon he'd be up and off, half way to his safe overnight stop. We'd stay the night, make a slow journey of it and meet him there by the morrow mid-morning.

We sat on the settles, drank ale, smoked a pipe, and talked of a London without the King, and with Parliament in control. The sisters pressed me to agree that I'd take Will to find them presents of lace or ribbons, and I promised to send him home with the latest news sheets, ballads, and my mother's newest cap and sleeve patterns.

One sister wanted to know if I had heard any of the sermons of William Gouge, John Owen or Thomas Goodwin. Everyone present hoped the King would change his mind.

"He didn't when it came to foisting his prayer book on the Scots. We had to pay for that war," said Master Verne.

War, it was said and sat there, the great terror for all of us.

"It's not only the King who needs to think again," I said. "There are Puritans who would do well to give way."

Will arrived in a clatter of booted feet, with a packed saddle bag, determined to ride back with me to the parson's, and probably hoping to persuade me to take him to the London playhouses, bawdy houses, taverns, anywhere his parents would disapprove.

"What have you yet to do, Will?" His father looked stern.

"You mean, the building work to complete, there's a muster of the troop tomorrow, and Mistress Paske..."

"And work to do here, this afternoon." Hamnet was firm and Master Verne firmer.

Will looked to turn mutinous, but I forestalled him. "Tomorrow, Will, be ready to come early, we can ride to where No...Noah will have a horse waiting for you. There you can leave your father's horse safe at the farm."

Murmurs of approval greeted this, and without much difficulty I escaped the house and then the barn, finally getting to the parson's as Mistress Paske set out the supper.
***

Leaving Eikenthorpe the following morning was all the farewell I'd been denied under the previous forced departure. I rose early enough to oversee my horse's morning feed and grooming. I'd wanted a quiet swift leaving, but the three Graces caught me breaking my fast, coming from their father's study where they'd attended some early scripture lessons. They slipped into the kitchen, expecting their mother, and found me, chucking Lizzie under the chin, making Tabitha laugh, and eating hot griddle cakes.

After that it was Mistress Paske herself who arrived and made us all wash before going to the dining room for a generous breakfast, despite the early hour. We washed hands and faces at the pump, me splashing the little maids, using again their rose scented soap. Mistress Paske herself brought warmed linen towels, thick home woven ones, also carrying a faint rose petal scent. Ever after I would associate that particular rose scent with those four faces.

Saying farewell proved difficult. Tabitha actually stepped out from the back kitchen to smile and wave as we moved into the stable yard. All was forgiven. The family stood by the yard gate, and the little maids did not cry out or fuss. Their father prevented any such tricks by standing nearby, but we'd been comrades for weeks and I would miss them. I had a fondness for sisters and when they came as three bonnie poppets, who could have cooed and charmed, using their appealing three-ness for gain, yet were without any such guile, well...what would you? I knelt and bussed each soft round cheek, as a cousin would, whispering a goodbye. Into Grace's ear I murmured a promise of a thank you parcel for their mother and father with some fairing and toy for each little girl. She sneaked her arms around my neck in a quick hug, sliding them away almost before I felt them. I gave her an extra kiss and rose.

Mistress Paske took both my hands, thanking me for giving Mattie a chance to choose. "She helped us find Loveday's message, her family will be safe within our community, and the Lord will shield and guard them. I thank you for that. With our guidance and the Lord's strength she won't steal again, nor will she become a thief or outcast. You used your wealth in a proper godly way. She, we, will remember that goodness."

Even my ears flamed. "Faith Paske." She released my hands. "Mistress Paske," I amended, conscious of Parson Paske within ear shot. "I am more accustomed to a scolding than such praise from you." I turned to include the parson. "I would like to thank you for your Paske hospitality and repay your kindness in keeping me imprisoned in your home and not the local goal."

If Parson Paske detected irony he betrayed no sign of it, merely gave the slightest of bows. "There is no need. You were safer under my eye."

"Then I thank you again." A parcel of music and books for them all, ribbons and dolls for the three Graces and some of Merchant Emerick's exotic foods and spices for Mistress Paske to enjoy in the kitchen, that was a way to send Emerick thanks. My mother would relish organising such a hamper, especially after she had the full Eikenthorpe story out of me.

The parson inclined his head. Mistress Paske smiled and shook her head. "You leave us with less mystery," she said, "but no solutions." Her tone softened. "You will write and give us as much news as you can?" Her involuntary gesture, a reaching out, she noticed and controlled, but I took both her hands, laid one atop the other and bowed low over them, as to a great lady. Mistress Faith Paske had been a support and strength, far more than she would ever know. She blushed to her hairline; and withdrew her hands. The three Graces gathered beside her, looking with round eyes at me. I straightened and gained a fleeting impression, an involuntary wince or pained expression on Parson Paske's face, although there was nothing to see when I looked directly.

"Farewell, gracious ladies," I gave them an extravagant flourishing wave, hat in hand, which made the little maids giggle, and allowed Mistress Paske to put a hand to her mouth to hide her laughter and therefore part of her face, if not her expressive eyes.

Parson Paske came with me to the stable door where his stableman had my horse saddled and waiting outside. I bethought me of that wince. How does one broach a subject as delicate? For if it was pain I saw, and I had inadvertently caused it, I had a responsibility to repay Mistress Faith Paske's many kindnesses with a kindness of my own. I must not leave a seed of possible discord between that good woman and her husband.

The stableman gave me a leg up and departed to his other tasks. I looked down into Parson Paske's face and words failed. I could not find a way to say, "I never made love to your wife, nor she to me." Or, "There is nothing between us, sir, just your wife's kindness and tender heart." I leant down and offered him my hand instead.

"You did your duty, Richard Paske, and I did mine. Thank the Lord your wife built a bridge between the two. She saved my neck. I owe her eternal gratitude for that and will ever be mindful of her kindness and charity." The best words I could find to give him peace.

The parson gripped my hand, and I hoped it was a flicker of understanding I saw in his hazel eyes. Gratitude from a young man to his wife might be acceptable, that his young wife might feel a tenderness for that same careless young man was not.

"Go safely in God's hands," he told me. I nudged the black gently and we walked away. I raised a hand, but did not look back. I would miss the three Graces, but I refused to accept that I would miss Mistress Faith Paske.

# CHAPTER TWENTY–SIX

Will dashed for his nag as soon as he saw me. He'd been on look out duty since day break. Turned out neatly and simply in Puritan breeks and tunic, (bulked out, by the look of him, with several warm layers under his tunic, his mother's doing, I'd be bound,) with a good wool cloak atop, he wasn't about to set fashionable London by her ears. His cup top boots were polished and oiled. His grin would not have disgraced a sailor given unexpected shore leave and a fat purse to spend. His eager enthusiasm made me laugh.

Mistress Verne asked me to stay and break my fast again, but my refusal, on a plea of haste, had Will's sisters bundle up fresh bread and pastries, with two leather bottles of the weaker last brew beer, which went into my saddle bags. "I'll return him safely, Mistress Verne." I gave her a half bow. "My word on it, Master Verne." I stretched out my hand and he reached up his hard brown one. I shook it and rode away with Will at a sober trot.

Will kept silent for the first part of our journey, delight and incredulity written all over his face. He beamed, his eyes sparkled and he seemed about to brim over into a torrent of words, yet restrained himself. We were over half way to Nowell's first stopping place before he uttered anything and then it was only, "I hope Nowell has a good horse for me to ride." Finally, as we rode the last mile to the farm, he loosed his tongue and questions poured out.

"What we might do in London? Where might we go? Who would we see?"

I don't know that he believed the streets were paved with gold, but he did think that anything marvellous could happen.

Nowell kept watch too. He rode Samson, so I knew his father had been as good as his word. Indeed Master Merriot was waiting for us. We ate at the farm, sorted out the horses and set Will, who was a natural rider and easy with any horse, on a fine bay. I missed my Perry and allowed Nowell to settle me on a steady dappled grey gelding which wouldn't skitter about, or drop a shoulder to unseat me. We farewelled Master Merriot, who took a group of well bred horses away with him, and would meet us at his home. Bound for the King's men? Perhaps, and they'd have a powerful cavalry with his mounts. Who bought mounts for Pym's cavalry? Knott's masters? Who would know to do it and how to do it? I shook off my despondent thoughts, and we took to the old lanes and bridlepaths again, reaching the ford as the light failed and dusk fell. We travelled slowly, talking about the contents of Loveday's box, the possible conclusions we could draw, and how any one of them would hurt Doctor Maye. We didn't have to arrive in Brockleford that day and decided, because Will pestered us, to spend the night at an inn.

There was an inn half a mile down river from the ford. Nowell recommended it for its quietness and good food. Will begged, so to the inn we went. We found the stable excellent, a safe box for Samson and stalls next to the box for the other two mounts. The one ostler handled the horses well. His eyes lit up when he saw Samson. Nowell insisted we take our saddles and bridles to lock in our room, after which we went to eat a simple supper of bean and vegetable stew, fried fish and raison pie. The beer was home brewed, dark and strong. We limited ourselves, and therefore Will, to one tankard. As Nowell had remembered, the inn was quiet, we dined in solitude in the small dining room. Just after we had strolled out to the stables, accompanying Nowell as he checked his horses to see all was well, another two parties of late travellers arrived. Two pedlars with heavy packs, a couple of laden asses, and a boy, shed their animals and the boy in the stables, to head straight for the dining room with their loaded packs. The other party of two men appeared out of the dark, turning into the bar with a familiarity which suggested they might be local. Two locals stopping in for a pleasant evening, or two travellers, I wasn't sure which, and the landlord merely nodded a 'Good evening' as he served them, which didn't help distinguish them. They joined us by the fire where we supped another beer with them and watched Nowell and Will fight a close contest at draughts.

They made easy conversation, introduced themselves as the Brewer brothers, seemed full of sport, laughing noisily whilst slapping each other on the back. They spoke as sailors do, loud but clear, and acted with genial good humour, borrowing a pack of cards from the Landlord. Nowell and I exchanged a cautionary glance, but they did not behave as gamblers out to fleece us. We played Thirty-One for sport and then the brothers taught Will and Nowell to play the more complicated version of Bone-Ace. I sat at Will's elbow to help him along. The pedlars came to watch, and stayed to play, so that we enjoyed one of those merry social evenings which pass the time before bed.

The pedlars' boy slipped in by the stable yard door as I spoke to the landlord about an early breakfast and paid him for our meal. He stood in the hallway, waiting until Pedlar Tom glanced his way then beckoned urgently. Pedlar Tom crossed the room to him. I strained to hear the whispered conversation. There had been something furtive about the way the boy pulled Pedlar Tom into the passage, out the sight of us all, as if he didn't want to be seen or heard. I nodded to the landlord and made as if to walk upstairs, which allowed me to cross the opening where the two whispered.

"I don't know what to do. I haven't eaten," the boy said. "They won't send me my meal, say I'm to come for it. There's another man. Came with them two playing cards. He's stopping out in the stables, been in at that fine stallion and those horses, tried to move the asses. He keeps telling me to get to the kitchen to eat and he'll watch the asses for me."

"Your pardon," I interrupted, moving them a little further down towards the stable yard door. "Did you say there's someone in the stables and he's been in to our horses?"

The boy glanced at his master, then answered, "Aye, sir."

"Where's the inn ostler?"

"The groom, sir? He talked with that other man, sir, and I reckon, Master Tom," here he gave the pedlar a knowing look, "that 'un slipped him a gold coin, for the groom went off to the kitchen, making me go with him, so I comes running for you."

Pedlar Tom swore under his breath. "Come quick," he said to me and had the boy half way down the passage before I'd understood. I ran after, bellowing for Nowell.

There came crashes and shouts behind us, but no Nowell. I didn't wait. The boy had the outside door open, and we ran into the yard. Pedlar Tom snatched up the candle lantern from the wall sconce beside the door, holding it high as he called to his beasts. A half moon in the cloudy sky gave feeble light, enough for me to be sure that the dark bulk of our horses did not loom in their stalls. An ass brayed. Pedlar Tom moved swiftly for all his bulk, and he whistled as he rushed to the stable. The boy and I ran down into the open yard, hoping to find the horses. The ass brayed again and suddenly animals, darker shapes against the night, shifted like shadows about us.

"Close the gate," I pushed the boy towards it, "hurry. And stay there, yell, wave your arms, do anything to stop the horses getting out." I knew by the drift of the animals that someone hid in the midst of them, directing them. Samson played the telltale, for he constantly sidled sideways, and kept being brought back to the centre. The asses trit-trotted everywhere on neat little feet, squealing and kicking, then one squeezed in towards the middle of the bunch, between Samson and the other horses. This forced the thief forward, tangling him in the ropes he used to lead them. The brief struggle to untangle himself, though only a breath's space, allowed me to see where he was and make for him. I thought I could fright him into swinging up onto one of the horses, and I knew I could catch him if he tried, but the arrogant knave wanted all the animals. He guessed we'd come in amongst the horses after him, so he exploded upwards like a pheasant breaking cover, clapping and yelling. The nags startled, snorting and shying in every direction, the asses ran towards the gate. The thief leapt onto Samson, hallooing loudly, driving all before him. I saw Pedlar Tom bustle along the stable wall, heading for the yard gate. "Stop him, boy," he yelled.

As I hesitated, wondering which horse to jump for, and praying not to be dashed to pieces in the swirling mass, Nowell erupted into the yard like cannon shot. He held a large lanthorn in one hand and waved a pistol. "Samson," he cried and whistled, a real ploughboy's two fingered, ear piercer. Samson squealed and reared up on his back legs. Nowell whistled again and Samson put his head tight down between his knees, kicking and plunging. The other horses crabbed sideways as he did so, to avoid the flying hooves. It became a melee of horse, ass, and men, the noise of Nowell's whistle, the horses' excited snorts and clattering hooves loud in the country night. Nowell's whistle went on and on and Samson jumped, twisted and jounced like a demon in torment. I almost pitied the thief, no one could hold on through that storm of movement. Finally the thief slid sideways, trying to catch himself on the back of an ass as he fell, but that too caught the demon fever, kicking and braying so that the thief landed in a heap surrounded by thrashing hooves. He was horse-wise, for he rolled and escaped with no more than a couple of glancing body blows. I went for my grey horse's head, he being the nearest and having a handy trailing rope. The boy rounded up the asses, cursing them soundly for a demon's brood. Pedlar Tom now stood at the gate, waving his arms and bawling, "Git, git away," to keep the horses back. The din should have brought all into the yard. That it didn't boded ill. Samson headed for his master. Nowell caught the stallion by his mane, raised the pistol, aimed over Samson's neck at the thief, and pulled the trigger. The flash and bang upset the horses again and only Nowell's cry of 'Missed him!' told me what had happened. Tom Pedlar roared as the thief kicked him in the knees and vaulted over the gate to freedom.

"Where's Will?" I called, struggling to settle two thoroughly upset nags and wanting his help.

"Here, permit me." Nowell took the second horse's rope, calmed the bay and led him and Samson back to their stalls. My grey now followed. "Will's holding one of their pistols on those two inside. I've used the other. I'll stay out with the horses whilst you settle the inside problem."

"I'll get Will to bring the saddles and bridles out to you, and we'll be away from here before that villain returns."

Nowell nodded. "I reckon the landlord is in with the group, and Will might need your aid."

I thrust my horse's rope into Nowell's hand. "I'm away." I ran, hoping that Will knew how to use a pistol and that the other pedlar had proved a help, not a hindrance. Raised voices came from the kitchen, but inside the inn bar I saw only overturned furniture, beer puddled on the floor, all signs of fighting. Heart beating hard, feeling responsible for the lad, I looked frantically behind the upset table.

"What did you lose?"

I whipped around. "Will!"

Will's eyebrows rose. "Who did you reckon on seeing?" He sported a developing bruise on his cheek bone and an incipient black eye.

I allowed a smile to express my relief. "Nowell told me you were watching the Brothers Brewer with a pistol in one hand and a pedlar to help."

Will gave me half a painful grin. "The landlord interfered. He came bustling in, demanding to know what was happening outside, went for me and the pistol, blocking me from the brothers. They nipped out and away through the lane door, thumping Pedlar Jack on the way. Now he's after the landlord. They're arguing in the kitchen."

"Aye me, lad." I looked closely at him and adopted a school master's tone. "And whence come those bruises?"

"I met the Landlord's elbow as I dived past to stop the brothers' escape."

"I think we had better join Pedlar Jack and find out what sort of inn this really is."

The landlord, his wife, an old crone and a skinny little maid, huddled in a corner behind the butchering bench, as Pedlar Jack ranted and roared at them. He was as big as his partner and looked to have a meaty fist at the end of a long arm. The landlord, a thin, pointy nosed man, did well to keep out of his reach.

I grinned at Will and tapped the pedlar's shoulder. "If you will allow me?" He halted his stream of abuse. "What do you know of these Brewers, landlord?

The landlord hesitated.

"Come, man. Where do they live? They knew this place and you knew them."

"They visit the village sometimes." A grudging answer, given only because his wife, who looked terrified, poked him.

"You knew what they would do. You prevented Master Verne here from holding them. You struck him." Will scowled and the landlord's wife hid her face in her hands. "How much do they pay you?"

The wife wailed, throwing her apron skirts over her head. The other females cowered, a clear sign of guilt, as was the landlord's swift sideways glance of annoyance at them.

"I'll have your licence for this and the local justice investigate you for consorting with thieves. I'll see your inn banned, a place for decent folk to avoid." The women wailed. The landlord's features pinched together, shock bleaching his complexion.

Nowell, coming up behind me, snorted, much as his stallion would have done. "Oh there'll be plenty more trying this on, when the King raises his standard, but these thieves were the boldest I've yet to meet, and a landlord like this rat had better be scarce or..." I'd never thought to see Nowell in such a rage. He had his hand on his sword hilt, looked likely to stab the landlord through the guts and hang him on his wall.

"Peace, Nowell. If these Brewers have friends somewhere in this locality we'd best move now. They might not want us free to speak of their charming habits to the local authority, whoever he might be."

Will, perched on the edge of the table, and calmly sampling the cheese and oatcakes set out there, spoke through a mouthful of crumbs. "I'll watch this lot with the pedlar here, you fetch the saddles and packs from our room."

The pedlar grunted agreement, his eyes still fixed on the landlord, and we hurried upstairs.

"Young Will was meant to have fetched these," Nowell said, as he struggled to heave one pack, the bridles and two saddles onto his shoulder.

"Not as slow as you thought, is he?" I shouldered two packs, hoisted one saddle and nudged the door open with my foot.

Nowell gave me his frog gape grin. "Quiet and devious is our Will. I can see you are going to have your hands full watching over him in London." He hooked his foot round the door to close it behind us, and we hastened down the stairs.

Saddling and departing took no time at all, We left no coin for the landlord, but a warning to the pedlars to sleep with their asses.

"Aye, we'll be doing that and we're moving off as soon as there's light to see," Pedlar Tom said, closing the gate behind us. "We'll take word to the local constable and make sure that rogue suffers. Do you make a complaint too, good sirs."

I assured him I certainly would, and we rode off into a velvet warm night, clouds cobbled over the moon, the scent of June and summer blowing in on a soft wind. We stayed on the King's highway, ears alert and eyes straining to see anything not in its proper place, or with its right shaped shadow. The horses caught our cautious mood and began eyeing the dark, shying when leaves rustled. We reached the farm in a state of nervous excitement, quietened the dogs, settled the horses, and sat above them in the hay loft, legs dangling, stable boy style, from the open loft door, watching the darkest time of night give way to that pale glow in the eastern sky which heralds the nearness of dawn.

"Nowell?" Will's voice told of his hesitation.

"Yes, my lad?"

Will made a rude noise. "Lad? Ha!" He paused, then asked the question. "You said the King will raise his standard. How do you know?"

"Ah, Will, we farm a good farm, but our wealth comes from breeding fine horses, gentlemen's horses like Samson." I heard the smile in his voice, no mistaking where Nowell's heart lay. "Only the wealthiest can afford them, and they are often the King's companions. In the last year we have sold every available horse to the men around the King. They speak of making one swift attack that will crush the Puritans and Parliament, to give the King London again."

Will scratched his head. I could hear his nails scritch through hair and scalp. "Will they succeed, Nowell?"

"I cannot see what untrained men, led only by religious fervour and without experienced and skilled military leaders, can do against the King's might, his trained soldiers and their generals."

"Jacob, is that what you think?"

I heaved a gusty sigh. "Will, I do not know. The King has military men, trained soldiers, and the might of Kingship. But there are some military gentlemen on Parliament's side. Parliament controls the army. There are bands in training, London is Parliament's and the King doesn't have the navy to support him. It's that loss, the navy, which may well be the vital blow. But I do not know and I don't want to find out."

"If it comes to fighting who will you fight with, Nowell?"

"Come Will, not one of us has a choice. We are bound to keep our oath of allegiance to the King. I must. We all should."

Will scratched his head again. "I don't see how...." His voice tailed away, heavy with tangled thoughts. He nudged me again. "What about you, Jacob, you've claimed to be Puritan?"

"The Merchants Emerick are Puritan by choice, Will. However we have a profitable trading business to keep safe. I do not have a choice in this. I can't stand up to fight for either side, but must fight to keep our business, our ships free to trade. I doubt we'd carry supplies for whoever pays for them - nay, Will, we'd not go that far." Will's mutter of protest stilled. "We'll hold off and pray for a King's Peace and not a King's War."

Nowell released his breath in a series of short huffs. "You'll not get that. They say war is the sport of kings. This King has fought Scotland and Ireland...."

"And lost in both events," I retorted.

Nowell punched my shoulder, I shoved an elbow into his ribs.

"The King has fought in Scotland and Ireland," he repeated. "Now he seems set on fighting in his own country. You will have to choose, Jacob. In the end you will have no choice. Where will you go? The King's navy or Parliament's."

"No navy for me." The hay rustled as both my companions turned to try and see my face. The scent of it, last year's hay, no longer green fresh, but drier, sweet and dusty, filled my nostrils. "Parliament's Cavalry if I must, but only if there is no other way."

Will's elbow nudged my ribs. "And for me. A horse charge, there's the thing. Make the King run." He prodded me again, this time with a knobbly knuckle. "Why not the navy?"

"You are about to meet my family. My brothers will take delight in telling you why."

Nowell gave a sleepy chuckle. "Ah, a member of a nautical family who can't stomach a sea voyage."

I leaned across to thump him, but he had stretched out on the hay, and that seemed a good idea. I heard him chuckle as I rolled Will to one side, telling him to bite his tongue on any more questions, and lay back myself. Will grumbled, but if he asked more questions I didn't hear them. I drifted to sleep worrying again over Loveday's death. Who killed her and why?

# CHAPTER TWENTY-SEVEN
Brockleford, 1st of June 1642

Nowell took us to Brockleford his way, by old pathways and bridle paths that were not the best of roads, but provided a private, gentle ride through leafy woodland and soft green countryside. We'd slept late, but the previous night's excitement kept us watchful. We saw only birds and beasts, flowers and the 'fair fields of England'. My mind was much occupied with Denzil Gamlen, and the obvious cause of his unexpected death, Jameson's death by that same devil's spawn, and how Loveday's death fitted there. The packets Loveday had hidden in her box had been given to Denzil Gamlen, and he died. The contents had killed Granny Tratt. The papers in the box had caused Philip Jamesons' death. Who had cause to strangle Loveday? The answers to all my questions lay in that box, a skein to unravel, and whilst the good Lord knew all, He did not grant me the same knowledge in a blinding flash of insight. What seemed, and what might truly be, I must carefully untangle until the truth stood clear and plain. I let my horse pick his path behind Nowell's and Will's and thought steadily about all four deaths and the reasons for them.

Will tried a few questions, but I gave him scant nothings by way of reply. I think I said 'Aye', twice and 'Nay', three times before sending him to pester Nowell instead. He rode ahead of me and did exactly that, to Nowell's amusement, for Nowell had never been to London either. Eventually I ceased pondering on murder and the problems of seeking justice by revealing the truth, for if I thought aright, then many people would not want to hear my conclusions. The tangle made my head ache, and such a mild early June day deserved better celebration than my ignoring it. I eased my nag between theirs, and Will began his questions again but on a different track.

"Do you think Master Thurloe will be in Brockleford still, Jacob?"

" I hope and pray not. He had a meeting in London." I laughed. "A meeting I was to attend and where I was to be told what the Merchants Emerick must do."

Nowell checked Samson's attempt to bite Will's bay. "And what of friend Knott?" he asked, with a quirk of his eyebrow.

"Let us devoutly pray that Master Knott has gone too. He claims not to have killed the lawyer, Jameson, but that he did bring the body to Eikenthorpe in one of the Fowkes' carts." I nudged my grey out of reach of Samson's snaking neck and threatening teeth. "I am inclined to beat the answers from him, but the parson won't permit it. He protects Knott, and Knott knows far more than he has told."

"Jacob, what do we tell Doctor Maye?"

I looked at Will and shook my head.

"Nothing? You know nothing about Loveday's death?"

"What have we to tell, Will? Before I name names, and disturb him again by visiting him with more sorrow and pain, I need proof of what I believe."

"Then tell me what you believe. "

"That Loveday's death is separate. It came about for another reason."

Both Nowell and Samson snorted. Will glowered, then

grinned at me, tilting his head at Nowell. Man and horse as one, something I'd achieved with Perry, but doubted I could with every horse as Nowell did.

"Why couldn't Lady Fowke have ordered Loveday's death?"

"None of her men at arms are with her. Her only personal servants in Eikenthorpe were Gif and Mary. Neither would harm Loveday." I leaned towards him, trying to poke him. "She would have used poison again if she wished to harm the maid. Quiet and convenient and not easy to discover. None of you noticed Denzil Gamlen had been poisoned."

Will's face darkened as he frowned in confusion. "That's not...it's not what...Nowell what do you comprehend?"

"That your wits are wandering." He laughed openly.

I chuckled too. Will scowled at us both and trotted ahead in a huff. He was still leading us when we reached the edge of Brockleford and came to the turn into Nowell's lane.

Nowell flashed me a grin and called out. "Hold, Will. Turn right into this lane. My home is down here."

Will stopped his horse and waited for us. He gave us a rueful grin. "Is't not enough, good Masters, that my sisters ride me hard, and my brother bates me hourly? Why then do you twit me as well?"

I reached across and patted his back. "Peace, Will. We jest in friendship. Nowell's good name was blackened in Eikenthorpe. I nearly had my neck stretched. That's not something we can talk about with ease. We don't feel kindly towards Eikenthorpe's people, but you're the exception, and we treat you as we'd treat a younger brother."

Will pondered a moment, then nodded. Nowell, holding tight rein on Samson with one hand, leaned over to grip Will's shoulder with the other. Will gave Nowell's arm a friendly slap, and we rode in amicable agreement down the lane and through the gate.

I looked forward to Will's amazement when he saw the Merriot home and met the family, but hardly had we ridden under the archway when we found we were not the only arrivals. Two menservants in dark livery lounged against the open stable doors. A glimpse through the doors showed several horses stalled within.

Nowell frowned. "Who can be trying to buy horses this time?" He looked round for the stable boys and ostler. No one came running as they had before. His frown deepening, he looked up at the closed hay loft doors. "Micah? Benjamin?" His voice bounced back from the stone walls.

They did not come, but one of the two servants straightened up, advanced four or five paces, and bobbed a brief bow. "Master Nowell Merriot?"

Nowell nodded.

"You have urgent business with my master. He's in the house with your father, waiting for you."

If we hadn't met trouble at that inn, back by the ford, I wouldn't have felt uneasy. The way the first servant told Nowell he had business with his master sent a nervous frisson along my spine. The second servant's trick of sneaking sideways glances at our packs and saddle bags, moving his eyes rather than his head, reinforced that faint prickle of alarm. The men wore half capes, although the day was mild. I wondered about the lack of family badges or coats of arms on those capes and about their ability to conceal weapons. Will scented something amiss, for he gave me a look as I tried to give one to Nowell.

Nowell squared Samson to face the men. "And who is your master? I see no badge on your livery." He swung his leg over Samson's rump, dismounting neatly on our side of the horse.

"I'll take your horse," the first servant said, coming forward again, "then you can go to the house and find out what you want to know." His tone should have sounded civil, but I heard something out of key. It was difficult to know how much was overstretched nerves from the previous night, or a real premonition of things about to go wrong. Nowell felt it too for his hands slid close to Samson's bit, and he tweaked the rein attached to the mouthpiece on our side. Samson stamped and swung his rump round into the path of the servant. "Steady now, boy." Nowell's voice soothed, but he kept tweaking the rein, making Samson dance around like a nervy handful. The servant stood off.

"We'll take our horses out to the paddock. You must have a mare coming into season, and I daren't trust my stallion near strange horses." Nowell walked briskly away, still giving Samson those small signals which made the stallion fidget and fret, giving all the appearance of a difficult horse. Will and I rode after him down the yard. The gate to the paddock, at the far end of the yard, was visible, the paddock itself was not. We moved the horses through briskly to unsaddle there.

"Hide the saddles and bridles, Nowell. Help him, Will. You don't want those menservants to forcibly remove your horses if your visitor cannot agree with your father about what's for sale."

Nowell gave me a dry look. "I'd already thought of that, Jacob."

A great chestnut tree grew in the centre of the paddock. I took surreptitious guard near the gate as Will hid the horses' tackle in the lower branches, and Nowell coaxed the horses to stand in the shade beneath the tree. Will beat Nowell in the race back to me. They both raised their eyebrows as I raised a finger to my lips. I'd been thinking some more. I lowered my voice to a murmur. "Leave the packs. Can we hide them too?"

"What's wrong?" Will's voice rose.

Nowell answered. "Our stable boys didn't come, Will, yet strangers were about the stables. They know to always be there when there are visitors. Oh, there might be good reasons, but after last night...." His voice tailed into a sigh.

I saw the remains of hay stacked in a lean-to by the gate. "Nowell, take hay to the horses. Give us a reason for delaying and keep the servants from seeing what we do."

Nowell began pulling hay free, and Will took the first arm load.

"We have our swords?" I touched mine, saw Will's plain band

issue, then Nowell's. "I'll empty the packs of the pistols." Will returned for the next armful of hay. "Have you a dagger, Will? No? Then have a pistol. Good. Now I'll hide the packs."

Will ran with me, carrying the third bundle of hay. He climbed into the tree, and I handed him the packs. He climbed high to hitch them in branches, leaving them well hidden amongst the leafy canopy. Then I unhooked my hidden doublet purse bulging with all the Emerick documents. "Stow that safely in a crotch please, Will." He nodded, clambering up almost to the top to do so, and swung down, branch by branch, to drop beside me, light as a falling leaf.

We sped back to Nowell who was watching his horses unhappily. "Not the way to treat fine horses, young Will, after a long ride, but this time...." His voice faded away, and he looked at us with an unhappy face. "Come, then," he said and the three of us strolled through the gate, carefully fastening it behind us. Neither servant had observed us, for both had disappeared.

We stopped to consider, shrugged and walked on. We had to walk the length of the dividing fence to reach the gate to the house and garden, which was at the farther end beside the main entrance arch. It felt a mile away, and I found it difficult to affect indifference when the hair at the nape of my neck bristled. We were all uneasy. Will kept silent, and Nowell scanned the stable block and barns as we passed each building.

He turned to Will and me. "Where are they? Where did they go?"

I took his arm. "Those servants? In the house perhaps? Keep moving, don't show watchers that we expect difficulties." Nowell grunted and walked on.

I turned to Will. "Will, your pistol may be unloaded, but the butt is of good solid wood." He grinned and patted the front of his cloak which covered the pistol. "Have a care what you try to spit with your sword. Insolent servants usually have an arrogant master who might stick you for waving it about near his noble self." He thought about that and pursed his lips as if to whistle.

I addressed Nowell. "What might be happening in the house, Nowell?"

"Arguments. Mayhap an unhappy purchaser who bought a horse which fell lame. 'Tis never through his own fault, or poor horsemanship, but always ours for selling a bad animal." Nowell's scornful voice told us his opinion. "Sometimes a lady's horse is beyond the lady's skills." He shrugged, gave a faint smile, "Or, as we are careful to say, not mannerly enough for the rider, but, I think, from seeing those menservants, some lord noted one of our horses and wants several, all of the best, today, not tomorrow, and he intends to have them, whether we will or no."

We crunched our way across the gravel to the front door, scanning the windows for unfriendly faces. None. A yard before the first step I felt certain we were three ninnies afrit by moonshine.

Nowell felt it too, for he grinned and spoke up. "My father will have all in hand, everyone polite and courteous, supping and discussing in the eating room, with the ostlers and boys standing round to reinforce his decision." He opened the front door as he spoke, gesturing Will and myself inside. The three of us paused on the threshold, saw the empty hall, stepped inside, and moved off down the hallway. "To my mother's parlour, and you, young Will, doff that hat, in the presence of my lady mother and fair sisters, with the true courtesy they merit." Nowell, watching Will, crowed with laughter at his scowl, and patted his back.

Will held his tongue, with difficulty, judging by the mumbling in his throat.

"Now then, Master Merriot, our Will was taught his manners as well as you," I said, pitching my voice to prate like a parson's clerk.

Nowell laughed some more and stretched over to pat my back. I elbowed him out of the way and opened the parlour door before he had reached the latch.

"Wait 'til you meet Mistress Merriot," I murmured in Will's ear, as he brushed past. He cocked his head in my direction, eyes bright with interest.

We entered with a fine flourish of hats and courtly bows and a chorus of "God give you good day, Mistress."

"I've been waiting for you, Master Nowell Merriot. For you and your companions." The voice was not Mistress Merriot's. "Ah, good. We meet again, Master Jacob Emerick."

We stared at the finely dressed young gentleman, resting easily in Mistress Merriot's carved oak chair with his elbows supported on the chair arms, his fingers steepled under his chin. He was my age or older, certainly only in his twenties, but full of confidence, no, not merely confidence, filled with an arrogance of self conceit.

"Both of you in my net. My waiting has been worth the tedium."

Nowell halted abruptly. Will and I stepped back a pace, flanking him. Where had I met this man? Recently too, for I knew the voice. I observed Mistress Merriot, sitting on a child's stool at the man's feet, spine straight, head high and her hands politely tucked behind her. Nowell took note of her, started towards her, then stopped, his gaze fixed on her. She looked directly at him for less than an eyelid's blink. A breath of ice chilled my spine; her glance held a frantic warning.

"I regret, sir, that I have failed in courtesy and have not accommodated your wishes. My mother taught me better." Nowell bowed to his mother. "And I apologise, Maman, for failing you." Whatever message he had delivered to his poor mother, reduced to sitting humbly at this man's feet, her face did not betray. "How long have you been waiting, sir?"

The door slammed shut behind us. Will whirled round, I turned more cautiously. A thickset gentleman, middle aged, well dressed, though not finely garbed, yet not in livery, leant against the door, his right hand flat against the wooden panels. His left held an unsheathed sword, poised for use.

I grabbed Will's arm and swung him to my right, to prevent

one of his impetuous fits endangering us all. "Easy. Wait. Watch for me." I spoke on a breath, my voice a trickle of sound, barely reaching Will as I gripped his arm to steady him.

He gave me a look, but his eyes said he'd heard.

I rested my hand on his arm a moment longer, then turned my back on the swordsman, bringing Will with me to face the stranger in the chair.

The visitor regarded us with a sardonic smile. "That's wise. Ned is a trained swordsman." He looked at each of us again, then addressed Nowell. "I have waited far too long, Master Merriot. There is little to amuse a gentleman in these rustic surrounds amongst such peasantry." He gestured with a flick of his hand at Mistress Merriot and her beautiful room. It was a wicked spur to goad Nowell's temper and force a reaction, but in that room, surrounded by anything as costly and gracious as could be found in a nobleman's great house, it failed to move Nowell. His control astounded me. I knew what I'd feel if it were my mother sitting at that man's feet.

His lack of reaction did not please the man. "I know you will help me, Master Merriot." His words made a statement, a demand, and, despite the civil modulation, a threat. It was the manner in which he said 'Master', the word polite, yet something beneath the tone belying that civility, which struck a chord in my memory. He had tawny eyes, eyes that looked down a handsome large nose in the manner of one trying to see an insignificant nothing. His nostrils pinched then flared as he regarded us. Contempt? We were beneath his contempt, an unpleasant odour. His clothes, those velvets, that silk and lace, the gold in his ears and on his hands, said lord, his manner recalled someone else I knew from the King's Court.

"If you wish for horses, sir, you must speak to my father. I may not sell or deal without his permission. Where is he?" Nowell remained polite, but wary, and if I had reasoned correctly, and guessed aright, he was wise to be so, for the whole household faced a great danger. My prayers, swift and fervent, begged, not for a miracle, we were too late to ask for that, but that my wits should prove quick enough to outpace this murderous knave.

"Ah, but it's you, not your father, who have something I would like, Master Merriot Just a small thing I want, and you will give it to me."

"Let me speak to my father then. Believe me, I do not have the right or the power to sell or trade." Nowell kept his eyes on his mother, only looking directly at the man as he finished speaking. Something had passed between mother and son. I'd seen Parson Paske play the statue, the enduring man of stone, but Nowell outdid him in stillness as ice to water. "I may not deal with you, sir." His voice, determined, breathed frost and snow, his words struck cold and decided.

"Ah, you play the simpleton, pretend you do not understand." The man scoffed at Nowell. "You will give me Mistress Loveday Maye's writing box and all its contents. I have been waiting here with your family all the weary long day. When I am thwarted, then others suffer. It took time, and some persuasion, to discover that you were not yet returned." The man looked down at Mistress Merriot's head, smoothed his moustache, smirked, and rested his chin again on steepled fingers again. His voice remained as silk smooth as the wall coverings in this elegant parlour, but his boot heel dented the nap of the plush carpet into ugly scars as he ground it in. His nostrils flared, he looked down that long nose at Nowell, then turned his gaze to me. "Master Emerick?" This time his voice barely hid the underlying triumph. "You are to accompany me. You have papers to sign."

I watched him closely. His absolute certainty that we would all comply might prove his undoing, if I could but find a way to use it. "For your lady mother, Master Fowke?"

Beside me Will startled, then eased closer to me. "Who? A Fowke?" he muttered in my ear, but I dared not slacken my attention to make him a reply.

Nowell remained a pillar of adamant, but his mother blinked and blinked, speaking with her eyelids, telling me I had guessed aright. I repositioned my head so that I appeared to gaze fully at Master Fowke, yet I was able to watch Mistress Merriot from the corner of my eye, without showing Fowke what I did. Her closeness to Fowke worried me.

"My lady mother told me you were not quite the unlettered buffoon you seem. Yes, Master Emerick, you have some papers we want. Your brothers prevented me catching you last time, they won't this time."

That was him. In London, those men waiting for me at the foot of the lawyer's stairs. Ah, now I saw clearly the pattern to two, no, three, deaths.

Rolph Fowke looked at Nowell and then back to me. "A long day here in this pigsty, with little to amuse us, has put me out of temper." His voice lost the courtly surface, demanded harshly. "Now, give me what I want, and I will leave."

"The papers..." I paused. To tell him how much I knew jeopardised, not only my life, but the entire Merriot household. We'd seen several horses in the stables. Rolph Fowke wouldn't have ridden into Essex on this errand without a discreetly armed escort. How many and where they were, and where all the other Merriots were, we needed to find out.

Fowke raised his voice. "Ned, persuade the Merchant."

I whirled Will round. "Now, Will." I had my sword out, and Will brandished his pistol before Ned had taken one step.

"I think not." Fowke's voice held a hint of amusement.

I moved sideways so that I could see both Fowke and Ned. Nowell's sword threatened Fowke, but Fowke rested one relaxed leg across the knee of the other. In his hand he held a thin twisted cord of shiny peacock blue. It looked like a hank of the Merriot ladies' embroidery silk, and my heart quailed, for it led from Fowke's hand, under the chair arm, then disappeared beneath the linen and lace collar around Mistress Merriot's neck.

"Touch me, or my men, and your mother will feel it." He leaned forward and raised his hand. "Allow me to demonstrate." His hand ascended, exerting steady pressure on the cord. Mistress Merriot shrank, hunched her shoulders, pulling her head into her neck, bending forwards, trying to avoid the choking he inflicted. That it was painful, her face revealed. Her hands she could not use to try and ease the pressure for they were behind her back, not for polite appearance as I'd thought, but because they were tied there. As she bent lower and lower, I could see her fingers writhe in mute agony.

We all exclaimed in fury. Will and I held off Ned. Nowell, snarling, advanced on Fowke, but Fowke continued to throttle Mistress Merriot.

"Let my mother go."

"For the moment." Mistress Merriot collapsed forward into her lap, breath returning to her throat in harsh gasps, tears turning her eyes to brilliants. "Now put up your sword, and call off your companions."

Nowell grounded the tip of his sword, and I followed his lead. Will, testy as ever, turned on Ned. "Lower your sword," he snapped, pointing his pistol.

"Ah, Ned, we can afford to comply. Lower it, then fetch the others. I am quite safe here." And Fowke was. He gave a vicious jerk to the cord to show us and Mistress Merriot almost tumbled from the stool, her mouth opening and closing as she struggled to breathe again. Ned leered and departed, leaving the door wide open. Nowell did not move, although his hands, held behind his back, curled into fists so tightly that the knuckles made white mountain tops.

"As for you, Master Emerick, you have no choice, we will take you and the papers where you can do no harm. But you, Nowell Merriot...."

Will quivered beside me like a scenting hunting dog; Nowell turned again to adamantine. I broke into Fowke's speech to divert his attention and allow Nowell to steady himself, for we must not act until we could separate Fowke from his men, and disarm them all. "I don't have the papers. They are preserved in Kent where they will be safe and can be presented to the Gamlen heir. I would be a fool to carry them without a safe escort, and a fool? Well, that I am not." My declaration made no impression on Fowke. He simply dismissed my comments with that look down his nose and turned again to Nowell.

"I have your family. My men hold them. Give me my cousin's writing box, and all its contents and I will leave you and your family alive."

Nowell's hands, still firmly behind his back, opened, his fingers splayed out, then bent in a beckoning motion. He shook his head. "Nay, sir, Mistress Maye's box is, by lawful right, her father's and he has it."

Will and I eased forward.

"How now? Puritans who bear false witness. And did you not learn the Ten Commandments at your mother's knee?" Fowke jeered, a quick contemptuous 'Hah'. "I have a man watching the doctor, and I know you have not been to see him yet." He raised his hand, the cord visible. "You two, stand still or...."

We stopped moving.

"The Merriot family is not Puritan. I work for the King, sir, as does my father. The King values our contributions highly, knows our loyalty. I have been gathering information for him in Kent and am shortly to take it to him."

"Be silent." Fowke smoothed his moustache and nodded. "I have heard something of this." He looked at Nowell, and my flesh crawled. "I hear the King pays well for what you bring him. This time I will bring him your lists. His gratitude is all the payment I need, not the gold he pays you. Let that be a lesson to you, who ape your betters." He gave Mistress Merriot's beautiful parlour a disapproving glance and disdainfully toed the carpet with his boot.

Footsteps sounded in the hallway behind us and Fowke smiled. "Ah, my man, Ned, returns with your escort, Master Emerick."

Will quivered, leaning into me, his elbow nudging my ribs. Now was the time to slip his leash. "Out," I murmured, and we charged through the door, swords ready, cannoning into Ned and the two menservants, carrying them down the hallway in a melee of clashing weapons, overbalancing bodies, and multiple collisions. Nowell, Praise God for his quick wits and brave heart, came clattering behind, close on our heels.

"Trap Fowke inside," I called back to him. His expression, the anguish at leaving his mother helpless, when he slammed the door, flamed my anger into burning rage. I freed myself from the heap of bodies, saw Nowell thrust his dagger between the latch thumb piece and catch to hold the door. Will untangled himself from Fowkes' three men amidst curses, flailing elbows and the scree-screeing of metal on metal. He put the pistol butt to good use, crashing it down with a crack on the head of one servant who had fallen to his knees. It was a hard blow. The servant sprawled across the floor, an untidy bundle that tripped Ned, who stumbled towards me. I gathered him close, staying inside his arm reach and away from his dangerous, left handed sword play. We tussled. I tried to bring my sword hilt up under his chin to render him senseless. Ned tried to thrust me away. Will flailed around behind me, crashing his sword against the other manservant's with a horrible screech, fending him off my back. Ned's sword hilt caught my shoulder a painful jar, then he dropped his sword, and swung his fist into my face. I ducked, missing the worst of the impact, catching the end of it on my ear, which vibrated like a struck cymbal. Ned, curse him, fumbled at my belt, for my poniard. I used the short man's advantage, driving my head up into his face, striking him under his chin, but he didn't drop like a log of wood. He staggered back, pulling me with him. We reeled round in a drunken embrace, struggling to catch our breath, panting, feet slipping and sliding on the polished oak floor. Nowell, waiting for an opportunity to intervene, moved round behind Ned, sword ready. Ned knew. He tried to turn and push me away. Will rose from the floor, in front of Ned, dragging the other manservant with him, half choking him. To avoid falling over Will, Ned had to come towards me, and a quick lunge put my sword through his gut. He gave a gasping cough and crumpled at my feet.

It was the first time I had run a man through and the sound of the sword piercing his doublet and entrails, coupled with Ned's spewing up, overset my stomach. Will's white face, and Nowell's down turned mouth told me they felt the same. I withdrew my sword swiftly, leaving the twitching body, the smell of the burst guts, and the blood on my blade as reminders that I had broken the fifth commandment. "Don't look like that, Will. Think what Fowke and his men would do to us." At least the anger washed the guilt away, for a time.

"Or what they have done to my family." Nowell's face told of his fear.

My anger fled, I merely felt sick at what we might discover had been done by these men, and who else we might have to kill. We had so little time to act before we were discovered. I turned to Nowell.

"We must hurry, man. Fowke will be plotting how to defeat us. Hold on to that servant, Will. He'll be useful. Nowell, one nearly dead, one to tie up, what do we do? Can you drag them outside or to somewhere safe?"

"Outside is safer, Jacob, but help me."

Together we pushed and slid the two bodies down the hallway and out of the front door. I stripped off their garters, and Nowell tied up the manservant with them. Haste and anxiety made us clumsy. We fumbled when wrapping up wrists and ankles and I doubt my brothers would have approved any of the knots we used.

"One day, one long day," Nowell repeated as he worked, "one day, Fowke's men have been in my home for one day...one day...Dear Lord, my mother, preserve my mother...one long day...God keep my family."

I let him fret as I considered how many men Fowke had and where the family would be held. I tied a last knot, and we hurried into the house.

Will had the manservant in an arm lock. "I'm persuading him to talk." He noticed our raised eyebrows. "My brother did it to me," he bared his teeth in a kind of grin, "I know it's effective."

"I think," my heart thumped out the moments fleeing past, I had to pause and steady my breaths, "I think if you apply a headlock, Nowell, and you keep tightening that arm lock, Will, but we promise not to kill him, he might speak."

Nowell applied the headlock. Will twisted some more and the combination, plus my promise and request eventually forced the manservant to agree. Will set him on his feet and, as smallest of the three of us, I dodged behind him, twisted his arm up his back and made him walk down the hallway, myself hidden by his taller body. Nowell and Will stalked behind me. I urged the servant on. "Step out, man, and be warned. I made you con the words, remember them. Repeat it to me again."

He mumbled something, and Will jabbed him hard in the ribs with the pistol butt. "Speak clearly, man."

"I'm to look-see if my lord's men are there. If they are I'm to ask pardon and say my lord needs them."

"You'd had better pray you speak right without nods or winks or suchlike hints." Nowell's voice shook. "Give us away and I'll gut you on the spot. This is my home and my family you've been mistreating."

"I will do all you told me." The servant's eyes showed much white, like a spooked horse. He had seen us fight, he knew I'd killed Ned, he believed Nowell's threat, but he hoped, pray God he hoped. He had to. Our word that he and his master could leave was honestly given, although it had grieved Nowell to say it.

I harried our prisoner along. "We must search every room, we can not leave one of Fowke's men overlooked, nor any member of your family, Nowell. But use great care."

Will and Nowell nodded.

I wanted to tell Nowell that I was sure his family were safe, all together. Even a lord like Fowke would surely think to have a mind for the welfare of the Merriots, but I did not know, and to give false hope without certain knowledge was cruel. I held my tongue.

First the eating room. The servant knocked and entered. I crouched low behind him. Will hovered behind me, ready for action, as Nowell squinted through the crack between the open door and door frame. The room was empty. The table, a large and highly polished one, stood bare of any signs of meals taken there. Master Merriot's little room, likewise, held only books and papers.

My hopes raised. It must be as I thought. They had been sensible and taken themselves and their prisoners to the kitchens. They could guard them, be comfortable, and wait for us at their ease.

"I believe we'll find all in the kitchens." I shoved the servant in that direction, but Nowell slid in front and stopped us.

"What of upstairs, Jacob? There are several rooms and the servants' rooms beyond the main bed chamber."

No time to wait, for Rolph Fowke would not wait for us. Time to make a choice and pray it was correct. I turned the servant to face me. "How many men came with Fowke. How many are in this house. Speak man, for if you do not I will take back my word.

"We ought to slit his throat." Will glared.

Will's comment ruffled the servant. He turned sullen and wouldn't reply, no matter what threats and force we applied. It boded ill, but time sped. "Will, deal with him." The pistol butt descended with a thunk and the servant collapsed. "We'd better strip him, with your help, Nowell." Nowell and Will stripped him of cape, garters and hose. I tied him tightly. We dragged him to the front entrance, sliding him on his cape, and rolled him out onto the gravel with the others.

"Nowell, how many horses did you see? You, Will? Could you count them?" They strove to recollect.

"Five, I recollect only five," said Will.

"Two more stalls in that line where we saw them. Better assume seven, and pray God there are no more," Nowell added.

I nodded. "It would be difficult for Lord Fowke to ride openly here with more. I think we can assume we have at most seven men including Fowke, but these men are his lifeguard, and trained to kill as we are not."

We looked at each other, calculating the risk, remembering that silken chord, and wondering what Fowke plotted.

"The man is over confident." Nowell spoke for us all. "He believes we must let him walk out, for he has my mother."

"Come then, back and quickly. Three men accounted for, four to seek. We'll take the kitchens. Quiet in those boots, Will. No, let's leave our boots and slip along in stocking feet. Off with them. Now lead on, Nowell." I picked up the servant's cape as we went.

The hallway turned sharply away from the main rooms towards the kitchen.

We slid our feet over the wooden floor, close against the wall, flattening ourselves against it as Nowell did, when we neared the arched kitchen entry way which led to the pantries and the kitchens. We had to pass through the arched space unseen in order to reach the main kitchen door and that door was open.

A voice called out. I called back, making my voice gruff, flapped the cape before me as though I were doffing it in a huff and we all got into the kitchen behind its swirling movement. Two men guarding the group huddled near the fire began to turn towards us.

"What...?" But Nowell demolished the gaping man, as I tackled the other. Nowell struggled to hold his captive down, called for Will as I finally subdued my man, sitting on his back and banging his forehead against the stones flags. Will dived to Nowell's aid, sank his weight onto the kicking legs and between them they turned their man over and trussed him up in the cape. Nowell left Will to tie the oaf and ran to release his family. I flipped my captive over to tie him and shouted out in surprise, "Knott!"

Now I knew why Fowke came to be here. Now I understood who had told him of Loveday's box. "You Godforsaken traitor! You Satan's spawn! You murderous misbegotten devil!" I shook him. He used the movement to crack his head against mine, freed an arm, and punched me hard in the ribs. We rolled over and over in a tangle, coming to a halt against legs of the kitchen table and, bracing myself against them, rage giving me strength, I managed to heave myself up, bringing Knott with me. I held him tight by the throat, all but throttling him. He choked, sagged, and I changed my grip, twisting him to hold his body tightly against me.

Will and Nowell ignored us, busy freeing the Merriots. I swayed, gripping Knott from behind, bending him backwards, my forearm choking him. I expected a great clamour of crying and wailing from the servants and children, a babel that any other of Fowke's men still free would hear. I had been anxious to hush them, but as Nowell's sisters, brothers and the servants became free of restraints they collapsed into each other's arms. I only heard whimpers and choked sobs. The poor abused souls had wept themselves dry. Why? What had happened to them all? I dragged Knott, who was slowly turning blue, to see what his meddling had done. They sat in a shuddering mass, looking much like they had when we arrived.

"Where's our father, our sister?" Nowell counted heads, looking anxiously over the group several times. "Cissy? Where's Marianne?"

She did not reply. The poor maid, fourteen at most, I'd hazard, appeared whey faced, flesh drawn to bone, her eyes empty. The older servants, women, turned faces full of fear in our direction. The little children huddled, hiding their faces.

I pressed my forearm tighter against Knott's throat, bringing him near. "See what evil you have done, you monstrous beast. How have these folk deserved such treatment?" Will, his mouth as round as his eyes when he beheld who I was throttling, came to help, and as I released the man, he shoved Knott towards Nowell.

"Where is my father?"

Knott, his face still empurpled, voice uncertain, pointed a finger towards the ceiling. "He objected to the treatment of Mistress Merriot and was much beaten about the head. They carried him upstairs. I doubt he survived." His voice held not one vestige of concern.

Nowell swore, cracked his palm across Knott's face, then threw him at Will. "You callous monstrosity." He could not say more. Will caught Knott and dragged him away.

I looked at the hostages. They also thought Master Merriot doomed, their troubled faces told us.

Nowell's skin stretched across his face so tightly that every bone stood out. I think we both knew then. "My sister, what of Marianne?"

More wails and sobs. "We told them, we said she was our sister, but they took her, dragged her off with Agnes." Cissy could barely speak.

Knott, pushed down on a stool beside the table, raised his head. "She didn't look like her sisters. They thought she was a maidservant like Agnes." He shrugged.

Nowell exploded, a tempest from hades, whirling across the room to crash into Knott, fists pounding him, like storm waves crashing against a ship's hull. "And you did naught to prevent them." Thud, crash, Knott's face bloomed scarlet. "God forgive you, for I surely never will." Knott went down under the rain of blows. It was a brutal attack. Will wrenched Nowell away, begging him to be steady, to be rational for his mother's sake, but he shook Will off and dashed out of the kitchens.

"Tie Knott up, Will." I fled after Nowell and caught him before he mounted the stairs. I dragged him back. "Your mother..."

"My sister..."

"Nowell, a day, they've been here a day, you know what men like these do to serving lasses. It will be too late for your sister, you know that, but not your mother. We can save your mother." Some truths should never have to be spoken, so painful are they. Nowell's face bore such pain no man's face ever should. "Nowell, steady man. Reason it out."

He shuddered with something part sigh, part sob, I grasped his shoulders to hold him upright, but he shook me off. "I am going to kill them," he hissed, "every man jack of 'em."

"Permit me to accompany you. Slowly and softly, friend, we must save your mother and that means taking every Fowke man unawares."

He sped up the stairs, ascending on cat's feet. I followed as quietly. It took little skill to find them. The rooms upstairs had their doors flung open, their contents tossed and turned. Only one, the great bedchamber as it turned out, had a closed door. We paused, eyed each other, nodded, then Nowell stealthily lifted the latch and eased the door open. It swung inwards without complaint, giving us clear view across the room to the carved great bed. What I saw in an eye's blink seemed to imprint itself across my very soul and sear it there in all the horrific detail for the length of my life.

A maid, not Marianne, for straggles of fair hair trailed across her back, cowered naked, curled up like a whipped puppy, at the foot of the bed. She looked all over blotches of blue and purple, her pallid flesh showed as rare white spots between the bruises, streaks of dried blood darkened her upper thighs. Her wrists were bound together with bed cord and she whimpered, occasionally shuddering.

I had two sisters, as dear to me as Marianne was to Nowell, mine I'd seen put into the cold clay last winter, but I'd rather have them there than be hurt as Marianne was. Two sniggering men held her between them. Her arms, raised above her head, were tied at the wrist on a long piece of bed cord, then tied again high up on a bed post. The men jeered, and called her foul names. One would grip her tightly by the breasts, squeezing, and brace her for the other to drag her legs apart and force his engorged cock into her, ramming it like a spear. Their vicious enjoyment, the evil cruelty and bestiality of their acts sickened me so my gorge rose. I doubted that our rescue would ever remove the anguish and misery engraved deep in lines on Marianne's face, and that piteous face would have made a rock weep.

I fought down vomit. Nowell's knees buckled. I grasped his elbow and whispered into his ear, "Hold up man." I had thought him pale before, now every freckle looked black. He swallowed, drew his knife and indicated the near man as his goal. I loosed my sword and slid across the floor to the farther man as Nowell ran at his.

Two devils, with their breeches loose and like to slip down to their ankles, busy about their filthy work, would, I reckoned, present no complicated task. The difficult task would be to stop Nowell gelding them. Nowell arrived like an avenging angel and had his man down, dagger in his neck, before they knew of our presence. Mine had been the cautious one. His sword lay on the bed coverlet. He thrust the hapless Marianne into me and reached for it, kicking off his breeches and leaping onto the bed. He was a swordsman, this one, for that sword came at me like a lightening bolt.

Nowell, anxious to cut Marianne down and cover her, reached out and tugged the quilt, which saved me, for the man overbalanced and his thrust went wide. I skewered him without compunction, but with a prayer, and left him on the bed. I seized another cover for the maid. Neither one could speak, although Nowell reassured Marianne repeatedly, calling her name again and again, assuring her that all now was well.

It was as I bent down to wrap the maid in the cover that I found Master Merriot. He lay on the floor on the other side of the bed, his face swollen and battered. His breath came in slow gasps, and rattled. He seemed barely alive to me. Someone, possibly Marianne, had tried to wash and bandage his head, but he needed swift medical aid. We wanted Doctor Maye urgently.

I left Nowell weeping over Marianne and his father, went to investigate each room. Indeed they were empty. Fowke must have sent his men searching for Loveday's box, and they had not been careful how they had hunted. The last room had a window overlooking the garden and yard. I gazed out, looking across at the stable, I reckoned the ostlers and boys were shut up in the hayloft, and wondered if we could free them. Then I heard horses on the gravel and a voice issuing commands. It was an answer to my fervent prayers, for this was not more Fowkes. I knew that voice.

I hurtled along the passage and down the stairs, cursing under my breath as my feet slipped and slithered. The commotion outside the front door, where we'd left bodies, confirmed my belief. I wrenched open the door and saw the group. Praise the Lord, indeed. "A God's name, why didn't you arrive earlier?" I darted out and seized the doctor's arm. "Up the stairs with you, doctor, and pray make haste, Master Merriot is in sore state, like to die, and there are two young women most evilly used, in great need of your care." He hurried away and left me looking daggers at John Thurloe, the Tunnaces and three other soldierly men.

"Did one of the stable boys get free of the loft and inform you of the Merriots' plight?"

Thurloe shook his head.

"Then one of you men need to let them out."

Thurloe waved a hand and two of the three men set off. "Guard all the horses and see to these captured men," he called after them.

"Do you have him?" Thurloe turned to me, pushing me before him so that we now stood in the entrance hall. The others loomed behind him, black hulks against the sunlight.

"Who?"

"Rolph Fowke, Master Emerick. Is he here?"

"How do you know to expect Fowke?"

"We set a trap, of course. Jacob, is he here?"

"Aye, and like to choke Mistress Merriot. What trap did you set? Did you send that hell hound, Knott, to Fowke." I was nearly incoherent, thinking on what the Merriots had suffered all this long day.

Thurloe's eyes narrowed, he gave me a measuring look. "What has gone on here?"

"Don't play an innocent, Master Thurloe." He continued to stare. "Had you no notion of what would happen if you told Rolph Fowke how to get hold of Loveday's papers and the Merchant Emerick's lawyer? Come and see."

I grabbed his arm and towed him roughly, he protesting at my grip and haste. The Tunnaces came behind, objecting to my behaviour. We entered the kitchen amidst much racket and fuss. The Merriot children and servants, still huddled in disarray, gazed at us in a panic. Will, guarding the two men, looked anxiously at us over his pistol as we entered.

"Aid and rescue in your present distress, oh, Merriots. Look who has come, Will." His frown faded. He gave us a relieved grin. "Doctor Maye is here to help," I told the huddle.

"The family need aid, Master Thurloe. These poor ill-used little ones have been tied and kept here since the Fowkes first came." I whirled him round to my other side so that my voice went to his ear alone. "Their father is upstairs, much beaten about the head and their oldest sister and a maid were kept in the same room, tied and raped for sport and amusement." Thurloe gaped at me. "What did you expect when you sent Knott off?"

"We expected you to return swiftly before Rolph Fowke arrived. We have been waiting for you since yesterday."

I swore bitterly. "No blame is mine, John Thurloe. Your plan was ill-conceived, bound to go awry." I gestured towards Will. "Release Will from his guard duty, set one of your men to take these," I prodded the trussed up servant and Knott, "to the others outside and get another to bring down the bodies from the master bedroom. Then let us gather a company of armed men, there are enough ostlers and grooms to help, for we must make a show of might to overcome Fowke." Thurloe regarded me, face as unrevealing as ever. I cursed him, raised my hand to hit him and yelled, "Hurry, man, for Mistress Merriot's sake."

He blocked my blow, gave his orders. The Tunnace brothers dispatched them and sent a man back in to Brockleford to fetch their women to give aid. "Bring Doctor Maye's servants too," Thurloe added.

Will, I wanted safe away from possible danger, and those sights upstairs. I took him aside, and, under cover of getting the fire fed and water boiling, asked him to slip away quietly to fetch Loveday's box from the chestnut tree to give to Doctor Maye.

"Watch yourself lest a Fowke is loose in the stable yard or hiding in the hay lofts."

He grinned. "I'll take my pistol and ward off any such." He departed.

I left Thurloe to organise the kitchen and his men, and ran upstairs to Nowell. The doctor had Master Merriot in his bed. Both Marianne and Agnes had been removed to another room. Nowell still raged, and the doctor was frantic for useful assistants.

"Come Nowell, we'll set your mother free and she will organise all for the doctor." I looked across at him. "We've sent to Brockleford for your servants, and the Tunnace womenfolk will be coming with them, doctor."

Nowell remembered his mother, stood undecided, looking to his father's body on the bed, then through the door to the room where his sister lay. Finally he drew himself up, ceased shivering and clapped my shoulder. "Let's be doing it then."

In the hall way beside the parlour door Thurloe, and his men waited. The Tunnace brothers and their two companions drew pistols, half cocked them and looked to Master Thurloe. I caught him by the elbow. "No, let Master Merriot go before us. He might, God willing, find a way to prevent more harm."

Nowell withdrew his dagger from the latch. The catch clicked, a metallic sound louder than a canon blast to my ears.

"Open the door with care, he may wait behind or near it, ready to kill you." Noah Tunnace should have saved his breath, for already I had edged to the hinge side of the door, intending to peer through. Nowell eased open the door, keeping it between him and any waiting swordsman.

"Come in, pray do." The same voice, as calm and arrogant as before. "Let me see you all."

Nowell had his sword out, and we walked in behind him. Rolph Fowke sat at his ease, left knee hooked over the chair arm, left hand holding the silk cord resting on that knee, his sword, in his right hand, at the ready. Mistress Meriott sat as she had before, but the silk rope was visible round her bruised neck.

Rolph Fowke gave us his calm dismissive stare. "Ah, and you hope to detain me. How?"

"Your men are dead or captured. Leave my mother and come with us in safety."

Fowke threw back his head and laughed. "I am a Fowke, one of the King's Court and a close companion. You cannot touch me, for his Majesty will most surely touch you, and all that is yours, if you dare."

His arrogant confidence amazed me. "The King will return to London will he? He will come specially to this place to release you? And does our King support proven murders, men who invade the home of one of his loyal subjects and raise havoc?"

"His Majesty is always grateful to the Fowkes."

Nowell slipped a little closer. "His Majesty is always grateful to the Merriots. Who will he support in the case of murder and mayhem we Merriots shall bring?"

Rolph Fowke did not own remorse, why should he? He sneered. "Merriots speaking against we Fowkes? His Majesty knows how to deal with overweening presumptuous citizenry like you.

"You mean he is about to declare war on his own people." This from Master Thurloe in a quiet voice.

"On rebels. Those who ignore the King's commands are insolent traitors," Fowke snapped. "I am one of those who will assist him. He will aid me." He expected his words to free him, but he prepared himself, dangerously so. "Bring my horse to the door and I will exchange this old jade," he tugged the cord and Mistress Merriot swayed, "for my stallion."

"No." The cry came from Mistress Merriot. "Never, Nowell, never turn this animal loose." Fowke jerked the cord and she choked, her voice dwindled to a gasp.

"Be silent, wretch."

She sucked in air and struggled on, defiant. "I will see you hang as a common criminal for my husband's hurts."

Fowke's face twisted. "Silence, you drab!" He choked her again, but instead of sinking onto her stool she found hope and strength in our presence. That brave lady threw herself against his side.

We moved together. A Tunnace sword sheared the silk cords, Nowell caught his mother, but Rolph Fowke held the other Tunnace and his companions off at sword point.

"Pistols against a sword and at close range. Why don't you shoot?"

They did not, and Nowell swept his mother to safety on the window seat, then came from behind, sword thrusting.

Fowke fought and swore and struggled, but we closed in, knocked his sword away and surrounded him. Master Thurloe stepped forward. "You are arrested, Rolph Fowke, for numerous nefarious crimes, murder is one of the many, you have committed."

"You cannot arrest me."

Master Thurloe was unmoved. "You will be taken to London and tried, your crimes broadcast so that all may know what the King's men do for the King. Bind him well and take him into town, Abel." We watched as a livid Fowke was dragged away. Thurloe turned to me. "You must see why we need Rolph Fowke alive. His trial will give us much support from those hesitating to choose."

So there was an end to it all. I breathed deeply in relief and left Nowell to see to his mother. I had to find Will and prevent him handing over the box in front of Thurloe or his men. I went to seek him, wondering how we could best help the Merriots. I had scant knowledge of the sick and ailing, but I could see to fires, organise servants to tidy those ransacked rooms and fetch and carry until the women arrived.

Outside, two of the Tunnace men had the Fowke servants and lifeguards roped together in a line, each well tied, ready to be led from horseback. Someone had fetched a small hay cart, and the dead were dumped upon it. Over in the stables, released stable boys and ostlers attended their neglected charges. Life began to resume again its familiar pattern for the Merriots. I ran to stop Will walking into the bustle, slid through the paddock gate and caught sight of him leaping down from the chestnut tree. He had my pouch purse, but he didn't place it on the ground and climb again for the box. Instead he rested his back against the tree trunk and unfastened it.

I expected Will to look round, make certain he was unwatched. I slithered down into the remnants of the hay, by the lean-to wall, but Will never lifted his eyes from the documents he pulled out. What did he seek? Then I knew and groaned aloud. The land deeds. He meant to take them. In any future dispute with the King's men those deeds would have the greatest legality. All the parts of the puzzle sprang together in my mind in one swift flash of comprehension, but I would not believe where my thoughts led. Yet, and yet...I rose and sped across the grass.

"Will, what ails you, you fool. I've promised your father a document giving him tenancy. You don't need the deeds."

Will started and thrust the purse and papers behind him. The guilt writ across his face and in his eyes told me.

"Oh dear God, no, Will. Not you, heaven forfend. What devil tempted you so? Did Loveday tell you she had your farm deeds?" I grabbed him by the shoulders and shook him.

He swung a hard fist in my ribs to make me release him. "Leave off, Jacob. It just happened."

"What? Explain yourself, you fool boy."

"She was there, down by the bank. I'd been watching, and I knew. She'd told me about your papers, she was going to get them to her father. I'd seen her leave the manor with a bundle. But I followed too cautiously, and she's hidden the box before I could see where."

"You didn't need to kill her, Will." My voice rose. "You didn't have to kill her." I looked at the boy and could not believe that this lad, impulsive and hot headed though he could be, had actually placed his hands around Loveday's neck and strangled her. Red rage surged. I hit him, smashed him back against the tree. His head thunked against the trunk.

He raised his arms to protect his head. "Let be, Jacob, let be. I didn't mean to hurt the maid. I loved her." This came as an anguished wail. "Jacob, I was desperate. I knew she had Emerick papers with our deeds amongst 'em. I jumped down to catch her shoulders and give her a shake. We slipped on the mossy rocks and I fell. My hands gripped around her throat as we fell. I didn't want to kill her." He wept. "We were clutching at each other and I...God forgive me...I grabbed her throat as we tumbled down. I didn't mean to hurt her."

I closed my eyes and tried to believe him. He was a quick tempered, thoughtless lad, but he had loved the maid. Yet, and yet, God forgive my thoughts, he'd shown no signs of remorse or torment all the days I'd known him. Will Verne had murdered Loveday. Yet I liked Will, who'd become a pesty younger brother to me, one who had supported me in the face of the community. Did he kill her in a fit of temper, regretting what he'd done the moment it occurred or was it an accident, as he claimed? And, oh dear God in Heaven, what should I do? Who to tell?

Before I could do or say more a furor began in the stable yard. I snatched my purse and documents from Will. "Come," I cried, "we'll sort you later."

We ran to the gate and into the yard. A fight had broken out down where the prisoners were.

I grabbed Will's arm. "My saddle pistols. I'll fetch them from the stable, you sneak up and see what's to be done. Have a care." We ran together, but my turn of speed was greater than Will's. I reached the stable doors with him pounding after me.

An ostler and two boys shoved at the doors, closing them. "Hold!" I slipped through. "My saddle pistols?"

The ostler waved one in his hand. "It's loaded, master, we..." but I seized it, yelled for them to bar the stable doors, and ran out. The doors crashed shut behind me as I paused in the shelter of the water trough and looked for the problem. One Tunnace brother lay on the ground. A man, dressed well but plainly, like Fowke's man,

Ned, had ridden into the yard and ridden him down. He flung himself off his horse to slash free Rolph Fowke, tossing him the sword. Fowke whirled to hold off two more of Thurloe's retinue, pinking one as I watched. The horse ran loose half way between me and them. I realised this must be Fowke's man who kept watch on the doctor and cursed my forgetfulness. We should have looked out for him. The man ran towards the horse, calling Fowke to come. I started for the horse and discovered Will before me, by the fence, screened by the greenery. He crouched, then ran beside the fence, that pistol still in his hand. He reached the place opposite the horse before the man and charged him down as he arrived. The pistol descended with a vengeance, and the man fell to the ground, clubbed into insensibility.

I waited, my pistol raised and ready to fire, covering Will, at the same time frantically urging him to bring the horse to me. The horse, with an unfamiliar hand on the bridle and panic in the air, proved difficult, tossing his head and pulling away from Will. "Mount and ride, Will," I yelled, "Fowke is upon you." Indeed he was fast approaching.

The wretched nag shied as Will tried a leap into the saddle and circled so that its body loomed between me, Will and Fowke. I dare not shoot and rushed forward to be sure of being in range as soon as I could see. Will scrambled himself up to dangle half over the horse and thumped its ribs with his fists.

The horse plunged, started towards me. Will raised his face, his grin touching each ear. "I have it safe..." Then he disappeared backwards, pulled off the horse, reappearing with a crump as he landed on his belly in the gravel.

I ran, calling Will by name, dodging the startled horse which careered past me to stop at the stable doors. Will lay still stunned, breath knocked out of him. Fowke stood over him, sword raised.

I stopped, aimed the pistol, braced my arm and yelled. "Submit, Fowke or, by God, I will shoot." Fowke looked up, his head turning from the horse behind me, to my pistol. "Make no mistake, Master Fowke, this is a good flintlock pistol, and I can shoot very well with it. Run at me if you will, you won't take more than three paces."

Will stirred, tried to roll over, but rolled the wrong way, into Fowke's feet. He began to push himself up, shaking his head and coughing the dust and gravel from his mouth. Fowke sneered at me. "Then I'll take another of you Puritan rebels with me." I squeezed the trigger, but Fowke had flipped Will over with a booted foot, plunged his sword into the boy's stomach, wrenching it viciously, slicing sideways, before the powder flashed and my bullet to his chest toppled him over.

"Will!" Oh God, not Will. I flung myself down beside the boy raging. How many times must I watch a friend die? Oh great God Almighty, was this thy design for Loveday's sake? Where would I find the courage to tell his parents. I'd given my word to them, promised I would take care of him. I cradled Will against my chest, turning his face to look at my face and away from the gaping gut wound and the rhythmic gush of blood.

"What...I hurt...Jacob?"

"Yes, Will. Hold hard, man, you're safe."

"Did we...stop him...that...Devil's spawn...."

"Fowke? Yes, you drove the horse away, and I shot him."

There were people round me now, legs crowded close, voices hushed and low. Doctor Maye pushed through, stood looking down, shook his head.

Nowell elbowed in, panting. "I saw it from my sister's room." He collapsed to his knees beside me, touched his hand to Will's cheek. "You did great work today, young Will, we thank you, my family thanks you, for what you did."

Will tried to speak, trembled, exhaled. Some of his dark curls fell over his forehead, obscuring his eyes. I pushed them away and saw the life light fading there, the rich brown darkening.

I leaned forward to whisper, "Be easy, Will. I'll tell your family only of your deeds today. God forgives all sins. Take Loveday

Nowell's love and mine as I will surely give your family yours." He managed the faintest flicker of a grin. I couldn't speak more for my tears stopped up my throat.

Nowell's voice sounded out with barely a tremor. "Go in peace, Will, in surety of God's great mercy and many blessings. Take our prayers with you."

And Will sighed, and left us.

# CHAPTER TWENTY-EIGHT

Eikenthorpe, June 1642.

We took Will home speedily the following day, changing horses regularly, riding through the night, speaking little. I still raged at Master Thurloe's interference, and he was angered over Rolph Fowke's death. A messenger had gone ahead. Parson Paske met us with Will's father at the hillock with two hawthorns, and we transferred Will's body from the Merriot wagon to a cleaned cart, the floor of which was decently covered with green boughs, bunches of fresh herbs hung at each corner. We placed the body there in silence; we rode to Eikenthorpe in silence. There the whole of Will's family listened and wept. I gave a carefully incomplete report. They merited only that truth, which would give them no more pain. I detailed each Fowke member's part of their family's villainy, and praised Will's good deeds. Master Thurloe witnessed my statements.

I doubt that Will's death as part of a larger piece of mischief comforted his parents, but one sister told me she was glad it hadn't been as the result of a foolish accident. It didn't comfort me. Guilt rode hard on my back, an imp whose vicious goading told me repeatedly that I should have fired my pistol as soon as I had aimed at Fowke. My conscience smote me. Had I deliberately waited, wanting Will's death for Loveday's life? And didn't his death ease the problem of telling Eikenthorpe that one of their favoured sons had murdered? My new flintlocks had a quicker, better firing record than my old wheel-lock pistols, even though the distance was at the pistol's limits. Why hadn't I fired sooner? I couldn't forgive myself, and I found it a shaming thought that I'd not taken account of the man Rolph Fowke told us watched the doctor. A guilty conscience weighted me down, peace of mind fled.

I carried a letter Nowell wrote for Will's parents. He could not leave his shattered family, but sent their thanks and the promise of two good horses from those left by Fowke, as Will's rightful share. That gave further proof of honour to Will's death. Let it be seen that way. I closed my lips over any words which might hint at other things and prayed for Will's salvation.

The following day we took Will from his home to the Eikenthorpe churchyard and buried him next to Loveday. All Eikenthorpe attended and I was subjected to much malevolent castigation and vilification for failing to protect him. The people of Eikenthorpe, only knowing that he had left, with me, to visit London, felt free to point out the error of my ungodly ways in not returning him safely.

After the ceremony I walked along the river path, living in my mind's eye the events of the last weeks, seeing again Loveday riding out on my Perry, Will coming to meet me on his shaggy cob. Nowell, Will and I hunting Loveday's box. I could not take back the time past, but, oh, I wished I had better spent it.

I went as far as Gamlen Manor in most melancholy humour and stared at the house. All this wanton mayhem for a title, that manor, and the Emerick gold. And all because a King stubbornly refused to be flexible. It sickened me. Denzil Gamlen, the lawyer Jameson, and Granny Tratt, their lives the cost of buying a title from our King. Loveday and Will dead because Denzil Gamlen died. All their priceless lives set against the value of gold, a useless metal, whose only worth came from the glitter of a King's promise, a King who debased the honour of a title to a mere commodity to be bought and sold.

I walked back to the parsonage shaking my head at humanity's evil and heart sore for the loss of my friends. Master Thurloe, already at the parsonage, would do well to hide himself. I began to see how he could be blamed as well.

On my return the parson bid me welcome at the front door, bustled me to his study and wished me to explain all. I promised him a full account after supper and he took pity on my sad state, allowing me to escape to Mistress Paske's room by the kitchens to weep and mope. Right glad I was to see friendly faces and be treated with kindly concern. The three Graces pattered after me, sat me down, sat round me and on my lap, then asked me to hear their recitations, Song of Solomon this time. Their mother and Tabitha never gave the little maids cause, by look or raised brow, to believe their behaviour improper, and the nearness of their chubby bodies, their gentle prattle radiated a physical warmth which nearly warmed my spirit. After their readings they requested music. I had neither the mirth for songs, nor the joy to shape my lips to the flute, but the twenty third psalm was always a comfort when belief wavered, and God's presence seemed more nearly an absence. They remembered my tune and Parson Paske had us all sing it at evening prayers. He, as at Loveday's death, would not be doleful, nor weep for Will, though Mistress Paske and the three Graces had eyes stained by weeping. Will had been one of Eikenthorpe's favoured sons. I saw how they hurt, as I did, for the space his death would leave in their lives.

Supper was brief, but comforting to the stomach, a custard, thick pease soup with fresh herbs and soft cheese dropped in it, small ale, and oatcakes dripping with honey. Tabitha fetched the three Graces away to bed and Parson Paske granted me permission to say 'Good night' and 'God Bless', as well as 'Farewell'. Master Thurloe and I had to be off by cock crow. I bussed the maids roundly and was hugged and kissed in return. I listened to Mistress Paske sing them to sleep, the lullaby an old old song, words so ancient they didn't make sense to my ears. Mistress Paske told them over as we walked down stairs. Very like the lullabies my mother used to sing, those same comforting words: be not afraid, sleep safe in God's hand, be at peace. I found myself wondering if Will had heard them too and felt that weight of guilt yet again. And what should I say? Did I tell the parson the truth about Loveday's death?

Master Thurloe attended our after supper conversation. I knew he acted as eyes and ears for at least two powerful men, men who supported John Pym's party, and therefore I had to check and choose every word before it left my mouth. Now I waited, willing to speak only after Master Thurloe had confessed, penitent for his part in the matter.

We settled in what had been the great hall where first I met Will. Building had finished on the one half now, the smell of the new building and brick dust damped down by the smell of Mistress Paske's cleaning and scrubbing. We sat within the space of the carved screens, huddled against the darkness beyond us, hovering over us, in the height of the hall. The ox sized hearth, empty of fire, Mistress Paske had filled with herbs and flowers, all tied in small bunches, hanging head down. She begged our pardon. "For there is a fine draught makes its way up the chimney, and my herbs dry well here."

Master Thurloe, seated with Parson Paske on the settle with its back to the door, gave his cousin a slight smile. "The scents will savour our sad tale and cheer Master Emerick and myself. He will be, I know, as content as I, to finish this mismanaged business and return to his home."

I gave him the kind of glance my mother called 'a look' and decreed to be impertinent. "Why a'God's Name did you begin all this, you Parliament men? How could you think we Merchant Emericks would pay our gold, yes, our gold, not Gamlen gold, and let our new ships be taken?" I couldn't help it, for all my wishing to be restrained, the words burst forth.

Master Thurloe gave another of his rare smiles, a self depreciating one. "Ah, Master Emerick, all knew the Merchant

Emericks had built two large trading vessels with money loaned by Denzil Gamlen. Now the King needed ships, offered much for them, and we knew Lady Fowke promised him yours."

"There are many Merchants with pinnaces as good which the King might seize." I gave Thurloe a wolf's smile, teeth bared.

Thurloe was no fool either. He returned my smile with one as empty of cheer and sighed. "Truly, Master Jacob, the Emericks are not the only merchant family to be requested to keep ships and gold from the King. Nor are they the only merchants who had someone working beside them to prevent the King receiving anything of benefit from them."

"Well then, let it be. The Fowkes have gained naught but Cain's reputation, and one day we will see them in a court of law to answer the charge. Will you, Parson Paske, hold onto the evidence, keeping it safe?"

The parson nodded. Mistress Paske lifted her head and spoke. "We know what Lady Fowke and her son have done and why. But what of poor Loveday. Who hurt that pretty maid?"

So it came to the moment where I must decide to speak or say nothing. To confess my knowledge of what Will had done, or to remain silent. My conscience begged to be relieved of the knowledge, my heart quailed at the destruction the truth would make. I did not know what to do, and the Lord provided no answer. Oh, I could make them swear on the great family Bible, but it says much of what I had learnt since coming to Eikenthorpe that I knew Mistress Paske would keep her word, as would, I was nearly certain, Parson Paske, but I had doubts that Master Thurloe would. Was the pain given to the Vernes, the whole community, worth knowing the truth? And Will had said it was an accident. I had no proof to the contrary.

Mistress Paske spoke again. "Let me understand fully, Master Emerick. Did Lawyer Jameson truly meet his death for the sake of mere papers?"

"Aye, Mistress, for that paper from Denzil Gamlen which he did not have."

Mistress Paske pressed her lips together, and her face showed such sadness I wanted to reach out and comfort her. "That poor man and his bereft family."

"Blame our King, Mistress, for that one paper would have gained an earldom for the Fowkes. The King would have given them any honours they asked for if they could have presented him with our ships and gold."

"To use in a war that need never be." Mistress Paske looked at both men. "Isn't there a way to stop it?"

Master Thurloe spoke with more animation than I'd ever seen in him, yet he sounded more hopeful than believing. "Those I work for haven't given up. His Majesty will not discuss, talk or reason with Parliament. He has made such a divide, a great earthworks between himself and his people. His Court and advisors are far removed from his people, but we hope, by removing all opportunities, to force him into a place where he has nowhere else to turn and would finally talk to those men of reason who want no part of warmongering."

Thurloe paused, looked at us in turn, rubbing his brow, as though by doing so he could smooth away the problems. "Your Emerick ships were all a part of the great whole, Master Emerick. Remove from the King any hope of winning a war and he must compromise and settle."

"Yet his Majesty is in York, refusing to talk to Parliament," said the parson, "where is his show of compromise?"

Mistress Paske turned our thought into words. "He won't will he? There will be fighting."

We said nothing, but we were agreed.

Mistress Paske shook her head. "It's all a part of something too evil to contemplate. And I dare not, cannot think that any of God's creatures could kill so lightly, for earthly privilege." Her voice fell away into a whisper. "Especially within a family."

"We know what Lady Fowke and her family have done, cousin. What provoked her to this action was our King. His stubborn...."

I could take no more. "And what of Parliament's actions, John Thurloe. There's a family in great distress in Brocklehurst because of you and Knott."

"Neither side," the parson spoke slowly, every word considered, "has done well." That was a rebuke to John Thurloe, and Thurloe knew it.

Mistress Paske sighed. "Can what we have and know bring Lady Fowke to justice?"

Master Thurloe's face registered a kind of grim satisfaction. "I believe we have her, enough to insist on questioning her and to demand justice from the King."

"Such evil." The parson closed his eyes, his lips moving in a swift prayer.

"If the poison is identified in the sachets," I looked to Thurloe, "there might be a strong case against her for the murder of her brother, and the old grandam. My brothers can bear witness that Rolph Fowke and his men were in London, but the Fowkes are presently surrounded by strong protectors. The King might well dismiss all, preferring to blaming her son, because he is dead, and cannot answer any questions. I doubt we can do any more."

Master Thurloe interrupted. "I think there are ways and means to make the information known to many. Rest assured that the Fowke family will become notorious for their evil ways."

"Then," asked the parson, "What of Loveday?"

I shook my head, "No Fowke hand touched her. Denzil Gamlen's murder created problems and Loveday died because of them."

Mistress Paske looked at me, "Master Emerick, Jacob, what do you know?"

"Nothing to share."

She knew I lied. Her eyes narrowed as she thought, and she blinked rapidly. Her husband stretched out his hand to touch hers.

"You will not say?" From Parson Paske that came as a polite request.

"I cannot. I have no proof."

"Friendship indeed." John Thurloe said. Mayhap he guessed, or perhaps sought to provoke the truth from me.

"You mean that Master Merriot...?"

"Nay, never think that, Mistress Paske. Nowell Merriot loved her truly." I raised my hands to heaven, dropped them to my sides. "God is all seeing, He knows." I stood, leaned over the parson. "I pray you leave be, and let that be enough."

Parson Paske attempted to out stare me. He failed. I held his gaze until he bowed his head, spoke of the duplicity of men and the Devil's work, assuring us that we might take comfort in God's all seeing and knowing. He then prayed us off to bed. Early it might be, but we were exhausted, wearied by the horrors of the past days.

In the morning, as Thurloe and I departed, four hands waved from an upper casement. Mistress Paske and her daughters, the only part of Eikenthorpe I would miss.

We rode hard from Eikenthorpe to the Ford, in one long day, but mindful of our horses. I found Perry her usual comfortable easy ride and her sensible nature allowed me a little piece of mind free to muse on the topic of retribution, not the Lord's, but legal, in the form of compensation to the Merriots. Master Thurloe rode his stolid horse with an easy hand, saying little, it wasn't until the ferry crossing that he broached the subject of what my future could be.

"There's work for a young lawyer of your mind and mettle, we could use you to find out and persuade."

"Oh, indeed, Master Thurloe. More murder and mayhem? More families like the Merriots deliberately destroyed? Would you have me play your role and be the informer, whispering secrets to those in fear of them, in order that they might smite the helpless? Do you want me to create more incidents like those at the Merriots?" My voice rose to bellow. Perry sidestepped, tossing her head unhappily. She nearly stepped off the causeway. I stopped roaring to guide her. We splashed through, side by side, Thurloe's voice rising as his anger rose.

"Do you not think that I regret my decision to send Knott to Rolph Fowke in London before I knew exactly where you three were on the road?" Thurloe's face, normally pale, suffused with blood, veins became visible at his temple. "We have all tasted shame and guilt over this, and I have been taught a hard lesson, that I should plan for every possible detail, including delays. I assumed you would hasten back and lost sight of what you might do in Eikenthorpe. I will never assume anything again."

"Is that an apology? Do you care? I had to kill men. Look how the Merriot family suffered, Nowell's father might die, his sister never recover her right mind. Is the cause against the King worth that? Is setting father against son, brother against cousin, destroying families who lived peaceably, what you wish for our England?"

"None of us do, you young fool, but when the King will not bend what can we do? We can say we tried. We did try to stop this happening, we did try to persuade the King. Think, Jacob Emerick. Stop feeling abused and sore for thyself, lad. There are greater things afoot. You know what is happening in our country. Brood on that and about the inevitability of war."

I pushed Perry ahead, biting my tongue on furious words, rife with indignation, and we started down the main highway to Brockleford. The horses quickened their pace, sensing our nearness to the night's stop. Thurloe caught up, his face darkened with anger.

"Jacob Emerick, use the wit the good Lord gave you. There is no going back. If we had held and tried Rolph Fowke, many people, people undecided, wanting to honour their oaths of allegiance, would have seen what the King's men will do for the King's rewards. Rolph Fowke, brought to trial, would have helped those unsure to see the untrustworthiness of the King. He has already set us at each other. We need all we can glean and garner to stop more killing before it goes farther than his hotheads and ours."

I shrugged. "You chose to work by deceit, threats and violence. How does that make you different from the King or the Fowkes?" With that message from Knott, you sent Rolph Fowke rushing to Brocklehurst and caused an innocent family much pain and grief." I almost spat Knott's name I felt that much disgust. "If you wished to shame the Fowkes and our King you could have published broadsheets with all the story and more."

Thurloe pushed his gelding closer to Perry. "I have thought about methods too. I cannot undo what was done. But I go to talk to my patron and to discuss using words, making a war with words. You might join me if you preferred to wage war that way." He raised one eyebrow, but I refused to comment. I turned Perry away from him, into the Merriot's lane, telling him I would see him at the Tunnace home in the morning. Any fighting I did would be for my family, but now I wished to learn how the Merriots fared.

The Merriots intended to stay safe. The great gates to the entry arch were closed, barred and bolted. A large bell hung outside. My ringing a peal started dogs barking, and a suspicious voice asked who I was and what I wanted. An opening had been cut into one door at eye height and covered with a grill of bars and a wooden shutter. I was well conned and peered at before the message came that I might enter.

Nowell fetched me to the house, although I protested that the hay loft would be comfortable. Mistress Merriot had made a remarkable recovery, insisted I dine with them, and her strength gave the family the outward appearance of ordinariness. The talk was of the new foals, the hay crop, and music. The Merriot maids played the lute, all the children sang, well taught by their mother. I borrowed a flute and we played and sang until dusk. Then Nowell and I walked the rounds, making all secure. Two ostlers and two lads slept in now, and a flock of geese ran in the small paddock where we had stowed our saddles.

"No one will surprise us again," Nowell told me. "We'll guard what's ours."

We spoke of what had been unspeakable at the dinning table as we strolled back to the house. "I dared not ask in the house, but how is your father?"

"Much improved, Jacob. He will, thank the Lord, recover most of his wits given time, although he will always be slow of speech."

"Praise God. I feared so for him."

"It is thanks to Marianne, with what care she gave at first..." Nowell's voice faded as we both thought of her.

"And Marianne? What says Doctor Maye?"

"The other, the maid, Agnes, so ill used she broke inside, she died, Jacob. Marianne, she won't speak, sees and hears nothing. My mother and sisters spoon food into her, talk to her, praise her care of Father. The doctor tells us only time will heal, makes her sleep and gives her his special potions. Pray, he says, and someone be with her all the day."

"And you, Nowell, how fare you?"

"Better tomorrow when I ride north to seek the King and claim retribution. I've spoken to my father, and we will give his Majesty the information I collected in Kent and be paid in gold for it. Then if he protects the Fowkes, I return and will not stay to aid his cause. There will be no more Merriot horses or information for his cause."

"Ah, Nowell, when his subjects are so divided he cannot demand retribution against those who support him as the Fowkes do."

Nowell whipped round to face me. "He should, if he is indeed, as he tells us all, our King and protector on this earth. In God's Name he should."

"Hush, man, don't disturb the night." I gripped his shoulder and shook him gently. "If King's justice were seen to be done in this case then that would be well done and good for his cause." I kept the rest of my doubts behind my teeth.

We parted the following morning, Nowell riding off to the King on a pretty brown mare, leaving Samson doing his duty to beget another crop of excellent foals. "God speed you safely, and pray the King listens, Nowell."

"Amen to that, friend. I know where I'll find you should it come to taking sides. Return to me when you want to breed Perry, and my thanks for what you did." He bent forward to shake my hand, nodded to Thurloe, and turned to ride off in the opposite direction. I knew how much I would miss him.

Thurloe and I rode further down river to where an Emerick lighter waited. I was going home, and Thurloe and his Masters or Patron could go to Hades. Thurloe had not argued.

# CHAPTER TWENTY-NINE

London, June 1642

Home at last, weeks overdue, but home. Home from whence I had departed in foul humour, ruing the day I was born into such a family, and vowing not to return until I had found a way to make a gentleman's home in some place like Eikenthorpe. Such hopes I'd held, all dashed. That comfortable Jacob Adam Emerick, the young man so well set up in his own conceit and belief in his abilities, had vanished, along with my hopes of a marriage which would give us influence at Court and enrich the Merchants Emerick. All had disappeared, died, wrapped in the shrouds of deceit and dishonesty which had surrounded me ever since I had left home. I'd take decency, honour and godly goodness above ought else. I'd value loyalty and honesty in a wife above riches, and I'd earn my way to be a Member of Parliament at the side of no man except an honourable one.

I rode Perry into our yard where the milk cows were wintered and appropriated a stall for her. No handing her over to stable boys here, not yet anyway. I saw to her myself and left her warm, dry, well watered and nosing beans and chop in her manger.

Hoisting my saddle bags and pack, I shoved my way through

the washing in the drying yard, crossed the brew and bake house yard, making for the side of the house where the kitchen door opened on to the pump, now surrounded by a newly paved surround. I'd won my bet, Caleb owed me an embroidered shirt.

The kitchen was empty, no Judith, kitchen maids, my mother, or the two young girls she was training. The chopping block, the tables, the hearth all left in disarray, fish, meat and vegetables lying in various stages of preparation.

I strode through the kitchen, hurrying to see what had upset them all, hastened down the passage and into the hall. There I heard them before I saw them. In the parlour my uncles, aunts, father and mother, servants, sisters-in-law, nieces, nephews and cousins crowded together, shrieking and exclaiming. I dropped my bags, fearing that one of the new ships had foundered, and hurried in.

"What is it? What's a do?" I could say no more for the constriction across my chest.

"Jacob." Various voices called out to me. My mother exclaimed, hurried across, catching at my hands to pull me in for a rare welcoming kiss.

My father straightened up to his full height to make his announcement. "He's done it."

I knew then.

My father continued. "King Charles, our Sovereign Lord and Gracious Majesty, has issued the Commissions of Array ordering all the Lords-Lieutenant throughout the kingdom to raise an army for him."

It was done. No stopping it now. The King intended to break all his many subjects who wanted him to give way. We fell silent then, wondering, and waited for my father to begin a prayer for peace.

But he shook his head. "I cannot," he said, "I cannot find the words to pray."

No more could I. Peace would take its own time in coming, and that time might not be ours.

# CHAPTER THIRTY

London, June 1642.

'Cry 'Havoc!' and let slip the dogs of war;'

There was no need for secrecy was there? The King had declared war so war it was to be. Still, a man might be observed and noted, and some men wished to go unseen. Who knew what would happen or might happen? A friend now could turncoat, be an enemy later, best be cautious. Who would win? King or Pym?

Those attending the meeting came secretly and privately. With hope of compromise gone, the middle way destroyed, the only path present was to aim for a swift resolution and bind the King through Parliament's winning.

"Well done?" The central man of the seated three spoke. "No. Botched, badly botched, Master 'Knott'."

Knott stood, full height, shoulders set, righteous. "I performed God's work as it was given me."

"In future let us direct you in that, your interpretation of God's work has not been ours." There was condemnation in all faces.

"We needed Merchants like the Emericks," the man by the fireplace walked to the table, "the Emericks will not support us now."

"Nor will they support the King." John Thurloe, sitting quietly behind his patron spoke when his patron nodded at him.

"And you, Master Thurloe, how came you to botch that meeting between Rolph Fowke and Jacob Emerick?"

His patron spoke. "Emerick delayed his return journey, unexpectedly, but what happened gives us powerful material to use in broadsheets against the King."

Thoughtful murmurs of agreement, heads nodding, no dissent.

"But you failed us, Clerk Knott. Be less zealous in your new duties and this time do only as you have been asked. I shall watch you." A wave of dismissal sent Knott out. He bowed to all present, turned himself into the humble clerk again and slipped out of the room.

"Now, Master Thurloe, this plan of your. It is ingenious."

Thurloe stood, bowed to all and began. "We need the Merchants. King Charles will offer them promises. We can offer them trade. Also I believe these merchant sailors may help us in quite specific ways."

"How so?"

"A link to the continent, carrying information both ways, moving supplies and arms round the coast to our armies, my lords."

"Spies, Master Thurloe?"

"You know how valuable our information gatherers have been. Men placed as Master Jacob Emerick, travelling to the continent, making trade agreements, can gather information just by using their eyes."

Further murmurs of agreement, further discussion, and a decision made. When dusk came the group dispersed, leaving at irregular intervals, one by one, as silently and carefully as they came. If there were to be any tomorrows for a Protestant England, they surely depended on working in secrecy today.

# HISTORICAL NOTE

I have always preferred historical stories about ordinary people, the ones whose names and lives we don't know much about.

The events leading up the English civil war are well chronicled in political histories. It is how those events affected ordinary people which interested me.

Reading the diaries and letters of parsons and farmers, merchants and tradesmen showed me how hard it was for them to choose what to do and what pressures might be brought to bear upon them. I thought it made a tale worth telling.

# ABOUT THE AUTHOR

p.d.r. lindsay (no capitals please in tribute to one of her favourite poets, e. e. cummings) makes New Zealand home, for now. Born in Ireland, educated in England, Canada, and New Zealand, and having worked in many different countries, she calls herself a citizen of the world. This wide experience of different cultures colours her writing and keeps her travelling.

# Writer's Choice
## a writers' publishing collective

## We publish quality fiction
## for readers' enjoyment

If you enjoyed this novel here are some other Writer's Choice novels you might like to read.

'A Woman Transported' by Sharon Robards
- www.smashwords.com/books/view/309773
- Kobo: www.kobobooks.com/ebook/A-Woman-Transported/book-buQO6oelekqY-8hzunYvZg/page1.html
- Kindle version: www.amazon.com/A-Woman-Transported-ebook/dp/B00CINRDXE/ref=sr_1_1?s=digital-text&ie=UTF8&qid=1367015750&sr=1-1&keywords=a+woman+transported
- Print Book version: www.amazon.com/A-Woman-Transported-Sharon-Robards/dp/0646579126/ref=tmm_pap_title_0?ie=UTF8&qid=1367015750&sr=1-1

South of Burnt Rocks, West of the Moon' by G.J. Berger
- Amazon UK: www.amazon.co.uk/South-Burnt-Rocks-West-ebook/dp/B009V2ZOL8
- Amazon USA: www.amazon.com/dp/B009V2ZOL8
- Smashwords: www.smashwords.com/books/view/247471
- Barnes and Noble: www.barnesandnoble.com/w/south-of-burnt-rocks-west-of-the-moon-g-j-berger/1113728010

www.ingramcontent.com/pod-product-compliance
Lightning Source LLC
Chambersburg PA
CBHW061324170626
46817CB00001B/297